FEAR ITSELF

novels by
Elena Santangelo

BY BLOOD POSSESSED

HANG MY HEAD AND CRY

POISON TO PURGE MELANCHOLY

FEAR ITSELF

To Gloria,

Enjoy!

FEAR ITSELF

A Pat Montella Mystery

Elena
Santangelo

FEAR ITSELF

ISBN 978-1-933523-76-7

First Edition, May 2011

Library of Congress Control Number: 2011926572

Printed in the United States of America on acid-free paper.

Cover painting by Joyce Wright – www.artbyjoyce.com

Book design by Bella Rosa Books

10 9 8 7 6 5 4 3 2 1

To
the memories of my mother,
Helen Theresa Chicco Santangelo
and my father,
Augustus Santangelo

Acknowledgements

If you helped me with this book and I failed to mention you below, I apologize. Your contribution was appreciated, despite the holes in my memory.

I couldn't have written this book without my dad. I spent many long walks with him, listening to his memories of life on East Main Street in Norristown during the Great Depression. When we would return home and I'd write it all down, he was infinitely patient as I questioned details. He even helped me diagram the complete interior of 349 East Main, the house he grew up in, which became my haunted house for this book.

My mom kept insisting she didn't remember anything from those years. With a little nudging, though, she recalled things like stopping on the way to school to roll up her long underwear so it wouldn't show under her dress. She helped me become at home within the mind of a teenage girl in 1933. Also, both my parents helped me recreate the interior of Mom's grandmother's house, which became Aunt Sophie's home. My only regret is that my parents didn't live to see this novel in print.

The Montgomery County Historical Society's Norristown *Times Herald* archive provided not only many of the quotes for the 1933 chapters, but much needed data on news, weather, advertisements, and even the comics of the era. The society was also a great source of information about Montgomery Cemetery, as were their and the W.S. Hancock Society's wonderful tours of the place.

I ran a contest on my website, searching for a feline on whom to base my fictional kitty. Out of what felt like a zillion entries, I found Chrissie, whose overall look and personality was perfect. I thank Joan Schramm for allowing me to make my Crisi a fun character. The runner-up in the contest was Karen Tannert's cat, who has a quick walk-on in the story.

I thank the Plymouth Township Police for the tour of their K-9 Unit, and Elizabeth Loupas, Carole Shmurak, and Mitchell Young for helping me learn Czech police dog commands.

My brother Bob (fellow author Bob Brooke) lent me research materials and his laptop, reworked my website, and generally made this writer's life easier.

Gretchen Hall once again tutored me in the use of hazardous materials. Leonard Greenberg taught me (and Aunt Sophie) the best way to cook fish. Jill Newnam needs thanking for being flexible and understanding. Without her, I couldn't be a writer and pay bills at the same time.

As always, my proofreaders were invaluable: Linda Gagliardi, Jean Geiger, Suzanne Pontius, and my brother Tom Santangelo. Tom also contributed from his stock of family stories, and was most responsible for keeping me sane when the going got tough these last few years.

And lastly, I thank my extended family. A few cousins answered research questions. Others have been super-supportive, showing up with mounds of food during difficult times, keeping in touch since. Mostly, though, what went into this book from them was a foundation of loving memories. Like Pat's family, they're all good people.

"We in America today are nearer to the final triumph over poverty than ever before in the history of any land. The poor-house is vanishing from among us."

—PRESIDENT HERBERT HOOVER, 1928

1933 – East Main Street, Norristown, Pennsylvania

What I recall of the Depression was everyone saying we didn't have enough to eat. And they always said the coal had so many rocks in it we couldn't make it last a week. Bootleg coal was all we could afford—the small slaggy bits left over after the good coal was shipped out.

Do I remember feeling hungry? No more than usual. What I got to eat was how much I'd eaten every day as long as I could remember.

Same with feeling cold in the winter, I guess. I wore flannel underwear beneath my dress. Over it I wore a heavy sweater, with thick stockings below, hand-me-downs from my cousins, knit in better times by my grandmother. We all called her *Nonna*.

At night Aunt Gina would put a hot water bottle under the sheets of the bed I shared with my cousin Delphina. After we were tucked in, my aunt would throw the rug from the floor over us. We couldn't move from the weight. Then our cat would jump up to nestle under the rug between our feet and the hot water bottle. She'd lick her fur for maybe twenty minutes, making the whole bed rock. With the bottle, the rug and the cat, we kept warm enough.

That's what a child remembers. Not the cold, but the way we kept warm. Not the hunger, but the days when we *didn't* eat macaroni for dinner. Or ate it, but with something besides beans or split peas or onions in tomato sauce. Sundays we had ravioli, or once in a while Uncle Ennio brought home a chicken. After he wrung its neck and Aunt Gina cut it up, we got the feet to play with. We'd pull the tendons to make the claws move.

I can't picture the hand-me-downs we wore so much as when one of us got new clothes, like the brown oxford shoes Del put on when she started junior high, and the white knickers Aunt Gina sewed for my brother Salvatore for his First Holy Communion the next spring.

It's the out-of-ordinary things that stick. That's why I can remember that one week in 1933 so vividly. Roosevelt became our new president right after Lent started. We listened to him on Mr. D'Abruzzo's radio. But that was also the week a rich man got deathly ill on our front steps, and when I heard voices in a room with no people, and when our black cat Crisi helped me and Del uncover a secret best left alone.

1

February 26, Present-Day

"Say *what*?!"

I was talking to a PC, to a laptop screen that seemed to float eerily atop the table in a kitchen otherwise illuminated by the glow stealing in from the hall behind me. I couldn't see wasting electricity by turning on the three-bulb overhead lamp when I didn't need it. The corners of the room were dark shadows, which some folks might think pretty spooky, given that the kitchen was in an 1870s farm-house with a history of ghosts.

Ha! You want spooky? The scariest thing in that room was the number on the screen. The hundred and thirty-two bucks Turbo Tax said I owed the government sent a chill up my spine, until that body part matched my nose, ears, and fingers, already cold from the draft coming through the north wall.

My "Say what?" was for the program's question about my car mileage deduction, which I couldn't seem to bend my brain around. I'd had similar reactions to the questions about accounting methods, 401K rollovers, and self-employment health insurance. Believe me, I wanted every deduction I could get for the latter, since my individual plan had covered all of two medical scans before my annual diagnostic benefits ran dry, six months short of the renewal date. I was supposed to have more tests for the knee pain I'd had off and on since Christmas. A bottle of ibuprophen was what I could afford, so I was going that route.

Most of my life, I'd filled in a 1040EZ. Piece of cake. Those years when I had to deal with inheritance after my mom and dad died, I let H&R Block handle it. Since neither of my parents had written a will (superstitious Italians until the end), and since they *had* left a mortgage, car loan, medical and funeral bills, et cetera, I had to sell the house to pay everything, including the tax filer and lawyer fees. I was back to an EZ the next time.

This past year, though, I'd been laid off, collected unemployment, then started a modest gardening business. The less money I made, it seemed, the more forms I was required to file.

Besides all that, I kept getting distracted by the gleam of the PC monitor off of the rock on my finger. My advice? Never daydream about your wedding while you're doing taxes, especially if Turbo Tax says you owe a hundred and thirty-two bucks. It's depressing. I pictured myself feeding my guests cornflakes. Food was my main concern. I didn't care about a gown, fancy hall, flowers or a limo, but everyone *had* to rave about the food, and "everyone" meant several dozen aunts, uncles and cousins on my side alone.

A hundred and thirty-two smackers. Doesn't sound like much in this day and age, but I also had big-ticket bills for health and car insurance coming due before tax day in April.

I was hoping to start this year's gardening season soon. My clients' flower beds would need cleaning up, and the soil at Mrs. Adams's ought to be turned over and fluffed up so I could get her turnips and radishes in by mid-March. (According to my family's age-old gardening traditions, root veggies *must* be sown March 19, St. Joseph's Day.) Thing was, the ground was too muddy to work, and we were still having hard frosts overnight. The leaves protecting shrub roots were best left alone for now.

Chances were good that I'd be borrowing money from Miss Maggie again this coming month.

Last May, I moved to Virginia to live with Magnolia Shelby, a.k.a. Miss Maggie, who was ninety-one at the time and claimed that it made sense for someone her age to have a live-in companion. That, at least, took care of my room and board. For my part, the experience so far had been rather like raising a two-year-old. Not that she was helpless—far from it—but she had the same sense of wonder and discovery as a tot. She could be just as stubborn, too.

We're not kin, yet somehow, since Fate threw us together, we've become a family, with her filling the void left by my mom and grandmother. She says I'm the granddaughter she never had. Sometimes I feel more like her straight man. Or Robin to her Batman.

As I sat in the kitchen, watching dollar signs swim across my screen, she was in her parlor, which she called her "War Room" because it was also her office. She's an historian who takes old diaries and letters, annotates them, adds other pertinent data, and voila! puts out books that actually fascinate people like me who hated history in school. These books have made her fairly famous in history circles.

Not bad for a woman who took up the career *after* retiring from teaching at age seventy.

Three days from now her revisions to her latest project were due back at her publisher's. That project was titled *No Borders From Above: The Vietnam War Letters of Louis Montella.* Lou was my brother, killed in the war, so the book was dear to my heart. I'd been doing my darndest to stay quiet and out of Miss Maggie's white hair all week.

So when the phone rang the next instant, I pounced. I assumed it was for me anyway. I was hoping my beloved, Hugh, was calling to commiserate after returning home from combat, that is, a field trip with his daughter's Cadette Girl Scout troop. They'd gone to a Sunday matinee of *CATS!* up in D.C. I'd been invited, too, but I'd begged off. For one thing, we'd spent nearly every weekend together for the last two months. He and Beth Ann needed some bonding time without me. For another, the trip cost eighty dollars a person. Too rich for my blood. Oh, Hugh would have insisted on paying for me, I'm sure, but it's the principle of the thing. Girl Scout trips shouldn't cost so much that it's a hardship for some parents to send their daughters. I was boycotting.

Anyway, figuring Hugh was on the other end of the jangling phone, maybe wanting to schedule a little Sunday evening snuggle time, I snatched up the receiver and said, "You home?"

"Uh, actually no. I'm at Ma's." The voice was feminine, the inflections pure Montella. "Where else would I be on a Sunday night?"

"Cella?" Her name's pronounced like the musical instrument, only with an "a" on the end. Why I put a question mark after her name, I don't know. I recognized not only my cousin's voice, but her attitude. After all, we'd spent most of our adolescence on the phone with each other. "What are *you* calling for?"

"Nice to hear your voice, too, Pat."

"That's not what I meant." I had to admit, it *was* good to hear her. Last January, right after I heard she and her husband Ronny had split up, I sent her a funny Hallmark card with a little note. Under my John Hancock, I wrote my email address (Miss Maggie set up one just for me, bless her). Cella dropped me a line the day she got it and we've been emailing every day since. Cheaper for both of us than long distance, plus we could say oodles more that way. If she was calling, I knew something must be up. "What happened?"

"Uncle Rocco died."

"Oh." Not the worst case scenario, at least. Half expected. Great-uncle Rocco was . . . come to think of it, I wasn't sure how old he was.

"He was a hundred and two," Cella said, reading my mind the way she used to in high school, "and the last few years, he wasn't . . . you know."

"Longer than that. He's been talking to himself nonstop for ages." I had a vivid memory of my mom's wake—Uncle Rocco sitting alone in the third row at the funeral parlor, holding a spirited conversation with no one I could see. The memory creeped me out all over again.

"Rocco was *always* a talker" was Cella's explanation. "Just, after a while, we all stopped listening. His granddaughter should have put him in a nursing home sooner, where he would have had other people to talk to all the time. I think he got too used to talking to the walls. Got to thinking the walls were better company. They don't up and leave on you."

I wondered if she really meant her own hubby, but all I said was "It's sad. I always liked Uncle Rocco." And I had. He told the most entertaining stories. As the youngest of eight siblings, Rocco always got into mega-trouble growing up. Being an adult hadn't stopped him. He told us how during the Roaring Twenties he had, à la Cyrano de Bergerac, helped his brother Tonio woo the honest-to-Pete flapper who became my Great Aunt Benita. Or Uncle Rocco would talk about all of his get-rich-quick schemes during the Depression, or how he learned to fly airplanes in a hurry for World War II, even though he was older than all the guys in his outfit.

Even after he'd begun babbling to himself, I liked Uncle Rocco. "He had one of those easy smiles and a hug for everyone," I added to my eulogy.

Cella agreed. "Lots of charisma. Never heard a mean word out of his mouth."

"You can't say that about most people."

"Especially Beatrice."

Beatrice was Rocco's only granddaughter. "Dad used to call her 'Miss Snooty.' She always thought she was better than the rest of the family from the day she was born." I stood to stretch my legs, then took the phone over to the sink to refill my tea mug.

"She still thinks so. Listen, Pat, I don't mean to cut you off, but Ma's giving me the eye. Gotta call my brothers."

"You called *me* before them?"

"What do you think? I *like* talking to you."

"Wait. Tell me when the funeral is."

"We don't know yet. Wednesday or Thursday. What? You coming up for it?"

I hadn't even been thinking in terms of choice. Montella funerals were like magnets that pulled us all home. Then again, when I thought of logistics—well, I'd just have to drive the distance. Couldn't afford a train ticket. The price of gas, though, would put a hole in my already Swiss-cheese pocket. But I said, "I have to. Rocco was the last of his generation. Dad would want me there. Can somebody put me up for a few days?"

"You kidding? I'll put you up myself."

"At your mom's?" Cella and her kids had moved back home after her split. I knew Aunt Lydia would take me in gladly, but there wasn't an extra bed in her place right now. I didn't relish sleeping on her couch. Aunt Lydia was a staunch believer in plastic slipcovers.

"No, no," Cella assured me. "I have a new place. It's a long story. I'll show you when you get here."

I pictured a small apartment, but at least Cella's couch would be comfy. We talked a half minute more, me saying I could get there Tuesday, her saying she'd email me details tomorrow. I hit the off button on the phone.

"Heat up some water for me while you're at it," said a raspy voice across the room. Miss Maggie was standing beside the table, leaning on her hands, her nose almost touching the laptop screen as she scrutinized it.

Miss Maggie was dressed in yellow sweatpants and a matching heavy fleece top, the collar up to keep her neck warm. In the dim kitchen, it looked like an ominous glow-in-the-dark blob had swallowed her whole, leaving only her head sticking out.

"I thought you were working." Reaching for the kettle, I flicked on the stove's hood light to give us more illumination and make her look less sci-fi.

"Needed a break," Miss Maggie said, working the full-sized mouse we always plugged into the laptop—her arthritis and my patience couldn't deal with the fingertip torture device on the machine. "If I sit too long in the winter, I stiffen up so much, I can't move." She pulled her attention away from the screen, straightening as much as a woman with advanced osteoporosis could. "Make mine hot cocoa, Pat. Yours, too."

I didn't argue. Cocoa sounded perfect right then and, since it was Sunday, I was allowed to break my Lenten fast on chocolate. Anyway, I'd figured a way to make a low fat, low cal, low sodium mix from scratch, so not much guilt was involved: five parts nonfat dry milk, two parts sugar, one part nonfat creamer, and one part cocoa. I retrieved the big Ziploc of the mix and bag of mini marshmallows from the pantry.

"I couldn't tell much from your side of the conversation," Miss Maggie continued as I filled the kettle, "but it sounds like you have a funeral to go to back home."

"I'll only be gone a few days." I explained about Great-uncle Rocco, giving his advanced age as an aside only. One did not imply a connection between age and death in front of someone who was in her nineties.

Miss Maggie expressed her sympathies first, then added, "You haven't been back to Norristown in almost a year. Be good for you to have a nice visit. I think we should stay through the weekend."

"We? You want to come? Not that it's a problem," I said hastily, hoping it wasn't. Miss Maggie could have Cella's couch and I could sleep on the floor. No big deal. "The family would love it. Aunt Sophie's been dying to meet you." For that matter, all my relatives were. They couldn't fathom an unrelated, non-Italian stranger more or less adopting me out of the blue. And truth to tell, I very much wanted Miss Maggie to meet them. "But, your revisions—"

"I'll finish them tomorrow. All I have to do is stop wasting time cursing out my copy editor every page. But I'll confess, I have an ulterior motive for wanting to go with you."

I spooned three tablespoons of the cocoa mix into my mug and two into Miss Maggie's. She likes her cup only two-thirds full. Lower caffeine and more room for marshmallows. "If it's that you want to eat gobs of Italian food all week, we're headed for the right place."

She rolled her eyes in anticipation of the ecstacy. Eating was a vocation of hers and Italian food, her favorite. "*Two* ulterior motives, then. The other is that I've been wanting to visit . . . actually, while I was tracking you down, Pat, I read all about Montgomery Cemetery in Norristown—"

"Montgomery? Up in the West End? You want to go *there*?" I knew it well because Aunt Lydia and Uncle Gaet (pronounced like Guy with a "t" on the end) had lived only a block away for the first twenty years of my life. Cella and I weren't supposed to play inside the cemetery gates, but we did anyway. Montgomery was an old Victorian graveyard, no longer active, complete with ornate angel statues and tall obelisks.

"A slew of Civil War generals are buried there," Miss Maggie said, "including Winfield Scott Hancock."

Ah, I thought. A pilgrimage. After all, she *was* an historian. "Sure we'll go," I promised. "I'll even call the historical society when we get there to see if they have a map of the place." The kettle whistled and I poured out the water.

"Good. I'll pay your train ticket for that. You make the reservations and—"

"I was going to drive." I reached for the vanilla extract. Secret ingredient. Two drops in each mug.

"Driving's not recommended." Miss Maggie swung the laptop around to show me the screen. She'd brought up the National Weather Service website. "Fixing to snow in Pennsylvania Tuesday and Wednesday. Maybe more for the weekend, too. March is coming in like a lion this year."

I brought our mugs over to the table and checked out the forecast. One of those Yankee clipper systems down from Canada, meeting moist air coming up the coast. Only three to five inches predicted, but not something I wanted to drive any distance in. And another possible storm behind it for Saturday.

So the train it was. To get to the cemetery, we'd have to bum a ride from one of my relatives, that's all. Just not Uncle Leo. I imagined us in his ancient Oldsmobile, Miss Maggie having a heart attack as he drove up the middle of Main Street at five miles an hour, oblivious to the 18-wheelers bearing down on him from both directions. Still, I had oodles of relatives. Maybe I could even borrow a car.

Then it struck me how much I was looking forward to seeing those hordes of kinfolk again. I'd been away too long.

2

February 27, Present-Day

The next day, as had become my habit in nice weather the last couple of months, I got up early, bundled up, and walked through the woods down to Hugh's trailer for breakfast.

A year ago, if some gypsy fortuneteller had told me I'd be taking winter nature hikes before eight A.M., I'd have yelled "Fraud!" and demanded my money back. But I'd fallen in love with Miss Maggie's estate, Bell Run. Mornings like this, when the woods were silent except for my footfalls on the wet leaves, the place seemed enchanted. I didn't mind the cold or the slippery footing, or even achy knees on the hills, if I could share in the forest for five minutes.

Above me, the sun was painting the bare tree tops a warm amber, and over them, a lone hawk glided by, looking for his first meal of the day. I stopped at the small footbridge over the creek to look upstream and down. In the shady areas, lacy ice still spread over the bank, but anywhere the sun could reach, new stubs of green growth were sprouting. A tiny chickadee, enjoying the protection of a rhododendron, loudly reprimanded me before flitting away, shrub-to-shrub, downstream.

The breeze caught me in the face, cold enough to make my eyes water. Yanking my scarf up to cover my chin, I hurried on.

The trailer was a double wide. Hugh and his daughter lived in one half and our local post office annex took up the rest. Hugh was postmaster.

Beth Ann let me in, balancing a bowl of cereal in her other hand. She was dressed in black jeans and a black sweatshirt with pandas on the front. I hated to see that much black on a fourteen year-old, but had to admit, it brought out all the gorgeous natural highlights of her long fox-red hair, which she almost always wore loose.

She was at least half responsible for my love of Bell Run's woods. Her favorite subject was science—botany and ecology in particular—though any topic of nature, from geology to meteorology, could hold her attention.

I peeled off my gloves, hat and scarf, tossing them on the sofa, then unbuttoned my coat as I gave her my report. "This morning I saw a chickadee and a red-tailed hawk."

"Cool," she said, shoveling a spoon of Corn Pops into her mouth. Around it she added, "Saw another flock of grackles yesterday. Spring's coming."

I heard the shower running. "Your Dad's still in the bathroom?"

"Running late. He overslept. We got in late last night."

I headed for their kitchen, a closet-sized nook separated from the living room by a built-in table. The aroma of fresh coffee hit me halfway there. Yes, I was marrying the right guy. Regardless of the late hour, he'd remembered to set up the coffeemaker and timer the night before. While I poured myself a cup, I asked Beth Ann about yesterday's field trip.

"It was fun." A mischievous gleam came into in her green eyes. "We drove our bus driver crazy singing 'Ninety-nine bottles of beer' over and over." She glanced at the clock on the stove. "Gotta get my stuff together or I'll miss the school bus." Dumping her bowl and spoon in the sink, she made a beeline for her room.

An eighty-dollar trip and she remembers the ride, I thought. Cup in hand, I wandered back into the living room. The shower cut off as Beth Ann reappeared, coat on but unzipped, backpack looped over one shoulder. Her opposite hand clutched a two-by-three-foot piece of green poster board which she maneuvered awkwardly, to keep me from seeing one side.

"No peeking," she admonished. "You'll see the finished product at Science Night."

"Science Night," I echoed, mentally flogging myself. I'd completely forgotten I was supposed to go to her school on Thursday. "I can't go."

Beth Ann looked as if I'd slapped her, making me feel like a total dirt ball.

"I have to go home," I explained quickly. "Back to Pennsylvania. For a funeral. One of my uncles died. I just got the call last night. I'm really sorry, Beth Ann."

"What'd he die of?"

I couldn't tell if the scientist in her genuinely wanted details or if she was measuring the tragic-factor to determine how to react, but it hit me that I didn't know what Uncle Rocco had died of. "Old age," I replied. "He was a hundred and two."

Beth Ann let out a whistle. "Wow." She still looked crestfallen as she headed for the exit, but when she got there, she turned and blurted out, "It's okay. I have uncles, too." Then she was gone, slamming the door behind her.

That was her awkward way of expressing sympathy and saying she understood. I fervently hoped that she *wouldn't* find out what it felt like to lose one of her three uncles for a very long time yet, but she meant that I was forgiven. I still felt like a dirt ball, though. To her, Science Night was the biggest event in the school year.

I made my way back to the kitchen, where I checked the fridge. Hugh and Beth Ann went through the essentials—milk, bread and fruit—at a phenomenal rate, I'd found. Sure enough, only about a pint of milk was left in its plastic container, and three navel oranges in the drawer. Well, I thought, since we were going away, I'd need to clean out Miss Maggie's fridge anyway. Hugh and Beth Ann could make do with skim milk instead of two-percent for a few days.

Yogurt oatmeal this morning, I decided, since Hugh was running late. A half cup each of light fruit yogurt (today blueberry), milk and oatmeal, with a handful of raisins, mixed together and nuked, made a decent, filling, hot breakfast. I placed bowls, spoons, oatmeal and raisins on the table, then once more took up my coffee, which was now the perfect drinking temperature.

After two mouthfuls, I headed for Hugh's bedroom, where I figured I'd make myself useful by straightening the bed. The sheets still smelled of him, making the chore was pleasingly sensual. I was fluffing his two pillows when he emerged from the bathroom, wearing nothing but his pajama bottoms. The aroma of steamy aftershave wafted into the bedroom ahead of him.

I dropped the pillow so as to turn my full attention to the view. Hugh was over six foot and built like a linebacker. Hauling mailbags and walking a letter delivery beat each day ensured that very little fat clung to his torso. He had the same red tresses as his daughter, softened at his temples by a few gray hairs that you had to look close to find.

Looking close at Hugh was a favorite hobby of mine.

He crossed the room in a stride and a half, folding his massive arms around me, laying on me a good-morning smooch that tasted of toothpaste and sent my head, and other body parts, reeling. Then, as he caressed my back and butt, he sighed and whispered, "Is that coffee for me?"

Miss Maggie said she thought Hugh and I were meant for each other because we've been acting like an old married couple since the day we met. Case in point. My mug was behind me, on his bureau. "You can have it, but it's black."

I felt him grimace. "How can you drink it that way?"

"Kiss me again, Romeo, and I'll go pour you a fresh cup with gobs of sugar."

"I don't need gobs. Just two level teaspoons."

"You want sweets? *I'll* give you sweets." I'd been running my fingers through the hair on his bare chest. Now, I brushed my lips up his breastbone, right above his sternum.

That got a gasp out of him, and I felt a stirring of interest under his pajama bottoms.

"Pat, I'm late enough as it is." Yeah, Beth Ann got her whine from him, too.

"So sort mail a little faster today." He'd already proven he could on other mornings this winter. Of course, those days we hadn't been as pressed for time.

"Can't. Ed's coming in at eight-thirty, remember?"

I'd forgotten about Ed. The housing development across the road had added another sub-subdivision to the north in the last year, and more houses were expected to go up between Miss Maggie's place and Route 3 next summer. Hugh's one-man post office was changing over to a two-man operation, starting this morning. The new guy, Ed, already knew the routine of the Bell Run Post Office. He was the usual substitute when Hugh took a sick day or vacation. But my beloved was nervous about the transition. Hugh liked doing everything himself and hated change.

"Oh, poo," was my mature reaction. I let go, thinking it a sorry turn of evolution that the need to make a living now trumped the propagation of the species. Mankind was doomed.

I reminded myself that Hugh would now be a supervisor, with a raise in pay, and that weddings have to be paid for. That, too, I felt, was a nasty turn of evolution. I was all for going back to a tribal culture where the village got together and killed a goat for nuptial celebrations. Better yet, a pig. I love roast pork. Better than cornflakes any day.

Hugh bussed the top of my head as an apology.

"Get dressed," I told him. "I'll go pour your coffee and make your breakfast, like a good wife."

Five minutes later, as I was firing up the microwave on Hugh's bowl of oatmeal while spooning mine, already cooked, into my mouth, he came out to the kitchen in his post office duds. White shirt today, under a soft blue pullover sweater, just the right shade to set off his hair.

"Hey, handsome, how 'bout a date tonight?" I asked.

He raised his eyebrows. "On a school night?"

I shrugged. "Beth Ann can bring her homework and whatever else she needs up to Miss Maggie's and stay over. I'll come down here and cook you dinner. I have a reason for asking." I went on to explain about Uncle Rocco and having to go home.

Hugh reached over, taking my free hand in both of his. "Honey, I'm so sorry."

He'd been calling me "Honey" in his mild southern tones for a few months now. It still sent an enjoyable little thrill through me. I'd never in my life kept beaus around long enough to earn such terms of endearment. Even so, I had to correct his assumption that I was in heavy grief. "I'm sad about Uncle Rocco—I liked him—but his death wasn't a huge surprise. And our families weren't all that close. We didn't see them very often, even though Rocco lived two doors down from Aunt Sophie. See, Dad and his siblings had some kind of falling out with Rocco's daughter after she had Beatrice, so—"

The microwave beeped. I pulled my hand away from Hugh's and set my breakfast down so I could extract his oatmeal.

Hugh looked disoriented as he mentally wandered through my legion of relatives. He'd been trying his best to keep them all straight. "Which of your dad's sisters was he married to?"

"None." I set the steaming bowl on the table. "He was Grandpop Montella's youngest brother."

"A *great*-uncle? Why are you going home, then? I mean, Beth Ann's got her Science Night Thursday and—"

"I know. I feel bad about that, but I talked to her. She seems okay with—"

"But you said Rocco wasn't a close relative."

I'd run into this same problem at my erstwhile employer, Dawkins-Greenway Corporation. My boss could never fathom why I wanted time off to go to the funerals of kin outside my immediate family. When Aunt Filippa's husband, Chicky, died two years ago, I had to call in sick. My cousin Alphonse, the podiatrist, even wrote me a doctor's note. I limped around all the next day to give it credibility.

"Doesn't matter if Rocco wasn't close," I replied. "When one of us dies, we all show up, for the viewing if nothing else. That's what Montellas do. It's like we have to make sure the family tree's still healthy despite losing a limb. Eat. Your breakfast is getting cold."

He took a seat, pulled the bowl toward him and chowed down. While I poured his coffee, he said, "I envy you. I don't know any of my cousins."

"You have cousins?" I set his coffee next to him, with a fresh spoon for sugar. "You never mentioned them."

"Dad's younger brother had two kids. Lived near Winchester, other side of the Shenandoahs, so we rarely saw them. I don't know where they are now." Hugh paused to dab his napkin along the edge of his moustache. "After Mom and Dad divorced, we didn't see them at all."

"How sad." I grabbed my oatmeal and sat down opposite Hugh. "So Beth Ann has a great-uncle and aunt, and first-cousins-once-removed, and maybe even second cousins, who she's never met?"

Hugh nodded, looking down at his reflection in his coffee. "Worse than that. She's got aunts, uncles, and *first* cousins she's never met. Well, not since she was four years old."

I was becoming well acquainted with that guilty crease of his brow, which appeared each time he thought about his late wife. Tanya had died when Beth Ann was only a tot. The crease was my cue to shut up and let him talk.

"Tanya had three siblings," Hugh said, "and they all had at least three kids apiece. I think her oldest sister had six."

"*Madonne!* A dozen cousins!" Why was I shocked? Like me, Tanya had come from good Italian-American stock. "What about Beth Ann's grandparents? Are they still around?"

"As of last year's Christmas cards, they were. They live in Baltimore." Hugh went back to work on his breakfast, maybe hoping I wouldn't make him talk with his mouth full.

But I couldn't let the subject alone. "You never take your daughter to see them?"

I got one of his smoldering looks, as if he was suppressing a psychotic urge to do violence to anyone who nagged him. When I first met him, those looks scared the bejeebers out of me. Now I recognize them for what they are: pure defense mechanism. Like that little lizard that stands on its hind legs and puffs itself up to fake out predators. I gave in. I hadn't come down here to ruin his day. Or mine.

"So what do you want for dinner tonight?" I asked.

Hugh grinned and shook his head. "You'll be busy packing all day. I'll take you out."

"I thought we were saving money for the wedding."

"We'll go cheap. Or better yet, I'll make *you* dinner."

"Now you're talking," I said with enthusiasm. Hugh was a decent chef, though his repertoire was limited from years of cooking for a fussy daughter. I promised to bring him supplies from our fridge, since Miss Maggie and I wouldn't be home.

"What?" he exclaimed. "Miss Maggie's going with you?"

I nodded. "She wants to meet the clan. I wish you could, too. And Beth Ann." Now I wanted her to meet all my cousins even more, to make up for not knowing her own.

He glanced over at the fridge, where a National Parks calendar hung from a hook magnet. February's picture showed steaming hot springs in Yellowstone in the dead of winter. A buffalo stood nearby, icicles hanging from his fur.

"Well," Hugh said, "after Science Night, neither of us has anything scheduled all weekend. If Ed doesn't mind flying solo Saturday, maybe Beth Ann and I could drive up Friday night—"

"That's perfect!" I declared. "You can stay through Saturday and drive us all home on Sunday. But wait, what if it snows in Pennsylvania this week?"

"I'll keep an eye on the forecast."

"I'll email you updates. Miss Maggie's bringing her laptop to record all my aunts' recipes."

"We'll get there. Take the train if we have to. 'Neither snow, nor rain, nor heat, nor gloom of night shall stay this courier from the swift completion of his appointed rounds,' " he quoted, then glanced at his watch. "Uh-oh. My appointed rounds won't wait any longer."

"These really are good times but only a few know it."
—HENRY FORD, 1930

February 28, 1933 – 349 East Main Street, Norristown

Del was in trouble before she got home from school that day.

Fat Tuesday it was, the day before Lent. Always meant a celebration at night. *Carnivale.* Cousins and friends would be coming over. Uncle Ennio would dust off his squeezebox and play the old Sicilian folksongs. We'd dance all night—*tarantellas* that I learned as soon as I could walk.

In the afternoon, Uncle Ennio ran the store by himself so everyone else could get ready. Aunt Gina made sesame seed cookies, not too sweet—we couldn't afford much sugar—but they'd be something to dunk in coffee between dances.

Del's oldest brothers, Pip and Vito, pushed all the dining room furniture back against the walls, the cat, Crisi, getting between their legs because she always wanted to be in the middle of everything.

Her real name was Cristiana, named by Father Travi when, as a stray kitten, she got inside the church twice. He said she must be a Christian. Del caught the stray kitten and carried her home, and Uncle Ennio said she could stay 'cause he needed a good mouser for the store. From day one, they all called her *Crisi*, the Italian word for "crisis," which is what it sounded like when she howled some nights. She was black, and had grown to be about the same size and shape as the worn leather football the younger boys sometimes tossed around the yard.

Anyway, that afternoon, Nonna unpacked and ironed the traditional outfits she and Aunt Gina would wear that evening, brought by Nonna from Sicily a quarter century earlier. Midnight blue skirts, embroidered all around the bottom and up the sides, with a lace-up vest that would go over a white blouse. A red apron, too, trimmed with yellowed lace tatted by Nonna's mother. Or maybe by her grandmother? I don't remember.

Nonna had a third outfit that she'd been saving until Del grew into it. Del didn't know it, but Aunt Gina and Nonna were going to try it on her as soon as she got home from school.

That's why Aunt Gina had a fit when Del didn't walk in the door the same time as her brothers Charlie and Gussie. Their real names were Cologero and Accursio, respectively. Everybody had nicknames back then.

I followed Aunt Gina up the stairs to the third floor, to the bedroom that Vito and Pip shared, where she stood on tiptoe to look out over the condensation on the back window. This side of the house didn't get the sun in winter. Middle of the season, these windows got ice an inch thick on them. That Tuesday, though, the whole day was above freezing. Even though our only source of heat was the coal stove in the kitchen two floors below, the back windows were half clear.

I couldn't see, but from Aunt Gina's reaction, I knew Del was playing baseball over in Jock Ranelli's yard. Del was crazy for baseball. Jock used to call her Lefty, never mind she was right-handed. He said she could pitch like Lefty Grove. She loved that 'cause Lefty was her favorite player on her favorite team, the Athletics.

Aunt Gina raised the window and yelled out, "Delphina Mariana Trepani!" A chilly breeze wafted inside. I retreated to the doorway. "Delphina, you come right home!" My aunt was mad. She didn't think girls ought to play boys' sports.

Aunt Gina said when Del started junior high she'd become a young lady and she couldn't play baseball anymore. Del did anyway, but she played farther from the house, where her mother couldn't see her. She did that until last November, when it got too cold to play outside.

Today, well, likely Jock was the only one Del could get to swing a bat this early in the season. And I knew Del *had* to play today 'cause she was giving up baseball for Lent. She had to get her fill enough to last her 'til Easter.

When Del walked into the house, Aunt Gina hollered at her but good, threatening to have my Uncle Ennio take off his belt and beat her with it (which she always threatened but Uncle Ennio never did).

"You'll go up to your room and do your homework right now," Aunt Gina told her. "And after supper, you'll go to bed and stay there. No *Carnivale* for you. No dancing, no cookies. You can just lie there and think about how you'll tell the priest at confession this week about disobeying me."

Del hung her head. "Yesmama." She said it so often, it sounded like one word.

Nonna shook her head sadly as she folded up the third skirt

to pack it away.

"Take the baby with you, Delphina," Aunt Gina added, "so I can finish cooking."

Del turned to me, not looking especially penitent when she wasn't facing her mother. "Come on, Bambola. Come help me with my 'rithmatic."

Bambola. That's what everyone called me back then. Italian for "baby-doll." I liked that nickname.

3

February 28, Present-Day

"I love trains," Miss Maggie breathed through the large scarf covering her mouth and nose. Our train, silver and sleek in the midday sun, had just pulled up to the Fredericksburg platform. "I get such a thrill riding them. For some reason, I always feel like I'm off on an adventure when I board a train. Maybe because the old steam engines I remember from my childhood *were* an adventure. But they always got you where you were going, unlike the automobiles back then."

The eleven-fifty-four to Philadelphia and points north was already crowded. We couldn't sit together, but were able to find seats across the aisle from each other. I squeezed our two suitcases onto the overhead rack a little way down the aisle and opted to hold the laptop case on my lap.

Miss Maggie sat next to a businesswoman who talked into her cellphone about synergies and paradigms nonstop until we reached Washington. I had a twenty-something man who played computer games on *his* phone. I swear, half the folks in our car were doing something or other on *their* phones. Whatever happened to the days when passengers brought crossword puzzles or a good book to pass the time?

The day began bright and sunny, and the ride up through Virginia, D.C., Maryland, and across the Chesapeake was pleasant. In Washington, the businesswoman disembarked, so I moved over to sit with Miss Maggie. We chatted, pointed out the window, and used the decaf coffee I fetched from the snack car to wash down the granola bars we'd packed.

Halfway between Baltimore and Wilmington, clouds began rolling in. By mid-afternoon, the sky was packed with gray fluff. As we reached Philly, before the tracks went underground, I spied the first flurries floating down from above.

Cella had emailed me last night that the viewing would be Wednesday evening and the funeral Thursday. Good thing, I thought, not only because of the weather, but because our train was late. We missed the four-twenty local to Norristown and had to wait an hour for the next one. Just as well. After sitting so long, Miss Maggie's arthritic joints had stiffened up again and she wanted to stay on her feet a bit. Truth to tell, my knees needed a lot of loosening up, too.

I stopped at the payphones to call Cella and warn her of our later arrival, then we bought hot cider and muffins, not wanting anything more substantial since dinner would be waiting at Aunt Sophie's when we arrived. After standing to snarf our snack, we took a stroll around 30th Street Station, with me wheeling both our suitcases behind.

Miss Maggie, thrilled to have extra time to explore the terminal, regaled me with stories about the building of the great Pennsylvania and Union Pacific Railroad stations. You can't take her anywhere without getting a history lesson of some sort. I never minded. She always managed to fascinate.

A little after five-ten, I herded Miss Maggie and our suitcases onto the tiny elevator up to the Norristown track. The platform was packed with rush hour commuters. On the bright side, I thought, all those people helped to block the cold damp wind that was whipping through the train shed. I shrugged my coat up to cover my neck. The air felt at least fifteen degrees colder here than in Virginia.

This time of day, trains pulled in every few minutes and you had to keep an eye on both the electronic scheduler and each train's signs to make sure you got the right one. When I spotted the green "Norristown" label, I urged Miss Maggie forward and inside, causing a logjam as I lifted our suitcases up onto the inadequate shelf over the seats, designed at most for briefcases and backpacks. But at last we were settled and chugging our way down into the dark tunnels through the city.

Our ride up along the Schuylkill River took not quite an hour and Miss Maggie found something to ask about or point out nearly every minute of the trip. The station names intrigued her—Wissahickon, Manayunk, Miquon, Conshohocken. She made me repeat them aloud until she could echo back my pronunciation like a native: "*Wiss-uh-HICK-en, MAN-ee-yunk, MEE-kwahn, CUN-shee.*" And of course, the river's name: "*SKOO-kull.*"

We were sitting on the river side of the train. In the fading afternoon light, I spotted mallards and Canada geese bobbing on the water, oblivious to the dainty snowflakes landing on their backs. A few cute little chubby black and white ducks bobbed there, too. I made a mental note to ask Beth Ann what they were.

Night stole in completely before we reached DeKalb Street in Norristown. I was glad I'd called Cella, not wanting to hang around the station in the dark longer than necessary. Norristown calls itself a borough, but it's actually a small city, with its share of urban crime.

Cella was right where she said she'd be, in the parking lot behind the station, wearing a white ski cap that made her stand out in the dark. She was jumping up and down, waving her arms to get our attention. Or maybe to keep warm. The wind was in our faces as we crossed the lot to join her and felt way colder than the "33 F" on the lighted bank sign up the street. Snowflakes were stinging my skin and I was glad to see Miss Maggie tug her scarf back up over her nose.

My cousin and I have been mistaken for sisters all our lives. We're the same height, same age, and have the same unruly brunette hair. Her face and body are rounder than mine. I'm more of a pear, the Sicilian influence of my mom's side. Tonight, Cella's shape was emphasized by a well-insulated winter coat buttoned up to her chin.

She hurried forward, wrapping me in a bear hug. "Don't mistake this for affection, Pat. I'm after body heat."

Letting go of both suitcases, I hugged her back. "Same here." I started to introduce Miss Maggie but Cella cut me off.

"Into the car first, then we'll be social." Grabbing the handles of both bags, she wheeled them over to a black Neon parked just a few feet away and opened the passenger door.

"Where's the minivan?" I asked.

Cella reached around inside to unlock the back door. "Decided to shed the whole suburban mom persona. What do I need a van for anyway? Only got two kids. I traded it in on a used Neon. Same model as yours. We're twins."

"We're not twins unless your trunk leaks."

"Big time. In fact, I'll put your bags in the backseat so they won't smell like mildew. Get in, it's snowing harder."

The flurries had mutated to the large blowing flakes that signal the onset of a blizzard. Miss Maggie huddled into the front seat. She didn't get to be ninety-one by dawdling out in the cold. I took the back, squeezing in beside the suitcases, using my gloves to wipe the snow off the laptop case. Miss Maggie, with wool around her face, plus arthritis and mittens, was having trouble fastening her seat belt. I reached around to snap her buckle before strapping myself in.

By the time Cella pulled out of the lot, the white stuff was coming down hard enough that she needed her wipers. We didn't have much time for being social. At first, Cella needed all her concentration to make the left out of the lot. Then, the distance to Aunt Sophie's was less than a half mile, even counting the extra block my cuz drove so she could turn onto Main Street from the opposite direction and park on the same side as the house. Not that there was a free space. Never seemed to be one on this block, regardless of the fact that more than half the houses had been torn down to make parking lots. Of the row of eight homes, only two now remained, Aunt Sophie's and old Mrs. Ranelli's next door.

As we slowed to a stop beside Uncle Leo's Olds, a tall wiry figure came out of Aunt Sophie's house, jogging around the silver pickup truck in front of us, into the glow of Cella's headlights.

"Vinny," I said, identifying another cousin, one of Aunt Sophie's grandkids.

Cella nodded. "I told Aunt Sophie to hold him here long enough to save the parking space for me."

"He's not eating dinner with us?"

Cella shook her head. "Just stopped by after work to drop off a bag of rock salt. He wants to get home early in this weather."

I wondered if maybe we should go right to Cella's place, though missing dinner would break Aunt Sophie's heart. Miss Maggie's, too.

As we waited to park, I surveyed my aunt's home, a plain brick rowhouse, three stories, maybe eighteen feet wide, with about ten feet of pavement separating house from street. A bright outdoor spot lit the cement stoop, iron railing, and most of the walk. Above the door, the vestibule light shone through the half-round transom. In the front downstairs windows, a dim table lamp cast a warm, inviting glow through frilly white curtains.

Mrs. Ranelli's house next door, on the other hand, came across as an evil twin, upper floors dark and no windows at all on the first level. Used to be a store, my parents had told me, and when it closed, instead of putting in normal windows, they just bricked in the whole wall.

Funny, I'd been to Aunt Sophie's hundreds of times and never thought twice about Mrs. Ranelli's house. Tonight it spooked me a little. I guess I still wasn't used to seeing it without Uncle Rocco's home next door, snuggling up against Mrs. Ranelli's other side.

Rocco's had been leveled not long before I left for Virginia last year, when he sold it before going into the nursing home. Anyway, tonight Mrs. Ranelli's place struck me as lonely and deserted.

Vinny pulled away, Cella parked and we got out. The pavement, I noted, was starting to feel slippery beneath my feet. The unsure footing and weight of the laptop on one shoulder made me feel unbalanced.

"Good thing we wore our boots, Miss Maggie," I said, helping her out of the car. Last thing she needed was broken bones.

My mentor stuck her tongue out, not as commentary, but to catch snowflakes. "I hope we get enough for a good snowball fight tomorrow." Like I said, she had lots in common with your average toddler.

Taking her arm, hoping we wouldn't go down together, I helped her up the steps, which even in nice weather wouldn't have been easy for her with her arthritis, being fairly steep and only one railing to hold onto. At the top, I turned to ask my cousin, "Is the weather supposed to get worse? Will we be able to drive to your place later?"

"Don't have to. We're here." Cella was liberating the suitcases from the backseat, lifting them onto the sidewalk.

"You're staying with Aunt Sophie?" Made more sense to me. With my aunt's kids out of the house, she had the whole third floor empty.

"Nope," Cella replied. "You're staying next door with me."

"You're living with Mrs. Ranelli?"

"Didn't Aunt Sophie tell you? Mrs. Ranelli died right after Christmas." Cella gave me the kind of grin I hadn't seen on her since the last time she told me she was pregnant. "You're looking at the new owner of 349 East Main."

4

I had no chance to react to Cella's pronouncement because Aunt Sophie was at the door urging us to come inside quickly and not let the cold in. Too late for that on a windy night like this, but at least the cold had to run a maze before finding a living space.

First you entered a little four-by-five vestibule with shiny subway tile wainscoting on the walls and a cheap rag rug over the hardwood floor. The door at the opposite end had a gorgeous cut-glass panel, which Miss Maggie cooed over. Then her aged, rheumy eyes (which were the only thing you could see on her face between her scarf and hat) widened. "Something smells absolutely luscious!" she exclaimed.

The air was indeed thick with the aroma of homemade tomato sauce. I closed my eyes and breathed deep. Nirvana. My family still understood the importance of a proper olfactory welcome.

I gave my aunt a big hug and kiss, wiped my feet, and introduced Miss Maggie, in that order.

Aunt Sophie seemed smaller than when I'd last seen her. Sure, I'd outgrown her by two inches by the time I was fifteen, but she had the kind of congenial, slightly bossy personality that made up for lack of height. Now, though, she seemed a bit more bent and I swear she'd lost weight. The pink fleece top she was wearing under her full apron looked two sizes too big. Yet her vitality was still intact.

"Take off your coats," she said, shooing us through the vestibule into the hall beyond. "Marcella, leave their bags there by the door. Nobody else is coming tonight in this weather. Hang your things here on the wall. You know how, Tricia."

I'd always been and always would be "Tricia" to my aunts and uncles, just like Cella would always be Marcella.

The hall was lit by the same glary wall sconces I remembered. In deference to rising electric costs, Uncle Leo had put in lower wattage flourescent compacts, leaving the high ceiling in eerie bluish shadows. You couldn't read in here anymore without getting eyestrain, but we had enough illumination to hang our coats, scarves and hats on the long row of pegs along the left wall. A carpet remnant ran the length beneath our feet, soaking up the slush we tracked in. I found a dry spot against the opposite wall to park the laptop.

The theme for the *Nightly News* drifted down the hall to my ears. Behind us, the front parlor was, as usual, unoccupied, a dim lamp left on for security only, so the house would look occupied from the street. Ahead, the hallway widened out, with stairs to the upper floors along the wall and a doorway beside it leading to the back of the house. I could see the lights of the kitchen through the dark dining room.

On the right was a doorway into the sitting room where we found Uncle Leo in his Lazy-Boy, dozing before the TV, hands curled around the sports section of today's *Times Herald*, now flat on his lap. The room still smelled vaguely of stale cigar smoke, though Uncle Leo had given up the habit six years ago.

"Leo! They're here," Aunt Sophie shouted, making my uncle jump. The recliner righted itself with a bang and the newspaper slid to the floor.

"I heard them come in," Uncle Leo lied, standing up to greet us. That was for Miss Maggie, I assumed. I'd hugged and kissed him while he sat in his chair lots of times. So had Cella. He didn't get up for mere nieces. Then again, the embrace he gave me made me feel missed.

"How you doing, Tricia?" he asked in a gravelly voice that came from smoking too many stogies in his lifetime.

"I'm good, Uncle. How 'bout you?"

He let go of me with a shrug. "Can't complain. The Phillies haven't lost a game this season. 'Cause they haven't played one yet."

He'd been telling that same joke every February at the start of spring training as long as I could remember. Cella and I still laughed. Miss Maggie, too. I introduced her.

"Call me Magnolia or just Maggie," she said, offering her hand to my aunt and uncle. "Pat's told me so much about all of you." With a gesture of her other arm, she included Cella and every other Montella, too. "I'm pleased as punch to meet you."

All three reciprocated the feeling. Formalities over, Cella grabbed my left hand and pulled me over to the floor lamp, the better to examine my ring. Aunt Sophie came, too, so as not to miss the first ogle. Uncle Leo was content to wait his turn.

"Ooh," Cella gushed. "Four diamonds, and how unusual!"

"Unusual" was a polite word for "ugly." The ring had belonged to Hugh's Great-aunt Mildred and was the epitome of Roaring Twenties gaudiness. The diamonds were nearly microscopic, but the real stars were the surrounding blood-red garnets and all the ornate silver. It begged to be polished every month. I'd worn the thing three weeks before the weight of it no longer made me feel off-balance. Yet I loved the ring, partly because it was unique, mostly because I loved the man that came with it.

Cella kept her eyes on my finger as she relinquished my hand to our aunt. "Antique jewelry is made so much better than modern. Antique anything, for that matter. Ronny never got that. He wouldn't buy anything unless it was new."

I saw regret in her eyes, and a little envy. Made me want to give her a big hug, but I couldn't without rudely yanking my hand away from my aunt.

"This guy of yours—" Uncle Leo said. "What's his name?"

"Hugh." I'd told my uncle every time I'd talked to him on the phone in the last three months.

"Your aunt told me he works at the post office."

"He's postmaster where we live in Virginia." Admittedly, I was out to impress. I didn't mention that Bell Run's postal facility was only big enough for three people to stand in line for stamps at any one time, which you have to do because we don't have a stamp machine.

"They make good money at the post office," Aunt Sophie said as she let go of my hand at last. My aunt believed that everyone made "good money" except her own kids and me. Where I was concerned, her beliefs were justified.

Kicking back into hostess-gear, where her main duty was to stuff her guests full, Aunt Sophie shut off the TV and urged us toward the food.

Miss Maggie begged a bathroom break first and Aunt Sophie nodded her sympathy. "Top of the stairs." She hit the switch at the bottom of the steps and light shone down from the landings above. "Tricia, you show her where. You probably gotta tinkle, too, after that long trip."

None of my Montella aunts consider the discussion of bodily functions to be impolite, and they all use their own entertaining vocabulary.

I led Miss Maggie up the steps, her going slow, and not only because today's trek had done a job on her arthritis. She kept pausing to gaze up the stairwell, which was one of the house's prettiest features, forming a spiral square all the way to the third floor, with ornate balusters and newel posts.

"How lovely," she declared. "What a beautiful Victorian townhouse. Do you know when it was built, Pat?"

I shook my head. "I only know that my great-grandparents moved in here sometime before World War One, then my grandparents raised their kids here, then Aunt Sophie."

"Three generations," Miss Maggie said with approval. "They took good care of the place."

When we reached the bathroom, I said, "Dad once told me this used to be a tiny closet. Just before the Depression, Grandpop and Uncle Rocco put in a toilet, but no sink or anything. Wasn't until Uncle Leo and Aunt Sophie took over the place that they knocked out a wall and built a full bath."

Felt kind of neat to be giving Miss Maggie a history lesson for once, though I had to cut it short so she could use the plumbing. I did likewise, noting that both old porcelain faucets in the sink were dripping profusely. I made a mental note to change the washers for them while I was here.

Miss Maggie and I headed down to supper. I thought we'd be eating in the dining room, but that room was still dark. By the light stealing in from the kitchen I could see that the dining room table was in its usual state of double duty. Uncle Leo had his tax forms spread over half of it, and Aunt Sophie had baked goods and loaves of bread half hidden under clean dishcloths at the other end. Some folks used bread boxes, some pie safes, Aunt Sophie used her dining room table.

The kitchen was warm and cozy from the added heat of the oven. I'd always loved Aunt Sophie's kitchen, nice and big and bright, with white metal cabinets and a white hammered tin ceiling. Only the appliances and vinyl floor had been updated in my lifetime.

The large table was stainless steel with a speckled red top, circa 1950. Tonight it was set for five, which made me ask Cella, "Where are your kids?"

"At my mom's. Tomorrow's a school day, unless they get snowed out—"

"They aren't staying with you at your new house?" I asked, surprised.

"New, my foot." Uncle Leo settled himself at the head of the table. "Ranelli's place is a dump."

"It is *not* a dump," Cella protested, turning to reassure me. "Needs some work is all, but I've got the kitchen and bath done. You'll be comfortable. I just didn't want Janine and Joan to have to switch school districts mid-year. Living with Mom, they can stay in Methacton."

"Don't listen to your uncle, Marcella," Aunt Sophie said from the stove where she was making last-minute pot checks. "Gonna be nice having you and the girls next door. I put your mail on the dining room buffet like usual. Don't forget it."

"You don't have to take my mail in, Aunt Sophie," Cella told her, as if this wasn't the first time. "It's only junk mail, either for 'Resident' or still in Mrs. Ranelli's name—"

"You don't want to leave the mailbox full all week, Marcella." Aunt Sophie lowered the gas on the back burner. "Sure sign of an empty house. Somebody be breaking in if you're not careful."

Uncle Leo grunted. "Nothing to steal over there."

"Never you mind," my aunt said to her husband before turning back to Cella. "Besides, today you got a box of chocolates."

My cousin's eyebrows went up. "I did?"

"Not postmarked," Aunt Sophie said. "FTD, I guess, but they put it in the mailbox since you weren't there. I don't know who they're from. No card. At least not on the outside."

I could see definite disadvantages to living next door to Aunt Sophie. Lack of privacy for one.

Cella had already poked her head into the dining room, looking for her package. "Where are they?"

"Oh, I gave them to your mother when she came by to drop off cookies for tomorrow night."

"You gave them to Ma?"

"Sure. She said you gave up chocolate for Lent. She's gonna put them in her freezer so they won't tempt you and nobody else'll eat them."

"Swell," my cousin said with a pout.

I voiced what I thought was the important question. "Who's sending you candy?"

"I guess we won't know until the Easter thaw." Cella's tone was flippant enough to put any theory of a secret lover to rest.

"Somebody paying back a favor," Uncle Leo said. "Marcella's always doing favors for people. Didn't you help somebody clean out their attic last week?"

"Week before." Cella shrugged. "Could be."

Conversation waned as Aunt Sophie brought a casserole out of the oven—rigatoni baked like lasagna with ricotta and sauce and gooey mozzarella. Drool-inducing. I jumped up to help run filled plates over to the stove for extra sauce while Cella sawed slices of Italian bread for everyone.

Aunt Sophie turned to Miss Maggie. "Tricia told us you got to watch your cholesterol, so I didn't put meat in the sauce. Just onions and basil, like how we used to eat it in the Depression." An apology, as if she hadn't put out a hundred percent, hospitality-wise.

"I like it this way," grunted Uncle Leo, then he smiled. "Makes me feel young again. Like my mom used to make when I was in knickers."

Miss Maggie sprinkled Romano cheese on her helping. "My parents kept hens back then, so at least we had eggs to eat. I learned to cook 'em every which way, to make 'em seem different each day, but once we could afford meat again, my husband never wanted to see another egg."

Doing the math in my head, I realized Miss Maggie would have been a young wife and mother during the Depression, before she earned two degrees and became a revered teacher/historian/author. I tried to picture her in her younger days and failed. Almost everything I knew about her happened after 1940.

After Miss Maggie raved over her first taste, we all fell silent as we satisfied our hunger. The baked rigatoni was kind of heavy on the stomach after a long train ride and so close to bedtime, but it took the cold out of my bones. Did wonders for my psyche, too. As much as I loved living at Bell Run, I had to admit that part of me had needed a fix of hometown and family for way too long.

I turned to Uncle Leo. "I saw your faucets upstairs are dripping. I'll change the washers for you tomorrow."

My uncle scowled like he does when a Phillies pitcher blows a save. "Tried that twice already. The plastic washers they got these days are crap."

Aunt Sophie passed Miss Maggie the salad bowl. "Those old faucets are all stripped inside. We need new ones. Just like we need a new freezer down the cellar and the roof needs painting and the oil heater needs . . . something. Doesn't heat the water like it used to. But your uncle here, he's saving his money for a rainy day."

Uncle Leo, still scowling, said, "Aw, what do *you* know?" His standard retort to Aunt Sophie when she had the better of an argument. He turned his full attention to his macaroni.

I was sorry I'd brought up the subject and was hunting around in my head for another. All I seemed to find there was a new worry that maybe my aunt and uncle weren't quite making ends meet. Not that I could help. I wasn't making ends meet either.

Up on the wall, the phone jangled. It was one of those museum pieces with a dial and real bell, hung where Aunt Sophie could answer it from her seat, but with an extra long cord so she could carry the receiver around the kitchen or into the dining room. As with the discussion of bodily functions, none of my aunts considered calls during dinner to be impolite. The phone was simply another way to welcome guests into their homes, without the obligation of having to feed them. Even telemarketers were greeted like prodigal children. The latter always hung up on my aunts instead of vice versa.

Which is why I was surprised when Aunt Sophie raised her voice. "I already told you, no."

I could hear noise on the other end of the line—a high-pitched, rapid, angry buzz, like a bee caught inside the globe of a porch light.

"You saw everything I have here," Aunt Sophie protested. "Clothes, photo—" More buzzing.

Uncle Leo glanced up from his pasta, meeting my eye, as if knowing I'd want to be clued in. "Beatrice," was all he said, all he felt he had to say.

As I said, Beatrice was Uncle Rocco's only grandchild and none of my dad's siblings, or their spouses, or their kids, got along with her or her mother. But that didn't tell me what was going on.

Aunt Sophie was still trying to get a word in edgewise on the phone, so Cella explained. "Beatrice has been calling here since yesterday morning. Can't find her grandfather's money."

"What?"

Cella nodded. "Remember last year when Uncle Rocco was in the hospital?"

"He had a stroke." I remembered how we all expected him to die that weekend, but he managed to cheat the Reaper for the umpteenth time, and with almost no lasting effects other than a slight droop to his lip, weak legs, and a tendency to mix up past and present. "That's when he went into a nursing home."

"Beatrice didn't wanna take care of him herself," Uncle Leo grumbled. "Shoulda took him in. She got a big house and only her and her husband there."

"Uncle Rocco must have thought so, too," Cella said, waving her fork for emphasis, "because he told Aunt Sophie where he kept his safe deposit key in his house. Told her to take it and not give it to Beatrice 'til after he died."

"Get outta town!" I exclaimed, but really not all that surprised. My family's superstitious enough to avoid final arrangements like wills, yet where the inspiration is spite instead of generosity, all bets are off.

"Sophie did just what he wanted." Uncle Leo dragged a slice of bread through the sauce on his plate. "Put the key in a little envelope in the china closet, all safe. Gave it back to Beatrice Sunday night."

I was impressed that Aunt Sophie had been able to find that key again. The china closet in her dining room is packed with unmarked envelopes protecting everything from spare keys to old Miraculous Medals. You can barely see her good china anymore.

"First thing Monday morning," Cella continued, "Beatrice went to the bank—"

"Now you listen to me, Beatrice," Aunt Sophie shrieked, angrier than I'd seen her since her daughter Lucretia was in her teenage-talking-back stage twenty years ago. "Go ask the bank if I used that key. They'll tell you I can't. All I have from Rocco is old photos, his Knights of Columbus uniform, his—"

When the buzzing once more cut her off, Aunt Sophie simply hung up, an act so out of character for her, even Uncle Leo stopped eating.

Aunt Sophie exhaled an angry, frustrated lungful of air, then looked at our plates. "Who wants more macaroni?" Uncle Leo lifted his dish to pass it to his wife, but Cella ignored him.

"What did Beatrice say?" my cousin asked.

I grabbed Uncle Leo's plate and refilled it while Aunt Sophie replied. "She says I took her grandfather's money. She *accused* me. *Me!*"

"Wasn't there anything in his safe deposit box?" I asked, getting up to fetch my uncle some more sauce.

"Sure there was." Aunt Sophie passed the grated cheese to her husband. "Beatrice said she found the deed to the family grave, a life insurance policy—I don't know for how much—and his wife's engagement ring, not that it's worth anything. Rocco couldn't afford a good ring back then. Instead, he saved up his money and bought the house he had his apartment in."

I returned to the table and set the steaming dish before Uncle Leo. "Beatrice expected to find cash? Is that it?"

"Bonds, I guess," Aunt Sophie replied, "or C.D.s or something. I remember Uncle Rocco talking about stuff like that, but maybe he cashed them all in. He had a ton of medical bills this last decade."

"Long retirements can eat up your savings," Miss Maggie commented, the voice of experience. One reason she was still writing books at her age.

Uncle Leo stabbed three rigatoni with his fork. "Yeah, but Rocco had a nest egg someplace. Everybody knew it. He was like a magnet for money. Always drove a big car. Always flashing fifties at the grocery store. When he used to take the casino bus down Atlantic City, he won at the slots every time. Money loved him."

Aunt Sophie nodded. "He was generous with it, you gotta say that for him. When we were little, he gave us kids dimes every holiday."

"Us, too," I chimed in, "except by that time—"

"—we got Bicentennial quarters," my cousin concluded.

"Kennedy half dollars for First Communion and Confirmation," I added.

"I still have mine," Cella laughed. "And my girls got Sacajawea dollars."

Uncle Leo spoke around the pasta in his mouth. "He went back to quarters when they started putting states on them."

"Okay, we agree Uncle Rocco used to have bucks," Cella mused. "The question is, did he *still* have bucks when he died?"

Aunt Sophie's brow crinkled in thought. "He didn't keep much in his checking account. I know because I helped him balance his checkbook and pay his bills these last few years, after he started getting confused about stuff like that. He was living off his pension and Social Security."

Cella set her fork across her plate and pushed it away an inch. "If he did have money left, he must have invested it without leaving a record of where. Or maybe, like Aunt Sophie said, he got confused. Threw away the documents or—"

"Maybe he buried his money in his backyard," I joked.

Uncle Leo chuckled. "That would be a problem, 'cause now you got tons of trucks parked on top from that company over on Penn Street."

Cella was shaking her head like she took us seriously, or more likely, wasn't paying attention. "No, I bet he invested it. I wonder if we could figure out where." She was talking almost to herself, and enjoying the conversation. Then, as she met my eye, a look that was pure Indiana Jones spread over her face. "Let's go treasure hunting this week, Pat."

> "There is not an unemployed man in the country that hasn't contributed to the wealth of every millionaire in America."
>
> —WILL ROGERS, NOVEMBER 1931

February 28, 1933 – 349 East Main Street, Norristown

Somebody scared the cat and that started everything.

Relatives and friends were arriving, everyone coming in the kitchen door. Only formal guests ever came in the front, like Father Travi when he came once a year.

Crisi stayed by the door, inspecting every pair of legs that entered, as was her habit. I think it was Great-aunt Michaela who scared her. Aunt Michaela had that kind of loud voice and she didn't care what was in her way as she moved. Crisi scooted out toward the sitting room. I followed, not because I wanted to bring the cat back to the party, but to get away from Great-aunt Michaela and her sloppy kisses myself.

Crisi kept going, through the sitting room to the front hall—two halls actually, shaped like an L. One led straight to the front door. The other ran along the back of the store, parallel to the front stairs, and ended at a side exit into the narrow alley between the houses. Uncle Ennio sometimes used this hallway as a place to stack extra inventory, but not during the Depression. He couldn't afford extra inventory then.

In this side hall was the only door into the store from the house. Every night after the store closed, Vito and Pip boxed up any fruit that had become too ripe to sell—apples, oranges, pears, bananas—and carried them next door to Rocco Montella's apartment. Uncle Ennio said Rocco knew a guy who'd buy half-rotten fruit for two cents more a pound than it cost. Rocco acted as middleman and took ten percent of the profits to do the delivery, but Uncle Ennio could still make a little extra this way, instead of losing his investment when unsold fruit went bad.

The Montellas were Southern Italian, whereas we were Sicilian. Back then, that was like being from different planets. Sure, we all went to the same church, but we had separate dialects, separate clubs, separate holidays and separate friends. We didn't much associate with each other, except, of course, that Uncle Ennio would welcome anyone into his store as long as they had money to spend.

Rocco, though, had a smile for everyone. A year ago he'd extended a neighborly hand by coming over to help my uncle and the older boys run a new pipe up from the basement. Afterward, they struck up the rotten fruit deal. Since the deal allowed our family to put a chicken on the table now and then, Uncle Ennio decided Rocco was okay.

Pip and Vito were carrying today's boxes out the side door as I got out to the hall. Of the two older boys, Pip was tallest, though he was younger than Vito by two years and had only graduated high school last spring. They both towered over Uncle Ennio, who was five-foot-four. Like everyone in the family, the older boys had thick, curly, almost black hair, and warm brown eyes.

Vito saw me when he turned to close the door behind him. "Don't come out, Bambola. It's too cold. We'll be back in a little bit." He gave me a wink, then shut the door behind him.

I wasn't interested in going outside anyway. I could see Del's feet, in brown woolen stockings with no shoes, up on the stair landing as she sat in the doorway of our bedroom. That was odd, 'cause if she wanted to hear who was coming in, plus catch the heat wafting up from the kitchen, she would have been sitting at the top of the back stairs, in her parents' bedroom. See, we didn't have hallways in the back part of the house.

Crisi scooted up the steps and I followed. By the time I reached the top, the cat was settling in on Del's lap.

"Bambola, did Vito and Pip close up the store?" Del asked, petting the tiny tuft of white hair on Crisi's chest with one hand while using the other to hold her skirt, so the weight of the cat wouldn't pull the hem up past her knees. I don't know why. Nobody could see her flannel long underwear but me, and I saw them every night 'cause she slept in a pair of them, like all us kids did.

When I nodded to her question, Del set Crisi on the floor behind her, then stood up. Instead of going back into our bedroom, though, my cousin crossed the landing and went up three more steps, like she was headed for the bathroom, but she passed that door. Crisi and I followed her down the hall to the front of the house.

The room on the second floor front was a formal parlor. We weren't allowed in except when special guests came, like when Father Travi blessed the house every fall. Then we had to be all cleaned up and wearing Sunday clothes, and he made us all kneel on the carpet.

Anyway, the door was kept locked, but Del took a bobby pin out from where it was clipped on the inside hem of her skirt. She wasn't supposed to have bobby pins. Aunt Gina said regular hair pins worked just as well and we had plenty of them in the house without buying some newfangled product. Del told me that bobby pins held her hair better, even when she was playing baseball. She helped a girl at school do her homework for a month in trade for four bobby pins, which she kept hidden on her hem. She only wore them at school so her mama wouldn't find out.

I didn't understand then that Del was picking the lock, and even if I did, I was too young to realize there was anything wrong with it. I just knew she was going into a place we weren't usually allowed and I was curious enough to want to see. That and I didn't want to go back downstairs to Aunt Michaela yet.

"Don't let Crisi in, Bambola," Del warned me. "Mama finds one cat hair on the rug in here and I'll be in my bedroom through Easter." She caught Crisi by the scruff of the neck while she pushed the door open just wide enough for me to go in, then she came in after me, closing the door quietly behind her.

Aunt Gina kept heavy curtains on the front windows, to keep the sun from fading her carpet. The only light we had was the tiny bit that shone under the door from the bulb in the bathroom hall. I couldn't see at all at first and had to rely on my other senses. The room was cold. A big radiator stood in the corner, but in those days Uncle Ennio never fired up the cellar furnace. It wasted too much coal. The heat from the kitchen stove couldn't get in here, and directly below us was the store, which Uncle Ennio wanted cool so his produce wouldn't go bad too fast.

The air smelled dusty and stale. Not liking what I felt and smelled, I ran back toward the door, careening into Del's legs, feeling the scratchy wool of her long sweater brush my face. She took my hand and I felt braver.

"We're not going to turn on the light, Bambola. Somebody might see it from outside and tell Mama when they come in. Wait a minute while our eyes adjust."

In that minute, I saw eerie white shapes appear in the room, not ghosts but furniture covered with bedsheets. To a tot's mind, though, they might as well have been ghosts. I squeezed Del's hand tighter.

"We're going to walk over to look out the window," Del told me. If I hadn't been so young, I might have heard in her voice, well, not fear exactly. More like subtle misgiving, like she was having second thoughts, but she didn't change her mind. Del was always stubborn. *Testa dura*, Uncle Ennio used to call her, which meant she had a hard head.

"We'll go this way, over to one side, around the furniture," Del said as she led me past the white blobs. "That way the floorboards in the middle won't creak." That's why she waited for Pip and Vito to leave the store, so they wouldn't hear footsteps overhead.

We were halfway to the window when we heard murmuring, like somebody was talking to us, but from very far away, and yet the voice seemed to be right next to us.

Del froze in her tracks. "What was that?"

We both listened, and I realized in that moment how utterly quiet that room was. I couldn't hear the family downstairs anymore, nor anything outside. Of course, back then we didn't have much traffic on Main Street, not at night. During the Depression, you only owned a pleasure car if you were rich.

The murmur came again, so faint we couldn't make out words, but coming from right beside us, where the fireplace was. Oh, it wasn't a real fireplace anymore. The front was closed up with wood panels painted white. I could see that and the white mantel above it, framed by the darker, flowered wallpaper around it. The murmurs sounded like some tiny person was standing on that mantel, calling to us.

"Vito and Pip must be back down in the store." Del let go of my hand and, going down on her hands and knees, she put her ear to the floor. After another quiet moment, she stood up, unsatisfied. "No sound from down there. Must be someone next door, standing right next to this wall. Come on, Bambola, let's look out the window."

Del didn't like her explanation, knowing the second floor apartment in the house next door had been empty since last October. She was just trying to get us away from those murmurs. Over at the window, she pulled the drape back only far enough so she could peek out, but it was far enough for me to slip between the heavy cloth and the sill, which my chin just reached.

The glass didn't have condensation like the windows on the

north side of the house, but being short, I still couldn't see as much as I wanted to. I turned around and held my arms up to Del.

"Can't see, huh?" Turning me back around, Del put her arm around my tummy and lifted me until my feet were on the sill. She kept her arm around my hips, encouraging me to lean back against her. I wanted to lean forward onto the cold window glass, to see as much as possible.

Not that the view was anything special, just Logrippe's house across the street. Next to it was Ronca's, a big old Gothic double with gingerbread trim, set back far enough to have a yard with grass and, unlike the rest of us, a nice front porch. Cousins lived in both sides of that double, and I remember Mrs. Ronca or Mrs. Chicco standing at the wrought iron gate out by the sidewalk, talking to their neighbors on nice days. That night, all the lights were on in their front rooms.

I remember liking the perspective from here better than the same view from the floor above. I felt closer to the action. Yet, I honestly can't recall what action I noticed at first. Being *Carnivale*, likely I saw people on the street, going to and from various parties, and an occasional truck, simply because this was the main route in or out of Norristown's East End, but nothing sticks in my mind, not until we'd been standing there a minute or so.

I was just starting to mind the draft seeping in around the pane of glass when a large automobile came down the street, bigger than any car I'd ever seen in my life. Its green hood shone in the glare of the streetlamps.

"Holy cow!" Del exclaimed. "I bet that's a Duesenburg! And it's the color of money."

She didn't know from nothing about Duesenburgs, other than reading that rich folks like movie stars were driven around in them by chauffeurs. Pip told us later that the car was a LaSalle, and a small one at that.

All of a sudden, the driver swerved over to our side of the street, bumping over the trolley tracks, parking along the curb directly in front of our house.

"Holy cow!" Del said again.

The driver swung his door open and pushed himself out. "No chauffeur's uniform," Del observed, sounding like a live chauffeur done up in a fancy uniform would have made her day.

This guy didn't disappoint, all spiffed up as he was in a long, tailored wool coat, Homburg hat, white scarf about his neck, sleek dark gloves on his hands, and a long cigarette holder between his teeth. Reaching in behind him, he extracted a walking stick whose tip glittered like a star when the light hit it. He was on the plump side, reminding me of the mysterious gentleman in the Wash Scrubs comic that Pip read to me sometimes from the newspaper.

Only this man didn't have his nose in the air. In fact, he was swaying a little, and holding his middle like his gut hurt him. Once he got his car door closed, he leaned back against it while he surveyed the houses. When he caught sight of us in the second floor window, his survey turned to a stare.

Del quickly lowered me back to the floor and pushed up the window, letting in a blast of cold air. As she stuck her head outside, I squeezed alongside her, stepping up onto the baseboard until I could see again.

"Hey, mister!" she called. "You lost or something?"

That seemed to rally the man. He pushed himself off the car and took a few steps forward, letting his walking stick support him. Snatching the cigarette holder from his mouth, he called in a frail, throaty voice, "Young lady, please tell Mr. Montella that Mr. Lowell wishes to speak with him." Smoke puffed from between his teeth as he spoke, either from the cigarette or just 'cause it was a cold night.

Del didn't tell him he had the wrong house. She was too busy being agog. "Lowell! Holy cow! Are you Lloyd Lowell? The one who's in the newspaper all the time? The one who buries the poor orphans?"

What she meant was that when an orphan died and no one could afford a proper coffin and plot, Mr. Lowell allowed the use of his large family burial vault. During the Depression, he was the closest thing Norristown had to a saint, even though he was Episcopalian.

Del didn't give him a chance to answer. "You hire my brothers sometimes, to help you with the funerals. They worked for you just last Monday."

"You must mean Vito and Joseph," he said. Joseph was Pip's real name. "So this must be the Trepani house? And Mr. Montella lives—"

"Next door. Basement apartment." Del jerked her head to the right. "I'm guessing it's Rocco you want, and not Louis Montella? He lives on the other side."

"Quite right. Rocco Montella. And I'll want a word with your brothers as well. I have work for—" He cringed, bending at the waist, as if whatever pain he had in his gut tripled. When he straightened again, he said, "Young lady, if you would go fetch Mr. Montella for me, I shall give you a dime."

"Wait right there, Mr. Lowell," Del cried. Yanking me backward, she shut the window. "Come on, Bambola. We have to go help Mr. Lowell. Ten cents. Holy cow!"

She took me by the hand and led me back through the parlor, which looked even darker now that our eyes had adjusted to the brighter out-of-doors. Del felt her way with one arm stretched in front of her.

"No time to re-lock the door," she mumbled when we were in the hall. "I'll have to sneak back up here and do it later." The cat was gone, probably returned to the party.

Downstairs we could hear Uncle Ennio's squeezebox playing, the stomp of dancers' feet, and voices talking, laughing, singing along. At the top of the big stairs, Del swept me up off the floor by my armpits and carried me down so I wouldn't slow her up. At the bottom, she set me down.

"Listen, Bambola," Del said in my ear. "You go see if Pip and Vito came back yet." Then, with a fast, furtive glance at the sitting room, she ran for the front door.

Being too young to care about following directions, I toddled after my cousin, taking advantage of her tendency to leave the front door ajar—just far enough that I could peek out.

Del was nowhere in sight, but Mr. Lowell was now sitting on our stoop. The black wool of his coat looked so fine I wanted to touch it. He must have sensed me behind him because he glanced over his shoulder. He was about Uncle Ennio's age, that is, in his early forties, with light brown hair graying at the temples. His eyes were blue, but the whites around them were watery and red, and his skin was waxen. His walking stick was beside him on the step and he had one arm around his stomach like it was paining him awful.

"Hello, little girl." More smoke wafted from his mouth and his breath smelled bad, worse than Uncle Ennio's did after he ate garlicky pork sandwiches at St. Charles Club. "What's your name?"

"She don't talk," came a voice from outside which I recognized as my brother Tutti's (*his* real name was Salvatore). I poked my head out the door until I could see the front of the house. Tutti was standing right at the tunnel between the houses. He was seven years old then, still in knickers, with a heavy sweater like me and a too-big wool cap that he always wore to make himself feel older. Every piece of clothing on him was a hand-me-down worn by Vito, Pip, Charlie, and Gussie before him.

"She don't talk," Tutti repeated, as if that explained everything, or at least, everything important at the moment. "That your car, Mister?"

Mr. Lowell nodded. Even speaking seemed difficult for him at this point.

"Sure is swell," Tutti said, walking toward the auto, admiring its lines. "I'm gonna have a car like that someday, only red and with a breezer top."

Rocco Montella came bursting out of his front door, followed by Vito, Pip and Del, in that order. Del still had no shoes on and she had to keep her feet moving to keep them warm.

Rocco was in his shirt sleeves and vest, without the collar and tie he wore as a teller at Peoples Bank, up at the other end of East Main. His wavy hair, though, was as carefully slicked back as when he left for work in the morning. He was in his late twenties then, and a good-looking man. Del had a crush on him.

"Mr. Lowell!" Rocco gave the man a concerned once-over as he held up an arm to keep everyone else back. "You're sick."

"Damned flu." Mr. Lowell had difficulty saying even that.

"You shouldn't be out."

The rich man ignored the advice. "I had to come. I need to do another funeral this Friday. Another orphan."

"What?" That was Vito, seemingly incredulous. Pip had joined Tutti in admiring the car up close, but Vito was right beside Rocco. "But we can't be ready that soon. Only Monday we—" Rocco nudged him in the ribs and he shut up.

"Someone broke into my crypt," Mr. Lowell gasped out.

"You mean somebody was grave-robbing the dead orphans?" Del exclaimed. "Why would they? Orphans got no jewelry on them."

Mr. Lowell shook his head. "Vandals. When Officer O'Connor informed me, he said he found an empty bottle that smelled of liquor on the grass. You understand?"

"Vandals drunk on bootleg hooch." Del said it as if the offense had gone from mere crime to mortal sin.

"Hoh-lee smokes." Vito made it three even syllables, which was the closest he ever came to cursing in front of family.

Mr. Lowell tried to puff on his cigarette, but it had gone out. With one hand, he checked his coat pockets. "Damn. My wife's always taking my matches."

Rocco reached into his vest pocket, bringing out a match, striking it on his fingernail in one graceful movement. My brother Tutti tried that once and burned his finger bad enough he had to wear a bandage for two weeks.

Rocco held the burning match out to light Mr. Lowell's cigarette as he asked, "Did that policeman check for damage inside the vault?"

"No," Mr. Lowell replied, his speech becoming more labored. "Squeamish. Only looked in from the top. Told him I'd send someone out tomorrow to check the vault, put the slab back. . . ."

"We can do that, Mr. Lowell," Vito assured him.

"Yeah," Rocco added. "The three of us will ride the trolley out there before I have to be at work tomorrow. And if you do another funeral Friday, we can have everything ready, Mr. Lowell, I promise."

"But how—" Vito didn't get two words out before Rocco's elbow met his ribs again. Rocco glanced up and down the street. Sure enough, people had noticed the big car and were poking their heads out of doors and windows to see what was up. Three more young boys and two teenagers ran up to join Pip and Tutti.

Mr. Lowell coughed, not like he had the flu, but like he had a mouth full of cotton balls. "Your friend, Rocco . . . the one with the Studebaker . . . will he be able to . . . to pick up the coffin?"

Rocco nodded. "I'll walk up to Orazio's place tonight and tell him you need him. Don't worry, Mr. Lowell. I'll take care of the arrangements. You just go home and get better."

Mr. Lowell, satisfied, grabbed his cane and tried to push himself to his feet, but his legs wouldn't hold him. His cigarette holder clattered to the ground. Rocco ran forward to support him and Vito took the other side, ducking his head under the man's arm. Pip opened the driver's door for them.

"You can't drive this way, Mr. Lowell," Rocco said. "I'll take you home. Mr. Lowell? Mr. Lowell!"

As the rich man's head lolled to one side, his Homburg followed the cigarette holder to the pavement. He suddenly became a dead weight. Rocco and Vito almost went down with him. Even with only streetlights, I could see that Mr. Lowell's face had turned white. His eyes were half open, unseeing.

Rocco took charge. "I'll drive him to the hospital. Vito, help me get him in the passenger side. You'd better come with me. Tutti, hand us his things. Take that cigarette out of the holder before it burns one of us. Pip, lend me your coat."

As Rocco and Vito drove off in the big car, Tutti ran back up the tunnel, knowing he could sell that high-quality Cuban cigarette to one of his uncles for a penny. The rest of us went in the front door, and Del, back up the steps toward her room.

On the landing, though, she stopped and stamped her foot. "Doggone it! I never got my dime."

5

Aunt Sophie changed the subject from Uncle Rocco's money by fetching from the dining room a pan of a dozen hot-cross buns, their icing crosses sloppy enough that I knew these were homemade. I was glad because Aunt Sophie only put raisins in hers. All the store-bought ones have citron, which in my opinion means not enough taste for all the chewing involved.

Cella and I helped pour the coffee (a good perked decaf I was happy to note) and as we drank and munched, I caught up on all the other family news. From Aunt Sophie's family, I mean. Just going through all her grandkids' doings took an hour. I would have been content to stay another hour to hear about Cella's side, but I noticed Miss Maggie starting to sag. Long day. Time to put her to bed.

The blizzard was still raging outside. Cella swept the inch that had accumulated on the top step of both stoops so we could quickly go between houses. The worst of the wind was coming from the north. The white stuff was drifting toward the street. Cella's car had snow up to the bottom of her wheel wells.

The first thing that hit me inside Cella's house was the cold. Almost seemed warmer outside. "Jeez," I remarked, shivering. "Don't your pipes freeze?"

Cella shrugged. "I lower the heat to sixty at night and when I'm out. I'll boost it up now, warm the place up 'til we go to bed."

Like Aunt Sophie's house, she had a vestibule, but no inner door, and a plastic mat instead of a rug. Beyond was a long hall with no rooms off of it. Also like Aunt Sophie's, the hall was lit by sconces, but the glass in them was dingy with years of grime. The wall-to-wall rug was threadbare.

We hung our outdoor things on a tall brass coatrack and followed Cella as she pulled my suitcase along behind her to the end of the hall. She reached through the next doorway into a dark room, to the inside wall where the thermostat apparently hung. A second later I heard the welcome sound of the furnace going on below our feet. I also noticed that I felt warmer here than in the entry. Must be a nasty draft there.

"I'll give you the grand tour tomorrow," Cella said, "but if you need it, the kitchen's that way." She waved toward the back of the house. "Let me show you where you're sleeping." She hit a switch on this side of the wall, which lit up another sconce halfway up the steps beside her.

This wasn't a stairwell like in Aunt Sophie's house, but a single flight with a hall beside it. Following Cella's example, I pushed the handle of Miss Maggie's suitcase down, grabbing the top strap to carry it up the steps, so as not to nick the hardwood risers and treads more than they already were. Miss Maggie insisted on carrying the laptop. I was glad actually. My knees were throbbing.

At the top of the stairs, Cella led us to the right, up two more steps into a room, hitting another switch for the overhead light as she entered.

What with Uncle Leo's opinion of the house and what I'd seen downstairs, I expected more decor-fatigue up here. Not so. This room looked like something out of a bed and breakfast. The walls were painted white with a stenciled geometric pattern in the colors of warm sandstone and terra cotta. The woodwork, including a mantel and paneled-in hearth on the far wall, was the same sandstone shade. A faint odor of latex still lingered.

On the hearthstone sat an antique coal scuttle holding an arrangement of red silk flowers. Twin beds with matching star quilts formed an "L" anchored by a small table in the corner that sported a lamp made out of a terra cotta pot. The rug between the beds was a nice thick brown pile. Overhead, the light was another antique, an ornate mishmash of brass and crystal that looked out of place.

Seeing my gaze, Cella felt the need to explain. "I plan to replace the ceiling fixture with a fan. Picture this as Joan's room, with one of the beds next door in Janine's room." She gestured through a doorway directly opposite. "I still have to run phone, cable and electric for their computers. If there's enough room in that thick chimney wall, I'm going to put a closet on either side. Eventually, I'd love to put windows in the outside wall. But nothing'll happen before the school year ends. I didn't say it in front of Uncle Leo, but I'm guessing the kids'll have to live at Mom's place another year."

The thought seemed to discourage her, like she knew she might have taken on too big a project but didn't want to admit it. I pointed out, "You got an amazing amount done here in so little time."

"All cosmetic. Just cleaned the grime off everything, and splashed on some paint, mainly because I needed a nice room to sleep in on weekends while I work on the apartment."

"Apartment?"

"Front of the second floor and the whole third floor," Cella replied, wheeling my suitcase over to the far bed. "I'm going to make an apartment and rent it out to pay for the rest of the renovation. Eventually, I'd love to fix up the store downstairs and rent that out, too."

Now she sounded like my cousin. She had a plan.

"Problem is," she added, "I have to add a kitchen in the apartment and at least one bathroom back here for us. The only bath in the house is—well, I'll show you."

"If you're leading us to a bathroom," Miss Maggie said, "let me bring my peejays. Because when I come back, I have a date with the sandman under one of these lovely quilts."

I lifted her suitcase onto the nearest bed and let her rummage through it. She extracted a pair of yellow flannels and pink bunny slippers, plus a small toiletry case, false teeth container, and her pill case.

Cella led us back down the two steps, across the landing, around to the left and up three more steps. The first door on the right was the bathroom.

"I leave the hall lights on at night," Cella assured us. "Too easy to take a header down the stairs otherwise."

The bathroom wasn't as big as Aunt Sophie's, but had the same subway tile as the vestibules. No shower, only a claw and ball tub at the far end, in front of a large radiator which was beginning to hiss as the steam heat rose through the house.

Cella pointed out the towels and washcloths she'd hung on the towel rack for us. "To get optimal hot water in the tub," she added, "only turn the hot spigot until the 'H' is pointing at ten o'clock, no farther. The furnace can't keep up with the water flow otherwise. Something else I have to fix."

As we left Miss Maggie to her ablutions, Cella said, "Let me show you my favorite room." She led me around the corner, down another hall toward the front of the house. The door at the end of the hall was closed but not latched.

Cella pushed it open. "Ooh, it's cold in here again. The radiator knob is rusted closed, and the door isn't plumb. Swings shut by itself. The heat from the rest of the house can't get in. But you *have* to see this."

I felt the chill as she hit the light switch, bringing on an even more ornate ceiling fixture. This time it didn't look at all out of place because the furniture, rug, drapes, wallpaper, even the hand-tatted doilies on the arms of the chairs, were all high Victorian. The fireplace mantel, though, was like the one in the other room and seemed too plain by contrast.

"Like a time tunnel, isn't it?" Cella said, spellbound. "Mrs. Ranelli said she never used this room and neither did her mother before her. I'm guessing maybe her grandmother never did either. It's essentially the same as when it was first furnished in the early 1900s. Although I gave everything a delicate but thorough cleaning last summer. At least three decades of dust."

"Last summer?" I echoed. "I thought you didn't move in until after Christmas."

"I didn't." Cella drifted through the room, running her fingertips over the wooden scroll on the back of the sofa as if to test the finish. "But I helped Mrs. Ranelli fix things around the house the last few years. Even if nothing needed fixing, I used to check up on her twice a week. She didn't have anyone else. No kids of her own, and her nieces and nephews never bothered with her. Ronny had fits. Said I ought to be home looking after my own family. I told him when he got old and helpless like Mrs. Ranelli I would."

I pictured the Mrs. Ranelli I remembered, the one Mom used to chat with over Aunt Sophie's patio wall, while I played with my cousins in the backyard. Mrs. Ranelli had been a thin, wiry little woman who wore stretch pants and bowling shirts. "She never struck me as helpless. How old was she when she died?"

"Somewhere in her eighties, I think. She wouldn't tell anyone." Cella slumped into one of the plump armchairs. "As for helpless, she wasn't until the last two years. After she broke her hip, she didn't keep active like she used to. That's when she went downhill. But she had most of her mental faculties up to the end, except being real forgetful."

Since my cousin was making herself comfy, I wandered farther into the room, regretting that I had to leave the warmer air of the hall behind. I stuck my hands in the pockets of my sweatshirt and kept myself moving. "According to Miss Maggie, if you keep body and mind active, preservation of mental faculties follows. Been working for her for nearly ninety-two years."

"I like Miss Maggie." Cella glanced toward the doorway, down the hall toward the bathroom. "Wasn't sure I would. I gotta tell you, the whole family was floored last spring when you decided to up and move to Virginia after spending a mere week there, especially when you told us Miss Maggie made you heiress to her estate. Sounded like one of you was conning the other, and since I knew that a smooth scam like that required more smarts than you carry around—"

"Gee, thanks." She was kidding. Cella knew darn well that Miss Maggie was only leaving me Bell Run because of an ancestral connection I had to the place. Not Montella ancestors, but on Ma's mother's side of the family.

At that moment, the door to the room slowly swung closed. I froze in my tracks by the hearth to watch the eerie movement, but Cella just shrugged. "See what I mean about the door not being plumb?" She turned her attention back to the finer aspects of the room. "In a way, Pat, your experience with Miss Maggie is responsible for me getting this house."

"What'd you do? Talk Mrs. Ranelli into leaving it to you?"

"No." An "of course not" was implied in Cella's tone. "Actually, Mrs. Ranelli suggested it when I told her about you. I refused. For one thing, as good as her intentions were, I knew she might never make a will. That superstitious-Italian thing."

I nodded my understanding. My parents had been the same way. The feeling was inborn, the niggling fear that as soon as you make a will, you die.

"For another," Cella continued, "I knew she was having problems living on her piddly income, what with health care and fuel costs rising. This place desperately needed a new roof, too. I said if, instead, she put the deed half in my name while she was still alive, I'd take over paying all the house expenses for her. So that's what we did."

Sounded both philanthropic and opportunistic, and the latter bothered me. "What did Ronny say?"

"What do you think? He was all for calling a real estate agent the day after Mrs. Ranelli died. That's why I was careful to pay everything out of my own savings. Ronny's got no claim to this house. That's the way Mrs. Ranelli wanted it. She knew how much I loved the place and that I wouldn't let anyone take a wrecking ball to it."

"Yeah, but how much savings do you have left?"

Cella made a face, indicating I'd whacked the refinishing nail on its head. "About as much as you, I imagine. Are you still determined not to sell your estate to developers?"

I grinned. "Picture me running all carpetbaggers and scallywags off with the evil eye. We're turning Bell Run into an educational historic site and nature center. End of story."

Cella laughed. "Next time you give someone the *malorchi*, call me. I wanna take notes." (The word for "evil eye" is really *malocchio*, but we Montellas have been pronouncing it *malorchi* for at least three generations.)

"See, we both have the same type of rocks in our skulls," my cousin continued with a sigh. "I'd love to leave this room as it is. It feels *right* this way. But I *have* to make an apartment or I can't afford to keep the house at all."

"Why don't you live in the front and make the apartment in the back?"

She shook her head. "Only two bedrooms upstairs. Not fair to make Janine and Joan share when they never had to before. In the back of the house, I can make a third bedroom for me downstairs, where the sitting room is."

"And there's no other way to divide up the house?"

"On my income? Not and still be able to put in the extra kitchen and bathroom."

"Bummer." We were both silent a moment and that's when I heard a noise, like people whispering or murmuring near the fireplace mantel. "Did you hear that?"

"What?"

I described the sound. "Almost like someone was talking in the house next door—"

"Except Uncle Rocco's house is gone," Cella said. "Nothing but snow on the other side of those bricks tonight." She came over to the hearth, bending to run her palm around the panel that sealed the opening. "I wonder if the chimney flue is open."

The explanation put my mind at ease. "That's probably it. With the storm outside, if the flue's open even a crack, the wind'll make weird noises."

"And cause yet another draft." Cella straightened up. "Crap. I'll have to pry that paneling off to fix it. If I *can* fix it myself. This house is a money toilet."

The discouragement I'd glimpsed in our bedroom earlier was back in spades. "Come on, cuz. Worry about your house some other time. Help me plan my wedding this week."

She smiled again. "You're right. Let's go down to the kitchen and plot over snacks."

On the way back down the hall, I asked, "Is there a phone jack in this house anywhere?"

"Only in the kitchen so far," Cella replied, "and I don't have it hooked up at the moment. If you need to make a call, you can use my cell."

"Not a call. I wanted to send a couple emails tonight. One, anyway, to let Hugh know we got here safe."

"Your laptop does wireless, right?"

"Sure. That's what we use at home."

"Bring it down to the kitchen with you. Let me do a potty break first and I'll be right with you." The bathroom door was now open and Cella disappeared inside.

I continued down to the landing and up to the bedroom. The radiator on the outside wall was softly hissing now and the room felt nice and cozy.

On the near bed sat Miss Maggie, in her bright yellow jammies, fluffing the pillow. "Do you need anything out of my bag, Pat? I'm so sleepy, I can't think." She slipped her legs beneath the covers.

"Don't think, Miss Maggie. Go to sleep. I'm just going to grab an antacid. Got a little *agita* from dinner. And I'll take the decaf tea bags down to the kitchen." We'd packed a big Ziploc full in the front pocket of Miss Maggie's suitcase since I was sure my cousin wouldn't stock any. "I'll be downstairs a while. Going to see if I can email Hugh and Beth Ann."

"Give them my love. Do we need the nightlight or is the hall light enough for you if I leave the door open?"

Miss Maggie always packs a plug-in nightlight. Looking around the room, though, I didn't see any outlets. The lamp pinpointed a possible location, but I'd have to crawl under the bed to look and a nightlight wouldn't be any good there anyway.

"The hall light will be plenty." I unpacked my pajama bottoms and a long-sleeved tee, plus my toothbrush and such, so I wouldn't make noise doing it later, then sat on the bed to take off my boots.

"Don't go running around in your stocking feet, Pat. With your cousin doing remodeling there might be nails on the floor, or at least splinters. Take my slippers."

Her feet are a size bigger than mine, but I accepted the offer. Even flopping around a bit, the slippers would keep my feet warmer. Laptop and tea bags in hand, I said goodnight.

Cella met me on the landing and led me back downstairs and through what she called her future bedroom, which was bigger than Aunt Sophie's sitting room because it covered the full width of the house. In fact, we had to crisscross the room diagonally to get to the dining room, then again back to the kitchen, with Cella switching on ceiling lights at one end and off at the other as we went. Old, dirty wallpaper and worn wall-to-wall carpet gave a dreary feeling to the rooms, both bare of furniture, instead housing sawhorses, power tools, paint cans and cleaning paraphernalia like wet and dry mops and a vacuum. A vague smell of sawdust hung in the air.

"You'd never know it," said Cella, "but gorgeous parquet flooring lurks under this ugly carpet. I'm leaving the rug down to protect the hardwood until I'm done with all the work in the house. Most of the furniture was in bad shape. I managed to sell a few pieces. The really good antiques that I kept I put in the store for now."

The dining room was longer than Aunt Sophie's, and the kitchen not as wide. I remembered how, playing in Aunt Sophie's backyard, you could see the back of Mrs. Ranelli's house jutting out maybe another ten feet, meaning the kitchen was an addition.

Decor-wise, the room was newer than Aunt Sophie's, though still thirty to forty years out of date. The cabinets were dark cherrywood, and the floor, dark gold linoleum, both popular when I was growing up. The deep hues made the space feel smaller still. If it weren't for the white appliances, light Formica countertop—white swirled with gold—and lacy white half curtains on the two windows, the kitchen would have felt claustrophobic.

A rectangular wooden table stuck longways out from the inside wall, a portable TV and some grocery bags taking up half the top. I set my laptop at the other end, but Cella pointed to a stool in front of the counter under the back window. Sharing the counter with a small microwave was another laptop, plugged into an outlet, recharging. "Sit up there or you won't get a signal."

Even tired as I was from my trip, I figured out what she meant right away. "You tap into a signal from one of your neighbors?"

"Oh, don't look so self-righteous, Pat." She crossed to the stove in the far corner to fetch the tea kettle. "I only use it sparingly on weekends, and only 'til I hook up my own. Either that or you'll have to hike a mile down Main to the Mickey D's."

Since I'd promised the troops at home emails, I set up the laptop on the counter and waited for it to boot up.

Meantime Cella crossed behind me to fill the kettle at the sink, nodding to my Ziploc en route. "You drinking tea? Or cocoa like us civilized folk?"

"I gave up chocolate for Lent."

"You're nuts. Me? I gave up broccoli."

"So why does your mom think you gave up chocolate?"

"I gave up eating chocolate at her house. She just assumed I'm not eating it elsewhere. Next time I'm home I'll have to sneak that candy out of the freezer and bring it here. Get two mugs out of that cabinet, will you? The 'World's Best Mom' one is mine."

As she carried the kettle back to the stove, I fished into the indicated cabinet. Inside were three mugs, two being those oversized solid-color ones you can find at dollar stores. Also in the cabinet was a box of plastic utensils, an unopened bag of pretzels, a big Ziploc half full of Oreos, and a box of hot cocoa mix—full strength, not diet. Nothing resembling healthy food. I didn't expect to find any. One way that my cousin and I differ is that I love to cook and she hates it. On her weekends here, she likely mooched off Aunt Sophie or did takeout.

I selected the black mug for myself and handed her a packet of cocoa mix with hers.

"If you gave up chocolate," Cella said as she poured the mix into her mug, "you won't be able to have the donuts I bought for breakfast. Half dozen Boston cream and chocolate cake ones." She nodded to the grocery bags on the table.

"Where'd you get them?" I asked, knowing the answer already.

"Where else? Am-e-lyn's."

National brands I could resist, but donuts from the local shops could always make me do penance during Lent. "I'm doomed."

Cella's grin became impish. "If you don't want the occasion of sin under your nose, I'll take the donuts into work tomorrow and just leave you the sticky buns. Also Am-e-lyn's."

Sticky buns were a brilliant Pennsylvania Dutch invention—soft, rolled cinnamon buns saturated in molasses, with raisins or walnuts or both on top. The one thing that could make me refuse an Am-e-lyn donut was an Am-e-lyn sticky bun and Cella knew it. "I haven't had a good sticky bun in almost a year."

"Then you better have one with your tea tonight. Be good and send your emails first. And while you're doing that, I owe my kids their nightly nag call. Where'd I leave my handbag?"

"In the front hall," I called after her as she left the kitchen. I turned back to the laptop and brought up the email screen. Beth Ann's would be the easy one. I did hers first. "Yo," I typed, my standard salutation. "A blizzard is raging outside this minute. I'm guessing no school here tomorrow. Jealous?"

I left the laptop to walk around the stove to the window, pushing the half curtain aside to look out, curving my hand against the glass to block the glare from behind me. The streetlight over on Penn made details meld into the surrounding darkness, but still, I could tell everything was coated in white. Right under the streetlamp, though, I could see that the snow wasn't swirling anywhere near as hard as it had been earlier. Okay, not a blizzard anymore, but I left the beginning of the message as is. Returning to my email, I went on to describe the ducks I'd seen that afternoon and ended with, "Miss Maggie sends smooches. Be cool. Pat." No blatant expressions of affection or Beth Ann would be too embarrassed.

Cella came back into the kitchen, cellphone cradling her cheek. "Wha'd'you mean, you forgot to ask me to sign it? How long was it in your backpack? No, I can't get there to sign it before school tomorrow. Ask Grandmom to sign it for you, then explain why to your teacher. Tell him to call my cell if he has to. Maybe you'll luck out and get a snow day."

Cella's daughters were right on either side of Beth Ann's age. No doubt I'd have similar crises to solve after my wedding. I hoped nothing worse. I scanned my message to Beth Ann, and the "Pat" ending it, wondering if I'd ever sign a note to her "Mom." In truth, I wasn't sure I wanted to, even if I was more accustomed to the whole maternal concept now than I had been a few months back.

Cella sat at the table, listening to whichever daughter. I felt an odd lack of privacy as I tried to construct an email to Hugh. Not that we ever said much kissy-kissy stuff over the Internet. A techie where I used to work once told me to construct emails as if they'd be front page headlines in a national newspaper the next day. And that was *before* wireless Internet existed. The lack of security in this particular signal made it a no-brainer. Besides, a couple like us, both in our late thirties, didn't need the lurid love letter content as much as simply touching base at the end of each day.

I wasn't so mature that I could resist a little teasing. "Cella's new place," I typed, "is like an urban version of Casper's Haunted Mansion. Doors close by themselves and fireplaces talk to you. I feel right at home."

I should explain that since I moved to Virginia, I've had a few run-ins with ghosts, as corny as that sounds. Hugh tried to get me to promise not to communicate with them, until he realized the ghosts pick on me, not vice versa. Hugh's reaction to my email would probably be to huff and puff and say "Don't even kid about that," which would make me tease him more. That's how we're built.

Thing is, I'd never encountered ghosts in my hometown, only in Virginia, so I felt protected here. Boy, was I a dope.

6

Family communication chores done, I closed the laptop and sat down with Cella, her with cocoa and a chocolate donut, me snarfing tea. I resisted the bun. My acid reflux from the heavy macaroni was still percolating.

The grocery sacks also contained packs of paper plates and napkins, adding to my suspicions that she had little else in the kitchen, so I asked.

"I need to give Miss Maggie a decent breakfast," I explained. "If she eats too much processed foods and non-whole grains, she'll blow up like a water balloon and I'll be rushing her to the hospital with congestive heart failure."

"Go next door," my cousin said. "Uncle Leo's on the same regimen. Bound to be something Miss Maggie can eat. Besides, Aunt Sophie told me to send you over as soon as you got up. Maybe she wants you to help her get ready for the wake. Everyone'll be coming back here after the viewing."

"I don't mind helping, *if* my aunt lets me."

Cella knew what I meant. "She likes doing everything herself. Ma's the same way."

"So's Aunt Florence."

She nodded. "Problem is, now that they're older, they *can't* do everything."

"Try telling them that."

"And get my head slapped?" Cella reached for a second donut, killing me with the smell of chocolate. "That's why I told Ma I'd pick the kids up from school tomorrow. That way she can come here earlier. She and her sister can slug it out over who does what."

"You're leaving work early *and* taking Thursday off for the funeral?"

"I was going to leave early anyway. Figure I'll complain about a stomach ache from the moment I arrive—"

"Keep eating those donuts and you won't have to act."

She ignored me. "I won't put on makeup so I'll look pale. That'll lend credence when I call in sick Thursday for the funeral. In fact, I think my stomach flu will reach critical mass by noon tomorrow."

"So you can come protect me if I get caught between your mom and Aunt Sophie?"

"Not *if*. *When*. And no, you're on your own." Cella swigged the last of her cocoa. "I'm gonna drive out to Uncle Rocco's retirement home. Talk to people there who knew him. Maybe he told someone there where his money's hidden."

"I doubt it."

"You never know. He might've dropped hints. Or maybe he had a girlfriend there. I'm guessing Beatrice hasn't thought to ask. Too subtle for her."

That last idea intrigued me. I could imagine Uncle Rocco picking up some chick thirty years younger than him, in her seventies. "You might be right, cousin."

That brought a smug smile to Cella's lips. "Tell you what. I'll pick you up after work and we'll go out to Evergreen Manor together. We'll grab lunch first. Miss Maggie can come, too. My treat."

I suspected Cella's idea of lunch would be something Miss Maggie shouldn't have, but I said, "I'll ask her tomorrow morning. Call Aunt Sophie's place on your cell when you leave work and I'll let you know if we're in, okay?"

Nodding her agreement, she stood to take her mug over to the sink. "We'll have to show Miss Maggie around all the historical sites this week, Pat. Valley Forge, the Peter Wentz House—"

"Actually, she's dying to see Montgomery Cemetery. She's a Civil War buff."

"I *love* that place. Remember how we used to play there? Now my girls and I go on their ghost tour every Halloween."

The word made me wary. "Ghost tour? Since when is it supposed to be haunted?"

Cella gave me a when-did-you-get-wimpy look of incredulity. "Since the word 'ghost' brings out hundreds of people and their kids, all willing to fork over some bucks to hear grave-robbing stories. It's a fund-raiser. The Historical Society's done wonders restoring the place, but they still have a long way to go, not to mention the maintenance costs."

She retrieved a small bottle of dishwashing soap from under the sink, dribbled a couple drops in her mug, then added some water.

"We'll go out to the cemetery after the funeral Thursday. I'll give you guys a full tour."

We talked about other historic sites to visit, especially after Hugh and Beth Ann arrived. When I mentioned Beth Ann's interest in nature, Cella suggested Mill Grove, which was where Audubon had lived while checking out Pennsylvania birds. That sounded perfect, but Cella also told me about a few nature trails her daughters both like.

Which is how we ended up talking about teens for the next hour, until I was yawning so much, my cousin said, "Bedtime for you, Pat. We'll talk wedding plans tomorrow night after the wake. Here, I'll show you the back way upstairs."

She walked over to a door in the corner, opening it to reveal an enclosed stairway. "This leads to the room next to yours. No ceiling light, so watch your step, not that there's anything on the floor up there to trip you. If I leave this door open, the light from the kitchen should be enough."

Too sleepy to worry about it, I said goodnight and moved toward the stairs, but no sooner was I through the doorway than I got a whiff of . . . thing was, I couldn't pinpoint it at first. The odor was faint, elusive, yet nasty enough to wrinkle my nose.

"What are you stopping for?"

I shook my head. "Thought I smelled something."

Cella stuck her head through the doorway and sniffed. "I used some Murphy's Oil Soap on these stairs last fall—"

"No, it wasn't that kind of odor. Wait, there it is again." This time my brain got enough data to do a comparison with my memory banks. Litter box? "You don't have a cat, do you?"

"Would I be standing before you breathing if I did?" She meant her animal allergy, inherited from the Montella side. My dad had it, too, as well as all his siblings. I lucked out and missed that genetic fiasco, but Cella had gotten a lion's share. I'd seen her go into asthmatic fits if she was in a house with an animal more than twenty minutes.

To her answer I shrugged. "Thought you might be getting shots for it by now."

"Shots are expensive. Don't need 'em if I avoid pets. That's what you smelled? Cat dander?"

"More like litter box. Did Mrs. Ranelli have a cat?"

"Not recently. We're talking 1970s." Cella retreated into the kitchen to tidy the table as she spoke. "I came across a photo of her cat while I was moving furniture around—one of those fluffy, long-haired, white creatures, where you could barely see the eyes for the fur. Professional-grade shedding machine. Which explains why my allergies still bothered me when I first started coming here. Mrs. Ranelli didn't believe me, I think, but she didn't mind me donning an allergen mask and cleaning her whole house best I could, stem to stern. Sure enough, most of my stuffiness cleared up. These last months, now that I've sold most of the upholstery, I don't need antihistamines anymore."

"Doesn't the upholstery in that front parlor bother you?"

"Mrs. Ranelli never allowed the cat to go in there." Cella grabbed her cellphone off the table, taking it back to the corner where her laptop was. She unplugged the latter, set the phone into its recharging cradle and plugged that in. "You must have some kind of sensitive nose to pick up that odor after all these years and all my soap."

I shrugged, said goodnight again and headed up the stairs. At the top, I could see the glow from the hall light coming through the doorway to our bedroom and, from a doorway behind me, the glow of the streetlamp coming through the back windows. Enough light to show that the floor in this room indeed had nothing on it.

Yet, as I started to shuffle forward, going slow because the floorboards were squeaky and I didn't want to wake Miss Maggie, I thought I felt my shin brush against something. Or more like something brushed against me. I looked down. The dim light showed nothing but the hem of my jeans above the fuzzy bunny heads of the slippers. Just fatigue, I told myself.

I got ready for bed, treading lightly over to the bathroom and back, draping my jeans and pullover across the foot of the bed before I crawled under the quilt. I drifted off almost at once, and had one of those dreams that you get right on the brink of sleep, when you're still half aware of where you are.

I dreamt I felt a sudden weight on the bed, down beside my feet. Not heavy, like a person sitting down, which would have scared the moles off me. No, this was light and compact, exactly like a cat jumping onto the bed and snuggling against my ankles. Not frightening but startling enough that I sat up and my eyes popped open.

No kitty. Just the weight of my jeans and sweater.

Felines on the brain, I decided, as I rolled over, then drifted off again.

I had no more cat encounters that night. In fact, I slept more soundly than I have in years, with only two more dreams, neither disturbing. One was of a family reunion. Instead of just Montellas, Mom's whole side of the family was there, too, including the Bells, all dressed up in their Antebellum South duds. The other dream was about donuts, but that's par for the course during Lent.

Wednesday, March 1

I was awakened first by the sound of the radiator hissing, which should have told me that my cousin was up. But I'd grown up with radiators hissing on winter mornings. My brain merely registered "heat" and that encouraged me to go back to sleep.

Next I heard an electronic rendering of "That's Amore" somewhere in the house. If I'd been awake enough, I would have realized it was Cella's phone down in the kitchen. Before I could doze off again, I heard the squeaky floorboards in the next room heralding someone's arrival. A moment later I identified the someone by her raspy alto as she softly sang "That's Amore." She knew all the words.

I said, "Morning, Miss Maggie," then opened my eyes.

"Oh, good, you're awake." The room was fairly dim since it had no windows, but the hall light was still on and I had no trouble seeing my mentor standing in the doorway to the next room. Wearing a bright green fleece sweatsuit, she looked like a leprechaun two weeks early.

"Your Aunt Sophie called. Wants to know if you'd mind cleaning off your uncle's car. She said he's determined to drive to cardiac therapy this morning, snow or no snow. He's not leaving for forty-five minutes, so you have time."

"Did Cella go to work?"

"She's outside cleaning off her own car. Looks to be about four inches of snow, but the sun's out bright. Won't last." I detected a hint of impatience in her usual easy Southern inflections. She wanted to go out and play.

I sat up, stretching. "Did you eat anything?"

"Oh, I can't yet." She came over to sit beside me on the bed. "With my one morning pill, I'm not supposed to have food for an hour after. Got fifteen minutes yet. Didn't see much to eat downstairs anyway, just some scrumptious looking buns, and I *shouldn't* have one of those."

Which meant she wanted to taste them in the worst way. "We'll split one, Miss Maggie. That way neither of us will feel too guilty. Then we'll get something healthy next door. Be down in a few minutes." I opted to just wash up a bit and get dressed, figuring if I got all sweaty shoveling, I'd get a shower over Aunt Sophie's later.

Cella and her phone were gone by the time I went down to the kitchen, but she'd left behind her the distinct smell of new Lysol in the stairwell.

Miss Maggie was licking her fingers and raving about her half of sticky bun. The other half was on a paper plate, along with the knife that cut it. I sat down and took a bite. The bun had half an ounce of sweet gooey raisins on top. Absolute heaven!

"I promised Cella we'd lower the thermostat," Miss Maggie said as she washed her hands at the sink. "She left us a spare key and said to make sure the deadbolt was all the way over. Hand me a napkin to dry my hands, will you?"

Using my non-sticky hand, I complied, then gave in and took a second bun. "How do you like my relatives, Miss Maggie?"

"They're the nicest people. Lots of folk I know in Virginia who brag about Southern hospitality could learn a lesson from them." She looked under the sink for a trash can, found it, and disposed of her napkin. "You and Cella act almost like sisters."

I shrugged. "Neither of us had a sister of our own. She's got two older brothers. We're the same age, and when we got to high school, we ended up in the same homeroom plus a bunch of classes together. Her maiden name was Napoli and most teachers sat us in alphabetical order, so she was always right behind me."

"I never put my students in alphabetical order," Miss Maggie said. "Put them in size order instead—shortest in front—so everyone could see the board."

"Makes sense. I was always stuck behind a football player named Doug Monroe who was built like Hugh. Cella and I took turns having a crush on him. But I never could see the board."

Breakfast consumed, I stood to wash my hands. Now Miss Maggie sat, as if she wasn't ready to go yet. "Pat, what do you think of Cella's house?"

"Architecture-wise? Or do I think she took on more than she

could handle fixing it up?"

Miss Maggie hesitated, which was so unlike her, I turned to meet her gaze. Smiling as if she were giving a quiz and this was a trick question, she said, "Start with the architecture."

I leaned against the sink as I considered it. "I like the layout of Aunt Sophie's better, where the hallways lead you through the house. This is more maze-like, at least the back of the house is. Did you see the parlor on the second floor?"

She nodded. "Walked through the house while you were sleeping this morning. The parlor reminds me of the way my grandparents furnished my house when I was young. The front hall leading to it looks like it was never redone, except to put in the bathroom. The third floor seems pretty much intact, too. Everything else was remodeled. The woodwork in the rear of the house has clean lines with no rosettes in the corners of the doorways. And the back room, second floor has a row of four casement windows. *Art Deco*, 1920s."

"Plus you'll note," I added, using my best Home-and-Garden-Channel voice, "the kitchen was done in the popular hobbit-hole style, circa 1970." I had to admit, daylight helped relieve some of the gloom. Still, the linoleum had to go.

"Okay, Pat, now, what do you think of your cousin's plans?"

I took a moment to consider that as well. "Complicated. I think she genuinely loves this place, but that feeling is likely bound up with an affection for the previous owner and with the fact that the house is an endangered species. Also, I think this has something to do with not wanting to abandon Aunt Sophie."

Miss Maggie nodded. "More than that, perhaps. Maybe Cella doesn't want to let go of the last trace of 'the old neighborhood.' Your aunt's house *is* a Montella landmark."

My turn to agree. "Beyond that, I figure this is a knee-jerk reaction to Cella and Ron's separation. Like her getting a different kind of car. She's redefining herself. Wants to prove she can be independent. Prove to the family, I mean. All my aunts think no woman can live without a man."

"Can she? Financially, I mean."

"Of course she can!" That was pure defense mechanism. The liberated woman in me was loath to admit that women's salaries on average were still far below men's. Heck, I even had trouble acknowledging that marrying Hugh would solve some of my own monetary hardships. I wasn't marrying him for his health insurance, I told myself. That was simply a happy turn of fate. I'd love him even if he quit the Postal Service to become a starving artist.

"Single moms have it pretty rough, Pat."

"I know that, Miss Maggie, but Cella's a budgeting wizard. In high school, she used to bring peanut butter sandwiches every day so she could pocket the lunch money Aunt Lydia gave her."

"Do you think she'll want to feed her daughters peanut butter every day?"

I didn't answer right away, though the reply would be a simple "No." Cella's aversion to cooking meant that, when not at her mom's house, she fed her kids mainly packaged meals or fast foods, neither cheap. Beyond that, from what I knew of my cousin's life the last fifteen years, she hadn't let her daughters want for much. Now, Cella was taking on this rehab project. I hoped Ronny would be paying child support and that they had college funds set up.

Miss Maggie had remained quiet, letting me think over the ramifications. In the silence, I heard the scrape of shovels on pavement over on Penn Street, reminding me of duty.

So in lieu of an answer, I said, "I'd better go shovel."

"One more question about the house, Pat." She smiled so innocently, I should have known what was coming. "Is this place haunted?"

"*Memento, homo, quia pulvis es, et in pulveram reverteris.*"
Translation: Remember, man, you are dust, and to dust you shall return.

—From the Roman Catholic Ash Wednesday rite of the 1930s

March 1, 1933 – 349 East Main

Aunt Gina wouldn't let Pip go out to Montgomery Cemetery with Rocco and Vito the next morning. She wasn't crazy about Vito going either. She said, with Mr. Lowell sick in the hospital, likely nobody would be paying even the nickel trolley fare for his cemetery vault to be put back in order right now.

"Mr. Lowell will pay us when he gets better, Mama," Pip argued. "He's always paid us before, hasn't he? Good money, too. We can't leave the grave open like that, can we? And it takes all three of us to move the slab."

We were down in the kitchen—everybody but Del and the younger boys who were upstairs getting ready for school—but nobody was eating anything because we were fasting for Ash Wednesday.

"Vito and Rocco can do it alone," Aunt Gina insisted as she raised the window to take the last of yesterday's milk out of the cold box that hung on the wall outside. "You're coming to mass with me and Nonna and the baby this morning, to get your ashes."

"Aw, Mama."

"Don't you 'Aw, Mama' me. Better to go to mass today than fool with an open grave." Aunt Gina poured a half cup of milk for me. Mornings like this it always had little chunks of ice in it. Then she put the last two mouthfuls in a saucer for Crisi, who was waiting at her feet. "They don't bury people the way us Catholics do, under the good earth and nobody gonna disturb you ever again. They put doors on their graves. A dead person can't rest in peace like that."

"It's a mausoleum, Ma," Vito explained. "Just underground is all. We got mausoleums at St. Pat's Cemetery, don't we?"

"Rich people have them." My aunt let a little bit of water run into the empty bottle. She swished it around as she talked. "You know why? 'Cause rich men can't get into heaven anyway. Says so in the Gospel. But they shouldn't allow mausoleums. People ought to be buried under the dirt. It's not sacred otherwise."

I cried, I remember, not because all that talk about burying people was scary, but because my milk was too cold. Nobody understood that, though. Nonna took me on her lap. "Hush. You're frightening the baby." She said it in Sicilian. She could speak a little English, but since we all understood Sicilian, she didn't bother around us.

Aunt Gina added the milk-water to the cat's saucer. "Vito, you let Rocco go into that grave today. You stay outside. And say an *Ave*. One before you start and one when you're done."

"I'll say three, Mama. I promise. And we can get the gravedigger to help us put the slab back."

That satisfied her. Uncle Ennio and the older boys were able to talk about the sports news in yesterday's *Times Herald*, about how Lefty Grove had hopped a train to Florida at the last minute 'cause his wife had an operation and how Babe Ruth claimed he wasn't gonna manage the Red Sox this year 'cause he was still playing for the Yankees.

Then, out of the blue, again in Sicilian, Nonna asked, "What made that man sick last night?"

Uncle Ennio set down his coffee cup. "Tuberculosis, I bet. It was in the paper Monday how everyone's catching it."

Pip shook his head. "No, Papa. The article only talked about medical science curing tuberculosis." Pip read the paper all the way through every day, then told us all about it. Fact was, he read anything he could get hold of.

Vito added, "Mr. Lowell told us he had the flu, but I think maybe he had some kind of attack in his gut. A busted appendix or something."

Rocco knocked on the back door and when my aunt opened it, he brought in today's two fresh milk bottles. Aunt Gina made the milkman put her bottles on the back porch because boys had been stealing them off people's front steps. We always knew when it was below freezing outside, like this morning, because when the cream at the top of each bottle froze, it rose up in a column that pushed the cap off.

Rocco was all dressed up for his job, with his starched collar, tie and vest showing under his unbuttoned wool coat. Instead of a cap like most young men wore, he always looked like a businessman in a classy Fedora that Del said cost him a good two bucks. He removed that hat now out of politeness.

"You gonna have a job much longer?" Uncle Ennio asked

bluntly. Everybody knew what he meant. The *Herald* had been warning of an impending bank holiday all week. Once the banks closed, who knew if they'd open again? Not that our family ever had enough money to deposit, but if one of Uncle Ennio's customers paid with anything more than a five, he had to send Pip or Vito up to People's Bank to get change.

"The Pennsylvania legislators promised to keep the banks open," Rocco assured us, waving off Aunt Gina's offers of coffee.

"Bah," Uncle Ennio groused. "Since when can you believe *politicos*? Might be better if you gotta look for other work, Rocco. Bankers like to keep their money too much. They don't pay you hardly anything. And they only got you working six hours a day. You got a gift, the way you can talk to people. You could get a better job like that." He snapped his fingers.

Rocco shrugged, not wanting to argue, I think. Everybody in that kitchen, even me, knew jobs were scarce. Only reason Rocco had one at all was his personality. Vito and Pip hadn't been able to get steady work. Neither had my own papa two years before. That's why he left.

Vito put on his coat and cap and left with Rocco. As Aunt Gina latched the door after them, she said an *Ave*, to which everyone buy me responded, mostly out of habit, "Amen."

7

"Haunted?!" I don't know why I was surprised. Miss Maggie loves ghosts. They're witnesses to history, after all. But her question still made my jaw go slack. Recovering, I said, "Oh, no, Magnolia Shelby. Don't you go assuming that I'll find you a phantom in every new place we visit—"

"I simply thought—" She grinned up at me, her green rheumy eyes impish. "You were awfully cold when we walked in the door last night. I mean, yes, it was chilly in here, but I thought you over-reacted. Your cousin thought so, too. And this morning Cella told me your senses seem much more sensitive than they'd ever been before. She said you heard noises she couldn't hear and smelled odors—"

"A leaky chimney flue and old cat urine," I assured her. "Nothing spooky about either."

"Are you sure, Pat? Most other times you've encountered ghosts, well, you didn't feel spooked then, did you?"

I had to admit, she had a point, but I still wasn't convinced.

"Any other odd sensations since you've been here, Pat?"

One of my mischievous moods took hold of me. "Now that you mention it . . ." I told her about feeling something brush up against my leg, followed by the weird half-sleep dream of something like a cat on the bed, cozying up to my feet.

Miss Maggie's scanty eyebrows seemed to climb up three ridges of wrinkles on her forehead. "You're saying the house is haunted by a kitty cat?"

I laughed. "Why not? Anything in the rule book that says ghosts have to be people?"

She frowned, knowing there was no rule book.

I continued, enjoying myself. "Tell you what, if I make contact, I'll ask him if he's seen any ghost mice hanging around."

Giving up, she stood. "Come on. Time to play outside."

The morning sun glinting off the new snow was almost blinding, yet Cella's stoop was still in shadow and the breeze coming up the street from the west felt frigid.

Out in the street, the traffic lanes were worn down to the blacktop, with a strip of crunching gray slush down the middle and on either side. That made me feel a little better about my uncle driving up to the hospital for his therapy session. The slush might keep him in his lane and other cars would have a better chance of avoiding him.

Across Main Street, people were out shoveling sidewalks and cleaning off cars. On our side, both sets of steps were already clear, plus shovel-wide paths on the sidewalk and out to the street. Cella's handiwork. I knew this because with the snow she'd shoveled into the narrow space between the stoops, she'd built a foot-high snowman as a sentinel between the houses. Two toothpicks formed arms and a third made a stake through its heart. Her signature.

Aunt Sophie must have been listening for the sound of us slamming Cella's door, because she opened her own to pass me Uncle Leo's car keys. I told her to give me a shovel and rock salt, too. Yes, the sun was bright and if we were in Virginia, the snow would already be melting. Here it wouldn't get warm enough 'til at least noon and as soon as the sun set, everything would refreeze.

My aunt tried to bribe Miss Maggie inside with the promise of breakfast, but my mentor elected to stay out, "in case Pat needs a hand," meaning she intended to pelt me with snowballs. She brought our stuff inside first—her handbag, my change of clothes which I'd put in one of Cella's grocery bags, and the laptop, which Miss Maggie wanted in case any Italian recipes appeared under her nose.

Meanwhile I began clearing a path in front of Uncle Leo's Olds, until I could get around to the driver's side and get inside to crank up the ignition and defrosters. Then I retrieved his squeegee from the back seat. The snow was wet and therefore heavy—three inches equaling about the same weight as a foot of powdery snow—but it easily slid off the roof, hood and trunk when prodded.

Miss Maggie came back out. I went over to the stoop to help her down the steps. Keeping her back to the breeze, she inspected the snowman. "Why the stake, Pat?" she asked through the scarf wound around her face.

"It's a voodoo snowdoll," I explained as I returned to bulldozing all the snow between the front of the car and Cella's empty space to give my uncle a clear runway for takeoff. "When we were kids and snow was on the ground, Cella and I would make little snowmen, about a foot high. We'd name them after her brothers, then stake them through the heart."

"How barbaric of you." Her voice rang with approval.

Uncle Leo came out, bundled up with a scarf across his face à la Miss Maggie, so the cold air couldn't get in and constrict his already stopped-up blood vessels. He came down the steps like Miss Maggie, favoring one leg. Then he gave me a good morning hug, thanked me, and drove off up the middle of Main Street, flattening out slush as he went.

"Take a break, Pat," Miss Maggie urged me. "You're all out of breath. Besides, I want to build a voodoo snowdoll myself, and I need help. Can't bend over like I used to."

I agreed, wanting her to get the urge to play out of her system, so she'd go inside and warm up. "I'll push the snow from the sidewalk up toward the house and you can build it up on a mound where you can reach, okay?"

We built her little snowperson beside my aunt's railing, patting the snow tight so it wouldn't melt too quickly. I found some cinders in the gutter that we used for eyes, nose and mouth but, since these houses had no trees out front, and therefore no twigs on the ground, we left our creations armless.

"No matter," Miss Maggie said. "Better they can't fight back. I'll name mine after one of those idiots in Washington. Hmm . . . to do this right, we ought to build a snowman for every member of Congress, the Executive Branch, and at least half of the Supreme Court judges."

"We don't have enough snow." I amputated one of Cella's toothpick arms for Miss Maggie to use as a stake. "Besides, you're getting too cold out here."

Not denying it, she stabbed her snowdoll, then headed inside for breakfast.

I promised I'd be in as soon as I finished Cella's walk. I cleared it the same way I did Aunt Sophie's, plowing the snow toward the house.

Pausing for a breather at the edge of the property, I took a moment to scan the block. Up the street, the old Borzillo Bakery was all boarded up, plain wood on the upper windows, white-painted plywood over what used to be the windowed store fronts at street level. A sign in Spanish proclaimed half the downstairs to be a

Hispanic mission. The other half had a big "For Lease" sign on it. Between that and Aunt Sophie's were rundown houses and empty lots, the latter overgrown with weeds behind tall, ugly chain link fence.

On the other side of the street, all the houses were, at least, still standing. Most had that forsaken quality half-leased rental properties take on.

In my own mind, I labeled the houses on this block the way my parents had always referred to them, by the names of the people who'd lived there seventy-plus years ago, when Mom and Dad were kids: Logrippo's, Ronca's, Salamone's, etc. But those families were long gone.

I imagined how this neighborhood must have been during the Depression, all the buildings still up, small stores in front, big Italian families living behind and above. Hard economic times then, too, but I pictured more life, more animation. Now, except for the occasional food take-out, you pretty much had to go to the malls to find stores.

Beside me, Uncle Rocco's old lot was the latest victim of progress. This morning, completely shaded by Cella's house, it was covered with a pristine layer of snow in front. Trucks were parked at the back end. Glancing at the wall of Cella's place—the wall that had once connected the houses on the second and third floor—I noticed that the painted or papered inside walls in each of Uncle Rocco's rooms were still visible. The back room third floor had been painted a really ugly shade of purple. I wondered if that had been Beatrice's mom's room.

On the first floor, the tunnel-alley separating the houses and leading to the backyards was also still intact, looking superfluous. An open sidewalk would do just as well now beside the fenced-in truck lot. Maybe the outer wall of the tunnel was necessary to help carry the weight of Cella's wall down to the foundation.

A gust of northerly Arctic air blew across the empty lot, directly into my face, making me turn away. Break's over, I decided. After finishing the walks, I even made a narrow path in front of the truck lot on the other side of Aunt Sophie's, then spread rock salt over all the bare cement. The funeral parlor was up on the next block. We'd be walking to and from the wake tonight and people would be coming to Aunt Sophie's afterward. I didn't want broken limbs on my conscience.

Exhausted but determined, I built my own voodoo snowdoll on

the other side of Cella's steps and stole her snowman's other arm to use for my stake.

I wasn't sure at first what to name mine, but Miss Maggie's frustration with government mixed with all my depressing economic musings suggested "I.R.S."

As I pushed the stake home, someone pulled into Uncle Leo's spot behind me. I spun around, ready to lecture that an elderly cardiac patient would be home in an hour and would need a spot in front of his house today as much as disabled folks needed the handicap spaces in front of supermarkets.

The car was actually a small pickup, and the man who got out left it running as he ran around to me. He was Hispanic, in his twenties, wearing jeans, work boots, and a short heavy jacket.

"You're one of the Montellas, aren't you?" He gestured to Aunt Sophie's house.

"I'm their niece."

He nodded as if to let me know I'd given the correct answer, then unzipped his jacket and reached inside, pulling out a greeting card-sized envelope. "We saw Rocco Montella's obituary in the paper. My father asked me to drop this off. It's a mass card." Then, seeming to feel the need to explain further, he added, "We used to live across the street, nearly twenty years ago, when my family first came from Mexico—"

"Wait," I butted in. "You mean the Garcias?"

He nodded again. "You remember us?"

Only vaguely. I didn't tell him that. Aunt Sophie had mentioned their last name. She might have said first names, too, but they hadn't stuck with me. However, I did recall a small, exuberant boy, maybe six or seven, learning to ride a two-wheeler on the wide sidewalk. "You were this tall last time I saw you," I said, holding my glove waist high. "Tell me your first name."

"Javier." He smiled as he handed me the card. "My dad says he's sorry he can't get to the viewing or funeral—we all have to work—but he wanted to do something. He said if it weren't for Mr. Montella. . . . See, when I was little, my dad and his brother were laid off from their factory jobs. Mr. Montella lent us some money to hold us over. Said he remembered the Depression all too well, and how his parents had been immigrants, too. My dad never forgot that."

"Tell your father how much our family appreciates his thinking about us."

"I will. Gotta run. Late for work." He hurried back to his truck and sped off.

Not wanting to get the mass card wet, I tucked it inside my own jacket. Then, so I wouldn't track a lot of wetness through Aunt Sophie's house, I carried the shovel and rock salt through her tunnel to the back. The tunnel, out of the sun and positioned to perfectly channel those occasional Arctic gusts, felt at least ten degrees colder. Snow runoff had already pooled at the north end and turned to ice. I spread salt on it.

A cement patio hugged the rear of the house. Because Penn Street back here is higher than Main, four steps led from the patio up to the yard. In the summer, shaded by the house, this patio was a pleasant and fairly private place to sit in the evenings. In winter, snow and rain runoff from the yard made the patio a skating rink.

Giving the shovel a test push along the house wall, I could feel the ice underneath. I knew I ought to at least clear and salt a path from the door to the trash and recycling containers near the steps, but I wasn't thrilled by the prospect. Here I'd have to lift the snow instead of plowing it, plus chop ice.

Aunt Sophie heard me and stuck her head out the back door. "You did enough, Tricia. Vinny's coming on his lunch hour to do the rest. Come in. Get warm and eat."

Relieved to leave this chore to my cousin's young, strong back, I went inside, leaving my wet boots by the back door. Aunt Sophie set my gloves on top of the radiator cover to dry. As I slipped out of my coat, I handed my aunt the mass card, describing its delivery as I hung my coat on the back of one of the kitchen chairs.

"Nice of them to have a mass said," Aunt Sophie commented. "I didn't know Uncle Rocco lent the Garcias money. I wonder if they paid him back?"

Leave it to my aunt to turn a good deed into a guilt trip. I changed the subject by mentioning that Miss Maggie's big bowl of Cheerios, Wheaties, chopped banana and skim milk looked good and that I was going to have the same, only half as much (since I'd had the second sticky bun).

As I ate, Aunt Sophie put a steaming mug of decaf coffee next to my bowl and pushed the sugar bowl and milk jug my way. "Tricia, I got something else you can do for me today, if you wouldn't mind?"

My mom used to phrase requests this way, too, knowing I couldn't say I minded before hearing the task. Still, this aunt had looked after me like I was her own since my parents died. Praying her next job was something easier on my back, I asked, "Need help cooking for the wake tonight, Aunt Sophie?"

She shook her head. "Hardly anything to get ready. Your cousins have all been dropping food off all week. Got a full refrigerator. No, I was wondering if you'd go through Uncle Rocco's things upstairs for me? Just separate his clothes into what I can give to Sisters of Charity or Purple Heart and what ought to go into the rag bag." Then she blushed a little. "Maybe you could check the pockets, though, in case I missed something when I packed them. I felt them all, but—you know."

She was asking for a second opinion. Wanted to make sure Uncle Rocco hadn't left a clue to his missing money in his good suit. "Sure, Aunt Sophie. No problem." I glanced over at Miss Maggie, not sure if she'd rather help me or work on her laptop.

She got the unvoiced question. "I believe, Sophie, that you said you had old photographs of Rocco's as well?"

My aunt nodded. "Most of them are of this neighborhood. That's why I kept them. They're a mess. Need to be sorted, put in scrapbooks."

"Perhaps I can help," Miss Maggie suggested. "I should at least be able to put them into some kind of chronological order, by the clothes folks are wearing or the cars they've got. Easier than these young'uns could." She gestured to me, implying that I wouldn't know a Model T from an Edsel. She was right.

Still, I should have guessed she'd have ulterior motives.

"All the really important millionaires are planning to continue prosperity."

—ARTHUR BRIBANE, NOVEMBER 26, 1929

March 1, 1933 – Trepani's Store

Later that morning, Pip and I were in the store by ourselves because Uncle Ennio got a ride with Mr. D'Abruzzo to go buy more wholesale fruit. Pip did a better job keeping a record of sales, anyway. The last six months he'd reminded his father every day to charge the one percent sales tax and keep track of the amounts. Uncle Ennio never did either, not when he was minding the store alone. Yesterday, the last day of February, the sales tax ended, and nobody was happier about it than Uncle Ennio.

So far, no customers had come in today. Pip was sitting on a stool at the back of the store, behind the glass display case that doubled as a counter. Inside the case were little toys and candy that no one ever seemed to buy. This morning Pip was reading a battered Zane Grey paperback that he bought off somebody for a penny.

I thought the ash smudge between his cap brim and brow looked silly. Aunt Gina had held onto my hands so I couldn't wipe mine off in church, but as soon as we got outside, I'd swiped my sweater sleeve across my forehead.

Now I was sitting on an orange crate by the store's front window, enjoying the warmth and brightness of the sun each time it peeked out from behind the fluffy clouds. Crisi sat near me, close to the door so she could inspect customers. She watched intently as people walked by on Main Street, swishing her tail as each person roused her curiosity. She would run behind the pickle barrel each time the trolley went by, but she came back out right after.

Our usual customers were neighborhood kids sent by their mothers for a head of cabbage or three cans of tomato paste or some such. Or the mothers came in themselves. I hated that. They always asked whoever was behind the counter if Aunt Gina had heard from her brother lately, meaning my papa. The answer was always the same—he sent some money last

Christmas, we'd heard nothing since. Not even a postcard. No one thought I understood or even remembered my papa, but I did. Tutti did, too. My brother acted tough so no one would know how sad it made him.

As usual, I held my ragdoll that Nonna had made for me. When FDR won the election, Del started calling my dolly Mrs. Roosevelt. I liked that. Today I was making Mrs. Roosevelt wave one stuffed arm at passers-by on the street. All the neighbors knew me and waved back. Strangers—walking to and from the church or Borzillo's Bakery or wherever—sometimes they waved, too, if they looked my way.

That's when I saw the lady walk up the street. She was young and slender, wearing a short wool coat over a pretty tartan skirt and real silk stockings. On her head was a stylish but functional blue hat that kept her ears warm, yet showed little bangs of chestnut hair at the front and longer ringlets at the back where her hair was shoulder-length.

The lady was looking at the houses as she came up Main, as if searching for a certain one, unsure of the number. She stopped in front of the house next door, then saw me. I made Mrs. Roosevelt wave. That got a smile out of the lady, but she didn't wave back. Instead, she came inside the store.

"Hello, little girl." She had a low, musical voice.

I froze, transfixed, like I usually did when strangers talked to me. More so with her, because she had bright blue eyes and in my neighborhood, I saw mostly brown and hazel ones. One thing I did note was an unmistakable ash smudge lurking behind her carefully arranged bangs.

Crisi, of course, met her at the door, circling the newcomer once, brushing against both her legs. The lady stooped, offering our cat her fingertips to sniff.

I heard Pip's stool push back as he stood and cleared his throat. "Can I help you, ma'am, uh, I mean, miss?" Despite Pip's question, I don't think he saw this lady as a customer so much as a very pretty specimen of the opposite gender. I knew by the way he took off his cap.

"Mr. Trepani?" Easy deduction on her part, considering the surname was painted on the store's front window. But when he nodded, she asked, "Are you Vito?"

"I'm his brother Joseph. Vito's not home right now. He'll be back soon, if you want to wait."

Crisi stayed by the window, but I followed the lady up the single aisle toward Pip, past shelves of Campbell's soup and canned beans, open crates of apples and onions, and the big pickle barrel.

"I heard that Vito was one of the men who took Lloyd Lowell to the hospital last night?" she said, making it a question.

Pip nodded again, hesitantly this time, like he was trying to figure her reason for asking.

"Did you see what happened?" she persisted.

"See Mr. Lowell get sick, you mean? Sure! I saw the whole thing." Pip could boast about that without bringing Vito into the picture. But then he seemed to realize that it sounded callous. "I mean—half the neighborhood saw him, but see, Mr. Lowell was sitting right on our front step, so—"

"Was he really?" She turned her shoulders to look out the window, to view the perspective herself. "What was Lowell doing down this end of town? Do you know?"

I thought Pip would boast again, but instead he shifted his eyes down to look through the top of the glass case, like he was taking inventory or something. "Said he had work for me and Vito. See, we help him when he buries orphans."

"He had work for you? He was planning another burial? Didn't he just do one recently?"

Pip looked uncomfortable now. "Yeah, so? Poor kids die every day."

"Do you know the name of the child? Or the orphanage?"

"No." He got this look, as if she'd changed from a pretty lady into something evil, like the women always did in the detective novels he read.

"Do you know the name of the child buried last month, Joseph? I think you must know, because you were there to hear every word said at the graveside. And I'm sure you'll tell me the truth, since a good Catholic like you—" she gestured to his forehead "—wouldn't want to be going to confession after only the first day of Lent."

Pip looked like he'd been backed into a corner, but he was saved from saying anything 'cause Vito and Rocco came in at that moment. Vito was carrying a big beat-up macaroni pot and lid that he must have rummaged off some junk pile. As usual, Rocco was doing most of the talking. ". . . Sure we can make it work. We got two whole days and—" Then he laid eyes on the lady. The sight of her shut him up like nothing ever did before. He removed his hat, which reminded Vito to take off his cap, too. He had to set the kettle down to do it.

"Rocco, why aren't you at work?" Pip asked. "They close

the banks already?"

Rocco let a moment go by, having trouble taking his eyes and apparently his thoughts off the visitor, but then he answered, smooth as always, "No, no. After I got to the bank, I felt under the weather, that's all. Thought it best to come home."

Later, when Del heard Rocco came home early, she said he must have put in a performance up at People's that morning—sniffling, chesty cough, threats of upchucking, the whole nine yards. Enough for bank customers to be put off their breakfasts. "Bosses don't just give you days off for feeling 'under the weather,' " she told me. In those days, nobody got paid for sick days. Del was figuring, for Rocco to be playing hooky, something big was up.

That's why Rocco changed the subject, putting on all his charm, saying, "Fellas, where are your manners? Take care of your customer."

Vito was also a bit spellbound at first. You'd think the three of them had never seen a female before, though she knew darned well how pretty she was and made it worse by flashing her white teeth from one to the other. At Rocco's prompt, Vito asked, "What can we get for you, miss?" implying the moon wouldn't be out of the question.

"She's not a customer," Pip said. "She's asking questions about Mr. Lowell being sick, and the orphans."

Rocco's dark eyebrows rose. "Miss . . . uh . . . ?"

"My name is Farrell. I guess you three haven't heard that Lloyd Lowell died this morning."

At first, none of them could speak, they were that stunned. Then Vito said, "Hoh-lee smokes."

Rocco, face unusually grim, said, "So Mr. Lowell's family sent you to ask about his illness?"

"No. The *Times Herald* sent me."

"The paper?" Vito looked confused. "You want to sell us a subscription, we aren't interested. Mr. D'Abruzzo sends his paper over every day, soon as he's done reading it."

Rocco set his hat on a shelf, so he could use his hands to talk. "I believe Miss Farrell means that she's a reporter."

"Can't be," Vito said. "No such thing as a girl reporter."

"Must be," Pip argued. "Who writes all the fashion items? And those 'News of Interest to Women' articles? Not guys."

"Oh, right." Enlightenment lit up Vito's face. "I bet you do the society page. That's why you're asking about Mr. Lowell."

"That's where they put my last piece," she conceded, not looking happy about it. "Maybe you read it? All about the orphan funeral last month?"

Vito shook his head. He only ever read the sports pages.

But Pip said, "I saw it. You wrote that?"

As she nodded, Rocco asked, "Were you at the funeral, miss?"

"I watched from a distance. That's the way Lowell said he wanted it when I called to ask him if I could write it up." Miss Farrell hooked her hands into her pockets. "Wanted, he said, to preserve the dignity of the rite. No reporters, no photographers. Funeral wasn't much, I thought—just Lowell, a nun from the orphanage, the man who drove her and the coffin there, and you two acting as pallbearers." She nodded toward Vito and Pip. "Not even a minister."

"The child was Catholic," Rocco explained, "and Montgomery isn't a Catholic cemetery."

"So no priest would come to the graveside," Farrell concluded. "That's what Lowell told me. I thought it was sad, though. Lonely funeral like that. Other folks in Norristown would have been glad to come and mourn, but Lowell never publicized when the funerals would take place. Only way I found out about the last one was to bribe Lowell's chauffeur to send word. I heard Lowell found out this week that his driver tried to let me know about Monday's burial. He fired him."

"So *that*'s why Mr. Lowell drove himself here last night," Pip said.

"Which explains," Miss Farrell said, "why you two—because if he's Joseph Trepani, I'm guessing you're his brother Vito—it explains why you and Rocco Montella here were the ones to take Lowell to the hospital last night? Don't deny that you did, the hospital has it on record."

"Why would we deny it, Miss Farrell?" Rocco made his voice softer, even a little seductive. "I'd be happy to tell you anything you want to know about last night. If you'd like, we can walk up to Woolworth's lunch counter and you can interview me over two sodas. Or coffee, if you prefer? My treat."

She seemed to hold in a laugh, as if to let him know his sexiness couldn't distract her. "I thought you were ill, Mr. Montella."

"Nothing catching, I assure you. I could also tell you what Vito and I discovered this morning, when we went to put

Lowell's crypt in order for the family. You know, of course, that the vault was broken into Monday night?"

Her gasp showed she knew nothing of the sort. That cinched the deal. Rocco let her precede him to the door, reaching into his coat pocket for his apartment key, tossing it to Vito. "Take my mail in for me, will you? And fire up my stove?"

"Sure thing," came the reply. When they were gone, Pip gave a low whistle. "Geez, he fell for her in a hurry."

"He didn't fall for nothin'," Vito said. "He was getting her out of our hair is all. Where's Pop?"

"Went to buy more fruit with Mr. D'Abruzzo."

Vito frowned. "Hope he doesn't buy too much. Rocco won't be paying for the rotten stuff anymore."

Pip's eyes opened wide. "No, I guess not. What a shame. Hey, what's that for?"

Vito had picked up his macaroni pot and was walking toward the back door. "What do you think? I'm gonna take it down the cellar, wash it out and fill it with Pop's wine."

"Pop's wine! You can't. He finds out, he'll kill you."

Uncle Ennio made his own wine each year, with all of us helping in some way. Me? I was small enough to fit in the barrels, so my job was to clean the insides. Most all the local Italian families made wine too, then we'd all trade bottles with each other, to see whose batch came out the best.

All through Prohibition my uncle made it, which was okay as long as we never sold it. Even later that year, after Pennsylvania ratified the repeal of Prohibition, opening State Liquor Stores and giving out licenses, Uncle Ennio still continued to make his own wine and trade with his neighbors, never selling it, never buying the winery brands. My uncle was adamant. *Vino per famiglie*, he'd say. Family wine. Meaning it was part of the glue that held us together.

So that's why Pip said what he did.

"Can't be helped this week," Vito replied. "We'll have to sneak some more later too."

"So we're going ahead with—" Pip looked over at me, then said, "—with the orphan funeral, even though Mr. Lowell died?"

Vito saw his glance. "You know she can't talk."

"Yeah, but she can hear, can't you, Bambola?" Pip winked at me. I smiled back, but he'd already turned back to his brother. "I mean, how can we? Mr. Lowell's gonna hafta be buried in that vault now, maybe the same day."

Vito shrugged. "Don't ask me. Rocco gave me his key and

instructions, meaning we get ready. Orazio said he'll drive. We asked him on the way home from the hospital last night."

"Yeah, but how can we open the crypt without Mr. Lowell?"

"We closed it without him this morning, didn't we?" Vito spun on his heel and left.

Pip called after him, "Hey, what did you and Rocco find out there this morning?"

But his brother was already out of earshot.

8

Aunt Sophie led Miss Maggie and me upstairs to the back room on the second floor. This was her catch-all room, where stuff she couldn't bear to throw out had accumulated over the last fifty-plus years.

The double bed in the middle of the room was more than half hidden by stacks of old blankets, quilts, tablecloths, et cetera, which were peeking out from under old sheets thrown over them to keep the dust off. The part of the bed closest to the door was clear and this, Aunt Sophie explained, was where I'd put the clothes that would go to charity.

Other than the bed, furniture-wise, the room only held a wardrobe, bureau and an old Queen Anne chair, the latter of which had shoeboxes piled on it. The top of the bureau had a small lamp, sans shade or bulb, a collection of religious statues and an archaic portable TV, the kind with dials for channels and volume. In the rest of the room, almost every empty bit of floor space was taken up by plastic and cardboard storage containers or large trash bags stuffed to the gills. Only a person-wide path was clear around the bed and over to the windows where anemic-looking African violets rested on the sills.

"Rocco's things are in those bags," Aunt Sophie said, pointing to three trash bags on one side of the chair, "except his good winter coat, his Knights of Columbus uniform, and one suit. They're in the wardrobe. He had two suits but I sent the other for him to be buried in. His photographs are in these." She tapped the shoeboxes on the chair, then looked at me expectantly, as if unsure I understood all the job requirements.

I assured her we'd be fine and shooed her back to her kitchen to prepare for the wake. Then I got to work, first clearing off the chair to give Miss Maggie a place to sit. Half the boxes felt suspiciously light. I looked inside. Only the top three had memorabilia in them. Otherwise, my aunt seemed to be saving empty shoeboxes. Like I said, she couldn't bear to throw stuff out.

"Good," Miss Maggie said, meaning the empty boxes. "I can use them to help sort the photos. Pat, could you run downstairs and fetch my handbag? I'll need my reading glasses."

I did and brought up a little TV table for her, too, so she wouldn't have to bend over as she sorted. I returned to find the ceiling lamp on, Miss Maggie with her nose in the wardrobe, and Uncle Rocco's Knights of Columbus hat on her head. Picture her in an oversized black Gilbert-and-Sullivan admiral's hat with a big purple plume down the middle, and singing "Columbus sailed the ocean blue in fourteen-hundred, ninety-two," to no melody I recog-nized.

"Look at this sword, Pat," Miss Maggie exclaimed, using two hands to bring the ornamental blade in its metal sheath out into the light. The surfaces needed a good polishing, but otherwise I only saw one small ding.

"Think that sword is worth anything, Miss Maggie?"

She frowned as she considered the idea. "Depends how old it is and who made it, of course. I'd say likely not much more than the value of the metal and craftsmanship. Not like it's a Confederate sword carried in the Battle of Shiloh."

"No historical significance, you mean?"

"No, I mean the sword's only worth what a collector might pay for it and collectors like blood." She set the weapon atop a stack of blankets on her side of the bed. "*Everything* has historical significance, Pat. Common objects often tell us the most about the former inhabitants of a place. This sword and uniform may have oodles of historical significance. When did your Uncle wear them, do you know?"

Deciding to work and talk at the same time, I went around to the wardrobe and opened the doors wide. The inside was crammed with Aunt Sophie's summer blouses, slacks and button-down sweaters, but at one end, under clear plastic dry cleaning bags, were men's clothes. "He wore them at least every August, when our church celebrates its two feasts. Italian festivals, I mean. The feast of San Salvatore on the sixth and *La Madonna del Soccorso di Sciacca* on the fifteenth."

"Our Lady of Help for Sciacca," Miss Maggie translated. "Sciacca's a city in Sicily, if I remember correctly?"

"You do." I spied the Knights of Columbus uniform in one of the bags. I pulled it out and draped it over the sword. "The Sicilians who settled here were almost all Sciaccis, like the Giamos on my mom's father's side. My grandfather was a member of the M.S.S.

lodge and helped carry the statue in the procession every year. Just like my other grandfather was in the Montellese lodge that did the San Salvatore procession and feast."

While I talked, I stripped off the plastic, then rummaged through the pockets of the black tuxedo coat and pants, even feeling around the lining, in case he'd hidden something inside it. No luck.

Miss Maggie, meanwhile, took up the uniform's matching cape—black with a purple lining—and draped it over her shoulders. "So, Norristown's Italian and Sicilian immigrants formed two separate lodges and celebrated different festivals?"

"More than two. The others just closed up over the years. I remember a Marchesian Club on the other side of Main when I was young. They were from Abruzzi. And Mom told me her great-uncle was in the St. Charles Society, another Sciacci club. Then there's the Our Lady of Mount Carmel Club. They're still around, but they don't do a procession anymore. Must have been others, too."

"The Knights of Columbus aren't a regional group, are they? I thought they were a benevolent society."

"Right. They don't represent any one part of Italy and they participate in all the festivals. At least, they do these days. When we have a feast day mass, or any other really special occasion, they escort the priest in, then stand and kneel in the aisles. Looks impressive, like our own version of the Swiss Guard."

"Then you should give this uniform back to them so they can keep up the tradition." Miss Maggie took off her cape and hat. "A new member might be able to wear it."

Agreeing, I proceeded to take Uncle Rocco's winter coat out for inspection.

"You missed the festivals last August," Miss Maggie pointed out. "You ought to make sure you get back for them this year. Bring Beth Ann with you. And take her on the train down to Independence Hall and the Liberty Bell."

I liked that idea. Those feast days last August and the Christmas holidays were when I'd missed my hometown and family the most. I liked the idea of starting new traditions with Hugh's family at Christmas, but if I could at least return for the San Salvatore feast, I'd be perfectly content in Virginia the rest of the year. "I'll talk to Hugh about it. You should come, too. They have lots of good food." I went on to describe the roast pork, grilled sausage and pepper sandwiches, and the *pizza frita*—fried pizza dough, coated with sugar, which are like heavy but yummy donuts. "Even tripe in tomato sauce, if you're brave enough to eat it. And the best birch beer, on tap."

"Stop, you're making me drool." She sat in the chair, extracted her reading glasses from her handbag, then lifted the shoebox of Uncle Rocco's photos onto her lap.

I searched the winter coat, which was in good shape except for two tiny moth holes. Also nothing in its pockets. I put it on the other side of the bed for donation to charity.

Uncle Rocco's remaining suit was another matter. We're talking the height of fashion maybe a quarter century ago. Vintage polyester. I remembered him wearing it to church and weddings. Besides looking way too retro, the trouser waistband and hems were frayed, as well as the cuffs on the jacket. But I did find five lottery tickets in the breast pocket. Dated 1993.

I used the suit as a base for a rag pile on the floor.

"Can you tell me who any of these folks are?" Miss Maggie asked. When I turned, I saw that she was examining two black-and-white photos with her magnifying glass. I'd seen her use it at home to read newsprint and package labels. She must have packed it in her handbag.

She held out the first photo, which was of two men and two little boys, the men in suits, the boys in white shirts, dark pants, and lighter plain ties. Both boys were standing at attention with their hands folded in prayerful petition. They would have looked like little angels if the grins in their eyes hadn't belied the fact.

"My dad and my Uncle Sal, he was Mom's brother. They were the same age. Mom and Uncle Sal lived up the street, across from the church, over Ronca's Bar. This must be Confirmation Day. The tall man's Great-uncle Rocco. He was Dad's sponsor. The other's my grandfather, Louie Montella. I guess he was Uncle Sal's sponsor. I'll have to ask Aunt Sophie."

"So that puts the photo in the 1930s?" Miss Maggie asked.

I did the math in my head. " '34 or '5. Look, they're standing in front of the stoops out front. You can see the glass where the store used to be next door."

Miss Maggie held the photo below her magnifier, nodding. "Your Uncle Rocco was a good-looking man."

Wasn't something I'd ever considered before, but I had to agree. Back then he had a full head of curly black hair, a trim body, and a roguish smile. Grandpop, on the other hand, a decade older than his brother, already had a pronounced receding hairline, a pasta-induced paunch, and worry lines induced by eight kids.

I went on to the other photo. "Uncle Rocco again. Sometime during World War II. He enlisted right after Pearl Harbor."

"That's a winter uniform he's wearing," Miss Maggie said, "but the woman and little girl in the photo are wearing spring coats. Around Eastertime?"

"Likely. That's his wife and their daughter, Zoe." Uncle Rocco was holding the tot with one arm, pointing toward the camera with the other, as if trying to get her to look straight at it and smile. Her face was half-hidden in his neck.

"Zoe looks shy," Miss Maggie observed.

"Everybody said she was," I recalled, handing back the photos. "She died the year after my brother. Breast cancer, same as her mother."

"Beatrice is Zoe's daughter? How old was she when her mother died?"

I hadn't ever thought about it before. As I undid the long twist tie on one of the trash bags next to the chair and started pulling out clothes, I said, "Let's see. Beatrice is going on fifty now, I think. I don't know, mid-teens?"

"Rotten age to lose a mother. Might have made her bitter."

That gave me something to chew on as I separated shirts and pants from winter wear—scarves, hats, gloves, sweaters, vests. Apparently Uncle Rocco had taken most of his wearable duds to the nursing home with him. The few shirts and pants left here were in poor shape. Nothing in the pockets. I fed the rag pile.

The winter things were in better shape. One sweater had pockets loaded with unused tissues. In with the Scotties I found a zinc lozenge and five more lottery tickets. 1999 this time. One pullover was fraying, but everything else went on the bed.

Meantime, Miss Maggie would ask me occasional questions about people in the photos. Sometimes I knew them, sometimes I didn't. Almost all the pictures were post-Zoe, as if Uncle Rocco didn't have a reason to keep mementos before her.

"Look at this one, Pat." Miss Maggie handed me a five-by-seven sepia done by a professional studio. Uncle Tonio and Aunt Benita's wedding picture, with a young Rocco as best man. I didn't recognize the maid-of-honor. The men had on black tuxes with stiff collars and bow ties. Both had their hair slicked back and a middle part.

But Miss Maggie wasn't looking at the men. "My wedding dress was something like that. Same style, less beads and lace."

Aunt Benita's dress had a narrow, midi-length hem, deeply scalloped with tons of beaded lace. Her veil was all lace, but fit like a cap, just showing the curled ends of her short hair. Very Roaring Twenties.

I tried to imagine Miss Maggie in it and failed. "Were you a flapper?"

"Oh, I wanted to be in the worst way. Born too late. Plus none of my crowd went to speakeasies. Too poor." With a laugh that was half sigh, she set that photo aside and went on.

I turned to the next trash bag, which held summer clothes—shorts, plain white tees, seersucker shirts, along with maybe twenty ties representing every fashion trend of the last sixty years. I couldn't bear to throw them out, thinking maybe a local theater group might want them, if not the Smithsonian. In the pockets of two pairs of shorts and three shirts, I found old raffle tickets, plus two door prize stubs for the San Salvatore feast, different years, and more lottery tickets. Did Uncle Rocco ever win?

"Newspaper clippings." Miss Maggie announced the discovery as if she'd unearthed a lost city. "Mostly soldiers in the war. Here's your father again."

One yellowed clip she handed me had society-page-like notices—small portrait photos of soldiers under the heading "Our Men In Service." My dad and Uncle Sal were listed, Dad in an Army uniform and Uncle Sal, Navy.

I looked through more of the clippings, finding similar notices for Dad's older brothers, Pasquale and Mario. I recalled how, when I was a kid, my mom had shown me pictures of Uncle Pasq at boot camp in the Midwest. He'd been in the cavalry, wearing britches and leggings. I'd been disappointed to learn that he hadn't ridden horses at all, just tanks.

Montella cousins—Uncle Tonio's boys—were mentioned, too, and I recognized names from other families who had lived in this neighborhood, like Joachim Ranelli. One picture was of a Ronca son from across the street, dressed in combat fatigues, standing on the streets of Colmar, France, grinning as he displayed a captured Nazi flag. And besides war-time notices, Uncle Rocco had saved family wedding announcements and obits.

"Now this is interesting." Miss Maggie scrutinized another piece of newspaper. "For one thing, unlike the others, whoever cut it out included the date and it's older than the other articles. March 2, 1933. For another, this fellow's not from this neighborhood."

Even as she held it out to me, I had no trouble reading the large headline: LLOYD LOWELL DEAD AT 53. Then, in slightly smaller print below: "Prominent philanthropist dies suddenly while helping the poor of Norristown." A photo showed Lowell with his wife and teenaged son posing with Republican dignitaries in front of, of all things, a big cemetery crypt. On a tall granite monument behind them was carved a large overlapping double L.

"What's it say, Pat?" Miss Maggie figured it was easier to use me as her magnifier than read it herself.

I scanned the tiny print, reading the gist of the article. "Here's the local connection. Lowell had come down to this end of town on February 28 for some goodwill mission when he took ill. 'He was taken to Charity Hospital by Mr. Rocco Montella and Mr. Vito Trepani, both of East Main Street'—whoa!"

"What?!" You can only test Miss Maggie's patience so far. She gets that "detention" look in her eye, a hold-over from her teaching days.

"It says the illness that led to Lowell's death may have been brought on by the shock of learning that his cemetery vault had been robbed the night before." I read the next part aloud. " 'In the last year, Mr. Lowell graciously allowed the burial of eleven deceased orphans in his family's crypt. According to Mr. Montella, who investigated the extent of the robbery for the Lowells, only one of the children's coffins remained yesterday morning. Stranger still, Mr. Montella stated that none of the four Lowell coffins had been touched.' "

Miss Maggie frowned. "How very strange."

"Macabre, if you ask me. My great-uncle was crawling around the inside of tombs."

"People did all sorts of odd jobs for money during the Depression." She took back the clipping and studied the photo with her magnifying glass. "What I mean by strange is, the Lowell family was obviously well-off. Look at the size of that tombstone. Yet the graverobbers—I'm guessing there must have been several of them to make off with ten coffins, even if they were child-sized—the graverobbers apparently didn't so much as look inside the coffins of the rich folk, where they might have a chance at finding jewelry."

"Maybe it was a prank?" I suggested. "Kids?"

Miss Maggie considered the notion. "Possible, of course, but back then, the teens I remember with a bent for mischief . . . Let me put it this way, Pat—America had two classes during the Depression, those who could afford to eat and those who couldn't. A less-than-ethical kid would more likely grab fruit off a grocer's stand, or vegetables from a garden, or milk from people's porches—"

"Stealing food," I summarized.

"Right, or if a teen had a true bad streak, he'd turn to regular thieving, stealing money and valuables. I can't imagine anyone wasting time on pranks that didn't produce food or money." Miss Maggie tapped the newsprint with her gnarled arthritic forefinger. "If teenagers did this, they were rich kids."

I slipped the article out from under her fingertip to rescan it. "The kid in this photo—the article says his name's Latimer, aged fifteen. Maybe he hated that his dad was giving more attention to orphans than to his own son."

Instead of commenting, she giggled. "Lloyd and Latimer Lowell. What were their mothers thinking?"

"Must have been a family requirement. Listen to this." I read from the article again. " 'Lowell's grandfather, Lucius, the son of Welsh immigrants, founded the L.L. Lucifer Company in Norristown in 1842. Lucius's son, Lawrence, took over the company and became a prominent member of the Match Trust—' "

Miss Maggie let out a guffaw. "Lloyd, Latimer, Lucius, Lucifer, and Lawrence. How silly of them!"

Laughing, I handed the article back to her and returned to my sorting. The next thing I pulled out of the bag was a plastic grocery bag that had been secured with another twist tie. Inside were plastic bottles and tubes of various kinds of herbal and natural remedies. I read the labels aloud: "Horse nettle, saw palmetto, feverfew, arnica cr—"

"Arnica!" Miss Maggie exclaimed. "That's leopard's bane. Granddaddy used it to make an ointment for sprains." Her grandfather had been a pharmacist in the late nineteenth century.

"These are all at least six months out of date," I commented. "Most more than that. Here's one that says 'Best if used before oh-three, ninety-nine.' "

"Did your great-uncle take all that stuff?"

I shrugged. "I'll ask Aunt Sophie."

9

Aunt Sophie came upstairs to use the bathroom soon after, then she stopped by the back room to see how we were making out. I asked about the natural remedies.

"Oh, I forgot all about these," my aunt said, fingering the little bottles. "Uncle Rocco used to try all sorts of these pills and lotions. He'd take 'em for a week and if they didn't do anything for him, he'd switch to something else."

"Without asking his doctor?" I asked, horrified.

"I think he told his doctor once and he got yelled at. He never mentioned them again."

"But he kept taking them?"

"Oh, sure. You get as old as Uncle Rocco was, Tricia, and you end up trying anything that maybe'll make you feel a little better without the side effects and cost of prescriptions. Even me and Leo, we take fish oil and glucosamine." Aunt Sophie began putting the bottles back into the grocery bag. "I brought these over here so I could flush the pills down the toilet instead of just throwing them in the trash. I forgot. I'll do it tomorrow, after the funeral, when I'm not so busy. Which reminds me what I wanted to ask you. When do you want lunch? Better come down before my sister Lydia gets here."

"Lunch?" I looked at my watch. Eleven-forty already and I still needed a shower. "I'll finish sorting later, Aunt Sophie." I explained that Cella and I were supposed to go out for lunch, before picking up Joan and Janine from school. I mentioned nothing about stopping by Uncle Rocco's retirement home. Some part of my conscience still wasn't comfortable with Cella's plan. I felt more as if I were tagging along to keep her out of trouble. Like I had umpteen times in high school.

"Good," Aunt Sophie said about our agenda. "I ordered two red pizzas and rolls from Corropolese. I was gonna send your Uncle, but you and Cella can pick them up while you're out."

I agreed, then asked Miss Maggie if she wanted to come.

"No, I think I'll go through some more of these photos and news articles this afternoon. For a historian, they're pure meat and potatoes."

Something in her manner made me suspicious of her interest in those photos. Silly me thought she just wanted Cella and me to have time alone, or that she wanted to compare notes with my aunts about me, or that she simply figured she'd get a better and healthier lunch here than with us, which was true.

Before I had time to read more into her intentions, she added, "But I ought to get up and walk around a little. My legs are stiffening up."

"You want exercise?" Aunt Sophie said. "We got a treadmill down in the front parlor. Leo's doctor says he got to use it the days he doesn't go to therapy. I walk on it, too."

Goodness, I thought, first lowfat and decaf foods, now exercise. My aunt, the health freak convert. No wonder she'd lost weight.

Miss Maggie's face lit up at the idea of trying out a new gadget. "That would just fit the bill."

"Don't overdo it," I warned.

"I'll tell her the right way," Aunt Sophie assured me. As I went off to get my shower, I heard my aunt lecturing Miss Maggie on their way down the stairs. "You have to stretch your legs first, then you start slow. . . ." My aunt, health freak convert *and* personal trainer.

When I came downstairs, I found Miss Maggie beside the treadmill in the front parlor, doing the cool-down stretches she always did after her walks in Bell Run's woods. On her face was the exhilaration of a new disciple. "We have to get one of these, Pat. Be great on those sloppy weather days when we can't get out for a hike." She stopped to take her own pulse. After a silent ten seconds, she exclaimed, "Exactly where it should be."

I heard newcomers at the back door, which meant Aunt Lydia, who always walked up the tunnel to come in the back door, even on bad weather days. Miss Maggie and I headed for the kitchen, where I found my two aunts talking a mile a minute about the grandson of someone who used to live on Violet Street. Uncle Leo ignored them as he sat at the table munching a sandwich on whole wheat. I could smell the tuna from the doorway.

I did hugs, kisses, introductions, and showed off my ring, in that order. Uncle Gaet came in the middle of it all, having dropped his wife off, then gone to find parking further down the block. As the door opened and closed, I heard the scrape of a shovel, meaning Vinny was here, doing the back walk and patio.

The phone rang. Cella, for me. I carried the receiver into the dining room so I could hear her over all the hubbub.

"I'm at the light at DeKalb and Lafayette," she said. "My mom there yet?"

"Just walked in."

"Then I'll pick you up out front. If I come in, we'll never get away. Be outside in two minutes."

Back in the kitchen, Aunt Lydia, Uncle Gaet, and Miss Maggie had made themselves comfortable at the table while Aunt Sophie brought out more sandwich fixings. My two aunts were still talking nonstop, now about some other former neighbor. Miss Maggie looked like a spectator at a close tennis match.

Grabbing my boots and jacket, I announced that Cella was picking me up. Aunt Lydia said, "Tell her not to forget the kids," as if my cousin abandoned her own progeny every day. Aunt Sophie gave me money and a list of things to get at the supermarket, since we'd be out that way anyway to stop at Corropolese's Bakery. The sisters went back to their gossip.

Outside, the day had warmed up a bit. Everything was wet from melting snow. As I got in Cella's Neon, she noted the addition of our voodoo snow dolls. "I named mine after my car insurance company," she said. "My biggest bill this week."

I filled her in on the identities of ours. "Too bad they won't last 'til nightfall." Then I told her about Aunt Sophie's errands.

"I figured she'd give you a list. Good thing we don't have to go out to Evergreen Manor after all."

"We don't?"

Cella pulled out into traffic. "I called there this morning and was told that Uncle Rocco's cronies would be coming to the viewing tonight. We can grill them here first, on our own turf, so to speak."

I was actually relieved to hear that she'd given up the idea of retirement home snooping, but I asked, "Why did you come home early then? I could have had lunch with Aunt Sophie."

"I still have to pick up the kids."

"Not for another two hours."

"You sound like Ma." Cella clamped her mouth shut, meaning she was annoyed at my nagging. But in another heartbeat she sighed, let her anger go and said, "Gimme a break. I haven't had lunch with my favorite cousin in almost a year. Speaking of which, what do you want to eat?"

"Hmm. I promised Hugh I'd buy him an authentic Norristown zep at Eve's Lunch this weekend. Today? A cheesesteak. You can't get either in Virginia. Not like they make here."

"Pudge's, Amadeo's, Via Veneto's, Lou's . . . ?"

"All exemplary. You choose."

"Tough call. Hmm. Okay, I haven't been to Amadeo's lately."

Cella drove up Main, through Norristown, clear to the other end, then most of the way through West Norriton Township, which altogether was only about three miles. Near the halfway point, we passed Hartranft Street on the left, which led to Montgomery Cemetery and Cella's old neighborhood. I remembered the clipping I'd read that morning. "Did you know Uncle Rocco once crawled around one of the crypts in Montgomery Cemetery?" I told her about going through our great-uncle's things and related the gist of the article.

"The Lowell vault?" Cella slowed to a stop at the next light. "I know where that is. I'll show you tomorrow. On the ghost tour they mention the grave robbery. The remains of ten orphans were taken, coffins and all. They were never recovered, the robbers never caught, and no explanation was ever found."

The light turned green and she put on the gas, yet was uncharacteristically silent for the last mile.

We settled into a table by a front window at Amadeo's and, after some discussion, we decided to split a pizza-steak calzone. It's sort of like a pizza folded in half, filled with shredded steak and mozzarella. Pizza sauce on the side for dipping. Diet Coke for her, root beer for me.

As we sipped sodas and waited for our lunch to come out, Cella began to muse aloud. "You know, if Uncle Rocco *did* work for one of the richest families in Norristown during the Depression . . . well, what if he was rewarded somehow? Say, a nice pocket watch or something. Or if he worked at the Lowell house and admired a piece of art, maybe they gave it to him. You hear stories like that all the time. Then decades later, the piece is worth a fortune. Maybe *that*'s what we're looking for."

Hating to squelch her daydreams, I shook my head. "If Uncle Rocco had money to throw around all these years, it means he sold an heirloom like that long ago."

She frowned. "What about the clothes?"

"Nothing valuable in the pockets. I checked."

"I was thinking vintage," she said. "Some old clothing is worth a lot in and of itself."

"Most of the stuff was seventies and later," I told her. "Except the ties. Some of them might be older."

"I'll look them over. What about war stuff? You didn't find his Air Force uniform, did you? Or anything he might have brought back from Europe?"

"No, but I'm not done sorting yet—" Our order arrived and all talking stopped for a while. You have to eat a calzone while it's hot. I ate slow, dunking my half in the sauce, savoring each mouthful. Might be ten more months before I had another.

We argued over who'd pick up the check since I knew, with the lack of Ronny's income, the needs of two teenage daughters, plus the new house, she likely needed every penny. But she also knew my employment situation.

"I said 'my treat' and I meant it," Cella insisted. "You can leave the tip, okay?" I grudgingly accepted the compromise and we left.

She drove across town to the north end, alongside Elmwood Park, past the bandshell made famous by Maniac McGee, past the swings I used to play on when I was little, past the bocce ball courts, past the zoo. As we rolled by, I got a glimpse of a mountain goat standing on top of a pile of rocks, in the same pose as the last time I'd seen him. Some things hadn't changed, for which I felt ridiculously grateful.

We picked up the order at Corropolese's first. I had to keep my hands in my pockets so I wouldn't be tempted to buy bags of Italian goodies to bring back to Virginia with me, but I couldn't resist a box of pizzelles (anise waffle cookies, that is). Not that they'd be as good as my own, of course.

The pizzas went onto the car's backseat—big rectangular boxes that took up most of the length. Corropolese's makes what non-Italians call the "tomato pie" version of pizza—half-inch crust of good Italian bread, spread with a thick layer of tomato sauce, sprinkled with Parmesan. No mozzarella. Served warm or cold. Our family calls it "red pizza" or just "pizza." Grandmom Montella used to make hers that way. That's how we Montellas prefer it. Oh, sure, none of us turn down the hot greasy slices dripping with cheese that my cousin Angelo churns out at his pizzeria. But at our family gatherings, this kind of pizza is essential comfort food.

As my cousin tossed the bags of rolls on top of the boxes, I asked, "Would you mind stopping at St. Pat's?" I meant the local Catholic cemetery, right down the road, where my parents and brother were buried.

"I was going to take a short cut through there anyway," Cella replied. After we'd turned in at the gates, she asked, "You want to stop at any graves beside your folks?"

For the past three generations, every deceased Montella, plus every dead relative on my maternal grandfather's side were buried here, so the choices were many. The voice of my mom in my head said I should at least say a prayer at my grandparents' stones. But as we moved down the lane, I saw that a thin layer of snow still hid the grass in places. Where it didn't, mud would abound. In the backyards of neighboring houses, the wind was bending the tops of trees, which meant, with all this open space, the chill factor would be nasty despite the sun. Since I'd left my gloves on Aunt Sophie's radiator, I declined the offer.

Cella drove around the circle in the middle and turned down the lane toward the newer part of the cemetery. As we went around the big mausoleum building—an apartment house for worldly remains constructed when I was a kid—I saw still another brand new addition behind it. "When did that go up?" I asked.

"Last summer. Place is getting downright urban." Around the other side, Cella parked in the center of the block. "I'll wait here, if you don't mind. I don't have boots on."

Smart move, because my family's grave was several rows in. When my brother's body had come home from Vietnam and my parents had to buy a lot in a hurry, Ma had fretted because the grave was so far away from the water pump, water being necessary to the Italian custom of covering every square foot in front of a tombstone with flowers. But then the mausoleum was built and a new pump installed right behind us. Ma was ecstatic.

I recalled all this while I was slogging across the squishy ground. The wind was coming from behind, at least. Once in a while a gust hit my left side, making me turn my head.

At the grave, I noted new hyacinth and daffodil shoots pushing up through the snow, between dead brown stalks from the geraniums and vincas I'd planted out here last spring. To one side were dried chrysanthemum leftovers from a small bush someone else had apparently planted later. Veteran's flag holders anchored either side, one for Dad, one for Lou.

The stone was small and pink marble—Ma had picked it out. "Montella" was in caps, with a small cross in the middle and flowers carved at the corners. I used my boot toe to wipe snow from the four inch shelf near the ground, where the first names were: Louis S., Carmen, Teresa Giamo.

"Hi, guys," I murmured. "Miss me?" It suddenly felt like eons since I'd planted those flowers, which made me feel guilty. "I've been tending your great-grandmother's grave in Virginia," I told my mom, knowing she'd approve. To cement her blessing, I held up my left hand, "And look, I'm engaged at last, Ma. Wish you could have hung around two more years to see it. You would have liked Hugh. Beth Ann, too. You always wanted grandkids."

I sighed. Besides a son-in-law and grandkids, my mom had never seen me with all the other things she dreamed of: a profitable career, a *Better Homes and Gardens* house, and a big luxury car with no leaky trunk. I felt like I'd failed her. "I'll stop by again before I go back to Virginia," I promised.

I mumbled three "Hail Marys", stumbling over the words, thinking how Mom would also want me to pray often enough that it was muscle memory. Then the gardener in me couldn't resist yanking out the dead geraniums and vincas. They came out easily with the ground so wet. The smell of mold on the roots tickled my nose, bringing on a sneeze.

I headed back to the car, the wind in my face making my eyes tear. At least, I told myself it was the wind. Turning my head to avoid the gusts again, I saw movement a few stones away—something black, like a small animal running between the stones, toward the older part of the cemetery.

I paused to look, wondering if a little dog had gotten loose from one of the neighboring houses, but now I saw nothing. I pictured him around behind one of the stones, peeing on it.

When I got into the Neon, Cella eyed the dead plants in my hand. "Collecting botany samples for your step-daughter-to-be?"

"Just weeding. Pull over at the next trash can."

She started her car, letting it roll slowly along the drive. "Weeds my foot. I spent half of last year waging war against the weeds on that grave. By October all the ground ivy and crab grass were too scared to go near it."

"Really? You tended my flowers? That's nice."

Cella shrugged. "Ma made me."

I knew, even if Aunt Lydia had made the initial suggestions, Cella wouldn't have done it if she hadn't wanted to. "She make you plant the new mum, too?"

"Ma bought it, but actually, Janine planted it. My kid decided she likes gardening. We started coming out once a week last summer to water plants and weed. Our afternoons to bond."

"Oh, then *Janine* did the weeding," I teased.

"You want to walk back to Aunt Sophie's or what?" Cella kidded me back as she stopped the car at the trash can. After I tossed my dead plants and got back in, she said, "Not too much mud along here. I'm gonna take a quick look at Mrs. Ranelli's grave. It's right up here. Okay?"

I agreed. Since we were now in the older part of the cemetery where my Giamo great-grandparents were buried, I decided to walk over to their grave. As I got out of the car, I caught a glimpse of that animal again, closer, near the fourth stone in from the road. Like last time, when I tried to get a better look, the animal disappeared behind the markers, yet the stones were smaller here than the rest of the cemetery. Thinking about the movement, I categorized it as more feline than canine. Made sense. This place probably made for good field mouse hunting.

As I walked up the drive, I recalled one Memorial Day weekend when I was in junior high. While my parents were planting flowers, I'd wandered up and down these older rows, reading names and dates. I'd been shocked to see how many were children. Quite a few had died in 1918. Influenza, I presumed.

Great-Grandpop Giamo had died only a dozen years after coming to America. I spied his distinctive grave marker—white limestone shaped like a cross with a pregnant base—and made a beeline for it. The carving was now so weather-worn, I couldn't read it anymore. The letters had still been there when I was young, though, and I remembered them. In Italian, it had said he was Salvatore Giamo, that he'd died on "20 *Agosto di Anni* 1914"—August 20, 1914—and that the stone had been erected by son Pete and brother Dominic.

My great-grandmother had a separate gray marble marker. She'd outlived her hubby by more than a quarter century. "Teresa Giamo," read the block letters. My mother had been named for her, following the strict Sicilian convention where first sons and daughters were named after the father's parents. Ma had followed it by naming her son Louis, but couldn't bring herself to saddle me with the name Monalisa. For which I've always been grateful.

Anyway, my great-grandmother's stone also had "Beloved Mother" beneath her name, and her dates. The single geranium I'd planted here last Mother's Day was nowhere in evidence. Unlike the Montellas, I had no Giamo aunts, uncles or first cousins to water flowers. I realized Ma's parents' grave was likely as barren-looking as these two. Graves needed flowers. Without something living and green, you saw nothing but the cold, deathlike stone marker. The flowers were like warm prayers.

I headed back toward Cella, who was standing with her back to me, inspecting the base of a stone not far from her car. The black animal was there, too, rubbing its neck against the granite. Definitely a cat. It turned to face me, yellow eyes meeting mine. I'd just noticed a wisp of white fur on its otherwise black breast when my foot caught on the uneven ground and I stumbled. When I looked up again, the cat was gone.

As I joined Cella, she was whining "Look at all this clay," as she gestured at the ground. The disturbed soil had flattened out where Mrs. Ranelli had been buried, but no grass grew there yet. The dirt was the color of red brick and filled with tiny stones, damp from last night's snow, but barely muddy. "Subsoil," Cella said, disgusted. "Be hard as rock come spring."

"Nothing a load of top soil and peat moss won't fix—" The inscription on the stone caught my eye. "Mrs. Ranelli's maiden name was Trepani?"

"Yeah. Why?"

"I remember Ma saying one of the Giamos married a Trepani. I wonder if she was some sort of cousin-in-law?"

"Maybe," Cella said. "She had four brothers. I bet Aunt Sophie knows who they married. She knows everything."

As we walked back to the car, I asked, "Can I somehow bribe Janine to plant something on the Giamo graves for me? Nothing high-maintenance. Vincas maybe. I'll pay you for the plants."

"I'll get her to do it, but don't mention the word 'bribe' to my kid or she'll ask for some incredibly expensive teen-fad thing. Last week she bugged me for a top that looks just like all the other tops she wears except the label on it made it cost three times as much."

We both slid into the Neon, which, sitting out in the bright sun, was now warm and toasty.

"You sound exactly like your mom did twenty years ago."

Cella stuck her tongue out at me. "You wait. You'll be sounding like your own mother soon, too. Stepmom."

I shook my head. "Beth Ann's not like that."

"Ha! Wait 'til you're her official mother. You'll be 'Patricia Marie, do what I tell you this instant, young lady!' all over again."

"We'll see." Oh, Beth Ann was perfectly capable of being a teenager from hell, I knew, but I couldn't picture myself turning into my mom. I'd be different.

The conversation made me think about Hugh and Beth Ann. Actually, these days, they were both always in my brain somewhere, hovering in the wings of my consciousness—Hugh especially, at the curtain's edge off left, constantly distracting me with sexy murmurs. But now, both of them came on stage, front and center, giving me the strong urge to hug them.

I'd check email when I got back to Aunt Sophie's, I told myself. Write and ask if they're okay, tell them how much I missed them.

I missed Bell Run, too. This time of day, speckles of sunlight would seem like jewels on the forest floor. I wondered if the tulips I planted last fall outside Miss Maggie's old farmhouse had poked through the soil yet.

How ironic, I thought. Now that I was back home in Norristown, I had a severe case of homesickness for Virginia.

"WARNING—Do not risk Federal arrest by looking glum!"
—FROM A SARCASTIC EDITORIAL CARTOON BY CORNELL GREENING, DURING HOOVER'S TERM

March 1, 1933 – 349 East Main

Little Carmen Montella knocked at our back door that afternoon. He and Tutti were the same age and usually walked home from school together, but today Carmen told us Tutti would be late because he was working.

"Working!" Aunt Gina exclaimed, shocked enough to stop chopping onions for tonight's tomato sauce. "Doing what?"

The gist of it was that two men were pointing bricks on a house up on Marshall Street. They couldn't reach the top corners from their scaffolding. Their idea was to put a belt around a small boy and let him lean out as far as he could stretch.

"*Madonne!*" cried Aunt Gina. "And you left Tutti there?"

"They said they'd pay him fifty cents," was Carmen's reply.

"Fifty cents!" Del had walked in the door from school two minutes earlier and was just coming back to the kitchen after hanging up her coat. "For fifty cents, I would have climbed up the bricks myself! Holy cow!"

"Me, too," said Carmen, "but Mama told me to come home early today on account of Ash Wednesday." Actually, I found out later that Carmen got dizzy from heights, only he didn't want to admit it. My brother Tutti, though, heights never bothered him.

Aunt Gina kept Carmen long enough to ask exactly where the house was, then, when he left, she asked Del where Charlie and Gussie were.

"Down the *Times Herald*. They had a nickel between them today." She meant they went to buy newspapers to sell. That's where they always went after school when they didn't have to be home for any reason and they had a few cents. If they could sell all their papers, they'd double their money.

"Find Pip, then," Aunt Gina told her. "Tell him to go keep an eye on Tutti. Make sure he's okay." She went back to chopping onions. Fifty cents, after all, was fifty cents. She could make us a whole meal with less than that. "And since Tutti's working, Delphina, I'll need you to sort the coal."

"Yesmama." She ran off, smiling, happy to get out of her regular afterschool chores, which today would have been scrubbing the bathroom floor. She preferred the boys' chores, always had.

Fetching Pip took a while. He and Vito were next door at Rocco's and nobody heard Del banging at Rocco's apartment door for a good five minutes. Then, after Pip went to find Tutti and somehow keep him from falling while he earned more money than the rest of us that day, and after Del changed into her old clothes, she went down the cellar. Mrs. Roosevelt and I followed her.

A single bulb on a short pull chain at the bottom of the stairs was the only light in the basement. Edison bulbs we had then, the kind with a point at the end and no coating in the glass. You could see the filaments inside. Del told me never to look straight at the bulbs when they were on or I'd go blind.

Yet, as bright as those filaments shone, the front and back of the cellar stayed fairly dark. The stoop into the store blocked where one front window would have been. The one window we had, over the sidewalk door, was dingy from coal dust, since the bin was right at the bottom of the outside steps.

The cellar ceiling was low. Since the house was only two blocks from the river, the water table was too close to the surface to dig the floor any deeper. The packed dirt was always damp along the back wall. Pip and Vito had to stoop over when they came down here. Del didn't, but she could easily reach up and touch the bare rafters.

The coal bin was merely a section of floor fenced off with boards. As Del walked over to it, the stark light made a long shadow of her that danced eerily over floor and walls. The shadows were what made the cellar fascinating. That and the dirt—the air down here always smelled grimy and dank.

That day I sat on the bottom step, under the light, because I had Mrs. Roosevelt with me and wanted to keep her clean.

"Nice and warm down here today, huh, Bambola?" Del observed. "Did Uncle Ennio run the furnace this afternoon? Or maybe Vito got hold of some railroad ties again or, remember last Christmas when Pip put pine knots in the furnace? Remember how hot they burned? I bet it's something like that."

The fact that the furnace was silent and cold didn't seem to faze her. She shoveled new coal into a metal bucket, making a racket, though the noise didn't compare to the clamor made when the coal delivery had come around noon. I'd run back to the kitchen from the store because I hated the banging of the coal tumbling down the chute into the nearly empty bin.

"Is Crisi down here, Bambola?" Del asked. Except for sunny mornings, the cat loved spending time down here. She'd stand on her hind legs and paw at the door until one of us opened it for her. I don't know what the attraction was. Mice, maybe. Or the big ugly water bugs that sometimes came in through the cracks in the foundation.

"Crisi! Here kitty!" Del called.

I turned to look back to where the clotheslines were strung across the cellar. Today Aunt Gina's and Nonna's white panties hung there alongside everyone else's long underwear. Against the wall, not far from the big sink and wash ringer, was a small crate filled with an old ripped blanket, a cozy nest that Crisi used for naps sometimes. The cat wasn't there now, though.

"Here Crisi! Come on kitty!" Del called again as she dragged her bucket back beneath the light, then went to fetch another pail, and a crate to sit on.

The coal had to be sorted since, like I said, it was bootleg, with slag mixed in. If too much slag was left in, the ashes would stick together and clog up the grate in the stove upstairs. The coal pieces ranged in size from pea to buckwheat, so Del needed all the light she could get to separate the bits.

She scooped up a handful, picked out the slag, letting it fall to the dirt floor at her feet, then tossed the good coal in the other bucket. "Did you get your ashes today, Bambola?"

I nodded.

"They don't show," she said. "I bet you wiped them off."

I nodded again.

Del continued to scoop coal and sort it as she talked. "I'm gonna get my ashes tonight. I'm gonna sleep on my back all night and go to school tomorrow with a dirty forehead. My homeroom teacher'll get mad and tell me to go wash as soon as she lays eyes on me, but I'll say, 'Sorry, Mrs. Wildermeyer, these are holy ashes and it's a sin to let water touch them.' That'll make her madder, 'cause she hates us Cath'lics—"

We both heard Crisi meow at the same instant. We still couldn't see her. The sound came from the opposite wall, near the first chimney foundation in from the street. In front of the foundation were floor-to-ceiling shelves. Every fall, when our garden was done producing, Aunt Gina and Nonna would fill the shelves with jars of cooked tomatoes, homemade catsup, sweet relishes. Now, only six jars remained.

The mewing came again, so Del abandoned her chore to find the cat. She peeked behind the shelves. "Where are you, Crisi? Come out, kitty." Her voice changed from her higher pet-calling tones to her usual range. "You know, it feels warmer over *here*, Bambola. Let me see something."

She walked back to the furnace and used the old fireplace poker Uncle Ennio kept handy to open the door at the bottom. Even from my seat on the steps, I could see only cold ash inside, no red embers.

"How 'bout *that*," Del exclaimed, closing the door and returning to the chimney foundation. She reached a hand back behind the shelves to feel the wall. "Yep, it's warm. Rocco must have his stove going full tilt, and it's heating up our cellar for us, saving us coal."

One of the cat's famous howls rang out. Del looked up. "How'd you get way up there, Cristiana?"

Now I spotted her, or I should say, I spotted only her golden eyes, peering out of the blackness between the rafters at the top of the shelves. I could see how she got there. Next to the shelves was an old chest of drawers where Uncle Ennio stored doodads like screws and washers and sandpaper. And next to that was one of the smaller casks he used to age his wine. This cask was empty 'cause it had a leak, but Uncle Ennio kept it around anyway. The cat had apparently climbed from cask to chest to top shelf, then ducked under two ceiling beams to get where she was now. She could get down by herself, but wanted to be carried.

Del reached up to lift Crisi down, soothing her. To me the cat didn't look upset. Impatient, maybe. As soon as she was within four feet of the ground again, Crisi jumped out of Del's arms, bounded across the floor, and tore past me up the stairs like she was late for an appointment.

"Now what got into her?" Del mused, heading back toward her buckets. "Sometimes I wonder if she's isn't batty or—"

Suddenly the shelf behind my cousin seemed to blow apart. Del fell face down, her back and legs soaked in red. I saw red specks on me, too, and on Mrs. Roosevelt.

I snapped my eyes shut to block out the scene, screaming until Aunt Gina came running.

10

We finished our errands and picked up Janine and Joan from school, squishing them in beneath the pizza boxes and other groceries. By four o'clock, Cella was parking in front of Aunt Sophie's. The snow was all but gone in the streets, with small mounds left where I'd piled it up on the sidewalk. Our voodoo dolls had shrunk a good four inches and lost enough weight to hype a new fad diet craze. My stake had fallen out completely, but Miss Maggie's and Cella's were still working their magic.

Uncle Leo let us in, and the luscious smell of Montella tomato sauce again greeted my nose. If I could figure a way to bottle that fragrance, I could make a fortune in aromatherapy.

Miss Maggie called to me from the front parlor where she was reading today's *Times Herald* funnies by the last of the afternoon sunlight coming in the front window, before the orb sunk behind the abandoned factory up the street.

"What'd they do?" I asked. "Banish you from the kitchen?"

In lieu of an answer, she abandoned Garfield and friends to shuffle out to the hall. I introduced Janine and Joan, who said, respectively, "Um, hi," and "Yeah, hi," proving Miss Maggie still retained her aura of intimidation from her years of teaching adolescents. The first time she'd fixed her eye on me, I'd had a strong urge to sit up straight and stow my gum under my desk lid. And I hadn't been chewing gum or sitting at a desk.

Cella sent the kids toward the kitchen with the pizzas and rolls while she and I brought the Genuardi bags in. When we paused in the hall to take off our coats (I hung my bag of pizzelles underneath mine), the girls came out to likewise lose their outer garments. Cella saddled them with another load of groceries. I was about to scoop up the one remaining sack and follow them to the kitchen, but Miss Maggie held me back.

"I found the cat!" she exclaimed, her green eyes glowing, making her appear feline-esque herself.

"What cat?"

"The one haunting Cella's house."

A laugh boiled up and escaped before I could stop it.

She gave me her Don't-titter-at-the-teacher look. "Land sakes, Pat. After everything you've been through in the last year, how can you still be so skeptical?"

"Skepticism has nothing to do with it. I just think it's funny that you searched for a ghost cat." I muted my mirth down to a grin. "Where does one look for such a wraith?"

"In your great-uncle's photos, of course. I found a picture upstairs that proves a kitty lived next door."

"I already knew that. Cella found a photo, too, maybe the same picture you saw. Big white fluffball of a cat, right?"

"White?" Miss Maggie frowned, perplexed.

I nodded. "Lived here in the seventies. Hey, if I make contact, shall I ask it about Watergate?"

"The seventies?" Miss Maggie's brow cleared. "My photo's pre-World War Two, and the cat in it is black with a tiny bit of white here on its chest." She touched her hand to a spot between her bosom and collarbone.

Black with a spot of white? I suddenly remembered the animal at the cemetery, hanging around Mrs. Ranelli's stone. Couldn't be, I told myself. Yet a cold shiver climbed the vertebrae on the back of my neck.

Miss Maggie didn't notice my reaction, lost as she was in her own predicament. "For as long as Mrs. Ranelli lived in that house, she probably had several cats. I wonder how we can tell which one is the ghost?"

"Where's the photo you found?"

"Still upstairs. I—"

Aunt Sophie appeared. "Tricia, do you have the carrots, peppers, and celery?"

I held up the bag in my hand. "Here they are."

"Bring them back." She waved me toward the kitchen. "Come in and talk to your Aunt Lydia," she urged. "She wants to hear all about this fiancé of yours."

"Let me hit the bathroom first, Aunt Sophie. I'll be right down." I carried the groceries as far as the stairs, then gave the sack to my aunt. Miss Maggie, knowing me well enough to recognize my evasive maneuvers, followed me up the steps.

"I need to see that photo," I whispered to her.

I knew we couldn't take long. My family bestowed privacy only for a limited time before sending out search parties. I also knew if both of us went into the back room, everyone in the kitchen below would hear the floor creak right above. Miss Maggie went to fetch the photo while I used the bathroom. When I opened the door, she bustled in, holding a small, scallop-edged black-and-white snapshot up to the light.

A twenty-something Uncle Rocco, white shirt sleeves rolled up to his elbows, lounged on the steps of the Ranellis' front stoop. Or, I should say Trepanis' stoop, because the window glass on the store to his left sported the name in curved block letters. Next to my great-uncle on the steps was a teenaged girl, hair pinned back on either side of the top of her head. She bore enough resemblance to the Mrs. Ranelli I remembered that I knew they were the same person. In the photo, she wore a huge grin and held a baseball in her right hand, at an angle that looked like she intended to throw it at the photographer.

Between my uncle and the girl, a black cat had squeezed. The pet was gazing at the ball above its head, one paw up as if waiting for the toss, like in basketball. I could clearly make out the small white tuft of chest hair. The spinal chill returned as, reluctantly, I confessed, "I think I saw this cat today, Miss Maggie."

"Saw it!" she exclaimed. "In a vision?"

Not an odd question considering that's where I usually see ghosts. In fact, I've only ever seen them once with my eyes open and that was more of a tableau. Under extremely emotional circumstances, I might add.

"No," I replied, "and I didn't see it next door either." I quickly described what I'd seen in St. Patrick's cemetery.

"How odd," she murmured. "Not like your other encounters."

"So maybe it wasn't *this* cat?" I said, even though I figured it was a false hope.

"Oh, we have to assume it was." Miss Maggie pursed her lips in thought. "And we have to assume you *saw* this particular ghost for a reason. I wonder why."

I replaced the photo in the top shoebox in the back bedroom before the two of us went downstairs. We found the kitchen crammed with females, all busy slicing veggies or arranging cooked salami, capicola, and provolone on a serving plate. My aunts had spent the afternoon rolling meatballs and the results were simmering on the stove in two big pots of sauce.

"Ground turkey instead of beef," my aunt the health freak proclaimed proudly. "Just don't tell my sister Filippa or she won't eat them."

"Neither will Dad," added Cella. Luckily, Uncle Gaet was in the sitting room with Uncle Leo, watching the opening spring training game from Clearwater. When we walked by, I heard the announcer say the Phils were tied with Boston, four all.

"What time is dinner, Aunt Sophie?" I asked, and before she could get defensive about the question, thinking I was trying to dictate her feeding schedule, which is a supreme no-no around Montella cooks, I added, "I'm asking because Miss Maggie and I will need to change before the viewing tonight. Better to do it now or after supper?"

"You'll have time after," my aunt replied. "I'll need to change, too. We'll eat early."

Miss Maggie, I knew, was disappointed, no doubt wanting to drag me next door right away for a cat seance. She directed me to pull two more chairs in from the dining room so we could join the food prep party. For the next hour, while I washed strawberries, drained olives and sliced tomatoes, I was grilled about Hugh and Beth Ann, then heard all the news from Aunt Lydia about Cella's brothers and their kids.

After that, Cella and her girls and I set the dining room table with paper plates and plastic utensils.

"When we were at the cemetery today," I asked casually, "did you see the black cat?"

She shook her head, half-distracted as she told Joan, "Forks go on the left."

"Ah, Mom." Joan's inflection was exactly like Beth Ann's. You'd think they graduated from the same whine-making school. "That's so antediluvian."

Cella raised her brows. "You know words like antediluvian? Why aren't you getting 'A's in English?"

Joan rolled her eyes and followed her sister back to the kitchen to fetch napkins and cups.

"Nice to know she's picking up *something* in school," my cousin mumbled as she rearranged the forks.

I tried to shift subjects. "The cat, Cella, it was hanging around Mrs. Ranelli's grave, while you were standing there. Sure you didn't see it?"

"Nope, missed it. Hope it isn't there once we start planting. I don't want it digging up my flowers."

I gave up. Cella had been looking right at the feline. She couldn't possibly have missed seeing it. That is, if we're talking a flesh-and-blood, dander-and-fleas entity.

Dinner was a preview of some of what we'd be eating later, after the viewing, meatball sandwiches and pizza.

Miss Maggie oohed and aahed over the meatballs, hinting that she wanted the recipe. Aunts Sophie and Lydia adroitly dodged the subject. They never gave recipes outside the family. My mom had to be married to a Montella seven years before Grandmom Montella told her what she put in sauce. Ma never did get the recipe for cannoli filling.

I made up my mind that, before the weekend was out, I'd cajole my aunt into parting with the recipe.

After we ate, Cella said Miss Maggie and I should go get ready, that she and her girls would clean up. She was still in her nice work clothes and therefore didn't need to change. I grabbed our things—Miss Maggie's handbag, laptop, my shoveling clothes, and the box of pizzelles. We went next door, using the spare key to let ourselves in.

No sooner were we hanging up coats in Cella's front hall than Miss Maggie asked, "Where shall we start, Pat?"

I didn't have to ask what she meant. She was determined to root out the ghost. Personally, I wasn't sure I liked the idea, but I replied, "Upstairs, I guess. That's where I felt it brush against my leg. Seriously, Miss Maggie, I don't think I can make contact with a cat. It can't converse, at least, not at a human level."

"All we want is a peek at what it's seeing and hearing," she assured me, flipping on the upstairs lights and starting up the steps, carrying her handbag and the pizzelles.

Clothes bag and laptop in hand, I followed. The house, though chilly, didn't feel as cold as last night. I told myself that the sun had been shining on it all day. Yesterday we'd entered in the middle of a blizzard. No doubt the wind had been coming in through every little crack.

An uncomfortable stillness seemed to hang in the air. My

rationalization was that we were alone in a nearly derelict house and my imagination was working overtime, the only part of me that ever did. Somebody ought to pay me time and a half for it.

My mentor switched on the ceiling light in our room. "Let's start here where you felt it at your feet in bed. Hold onto my arm, close your eyes, and I'll lead you around."

I set my load on my bed, thinking how I should point out how, when we'd used this technique before, our results were only passable. Granted, if a ghost was handy, closing my eyes usually produced some sensation—a sound, a smell, sometimes a whole vivid scene. But touching someone only seemed to make a difference if that person had a blood tie to the phantom, and being led around was distracting. Still, the touch of Miss Maggie's bony elbow beneath gave me backbone I wouldn't feel otherwise.

The odd thing was, as soon as I closed my eyes, I got the impression of something retreating, as if taken unawares, which startled me in return and my eyes popped open.

"What?" Miss Maggie couldn't handle me gasping without knowing the reason. "Was something there?"

Not only there, I realized, but close enough that I wasn't crazy about closing my lids again. I had to. I needed to find out more. Yet when I shut my eyes, nothing. "It's gone. I think I scared it away."

"Let's see if we can find it again," Miss Maggie said, putting her opposite hand over mine on her elbow. Her fingers were like ice. "Don't pursue it in your mind, Pat. You know that never works. Just relax and wait."

We circled the room to no avail. I had the giddy urge to make whispering sounds, which, when I was little, usually enticed our neighborhood cats close enough for me to pet them. I'd go home with cat hair on my coat and Dad would sniffle all night.

"I'm going into the back room," Miss Maggie murmured.

"Watch your step," I warned. "There's no lamp."

"I'll be fine," she assured me. "Between the last bit of twilight and the streetlamp out back, there's plenty of light."

I felt nothing in that room either.

"We'll go down the back stairs," she suggested.

"No, that's sure to be pitch black and I don't need you breaking a limb this week."

"We left the door at the bottom open and the kitchen's not dark yet. I'll go first. Here, put one hand on my shoulder and the other on the railing."

We descended slowly, her taking her usual one step at a time because of her bad joints. I couldn't think about ghosts on the way down, but I paused to sniff around at the bottom. No cat litter this time, just leftover Lysol.

"I really do think I scared it, Miss Mag—" All at once another odor filled my nose. I took another whiff.

"What?" Miss Maggie again.

"Tomato sauce."

"We just ate some. The smell might be in your sweater."

I shook my head. "This sauce has garlic in it. Aunt Sophie's doesn't. Basil, oregano, fennel, yes, but never garlic. None of the Montellas put garlic in their sauce."

The aroma was gone the next instant, yet its memory lodged in my brain, like a commercial jingle that refuses to leave you alone. The scent had been distinct but not strong, as if, like that same jingle, I'd sensed it from the next room.

"Take me into the dining room," I said, then realizing that without furniture, the function of the space wouldn't be apparent, I added, "The room next to the kitchen."

Miss Maggie was already leading me forward, then to the left. I ran my free hand along the cool, painted wood of the doorway as we passed through. She kept going, intending to make a circuit of the room, but I made her stop and let go of me.

I smelled garlic sauce again. A dimly lit scene faded in: a dining room table with a family around it, all viewed from an angle below table height.

Beneath my feet was a worn Mediterranean-style carpet—oval, with grayed flowers in the middle and fringe around the edge. The carpet was only under the table and chairs. Elsewhere the parquet floor could be seen. A different wallpaper covered the walls, yet seemed as old, tired, and in need of a redo as the current decor.

I counted seven people at the table, but I sensed more, as if I had on psychic blinders, blocking my vision of them. Sight-wise, nothing was really in focus. My senses of hearing and touch seemed muted, too, even more than sight.

Then someone grasped me around the middle and lifted me, until I was sitting on a lap.

> "Just keeping clean is a problem. . . . The purchase of soap or scrub clothes [sic] in a number of [poor] families is out of the question."
>
> —*Norristown Times Herald*, February 1930

March 1, 1933 – In the dining room

Most of the red on Del's back turned out to be catsup. One of the jars had exploded, from being warmed up, Uncle Ennio said.

Aunt Gina had a fit. "What's Rocco doing over there with his stove? Trying to burn the whole neighborhood down? It's a wonder all the jars didn't explode!"

Uncle Ennio calmed her, pointing out that the remaining jars could be moved to a cool spot, and as long as Rocco wanted to waste fuel that was his business, but our family could take advantage of the extra heat and save our own coal. That evening we left the door at the top of the steps open to allow the heat to rise to the first floor.

Del did get a couple pieces of glass in her backside, which Aunt Gina removed with tweezers. She and Nonna washed out the cuts with peroxide, which made Del screech like a demon. Next came a coat of iodine, which brought more yelling, though Del claimed later that she merely objected to having a yellow rump.

After they put gauze bandages on her, Aunt Gina told her daughter to lie on her stomach in bed. "You can prop yourself on your elbows to do your homework," Aunt Gina said. "I'll bring your dinner up to you."

But Del wouldn't hear of it. She was afraid that if she didn't come down for dinner, her mother wouldn't let her get ashes later, and then she wouldn't be able to bait her homeroom teacher tomorrow. She brought her pillow down to sit on while she ate.

Nonna had wiped the catsup off me and Mrs. Roosevelt as best she could, but my dolly was still stained. Del said I should pretend the stains were polka-dots. She said they were the latest fashion, that the real Mrs. Roosevelt wore polka-dots all the time. That made me feel better.

I can't remember what exactly we had for dinner that night. Probably macaroni with tomato sauce. No meat or even meat broth, of course, because of the fast day. And because we couldn't afford it anyway. We usually had pasta and even grated cheese 'cause Vito and Pip did odd jobs like shoveling snow for the family that owned the macaroni factory down Main Street past the church. That's how they got paid, with pasta and cheese.

Aunt Gina went on about Rocco making his stove so hot. "Didn't you feel it, Vito?" she asked. "You were over there all afternoon."

"It *did* seem warmer than usual," Vito admitted uneasily. When he'd come home, his face had been covered with soot, but Aunt Gina hadn't seen him before he washed up. She'd been busy tending to Del.

Pip broke in. "See, what happened was, Rocco gave me a dime yesterday to find some pine knots for him. I guess he put too many of them in his stove at once. You know how hot they get."

"Rocco never had any sense," Aunt Gina mumbled.

Uncle Ennio changed the subject by asking Tutti how he liked brick pointing.

"I like it fine," my brother boasted. "They said they'd come get me when they have another house to point. Okay?"

My aunt and uncle agreed. Aunt Gina hated that the work was dangerous, but willingly took the fifty cents when Tutti got home. She let him have ten cents out of it, which was more than Charlie and Gussie cleared together that day selling newspapers.

11

When I opened my eyes again, the glare from the ceiling light made me blink. My gaze met ugly carpet, paint cans lining the far wall, and two sawhorses supporting a sanded but unfinished door. In fact, the same things I saw last night in the same room. The aroma of garlic sauce had vanished.

"Well?" asked Miss Maggie, still at my elbow.

"I couldn't see much. Everything was blurred and dim." I told her about the people around the table. "One of them was the girl with the baseball in the photo—that is, a younger version of Mrs. Ranelli. She kept squirming like she wasn't comfortable."

Miss Maggie let go of me to rub her hands together. An expression of glee, I wondered, or were her fingers cold? After all, we hadn't turned the heat up when we came in. "What were the people saying, Pat?"

I shrugged. "Couldn't hear them very well at first, not 'til the end of the meal. Then they all turned their chairs around and knelt on the floor, facing the table with their hands folded on top of their chair seats, all except the oldest woman, who apparently had as much trouble with her knees as you do. She stayed seated, took out a rosary with big wooden beads, and led each prayer, which they recited after her in unison, in Italian. That part came through loud and clear, but then the scene faded. Like the audio finally tuned in just before I lost the signal."

"Hmm." Miss Maggie crinkled her sparse eyebrows. "Perhaps the cat was old and didn't see or hear well."

Nearly a year ago I would have scoffed and added, "Or maybe I imagined the whole thing." I knew better now. These ghost visions of mine had a feel to them unlike mere imagination. Yet this was different still. All the other ghosts had been anxious to tell me their stories, always in their own way, some pushy, some polite, some downright threatening. This one, I felt, was reluctant to tell me anything. Or maybe the glitch was in human-cat communication.

Wrong wavelengths or whatever.

"Time to go get changed, Pat," Miss Maggie said. "We can try again later."

We retraced our steps back upstairs. I washed up, but kept on my turtleneck, adding a pair of gray dress slacks and a nicer sweater, a cardigan this time. While Miss Maggie was changing, I took the laptop downstairs, set it on the kitchen counter, plugged in the mouse, and fired it up, the whole time looking over my shoulder toward the haunted dining room. The house didn't feel as ominous as it had earlier, as if the ghost, having had its say, went off to chase phantom birds or something.

When I tapped into the wireless signal, two emails were waiting for me. I opened the one from "AngelTrumpet" first. (Beth Ann chose that moniker not as a biblical reference, but because angel trumpet is a wildflower in the nightshade family). To this email, she'd pasted a close-up photo of one of the little black and white ducks I'd seen yesterday. Her message read: "is this what you saw? it's a bufflehead. my book says they hang out in northern estuaries during the winter, maybe some move up river until spring."

I made a mental note to lecture her on the need for capitalization even in cyberspace, but the name made me laugh. Bufflehead. Exactly how mine felt after my last ghost encounter. Her lesson in nature concluded, Beth Ann simply added, "dad's driving me nuts, as usual." and signed off.

I replied, saying that was indeed the right bird, thanking her for the photo, then describing the Audubon estate we could visit when they came up on the weekend. I told her how much snow we got, about building voodoo snowmen, and how most of the white stuff had melted already. And as I signed off, I told her to "break a leg" at her Science Night tomorrow.

I was tempted to mention the ghost cat, but knew Hugh wouldn't want me to. Despite the fact that Beth Ann had actually seen more ghosts in her lifetime than I had, Hugh was strongly opposed to the paranormal as a mother-daughter bonding activity. Supernatural stuff scared him like nothing else.

I couldn't help wishing I had more to say, because I missed Beth Ann and wanted to prolong the interaction. But the note was already more long-winded than I'd intended. I clicked on the send button.

Next I opened Hugh's email. "Don't even kid about that," was his first line. Took me a moment to figure out what he was talking about, then I remembered how I'd teased him about Cella's house, saying it was haunted.

I had a sudden empathy for the Boy Who Cried Wolf. When I'd first heard that folk tale in second grade, the teacher had made it clear from the get-go that something bad was going to happen as a result of the kid's prank. Now I realized the boy didn't have the benefit of foresight. Maybe, like me with ghosts in my hometown, wolves had been extinct in his part of the world for eons. Maybe he felt safe. The minute he broadcasts a fake wolf sighting, a real one shows up. Not the boy's fault that climate change altered lupine migratory patterns, is it?

Last Christmas I'd vowed that I'd keep no ghost secrets from Hugh. He had to know each time someone from the Other Side knocked at my door to ask directions, otherwise our marriage was doomed from day one. I fully intended to tell Hugh about the cat. Problem was, now he wouldn't believe me.

I scanned the rest of his message. First, a grudging concession that Ed was working out better than expected. This was a fast adjustment for Hugh, but his motive was clear in the last lines of the paragraph. "Ed agreed to work solo on Saturdays if he can have off Mondays, or Tuesdays on holiday weekends. Now I'll have an extra day each week to spend with you and Beth Ann."

That gave me a nice warm feeling inside. I was hoping it meant unrushed Saturday mornings in bed. More incentive to set that wedding date.

He ended with a last, terse paragraph, which completely floored me. "I've been thinking about what you said Monday, about Beth Ann not knowing her cousins in Baltimore. I'm going to talk to her about them tomorrow. Love you, Hugh"

The two topics this man *never* discussed with his daughter were (a) sex, and (b) anything to do with his first wife or her family. What brought this on?

I was almost afraid to comment. Too much enthusiasm on my part could daunt him. Then again, ignoring the subject might give him the excuse to chicken out. I simply highlighted his paragraph, copied it into my reply and typed, "Way cool. Let me know how it goes." Supportive yet not gushing.

Regarding Ed's schedule, I asked, "Does this mean you and Beth Ann are cleared for takeoff Friday?" I paused to bring up the National Weather Service site and check the forecast for Norristown, then added, "Forecast changed from snow to possible drizzles Friday, but the lows aren't supposed to dip below freezing."

Then, knowing I *had* to tell him about the ghost, if only for the sake of my conscience, I typed, "I WAS kidding last night, but found out Cella's house really IS haunted. Swear to God. Not to worry, though. Only a cat who doesn't realize his Little Friskies ran out decades ago." I reread it, unsatisfied, but the back stairs creaked, meaning Miss Maggie was coming down, so I declared my undying love to Hugh, signed off, and hit send.

"Ready, Pat?" She came into the kitchen, looking dapper in a forest green suit, white mock turtle and pale yellow V-necked sweater. Only the ankle boots on her feet created a jarring fashion statement, but they couldn't be helped, since we had a block to walk and the pavement was likely to ice up tonight wherever water hadn't drained.

I'd driven Miss Maggie to a few viewings and funerals in Virginia in the past year. She knew just about everyone in Stoke County, and had in fact already outlived a good percentage of her students. She felt it her duty to put in a live appearance and speak to the family when she could. On those occasions, she always wore green. The "color of life" she called it.

"Give me a sec," I replied, closing the laptop and fishing the plug out of the case. I tethered the machine to the wall socket to let it recharge while we were out.

"Any more encounters?"

"You mean with the cat?" I shook my head. "He let me email in peace."

I heard the front door, then Cella calling, "Hello!" out in the front hall. I yelled in return, "We're coming!" As Miss Maggie and I made our way toward my cousin, turning lights off behind us as we went, I glanced around the dining room, trying to re-imagine the scene I'd witnessed earlier. The sawhorses stifled the memory.

Cella and her daughters were in the front hall. "The others left for the funeral parlor twenty minutes ago," my cousin said. "You know how Aunt Sophie loves to be first in line so she can see who comes in after her. We said we'd wait for you."

While we wound scarves around our necks and slipped into our coats, Miss Maggie asked the girls what they thought of this house where they'd be living eventually.

Joan returned a mere shrug, either noncommittal or not wanting to speak up in front of her mom. Janine, though, murmured, "It's creepy."

"It is *not*," Cella protested defensively.

Miss Maggie nodded sagely, as if she'd heard what she had expected.

We all walked up Main, past the derelict bakery, gingerly stepping over the water in the gutters to cross the street. The night was clear. Few stars were visible through the streetlights' glare, but a nearly full moon was rising in front of us. The temperature had dropped considerably the instant the sun set, but at least the wind was at our backs. Hard to believe Easter was only a month away.

As we swung open the doors of the funeral parlor, loud voices blared out from inside. The front room was lit softly and furnished so as to give the hushed atmosphere of a formal parlor in an imposing mansion. The effect was ruined by a dozen or so Montellas, all voicing an opinion about the fact that Beatrice hadn't arrived. The room felt warm. I stripped off my coat, took Miss Maggie's, and went to hang them on the coat rack.

From there, I got a good look at Beatrice's husband, who was standing along the inside wall, cellphone covering one ear, opposite hand cupped over the other so he could hear above the din. I tried to remember his name but couldn't. Of course, I'd only ever seen him once before, at Grandmom Montella's viewing. They hadn't come either time when my parents died, or for any other funeral on our side of the family.

Beside him was the funeral director, a somber looking man wearing a black suit and tie. He was blocking the door into the room where, presumably, Uncle Rocco was laid out. A second, younger but just as somber man occasionally peeked out from within to get updates.

"Beatrice should have been here a half hour ago!" Aunt Sophie sounded as if she'd said the words ten times already and didn't think anyone was listening.

"She'll be late for her own funeral," Uncle Gaet commented.

"Won't matter," Uncle Mario said. "*I* won't be here." Not clear if he meant he'd be dead already, or if he intended to boycott the event.

"I hope she comes soon," Aunt Filippa fretted. "I'm gonna miss all my TV shows."

"You know why she's not here, don't you?" Aunt Florence

asked the world in general. "Not only did she go to work today, but she stayed overtime."

Everyone said something akin to "No!" at once, except Aunts Sophie and Lydia, who both nodded to prove they'd been here first and broke the scandal to their sister Florence themselves.

"Who's handling the funeral arrangements?" my cousin Portia asked. She had the same big hair she'd had the day she got married a quarter century ago, only now her dye job was conspicuous. I always found myself wondering how many bottles of Nice-and-Easy it took to cover all.

In answer to Portia's question, all four of my aunts rolled their eyes toward Beatrice's husband. Every Montella head swivelled toward him, as if he were starring in a freak show. Funerals had always been women's work in our family. Don't ask me why. Maybe because most of our men had such poor taste that no one wanted them picking out clothes for the deceased.

Still on his cell, Hubby turned his back to us, as if that would give him privacy.

The door opened again, and all heads did a one-eighty to see if Beatrice had finally arrived. She hadn't. I didn't know the four people who entered. Three were elderly, and the taller of the two men used a walker, while the other man limped slightly. The fourth person was a young man wearing a heavy green team jacket, the kind that in this part of the world usually had an Eagles logo across the back. This one didn't. Instead, the words "Evergreen Manor" were embroidered over the left breast.

"They're from Uncle Rocco's nursing home," Cella muttered to me. "The tall guy was his roommate."

"Hey, look, Tricia's here!" Aunt Filippa announced, pointing at me as if I were paparazzi fodder. Everybody gathered around for hugs and to gawk at my ring. I was trying to convince everyone that I genuinely loved living in Virginia and intended to stay there, when Beatrice made her entrance.

The opposite of most of us, she was a large woman, slender at one time except for her hips. They were fashioned from pure Montella DNA. She'd put on some weight since I'd seen her last (Grandmom Montella's viewing) and now her walk had a definite jounce. She wore no coat, only a navy blue business suit, the jacket too short for her build, the skirt too long, the white blouse too frilly, the black heels too pointy. Her attitude was the same as I remembered, perpetually confident and discontented. My aunts called it "spoiled."

Once Beatrice spied her husband, she put her head down and plowed through the crowd to get to him, ignoring sideline comments from my cousins. My aunts said nothing. They weren't speaking to her.

Beatrice and Hubby disappeared behind closed doors. Mr. Funeral Director stated that the viewing would begin in a few moments, voicing some nonsense about first giving the immediate family time alone to pay their respects to the deceased. Like any of us believed Beatrice was doing that. We all pictured her eyeing Uncle Rocco, wondering if she should go through the pockets of his suit one last time to make sure she got everything.

The funeral director asked us to line up. We ignored him, opting instead to socialize, especially since cousins from Great-uncle Tonio's side had come in behind Beatrice. Most of us hadn't seen them since my mom died.

When the doors finally opened, the family filed forward into a pecking order of sorts, aunts and uncles first, then Cella and her kids, since she'd volunteered to return to Aunt Sophie's house right afterward, to put on the coffee, lay out the food, and welcome guests.

I glanced around for Miss Maggie. There she was, perched at one end of an overstuffed sofa, chatting amiably with the woman who'd come from Evergreen Manor. The man with the walker sat beside them on the settee. The other elderly man stood next to them. I got the impression they were huddling together for protection against the size and animation of our family.

As I walked up to them, Miss Maggie said, "Pat, I was just telling Queenie here about you. Queenie Vanderhoff, Patricia Montella."

"Pleased to meet you," the woman said, her voice as sweet as her smile. She was younger than Miss Maggie, I estimated, though not by much. More petite, too, small to begin with, then shrunken even more with age. She reminded me of a thinner, more bent version of Helen Hayes.

Queenie turned to the man at her left and raised the volume of her voice a bit. "This is Iggy Jones. He was your uncle's roommate."

Iggy gallantly pulled himself halfway to his feet. He'd been very tall at one time. Now, with his shoulders slumped and his chest caved, he resembled a skyscraper frozen in the midst of demolition, the middle floors collapsed. He wore a heavy, padded jacket, still zipped to his chin. An Eagles knit cap covered his ears. "Rocco was great," Iggy grumbled as he sat again. "Best roommate I've had at Evergreen. Sorry to lose him."

"We all are." Queenie patted Iggy's arm. "He was an expert at pinochle. I don't know where we're going to find a fourth to replace him. And everyone wanted to sit with him at meals. Such a good conversationalist."

"Nice loud voice," Iggy said, nodding, as if that were the prime criteria.

Had Uncle Rocco told the same stories I'd heard all my life, I wondered, or had a new audience and new interests brought forth new topics?

I was glad to hear he'd gone back to the mental stimulation of pinochle. I swear he knew every card game invented, and had probably made up a few himself. One of my fond memories was of him at the first Montella New Year's Eve party he came to, the year after Beatrice got married. He taught us all a game called Seven-and-a-Half, basically blackjack with a smaller deck. We played for a penny a hand. I lost fifteen cents that night.

"Wait, where are my manners?" Queenie gestured to the other elderly man, who had a full beard and mustache beneath an equally full head of hair, all white. He would have resembled Santa except he was thin and fairly fit-looking despite the limp and the age spots below his eyes, which were hazel in color and droopy enough to look sad. His mouth hung slightly open, giving him an aura of perpetual confusion, like he didn't quite have enough blood bringing oxygen to his neurons anymore. Or the effect may have been caused by ill-fitting false teeth.

"This is Wyeth Adams," Queenie said. "He's a famous artist."

Wyeth blushed at the compliment. The color did his expression a world of good. "Not famous at all." His voice was soft, almost shy.

"What'd he say?" Iggy asked us.

"That he's not famous," Queenie repeated, close to Iggy's ear. To us, she said, "Don't listen to Wyeth. When he came to Evergreen Manor last month, Rocco told us he remembered seeing Wyeth's picture in the newspaper. More than once, too."

"Just a hobby," Wyeth murmured. "I taught high school art."

"You should see his work," Queenie went on as if Wyeth weren't there. "Real talent. And still at it. Stays in his room working all day."

"I don't paint anymore," Wyeth said. "Fumes would bother the other residents. Clay sculpture these days, when my arthritis allows."

"But you *do* stay in your room working all day, Mr. Adams." That came out of the young attendant, who had walked up behind me, presumably after having hung up his coat, since now he wasn't wearing it. His green polo had "Evergreen Manor" embroidered over the breast, the short sleeves showing off nicely toned arm muscles. I put him in his late twenties.

He offered me his hand. "Hi, I'm Darren King. I was Rocco's nurse on weekends. We're going to miss him." His broad face and blond buzz cut complimented his contagious grin. I thought, with nurses like him, old age might not be so bad.

"Tell Pat what you were telling me earlier, Queenie," Miss Maggie goaded.

"I only wanted to know if Rocco's granddaughter found what she was looking for," Queenie said.

Did she mean Uncle Rocco's money? "Beatrice?"

"Sure. She came over to Evergreen this morning, all upset because she couldn't find something of her grandfather's. Seemed to think we might know about it." Queenie paused to smooth out her stretch pants, a nervous gesture with both hands. "She wouldn't say what exactly was missing. That's what was upsetting. If she had told us, we could help search."

"She thought one of us took it," Iggy said, scowling. "Accused us of stealing."

Queenie soothed him. "She didn't accuse us, Iggy. Not really."

"She was grieved, that's all," Wyeth muttered. "Lost her grandfather. Hard on the young."

"What'd he say?" Iggy asked again.

"That she was grieving," Queenie yelled at him, then to us graciously added, "We didn't *blame* her, of course."

I was mulling over the notion that Beatrice had apparently gone into work late in order to drive forty minutes out of her way to interrogate Uncle Rocco's Evergreen pals about his missing money when Cella came up behind me.

"How long you staying, Pat?" she asked, as glum as I'd seen her since our grandmother died.

I shrugged. "What do you need?"

"If you're not going to be long, could you bring Joan and Janine back with you? They still have homework to do."

"Sure. Where are they?"

Cella cocked her head toward the line. "With Ronny."

Glancing over, I saw Joan and Janine, both smiling, happy, chatting with their father who had an arm draped around each. Ronny worked for an overnight delivery company and still had on his uniform. He was one of those delivery guys who wore shorts all year long. Even today, with this morning's snow and all, his knees were showing.

I thought all this in less than ten seconds, but by the time I swung my head back, Cella was already disappearing through the door, practically at a run.

12

My instinct was to go after Cella, but Miss Maggie was nudging my elbow, saying, "We'd better get in line," reminding me that my first duty was to my goddaughter Janine and her sister.

Between me and Ronny in line were three former neighbors of Uncle Rocco's who I recognized, two men from his bowling league who I didn't (Aunt Sophie told me later who they were), and my cousin Nicola and her brother Giacomo with their parents, Aunt Philomena and Uncle Mario. More hugging and introductions and ring gawking ensued, but I kept an eye on Cella's girls the whole time. As Miss Maggie and I passed into the inner room, Janine and Joan came out alone.

"Don't go back to Aunt Sophie's without me," I told them.

"We're going to wait for Dad out here," Joan assured me. "I've seen enough dead bodies for one night."

"Ditto that," Janine agreed. "Viewings are gross."

I nodded my understanding, having felt the same way at their age. Not that I liked viewings any better now. Back then, though, the feeling was selfish. I didn't like the way it made me feel to look at a dead person. Now I simply feel sorry for the deceased, because I think death's undignified enough without being put on display. Our ultimate bad-hair, bad-skin, bad-everything day.

Then again, when my aunts compare notes later about how Uncle Rocco looked, they won't be talking about *him*. They'll be critiquing the embalmer's skill.

Miss Maggie and I signed the guest register. She took one of the remembrance cards, which had always struck me as baseball cards for the dead, or anyway, that's the way Aunt Sophie collects them. She had a recipe card file filled with them in one of her kitchen cabinets. Catholic cards usually sported a picture of Jesus, the Blessed Mother, or both, in a typical Sunday School painting pose. Nowadays, with the magic of computers, you can get a photo of the deceased on them, too, but Beatrice had opted out of the extra expense. The other side of the card listed the dear departed's stats—full name and day of death, at least—with a prayer of some sort. Uncle Rocco's was standard Beatitudes: "Blessed are they that mourn, for they shall be comforted."

I glanced across the room, to where Beatrice was sitting, with her husband standing behind her. Her demeanor was appropriately subdued, but not at all mournful. Her husband looked merely ill-at-ease, uncomfortable at not knowing any of the guests, I supposed.

Aunts Sophie, Lydia, Florence and Filippa were sitting in the third row, heads together, no doubt gossiping. The collective noise of the mourners, even with everyone pseudo-whispering, was enough to mask their conversation. Uncles Leo and Gaet were right behind them, both looking like they'd rather be home channel surfing.

We reached the coffin, which was flanked by enough flowers to make my nose itch. On each side were the arrangements sent by each family on our side of the Montellas, some tasteful, some with big-and-gaudy leanings, like the one from my cousin Concetta who lived in California. In contrast, above the coffin was a small array of red and white carnations with a purple ribbon across the middle that said "Beloved Grandfather." I'd hear later from my aunts how Beatrice had skimped on the flowers.

I wouldn't judge her on that. From planning my mom's funeral, I knew coffin spreads cost big bucks. The same flowers in an everyday arrangement might be fifty bucks tops. Put them on top of a casket and the price could soar to seven times that amount.

Aunt Philomena went over to the kneeler beside the coffin, where, after lowering herself slowly to her arthritic patellas, she intoned loud, dramatic prayers for the dead, ending with "May the soul of our faithfully departed Rocco, through the mercy of God, rest in peace."

Everyone of us there, out of sheer habit, answered, "Amen."

As Nicola helped her mom up again, Aunt Philomena squinted at Uncle Rocco, then announced, "He looks good."

Personally, I thought Uncle Rocco looked awful. No smile, for one thing, and it just wasn't him without one. His long, once-graceful fingers, entwined with a plain black-bead rosary, seemed waxen. Even his best suit, a grey pinstripe, seemed to hang on him all wrong. Uncle Rocco would have hated that. He'd always been a snappy dresser.

Aunt Philomena could be forgiven for her poor observation

since she had cataracts, which was why her kids had to drive her everywhere now. She kissed her fingers twice, touching them to Uncle Rocco's forehead and hand, before moving on.

When it was my turn, I forsook the kneeler but still murmured a quick prayer. Nothing formal, just "Dear God, let him rest in peace." Given my last year, I knew some folks didn't.

Miss Maggie said a prayer, too, I think. Hard to tell without all the signs of the cross, et al, that we Italians do.

I shook Beatrice's husband's hand and mumbled, "Sorry about your loss," then offered my paw to Beatrice.

She ignored it, distracted by something going on behind me. "What's he putting in the coffin?"

I turned. The Evergreen contingent had been right behind us. Queenie, delicately touching a tissue to her eyes as she took a last look at Uncle Rocco, was blocking Beatrice's view, but those of us standing could see Iggy let go of his walker long enough to place a hand of five playing cards next to my great-uncle's rosary. I craned my neck to see what they were.

A royal flush. Hearts. That's when I got all choked up.

"Ozzie, don't let him do that," Beatrice hissed.

Ozzie. Right. *That* was her husband's name. I caught hold of his jacket before he could walk over and say anything. "They're only cards. Uncle Rocco would have loved it. Don't make a fuss, Beatrice. Let those people mourn in their own way."

Grudgingly, she gave in, with an air of fake indifference.

After expressing the standard condolences, I headed over to Aunt Sophie, who was waving to get my attention. Aunt Philomena had now joined their row and Uncle Mario perched beside Uncle Leo. Nicola and Giacomo sat two more rows back.

"You going back to the house, Tricia?" Aunt Sophie asked.

"Soon as I find Joan and Janine."

"Take my sister Lippa with you. She can watch her shows at our place."

So I waited as my Aunt Filippa sidled across the row in front of everyone.

Miss Maggie, I noticed, had been intercepted by Queenie. As they passed me, Miss Maggie said, "We'll be in the front room. Take your time."

Aunt Filippa stopped to chat with at least twenty people between the third row and the door, so it took a while. By the time we reached the front room, the Evergreen group had left, and Miss Maggie was back on the settee, this time with Joan and Janine beside her and Ronny standing facing them.

When I walked up, Ronny said, "Good to see you, Pat," as he reached over and bussed me on the cheek, something he'd done dozens of times over the last seventeen years. Tonight, knowing he wasn't planting real kisses on Cella anymore, it felt awkward. He'd been a total Italian hunk in high school, with a face and bod like a Roman statue and longish dark hair. His hair was short now, with a round, monk-like bald spot on the crown, but his job kept him trim and the added lines of middle age on his face only reinforced the impression of carved stone.

"Hi, Ron," I said, not about to return his opinion, holding my tongue so I wouldn't yell something like, "What the hell were you thinking, hurting Cella the way you did?"

"I heard you're getting married?" he said, eyeing my ring.

It was all I could do not to spit back, "And I heard you're getting divorced!"

Aunt Filippa saved me by poking Ronny in the ribs. Hard. "What are *you* still hanging around the family for?"

"I came to pay my respects to Uncle Rocco," Ronny said defensively as he rubbed his side. "He was a great guy."

We had to agree, of course. Before Aunt Filippa could continue, I spoke to the kids. "You guys have homework to do. Let's get our coats."

Ronny apparently didn't want a scene either. "I have to get going anyway." He held his arms out to his daughters. They gave him a long group hug as they said their goodnights.

Watching them, I got choked up all over again. I couldn't help wishing Cella's family was still in one piece.

Miss Maggie seemed quiet as we all walked back to Aunt Sophie's. Of course, she couldn't get a word in edgewise, with Aunt Filippa telling me in detail about every doctor's visit and medical procedure she'd had since I saw her last. Luckily most of it was pacemaker tweaking and blood tests. She wasn't due for another colonoscopy for two years yet.

Back at the house, Cella came to open the door for us, but after directing the girls to take their homework into the front parlor, she rushed back to the kitchen like she had something on the stove. Given her cooking aversion, I didn't think it likely.

I helped Aunt Filippa remove her coat and sent her off to tune in the sitting room TV while I hung my jacket and hers on the pegs. Miss Maggie did the same, still not saying a word. Worried, I asked her if she was tired.

"Not especially," she replied, "but I will need to talk to you later. Go tend to your cousin now. That's more important."

She refused to say anything more, which made me more curious. I left her at the sitting room, where Aunt Filippa was complaining that the cable channel numbers were all different from hers and she couldn't find *America's Top Model.*

The dining room light was on. On the table yawned a lavish spread of antipasto—pickles, olives and roasted red peppers, plus lunchmeat, cheeses, pizza, chips, pretzels, a bowl of fruit, sliced tomatoes, lettuce and other sandwich fixings, including hot and sweet green peppers. I grabbed a jumbo black olive to munch en route.

In the kitchen, Cella was standing at the table slicing rolls, almost viciously, maybe fantasizing that Ronny's neck was beneath her long serrated knife. She didn't look up as she said, "See if the meatballs are hot yet, will you?" Cella sounded nasal. I knew she'd been crying.

We'd been through enough emotional upheavals together that I knew to wait her out 'til she was ready to talk. Over on the stove, I heard the big pot of meatballs bubbling away. I walked over to lower the heat to keep the sauce from splattering Aunt Sophie's wall. "Need help with those rolls?"

"No, but you could put the desserts out on the sideboard." She gestured toward the corner of the side counter where I saw two huge plastic trays of Italian cookies, a cake covered in foil and an extra large bag of M&Ms. "There's a bowl of ambrosia, a tray of cannolis, and a key lime pie in the fridge, too."

Took all of two minutes to put everything out. The cake turned out to be a devil's food bundt with powdered sugar on top. Half of one minute was spent looking for Aunt Sophie's cake and pie wedges.

While I was retrieving two soup bowls to fill with M&Ms, Cella escaped to the dining room with one basket of rolls. I put the rest of the rolls up next to the stove for the meatballs.

Cella blew back in, zeroing in on the table where she fussily brushed crumbs into her hand, then carried the knife and breadboard to the sink. Looking around, seeing little else to do, she announced, "I should make up a plate for Aunt Filippa."

"Coffee done yet?" I already knew the answer. Up on the nearest counter, Cella had arranged tonight's beverage center: two-liter bottles of soda, an ice bucket, Styrofoam and plastic cups, and a large coffee urn whose little ready light was glowing red. "Mind pouring me a cup?" I asked, as if filling bowls with M&Ms required all my concentration and couldn't be interrupted.

Cella must have been looking for an opening, because she not only fetched my coffee, she poured herself a diet Pepsi and came to sit opposite me. I pushed a bowl of M&Ms toward her.

She scooped up a handful, popping four into her mouth in rapid succession. "You talk to Ronny?"

"A little."

"What'd he say?" The words "about me" were implied.

I related the brief conversation word for word, editing out what I hadn't said but wanted to. I paused to blow on my coffee, still too hot to drink. Decaf, I was sure, given Aunt Sophie's health kick, but it smelled good and strong. "You should have seen Aunt Filippa poke him in the ribs."

"Yeah?"

I nodded. "Basically told him he's got no business still hanging around the family." I put an M&M in my mouth, remembering too late that I was fasting on them. Vowing to do penance, I pushed the other bowl toward my cousin.

She popped another half dozen of the chocolate beads, talking around them. "Aunt Filippa didn't just mean tonight. I heard Ma tell her on the phone the other day." Cella took a swig of soda. "See, Ronny's been showing up in my parents' neighborhood, in his van, like he's making deliveries."

That gave me an uneasy feeling in my gut. "Coincidence?"

"What do you think?" More M&Ms. "I'm betting he asked for our route. Saw his van on Ma's block three times in the last two weeks, between five and six when I get home from work."

"He's stalking you?"

"No!" That came out vehement and Cella knew it. She took a deep breath. "I mean, jeez, Pat, Ronny's not the stalking type, you know? Probably he just wants to see the girls more. Right now they're only spending every other weekend together. Gotta be hard on him."

"Is he the one who sent you the chocolates yesterday?"

"Probably. Everyone else I know would send 'em to Ma's house. Ronny knows if he did that the whole family would be gossiping about us getting back together within two seconds."

"He wasn't bargaining on Aunt Sophie taking in your mail."

"Exactly." The doorbell rang and Cella jumped up. "Here come the troops. I'll get it." She dashed off, leaving me to mull over whether Ronny had come tonight merely to pay last respects to Uncle Rocco. At any rate, the sight of him had turned Cella into a basket case.

Or maybe she'd been a basket case since their separation and I was only now noticing.

Cousins started piling in, bearing more food—cupcakes, deviled eggs, and brownies (which, now that I'd tasted chocolate again, I wanted in the worst way). Miss Maggie appeared in the dining room to graze. She hit it off with my generation of Montellas, who seemed to adopt her as one more aunt. I, of course, didn't have to be coaxed to show off my ring and give full particulars about Hugh.

Cella retreated to the kitchen, to clear off the table, she said, because that's where the aunts would want to sit and hold court once they returned. She was right, I knew, but it was obvious she was shying away from the crowd. Not that she could avoid them completely, what with everyone migrating for meatball sandwiches and drinks.

So I wasn't surprised when, after she'd made sure her kids' homework was done, she said, "Pat, can you help Aunt Sophie clean up? I think I'll turn in early. Been a long day."

Aunt Sophie's oldest, Lucretia, had overheard. "You go 'head, Cella. You did enough today. I'll stay to help Ma put away everything. My sister Portia will, too."

Lu, of course, had also seen Ronny at the funeral home. As soon as Cella left, he became the main topic of conversation. "Can you believe he showed up tonight?" Lu exclaimed. "Like she needed to be reminded what a *porcellóne* he turned out to be."

"Ronny came to see Uncle Rocco, that's all," Cella's younger brother Chenzo protested. He's a bit of a *porcellóne* himself, that is, a man who shamelessly runs after women. Literally, a pig. Unlike

Ronny, though, Chenzo's unmarried.

Portia piped in. "Ma said Aunt Lydia told her that Ronny's been following Cella around like a lovesick puppy."

"What happened to his girlfriend from the Acme Market?" Lu wanted to know.

"Probably dumped him," Portia said.

"He dumped her," Cella's other brother Pasquale chimed in. "I think he wants to get back together with my sister."

"He realized his mistake." Narcissa, Aunt Sophie's youngest, nodded her approval. She was always the romantic among us cousins. Likely that was why she wasn't married either.

Lu shook her head. "Cella won't take him back now."

"Nor should she," Portia added.

Lu agreed. "If my Joey acted like Ronny did, I'd toss him out, too. And if he tried to get back in, I'd be waiting with one of my brother Angelo's sharp pizza wheels."

We Montellas tend to love fiercely, with acute tunnel vision. Problem is, we want our partners to hang out in the same tunnel. Always comes as a shock to us when a mate gets claustrophobic. I noticed my cousin Iris had stood by listening but hadn't offered an opinion. She divorced a year ago.

I made a vow to give Hugh breathing room, although the only woman he'd thought about in the last ten years was his dead wife. Tunnels aren't a Montella monopoly.

All tittle-tattle about Ronny halted abruptly with the arrival of the aunts, uncles, and the rest of the cousins.

"I told Beatrice to come over," Aunt Sophie announced as she passed through the dining room, "and to bring her husband—what's his name? I can't remember."

No one else could either, so I said, "Ozzie."

"That's it," Aunt Sophie said. "Doesn't matter. He didn't have a say."

The bottom line was, we were being snubbed. That, we all figured, gave us the right to gossip about Beatrice, particularly about her hunt for Uncle Rocco's legacy. My contribution was to mention how she'd gone out to Evergreen Manor that morning to cross-examine Uncle Rocco's pinochle cronies.

Instead of causing more scandal, the notion met with approval. Uncle Leo summed it up. "Makes sense to ask the people where he was living instead of us. I bet he had another safe deposit box and kept the key on him. Or maybe just kept cash under his mattress. Rocco liked to have his money handy. Liked to flash it around."

"But Beatrice didn't find more than pocket change when she cleaned out his room," Aunt Lydia reminded us.

"You know what those nursing homes are like," Uncle Mario said. "Somebody dies and I betcha the attendants go through all the deceased's belongings before the family arrives. Steal whatever they can."

Did Uncle Mario have a point? I screen-tested a mental video starring Evergreen's nurse, Darren King, ransacking Uncle Rocco's room for booty. Actually, the scene wasn't impossible. Sure, I'd liked Darren on first impression, but what did I know about him? Lots of criminals had wide grins. The better to con you with. Hadn't I learned that from my own experiences this past year?

Between nine and nine-thirty, anyone who had kids to get to school the next morning began to depart, including Cella's parents with Joan and Janine. In spite of the fact that most of us adults would play hooky from work for a great-uncle's funeral, nobody would pull their progeny out of school for anything less than an immediate family member. Education took priority in our family.

After noticing that Miss Maggie was practically nodding off on her feet, I also said my goodnights, promising Aunt Sophie we'd be over no later than seven-thirty tomorrow morning for breakfast before the funeral. Then Miss Maggie and I joined the mass exodus.

Next door, we tried to enter the house as quietly as possible so we wouldn't wake Cella. No need. As we hung up our coats, she came out of the sitting room. She'd changed into overalls covering a heavy sweatshirt, both of which sported a film of sooty dirt. On her head was an equally dirty painter's cap. An old plastic tablecloth was bunched in her arms, with a roll of duct tape balanced on top. Over her mouth was a dust mask. She pulled it down to speak.

"Party breaking up already?" Cella asked. She shifted the bulk of the tablecloth to one arm and reached up behind the wall. A second later I heard the furnace kick in. I realized the house, though chilly, didn't feel as frigid as last night and remembered Miss Maggie's observation that I was the only one who'd felt that cold.

But I refused to be distracted by ghosts. "I thought you were going to turn in early," I said to my cousin.

She shrugged. "My sleepiness passed. Decided to check that chimney flue upstairs. I was right. It's stuck open. Come help me cover the hole, will you?" She started up the stairs with her bundle.

I turned to Miss Maggie, not forgetting that she'd wanted to talk to me, but she anticipated my question. "Go on. Help Cella while I get ready for bed."

So I followed my cousin up and to the left. The front parlor door was shut, but Cella explained, as she closed it behind us again, she'd done that to keep the heat in the house from escaping.

Inside, the parlor was as cold as outside, making me wish I'd kept my coat on. The overhead light was on, but I didn't need it to see the hearth, which could be found easily by the draft. Some of the wood had been carefully pried from the fireplace, leaving an opening big enough to crawl through. Three tongue-in-groove slats leaned against the wall to one side. Tools were scattered on the floor—hammer, pry bar, flashlight, broom, dustpan, work gloves, and a half-full trash bag.

"Don't touch the panels," Cella warned. "They still have nails sticking out of them." Dropping the tablecloth and the duct tape, she got down on her hands and knees in front of the opening. "You can't see it from here, but there's a pipe running up the chimney back there. Probably when they first closed up the fireplaces, they ran the steam pipes up this way, then moved them later to the outside wall."

I followed the direction of her gesture to the big radiator over near the window. The pipe leading into it came through the floor in the corner to the right. Another pipe came out of it, running up the wall and through the ceiling, into the room above.

"But they never removed this pipe and it's keeping the flue from closing all the way," Cella explained. "I'll have to find it in the cellar and see if I can pull it out from below."

Following her direction, I helped her duct tape the tablecloth over the hole to stop the draft, my fingers getting colder by the minute. I kept my mind off the numbness in them by listening for sounds like I heard last night. Tonight, nothing, not even the wind whistling over the chimney above.

"That's it," Cella said when we were done. "Go get warm again. I'll clean up."

I was turning to make my escape when I saw a sleeping bag spread out on the sofa. "You're not going to sleep in here."

"This is where I slept last night. The sofa's comfy."

"Weren't you cold?"

"The sleeping bag's approved down to twenty-degrees Fahrenheit," she replied. "I wouldn't let Janine take it on Girl Scout camping trips if it wasn't warm."

"Yeah, but what little heat was here last night, you let out through the chimney tonight."

She couldn't argue with that. She simply shrugged, grabbing the broom as if to show that cleaning was more important than sleeping.

"You can have my bed," I said, "I'll sleep on the rug in your sleeping bag."

She shook her head stubbornly, making all the curls sticking out from under her painter's cap bounce. "No, you get the bed, I'll take the floor. But there isn't room—"

"We'll make room." Before she could protest further, I grabbed the sleeping bag, which felt as cold as the rest of the room, and made a beeline out of the parlor.

Miss Maggie had left the top light on, allowing me to see that she was already tucked in and asleep when I entered the room. No sooner did I spread out the sleeping bag on the floor, though, when her eyes opened. I'd seen her do this before. She had a precise internal alarm, allowing her to use bits of spare time to doze, the way others bided time doing crossword puzzles.

"There you are," she said, rolling with difficulty over on her side to face me as I knelt on the floor. "What's up?"

"Cella's bunking in with us tonight. Too cold in the front room for her."

"Then I'd better talk fast. I want this to stay between you and me for now. Come closer."

Intrigued, I crawled over to her bedside so she could keep her voice low.

"While you were busy with your Aunt Filippa at the funeral parlor tonight," Miss Maggie murmured, "Queenie and I had a little chat. She said I should tell you that your great-uncle was murdered."

> "In a roundup of boys and young men said to have trespassed on railroad property . . . the railroad police arrested 11 defendants last night."
>
> —*Norristown Times Herald*, February 1933

March 1, 1933 – Del and Bambola's bedroom

Del came back from getting her ashes that evening in a subdued mood. I heard Aunt Gina tell Uncle Ennio that she hoped their daughter was being pious, reflecting on the mysteries.

Pip said Del was quiet 'cause her derriere was still sore, then explained to Tutti that "derriere" was French for "rump."

"*Sedére*," Nonna told Pip, preferring that he talk Italian instead of French.

But once we were in bed, with the carpet on top of us and the cat licking herself at our feet, making the bed shake, Del told me what was on her mind.

In the light from the hall, I could see she was stretched out on her side, to keep her *sedére* off the mattress, yet had her face turned to the ceiling, to keep her ashes from rubbing off. She didn't look comfortable enough to sleep.

"Here's what's strange, Bambola." She used my nickname, but was actually talking to herself, thinking out loud. "When Gussie, Charlie, Tutti and I were walking up to church earlier, Carmen Montella and his brother Mario came out of the tunnel between their house and Mr. Fine's Dry Goods store. They were trying to scare us, but we heard them whispering beforehand."

Crisi, deciding her bath was done, abruptly hopped off the bed and went off in search of shoes and such, which she liked to drag around the house all night long. She did this most nights, howling as she went. If she howled loud enough, Uncle Ennio would put her down the cellar. Usually, though, Crisi took up her prowling later, long after I was asleep. Del's musing tonight must have thrown her off schedule.

"Thing is," Del was saying, "while I was waiting in line for my ashes, I got to thinking about those tunnels. See, we got one between our house and Rocco's, right? And it's what? Three feet wide? Doesn't that mean the cellar walls are at least three feet apart, too? They must be. With another foot each for the walls themselves. Even if Rocco had his stove blasting this afternoon, how could it make our cellar that warm?"

She kept talking, trying to puzzle it out. The soft babble of her voice lulled me to sleep.

13

"Murder?!" I exclaimed.

Miss Maggie didn't get a chance to elaborate because Cella stuck her head into the room.

I didn't know what my cousin had heard, or if simply seeing us whispering together made her insecure. "Sure it's okay if I sleep in here tonight?" she asked. "I could stretch out on the floor in the sitting room."

"The sawdust down there'll kill your sinuses," I argued. "I was only asking Miss Maggie if she'd taken all her pills today."

"Consarnit!" my mentor exclaimed, pushing herself up in as much of a hurry as a ninety-one year-old could manage. "Forgot my cholesterol whatzit. Pat, fetch me some water, will you?"

Her little collapsing travel cup was on the table between the beds along with her weekly pill case. I handed her the latter, noting that the Wednesday compartment did indeed still contain one tan tablet, then I took the cup and headed for the bathroom, passing Cella on the landing. She had her hands full, left one juggling the broom and dustpan, the other clutching the flashlight while dragging the trash bag. The hammer hung on her overalls loop, and the prybar and gloves were in various pockets.

"I'm heading down to the kitchen for cocoa." Her way of inviting me, hinting that she needed someone to talk at.

I was willing to oblige, but I needed to hear the rest of Queenie's story. "Let me get Miss Maggie settled and I'll be right down, okay? Put a decaf tea bag in a mug for me."

I made a pit stop in the bathroom, then fetched Miss Maggie's water. Back in the bedroom, while she downed her pill, I said, "Talk fast. I need to go play Dr. Phil downstairs."

Miss Maggie nodded her understanding. "I only had a few minutes alone with Queenie, so I don't know much. She said your great-uncle took ill Saturday night. They brought him over to the nursing wing at the Manor. Everyone thought it was a nasty stomach flu, but Queenie believes someone slipped something into Rocco's food. Maybe extra doses of his medications."

I sat down on the bed. "How does she know?"

Miss Maggie shrugged. "She said when he vomited, she smelled garlic. Thinks someone put it in his food to disguise the taste because nothing with garlic was served in the dining room that day. I asked her if he had any visitors Saturday who might have brought him other food."

I nodded, approving her process of elimination. Sleuth-wise, she was a regular Jessica Fletcher.

"Queenie said his granddaughter was in to see him that morning," Miss Maggie continued. "She wasn't sure if Beatrice brought him anything. About mid-afternoon, your Aunt Sophie brought Rocco some homemade ravioli, which he ate right away. After dinner, Cella stopped by to visit him. She was carrying a grocery bag, but Queenie didn't know what was inside. About an hour later, Rocco started complaining about his stomach."

Seeing I was impatient for more information, Miss Maggie apologized. "That's all I could get out of Queenie before that nurse—what was his name?"

"Darren King."

"Right. I used to be so much better at names," she lamented. "Anyway, he came to whisk her away."

I mulled over what I'd heard, still shocked enough that I could only repeat the word "murder" again, in disbelief.

Miss Maggie handed me her pill box and now-empty cup. "Don't get too het up about it yet, Pat. We don't know anything about Queenie, after all. She might have a peculiar kind of senility that has her imagining crimes where none exist. Old age can play odd tricks with the mind. Or she may simply crave attention, making up stories the way a child would. But I felt I should tell you, in case you think the family ought to look into the matter. You're sensible. You'll think it over and not do anything rash."

A nice way of saying I'm indecisive.

I went down the back stairs to the kitchen, wearing Miss Maggie's slippers like last night. No nasty ghost smells met me—neither used cat litter nor garlic—only the aroma of cinnamon from the two warmed-up sticky buns Cella was extracting from the microwave.

The tea kettle whistle blew while she had her hands full. I made a beeline for the stove to fill the mugs she'd put out, one with cocoa mix, the other with a teabag.

"No email tonight," Cella said. "I tried. No signal."

Just as well, I thought. After the evening I'd had, any email I sent to Hugh would need a board-certified psychoanalyst to interpret. With the word "murder" still ringing in my ears, I couldn't even let Cella bend my ear without asking a bunch of my own questions first.

As I carried the mugs to the table, I said, "At the viewing, I talked to a few of Uncle Rocco's friends from Evergreen Manor. You met them before, right?"

Nodding, Cella helped herself to one of the buns. "I swear Queenie was sweet on our uncle. Always hung around his room when I was there. And Iggy, of course, was Uncle Rocco's roommate—"

"So he told me." Taking a seat, I dunked my tea bag up and down. "Queenie said you came to visit last Saturday."

Cella stirred her hot chocolate. "Ma made up care packages for Uncle Rocco every other week or so. Either she and Pop would ride out to visit, or she'd rope me into it if I was making a run up that way. Once in a while I like to hit the flea markets and antique shops around Skippack, just to window shop, you know?"

She paused, blowing on a teaspoonful of cocoa before sipping it. Must have been too hot because she went back to stirring. "This week, we had pepper-and-egg leftovers from Friday supper. I took Uncle Rocco a sandwich the next day."

No garlic, I thought. Pepper and eggs are just that—strips of sweet bell peppers fried in a capful of oil until soft, then scrambled with eggs. Perfect on fresh Italian bread. My mother used to cook the same thing on Fridays during Lent, when meat is a Catholic taboo. For Miss Maggie, I scramble red bells with egg substitute and serve them on whole wheat toast. She loves it.

"Ma told me the pepper and eggs were the last thing Uncle Rocco ate before he got sick," Cella said. "I was afraid I gave him food poisoning, because I stopped a few places before I reached the Manor, and that sandwich was on my car seat the whole time. Not a hot day, though. Never got above forty Fahrenheit. And Ma wrapped the sandwich in three bags for insulation. But anyway, I looked up food poisoning online later and found out the symptoms don't come on that fast."

Food poisoning. An unfortunate but non-malicious explanation. "You mean, if Uncle Rocco had food poisoning, it was from something he ate earlier in the day?"

"Depends on the germ, but yeah, lunch at the latest. Maybe even something he ate the day before, or even Thursday dinner." Cella nibbled at her sticky bun, her appetite unaffected by the topic. "Nobody else got sick, though, which clears the food in the dining room."

I mulled that over. Aunt Sophie's ravioli sauce wouldn't have had garlic in it, but if Beatrice brought her grandpop lunch, she sure wouldn't have made it herself. Take-out from a supermarket or cheap restaurant, I bet.

"And if a food's been contaminated," Cella added, "the flavor isn't always affected. Even so, Uncle Rocco's stroke left him with a dulled sense of taste."

"It did?"

She nodded. "He said that was the most frustrating symptom. His balance and motor coordination returned, his cognitive confusion improved, his trouble swallowing liquids cleared up, but his sense of taste only came back halfway." She chomped down on her bun and talked around her chewing. "I can't imagine a world where I can't totally savor goodies like this."

"Me neither," I said absently. Despite my doubts, I was picturing how easy it would be for someone to slip Uncle Rocco an overdose, with perhaps a little garlic salt to hide whatever bad taste it might have. On an impulse, I said, "Do you want to take a drive out to Evergreen Manor tomorrow, after the funeral?"

Cella raised her eyebrows. "We never did get to ask Queenie and Iggy about Uncle Rocco's money, did we? But I thought we were going to Montgomery Cemetery?"

"We are. After that, I mean." I wanted to know more about how Uncle Rocco died, but I played to my cousin's sense of competition, telling her about Beatrice's visit to the Manor that morning to interrogate the residents.

"Did she really?" Cella licked her sticky fingers. "Well, we can't let Beatrice get ahead of us, can we?"

Cella and I stayed up, eating sticky buns and talking until after midnight, but not about Ronny. Turns out she didn't want Dr. Phil. She wanted distraction. She found it by turning the tables on me, asking why I hadn't set a date for my wedding yet. I spilled the whole saga of Hugh's first wife Tanya, of how he'd spent the last decade trying to erase her from memory and was only now beginning to mourn her properly.

Cella looked skeptical. "All this extra emotional baggage, is it ruining your sex life?"

I felt the blood surge into my face, but I'd always been honest with my cousin. I said, "Nope," unable to hold back a wide caught-in-the-act grin.

She grinned back, satisfied that she made me admit as much. "And baggage-wise, is his guilt worse than your basic Italian mother can generate?"

"*Nothing*'s worse than that."

"Exactly. Get him to the altar first, Pat. Don't give him the excuse to procrastinate."

I shook my head. "This isn't all about him. Since I came on the scene, Beth Ann's been asking questions about her birth mother. I don't want to take on the step-mom role until she's comfortable with it."

"Yeah? Maybe *you're* the one who's uncomfortable, Stepmom." Cella was still grinning, knowing I couldn't take offense as long as she kidded me, although we both knew she hit a nerve.

My Giamo-side Sicilian mulishness kicked in. "Beth Ann needs a better sense of who she is and where she came from, and the only one who can give that to her is her dad."

"Bummer," Cella said, backing off. "I was hoping for an August wedding—warm weather, at least—so I can wear a sexy matron-of-honor dress, tea-length and strapless."

"How are you planning to hold up your boobs?"

She frowned down at her mother-of-two, middle-aged, Montella-wide bosom. "Never mind. Strapless is a bad idea."

"We could get you a corset," I suggested.

"Then I wouldn't be able to eat."

"Sex or food. You can't have both."

"At your wedding? The food's bound to be better than the prospects of getting laid."

"Hugh's got a bachelor brother."

"Yeah? Is he cute?"

"He looks like Hugh, *and* he's a doctor."

"*Madonne!* Bring on the corset!"

Our conversation deteriorated from there, ending in fits of giggles, until finally we decided to wash up and close up.

Cella tried to shoo me off up the stairs ahead of her, but I hung back, telling myself I was keeping her from getting moody over Ronny again. In the back of my mind, I knew I was simply trying to avoid the cat ghost. Oh, I wasn't scared of it or anything. Just, with so much else on my mind, I didn't want the annoyance of a visit from the Other Side tonight.

Staying close to Cella seemed to work. No furry phantom brushed by my legs as I walked up the stairs and through the back room. I continued to put off sleep by taking my time in the bathroom, then rummaging through Miss Maggie's bag for her antacids because I had reflux again. Too many sticky buns, I told myself.

Nothing nestled against my feet as I hovered on the brink of sleep.

Unlike last night, though, my dreams were anything but pleasant. My brain ran a REM cycle marathon all night of vivid, disturbing nightmares, overlapping, interrupting one another, sometimes even simultaneously vying for my attention. Everyone was in them—all the Montellas, including the dead ones going back three generations, and none of those looked any better for being alive again. Ditto the Giamos, Ronny, the folks from Evergreen Manor, Beatrice, her hubby, the funeral director and clone, plus anyone else whose photo Miss Maggie had shown me that morning: men in uniform, Lloyd Lowell, his whole family including Lucius and Lawrence, the Republican dignitaries, and Mrs. Ranelli a.k.a. the Trepani girl, with her baseball and both of her cats.

All the dreams had next to no plot, but came with a huge sense of impending disaster, complete with dark storm clouds, the smell of garlic, and lots of guilt. Everyone seemed to want me to *do* something. No one would explain what. Or at least, they didn't have time before the next nightmare began.

The exception was Uncle Rocco, who appeared repeatedly, switching from young hunk, to buff Air Force pilot, to seventy-something teller of great stories, to ninety-something senile non-stop talker, to yes, even the corpse I'd seen in the funeral home. Only *he* asked nothing of me.

Thing was, I *knew* I was dreaming the whole time, but couldn't seem to wake myself up. The more I tried to get away, the faster the nightmares came and went. Nocturnal channel surfing, and I wasn't holding the remote.

Next morning my first thought was to wonder if those dreams had been broadcast by Spirit World Central, to get me back for my ghost avoidance the night before. Either that or something seriously Freudian was going down in my subconscious. At least the first explanation took the blame off my own shoulders. If true, it meant when I tried to contact the ghost, it retreated, but when I tried to avoid contact, it got offended.

I didn't have time to ponder further because we all had to dress for the funeral. I wore the same pants and sweater as the night before, but with a dressier white blouse. Miss Maggie redonned her green suit, this time with a pale yellow turtleneck. Cella wore all black, pants with a glittery top and longish blazer that hid her butt so she looked slimmer. We all wore boots. Not formal attire, but the cemetery was sure to be muddy.

Outside the sun was shining and the winds were calmer than the day before. Next door, Aunt Sophie had all her cereals out again. She'd added a plate of bagels, three kinds of cream cheese, and a loaf of banana bread, all brought by Lu and Portia, who were there ahead of us with their husbands. We pulled extra chairs in from the dining room and chowed down.

Aunt Sophie's youngest, Narcissa, came in next, and after her, the oldest, Angelo, with his son Vinny. They all greeted Miss Maggie like a long-lost aunt, with kisses on her cheek, even though they'd all just met her the night before. She beamed to let me know how she felt about this family who'd adopted her.

Our topic of conversation was carpooling for the funeral procession. Aunt Sophie's kids knew better than to let their father drive if they could help it. It was decided that Angelo and Vinny would take their parents, while Lu and Joey would go with Portia and Fred. Narcissa volunteered to drive me, Cella and Miss Maggie.

At ten of nine, the drivers left to bring their cars to the church lot and get orange funeral stickers for their windshields. The rest of us walked the block up to Holy Savior.

Our church had been built by the Italian immigrants of Norristown. Inside, it still maintains an aura of the old country, with white, pink, tan, lavender and green marble on the altar, terrazzo floors, and portraits of saints looking down from the ceiling. Lots of statues of saints, too. For the last weeks of Lent, they were hidden behind satiny, deep purple covers.

One of my earliest memories was of seeing the statues covered for the first time and getting thoroughly creeped out. I remembered snuggling against my mom in church, staring at those covers, convinced I saw movement from beneath them. Even then I had an uncontrollable imagination.

Now, taking a seat with Miss Maggie and Cella in the row behind Aunt Lydia and Uncle Gaet, I did a double take at St. Emidio up on the altar, certain the cloth over his upraised hand shifted. I was ridiculously grateful to spy St. Cologero's pet deer's legs sticking out below its purple shroud, a welcome reminder that mere painted plaster lurked beneath.

As usual for Cella and me, our minds were focused on the same thing, though she hit on the practical, whispering to me, "Don't have your wedding in here during the last weeks of Lent. All this purple would put a damper on things."

Wedding? Here? Actually, I hadn't thought about *where* I wanted to tie the knot. I guess I'd been thinking Virginia, but really, I had more family to transport than Hugh did. Maybe I *should* get married here.

The morning sun was streaming through the eastern stained glass windows, deepening the color of the pews' wood stain, giving the setting a warm, welcoming glow. The organ began the processional, not "Here Comes the Bride" but "Be Not Afraid." No matter, I pictured a wedding party entering and lining up across the front: Cella in her tea-length gown, Beth Ann in something less sexy. I'd ask Hugh's sister Acey, too, to give more height to the proceedings. Hugh would probably have his brother Horse as best man, but I'd need two ushers, one young enough to escort Beth Ann without looking like a dirty old man—

That's when it hit me that I was planning a real event, not just running one of those daydreams girls have during boring high school classes. I took a good look at the bride in that scenario and, sure enough, she really was me. Getting married. *Madonne.* And with that reality check came a little gasp.

Bad timing. The priest was incensing the altar and I got a snootful of smoke. As I started coughing, Miss Maggie pressed a clean tissue into my hand. Glancing at her, I saw she was wisely covering her own nose and mouth with one. I followed her example, taking a few deep breaths through the paper to clear my lungs. Most of the rest of my family began choking the same instant, especially Cella with her bad allergies. Miss Maggie passed her a clean tissue, too, for which she looked grateful.

I wondered if anyone had done a study on Catholics and incense-induced lung disease.

The incident brought me out of nuptial reveries and focused me on death. The occupant of the coffin was my Great-uncle Rocco, who Queenie Vanderhoff claimed was murdered. Within the next two hours, all physical evidence would be six feet underground. I couldn't stop his burial at this stage, not on the hearsay of a possibly senile octogenarian.

Yet I found myself wondering who gained from Uncle Rocco's death. Beatrice, of course, had made no secret of the fact that she *expected* to gain. Uncle Rocco's life insurance policy probably named her as beneficiary.

Beatrice was sitting up in the front row. I couldn't see much of her over the heads of my aunts, uncles and cousins, but I'd gotten a glimpse of her outside. Today she was wearing a black business suit with a blue blouse and looking appropriately mournful. Because her grandfather had died? Or because she still hadn't located her inheritance?

Behind us in the choir loft, the organist played a few bars of intro, then a lone singer intoned "Lord Have Mercy." Our response was anemic, half from shyness and half from our incense-asthma. As usual, Uncle Mario sang loudest and most off-key.

I wondered how Beatrice felt, having to pay for the whole funeral package, including the organist and singer. No cut-rate deals here.

Beatrice hadn't gained a thing. Not yet anyway. I glanced around at my fellow mourners, mostly family, who also hadn't gained. The bowling league guys were back, but not the former neighbors. That reminded me of the Garcias. Uncle Rocco had lent their family money. What if, like Aunt Sophie suggested, they hadn't paid it back? Isn't it gain when someone you're in debt to dies?

Or even if the Garcias paid my great-uncle back in full, who's to say he hadn't loaned money to someone else?

> "Elmwood Park zoo's groundhog was chuckling to himself today as the March Lion was regaining some lost ground in its duel with the lamb."
>
> —*Norristown Times Herald*, March 2, 1933

March 2, 1933 – Trepani's Store

The next morning, the younger boys ran down the steps, shouting to Del that it was snowing. Turned out to be only a couple inches on the ground, not enough to cancel school.

By the time they left, the snow had changed to drizzly rain and sleet. The air had a raw clamminess that made it feel wintry. Mrs. Roosevelt was cold. I held her close as we looked out the store window at the wet, gloomy day. Crisi had wisely remained in the kitchen, curled up beside the stove, and I was thinking of joining her.

"Brr!" Vito commented as he came back inside after going out front to see if the walk was slippery. "Hard to believe spring's just three weeks away."

Pip was the only one behind the counter because Uncle Ennio was up on the top floor, setting buckets beneath a new brown spot on the ceiling wallpaper, in case the leak started dripping.

As usual, Pip was reading. Today he had yesterday's *Times Herald* spread out on the counter, since he never got a chance to go through it last night. Over his head, the white globe lamp that hung off the back wall was glowing because the day was so dismal.

Pip tapped one finger at the weather article. "Forecast *said* it would get colder."

"Yeah, but it said 'fair,' too." Vito made his way back to the counter. "So how do you explain my coat getting wet?"

"Flying horses?" Pip glanced up, grinning.

"Maybe if someone put 'em in an icebox overnight. Anything worth reading in there?"

"Only if you like two full pages of sheriff's sales."

"I meant sports."

"Freddie Miller kept his featherweight crown." Pip peeled the page away and held it out. "Here. Read all about it."

Vito shook his head. "I'm too nervous. What do you think

about Rocco's idea? I'm guessing it'll make somebody real sore."

"Probably," Pip replied, "but like he said, this'll be the last time. What does it matter?"

"You won't be saying that if the somebody comes looking for us afterward."

Pip shrugged as he turned a page. "Rocco said he'll keep us out of—Aw Jeez!"

"What?"

Pip tapped his finger again as he read. "Reds Orazio was arrested for stealing gasoline, early yesterday morning. This says his uncle hadn't given him permission to take the Studebaker either, so he refuses to bail him out. Aw Jeez!"

"Hoh-lee smokes," Vito added. "Now what'll we do? We need a car."

Like an answer to a prayer, we heard an auto pull up out front. I turned back to the window. Along the curb was Mr. Lowell's big, green LaSalle, facing the right way this time. A chauffeur got out of the driver's side, hunching his shoulders against the sleet. No livery, but he wore a black cap with a short black coat and trousers. His pant cuffs and sleeves weren't quite long enough to cover the length of his arms and legs. He was husky as well as tall, and young enough that when I heard later that he'd dropped out of high school to take this job, I wasn't surprised. His face had big, long features, too.

Pip noticed. "Reminds me of Boris Karloff," he observed. "Same jowls."

The chauffeur opened the back door and, like the other night, out stepped a fine wool overcoat and Homburg hat, but this time they covered a boy about Gussie's age. He wore gloves. Expensive leather ones.

Vito whistled. "Hey, get a load of Latimer the Bratimer. What's he doing here?"

"And all of a sudden trying to look like his father," Pip observed.

"Yeah. Only last month I saw him in a leather cap and goggles, trying to look big and tough while he tore up the high school football field on that new motorbike his pop bought him. Now here he is, all spiffed up."

"Think that's his dad's coat and hat?"

Vito shook his head. "They'd be bigger on him. Besides, people like the Lowells don't have hand-me-downs. Against their religion."

"Betcha that get-up cost a good twenty bucks."

"At least. Think he's got a twelve dollar suit underneath?"

Latimer and his driver made their cautious way across the slushy walk to enter our store. The chauffeur opened the door, letting the boy precede him through it, but Latimer stopped just inside to survey the place before going any further. His face was on the chubby side, like the cherubs in the painting of the Blessed Mother that Aunt Michaela had on her sitting room wall.

Latimer's expression was anything but cherubic. He viewed our shelves of canned goods and boxes of produce and even our pickle barrel with open disdain. His driver squeezed into the two square feet behind his boss, shutting the door behind him.

"Morning, Latimer." Vito made his face somber. "Sorry to hear about your pop."

"Yeah," Pip said. "He was a great guy. We liked him."

Latimer raised an eyebrow. Just one. I tried to do it, too, but couldn't. Mrs. Roosevelt didn't even try.

"You liked my father because he paid you good money." The newcomer's voice was a little raspy, still trying to decide between tenor or baritone.

Neither brother contradicted the statement. Since Latimer didn't seem inclined to go any farther into the store, Vito strolled forward instead, hands in his pants pockets. "So what brings you down our end?"

"I'm taking over my father's business affairs."

"Are you really?" Vito glanced back at the counter, no doubt rolling his eyes in disbelief the moment his back was to the visitor.

Pip was careful not to so much as grin. "*All* of your dad's affairs, Latimer? That's a lot of work, isn't it?"

"Yeah," Vito said. "I heard you tell your pop you wouldn't go into the family business, that running a company was for stuffed shirts."

"Now you're wearing one," Pip pointed out.

Latimer turned to his driver, who took the cue, booming, "Show a little respect!" The big guy had that kind of deep, rumbly voice perfect for a gangster movie henchman.

Panicked, Mrs. Roosevelt and I ran back behind Vito, who said, "Hey, you're scaring the baby."

The Boris look-alike scowled, but he didn't yell again.

"He's right, though," Latimer said. "You need to show me respect. I'm your employer now."

"Yeah?" Vito asked. "Well, if you're here to pay me for

helping Rocco straighten out your family crypt yesterday, I'll treat you like you were the king of England come to tea."

Latimer's frown said he wouldn't have tea with Vito if it was the last liquid on earth. "My father never paid you until the week after each funeral, did he?"

Vito's eyes narrowed to slits, but Pip said, "You want us to help with your dad's funeral? We'd be honored."

The Boris-chauffeur laughed. "The family don't want no dagos at Mr. Lowell's services."

"They don't like Italians, but apes like you are okay?" Vito asked, his voice a blatant challenge.

Boris stiffened, taking a step forward, pushing against Latimer's back. "Thank your stars you got a little kid present, Dago, or I'd beat your face in."

Latimer held an arm out to restrain him. "Take it easy, Kenny."

Kenny? The name didn't fit the driver at all. I decided I'd still call him Boris.

"Let me talk business here," Latimer told his driver. "Go keep an eye on the car. Don't let anyone touch it." Through the front window, I could see that the LaSalle was attracting the curious again, like it had the other night. No kids today—they were in school—but two men were openly admiring the auto, one being Mr. D'Abruzzo. He held an old black umbrella over his bald head. Boris went outside to fend them off.

Latimer turned back to Vito and Pip. "My father had arranged for an orphan to be buried by Friday, didn't he? That's what he came to talk to you about Tuesday night?"

Vito and Pip exchanged glances, then Vito said, "Yeah. So?"

"My father will be interred tomorrow at noon." Latimer made a point to add, "Invited guests only."

"Naturally," Vito said. Even I recognized the sarcasm.

Latimer did, too, but ignored him. "My question for you is, are you two and Rocco ready to bury another orphan? You know what I mean?"

Vito looked at Pip again. Pip shrugged. Vito swung back, asking, "I'm guessing we do. What's the plan? You want the orphan's funeral after your dad's?"

Latimer shook his head. "I don't have my father's love of pomp and circumstance. I see no reason to have a funeral at all. Besides, after my father's service, reporters may hang around a while. We'll meet later, after dark. Can you be at the vault, say around eight o'clock?"

Vito rubbed his chin in thought. "We got one glitch. Our associate with the Studebaker won't be able to make it. We'll need Kenny-boy for transportation." He nodded toward the window where we could see Boris, shoulders hunched again, looking unhappy, either from icy drops going down the back of his neck, or from being in close proximity to people of Italian descent.

"No, you'll have to arrange your own transportation. I took enough of a risk coming here today." Latimer turned to leave.

"Hold on," Vito said. "If we need to get hold of a car, we'll need some cash."

Latimer shook his head. "I won't have money to pay you until at least Monday. Father would have paid you next week."

"He used to give us twenty bucks apiece." Vito said it with a perfectly straight face, but I heard Pip give a quiet gasp behind us.

Latimer smiled for the first time. "Lloyd Lowell didn't become a great businessman by making deals like that. I'll pay you three dollars each."

"Sez you!" Vito protested. "Your dad gave us eight! And don't forget that we cleaned up your crypt yesterday."

"That's included in my price. Be grateful. Most people don't earn as much in a week." Latimer opened the door behind him. "See you tomorrow night, gentlemen."

As we watched the teenager make his cautious way back to the LaSalle, Vito said, "I hope he falls on his well-heeled fanny."

"What are we gonna do, Vito?" Pip asked. "Rocco's not gonna like this."

"Mind the store." Vito buttoned up his jacket. "I'm going up to the bank to tell Rocco. Tell Pop I went for change or something."

14

Used to be, when I was a kid, funeral processions always passed by the deceased's home on the way to the cemetery. When folks moved out to the 'burbs, the processions stopped taking the detour.

I was reminded of this when Cella, beside me in the back of Narcissa's two-door coupe, pointed out that, ironically, since we were driving down Main Street anyway, we were passing the empty lot where Uncle Rocco's house once stood.

I leaned forward to look past her, out of her window. That's when I spied the cat on her house's stoop—small, black, and daintily licking one raised paw. I couldn't miss the white spot on its breast.

I swung around so I could see out the back window, but by then the cat was gone.

"What'd you see?" Cella asked, surprised by my fast moves.

"Nothing," I replied, slumping back in my seat. "Just a stray cat."

That was for Miss Maggie's benefit. She'd turned as far around in the front seat as her osteoporosis and seat belt would allow. Even though she couldn't look me in the eyes, I saw her brows go up.

At some point, when I had a free minute this week, I had to find out what that feline wanted from me.

The rest of the trip was uneventful, unless you count the pushy guy in a Lexus who tried to butt into the procession after DeKalb Street became one lane. Not only did he have to sit and wait for all of our cars to pass, but some of my relatives gave him a lesson in Italian he wouldn't soon forget.

At St. Patrick's, we headed for what I think of as the 1940s and 50s part of the cemetery, along the road to the back gate. That's where my Montella grandparents were buried with Aunt Paulina, who died in her twenties. Uncle Pasquale's first wife was there, too, and of course, Uncle Rocco's wife, and his daughter, Zoe, with her husband. I'd visited these graves before and knew the geography. Uncle Rocco's family plot was right beside my grand-parents. Seeing all the funeral trappings—the green turf rugs sur-rounding the hole and covering the big mound of fresh dirt—something about all that is disorienting.

Out here, as usual, the breeze was stronger, and I was thankful that the priest kept the graveside service short. The funeral director told us we were all invited to a luncheon at Presidential Caterers down the road.

We placed our flowers on the coffin, then headed back to the car, Miss Maggie taking my arm for support because the ground was seriously bumpy. Cella, ahead of us, stopped at the curb and was staring toward the back gate. I followed her gaze. Just walking out of the cemetery was a man in delivery-service shorts and jacket. Ronny.

His van wasn't anywhere in sight. Apparently he'd parked on a side street, or maybe even down in Corropolese's lot, and walked here. Did he come for Uncle Rocco's funeral? Or was he following his wife?

I wrapped my unoccupied arm around my coz. "Come on. Time for lunch. Beatrice's treat."

That got a smile out of her.

The Montellas almost always held their funeral luncheons at Presidential Caterers. Half our weddings had been here, too, Cella's and Ron's being the most memorable in my mind, since I'd been maid-of-honor at that one. Cella, Ronny and I had also come here for our fifteenth high school reunion a few years back. The two of them had danced to all the old disco tunes while I sat out in the big lobby chatting with five other dateless classmates.

Presidential was popular with our family because they had great food. Today's lunch was Italian wedding soup, Caesar salad, chicken Marsala, and chocolate fudge sundaes. I did my best to eat around the chocolate.

Beatrice and her husband, I noticed, sat with the priest and the bowling league guys, not with family members. Oh, everyone went up to her to express condolences before they left, but only as a formality. She was an outsider in our family, which struck me as sad.

So I was glad to see, as we filed out of the room afterward, all my uncles talking with the owner of the place. The few words that drifted over to my ears told me they were talking money. At my dad's funeral, my aunts and uncles had covered half the luncheon bill. At my mom's, they wouldn't let me pay anything. They wouldn't be as generous with Beatrice, I knew, but they intended to help in some way. Made me proud to come from such decent, unselfish stock.

By the time Narcissa dropped us off back at Cella's house, it was almost two o'clock. Remembering the cat on the stoop earlier, I had a Scrooge-like urge to look behind the front door as we entered. Nothing there, of course.

"Put on warm clothes," Cella told us. "Always feels cold at Montgomery Cemetery. It's on an open hill above the river." To me she said, "Still want to ride out to Evergreen Manor after?"

I hesitated, but Miss Maggie said, "Oh, I think that's a fine idea. Queenie was so disappointed at not being able to come to the funeral. She'll appreciate us telling her all about it."

My mentor's green eyes twinkled at me, indicating she knew darn well why I wanted to go out to the nursing home and she wasn't going to let me chicken out.

"Let me call them," Cella said. "Make sure it's okay for us to stop by later. Our luck, we'd drive all the way out and find they're off on a field trip to Canada to buy cheap prescriptions."

Turned out to be good thinking. When Cella flipped her cell-phone closed, she said, "They want us to come out now. Bingo Night tonight, so they'll be opening the dining room early for dinner." She checked her watch. "We can get there before three, visit for up to an hour, and still get to Montgomery Cemetery well before dark. Okay?"

Plans hatched, we hurried to change from dressy clothes to warm ones. I traded my blouse and sweater for my fleecy sweatshirt over a T-neck, and my dress pants for jeans. No time to devote to the cat, even if Cella hadn't been around.

The drive to Evergreen Manor took a little more than half an hour. This part of Montgomery County still had a few pockets of farmland left, though the rolling hills were now mostly blanketed with new housing developments. Evergreen Manor was an older assisted-living facility, fairly small compared to similar places around Philadelphia, but the main entrance was newly-renovated, with a shiny metal roof overhang the color of a new penny. Behind and above it huddled brick walls with dorm-like windows.

Inside was a double entrance with a guard station between, the guard being an elderly man himself, probably doing this part-time to supplement his Social Security. He recognized Cella and expressed his condolences about Uncle Rocco as we signed in. She told him we just wanted to drop by to check on Queenie and Iggy.

"Probably find them playing pinochle in the dining room," he said, hitting the button that triggered the inner door. As it slid open, a blast of warm air hit our faces.

All three of us peeled off our coats, hats, and scarves. I took Miss Maggie's to carry for her. As we walked up the wide corridor, I pushed my sweater and turtleneck sleeves up to my elbows, too. It was that hot. The air had an antiseptic smell. Still, the decor was welcoming, tastefully wallpapered like the hallway of a posh hotel. Only the waist-high metal safety rails along each wall, and padded benches at intervals, reminded me that this was a geriatric facility.

We passed a sort of parlor where some residents were reading or napping, then a TV room. The paneled glass doors were closed, but I could hear the soap operas as clear as if I'd been standing next to the set.

Just past an elevator, we turned into the dining room, which looked bright and airy. Temperature-wise, still stifling. The room had a two-story ceiling, with windows along the south wall, and held round tables that could seat six each. They were set far enough apart from each other to allow wheelchairs to pass easily between. Bland food aromas hung in the air. If I had to guess, I'd say chicken and peas.

We found Queenie and Iggy at the table nearest the windows along with another woman and man, the latter in a wheelchair. Queenie was yelling at him, "Put down your meld, Ned. King and queen? Or jack of diamonds, queen of spades? Here, let me see your hand—"

"You can't do that," Iggy protested. "Hoyle says you can't look at anybody else's hand, even if he's your partner."

"Ned's learning to play," was Queenie's rationalization, in a voice that was only slightly loud this time. The shouting was apparently for Ned's sake. He didn't move to show Queenie his hand. In fact, except for a slight shake in his hands and his eyes blinking, he wasn't moving at all. His jaw was slack.

Iggy spied us coming in and tried to rise gallantly to his feet. I waved him back down before he hurt himself.

Queenie's face lit up. "How was Rocco's funeral? I want to hear all about it. Wait, let me introduce everybody. This is Val—" The other woman, very thin with straight white hair, smiled up at us over her cards. "—and this is Ned. He's taking Rocco's place." Ned didn't acknowledge our presence at all.

Cella gave them a rundown of the funeral's highlights, including the menu for lunch.

"Chicken Marsala?" Queenie wrinkled her nose. "Isn't that when they cook it with mushrooms? I never liked mushrooms."

"Can't eat 'em anymore," Iggy said, touching his fist to his sternum to indicate that they gave him *agita.*

"We had chicken today, too," Val volunteered, more to feed the conversation than anything.

Before it lagged, I changed the subject. "Remember what you told us last night, about Rocco's granddaughter Beatrice coming out here yesterday?"

"She find what she was looking for?" Iggy asked.

"She wouldn't tell us what was missing," Queenie put in, repeating what she'd said at the viewing, practically word-for-word. "That's what was upsetting. If she had told us, we could have helped her search."

"We don't know what exactly was lost," Cella replied. "Did Rocco mention anything he had that might have been valuable? Some kind of antique or collectible? Maybe a piece of artwork?"

"If it's artwork you're looking for," Queenie said, "you ought to ask Wyeth."

Iggy shook his head. "Wyeth's only been here, what, two weeks? If Rocco didn't tell me he had something valuable, he wouldn't have told Wyeth."

"Maybe Rocco wanted an artist's opinion," Queenie argued. "He used to go talk to Wyeth—"

"Rocco talked to everybody," Iggy said. "All the time."

Val felt the need to explain to us. "He was trying to draw Wyeth out of his shell."

Queenie nodded. "You know what Rocco was like. Wyeth stays in his room all day, Rocco thinks he's being antisocial. He wasn't. He was working on his art is all."

"I don't like his paintings," Iggy groused. "These modern artists. You can't tell what you're looking at."

"Wyeth paints recognizable things at least," Queenie said. "Like that one on his wall you can see when you go by his room if he's got his door open. That's a pencil eraser."

"Is *that* what it is?" Val asked, surprised. "But it's yellow."

"That's my point," said Iggy. "Who paints a yellow pencil eraser? Why bother?"

"Why *not* a pencil eraser?" Queenie asked. "How's it so different than, say, a bowl of fruit?"

"Fruit's more colorful," Iggy maintained. "Harder to draw, I bet. And who doesn't like to look at fruit?"

"Where's Wyeth's room?" Cella asked. I could tell from the look on her face that she thought we'd hit on a lead, so sure was she of the artwork angle.

Queenie stood up. "I'll show you."

Val protested. "But our game, Queenie—"

"I'll be right back. Finish melding. Look, Ned's putting cards down."

Ned had indeed already put three aces down and was shakily setting a fourth beside them.

"A hundred aces!" Queenie exclaimed, shouting so Ned could hear. "Now we're sure to make our bid!"

Ned's smile was half toothless and his voice came out hoarse. "Four of a kind beats two pair."

"We're not playing poker, Ned," Iggy corrected him.

Queenie came around the table and looped her arm through Miss Maggie's like they were long lost sisters. She assured her pinochle mates that she'd be right back.

We took the elevator up a flight. Inside, Queenie asked Miss Maggie, "Did you tell them what I said last night?"

"I told Pat."

Of course, this meant we had to bring Cella up to date. By the time the elevator door opened, my cousin was saying, "Murdered! You knew about this last night and didn't tell me?"

I shushed her, but luckily, nobody was waiting for the elevator on the second floor. I couldn't answer Cella's rant without implying that Queenie might be nuts. I wiggled my eyebrows at her in an I'll-explain-later gesture which was lost on Cella. She kept asking why I didn't tell her.

Miss Maggie saved me by asking Queenie who she suspected. "You mentioned that you thought he might have been given an overdose of his medicines."

"Sure," Queenie said, sitting down on a padded bench across

from the elevator. "Or someone else's meds even. In a place like this, what could be easier? Everyone's got stuff like digitalis laying around. And you hear on TV all the time about nurses doing mercy killings."

All the time? I wondered what channels she watched.

"So you suspect one of the nurses?" Miss Maggie ventured.

Queenie shrugged. "They're the ones who give us our meds, aren't they?" She put on her sweet smile again, the one that made her look like Helen Hayes, only now she was Helen Hayes playing Miss Marple. "And what motive would any of the rest of us have for murdering Rocco?"

"Was Darren King on duty Saturday?" I asked.

"Darren? He's always here Saturdays. Works twelve-hour shifts Friday through Sunday. Rocco liked him a lot. Said more than once that he wished he'd had a son like Darren."

"I heard Uncle Rocco say that once when I came out to visit," Cella mumbled. "That makes sense." She had this look in her eye, like she was light-years ahead of us, deduction-wise.

"*What* makes sense?" I prompted, and Miss Maggie nodded, wanting to be clued in.

"Don't you see? Uncle Rocco had something valuable. Maybe he told Darren he'd leave it to him when he died. Or maybe not. But either way, Darren tampered with Uncle Rocco's meds to hurry the process along, so he could help himself to the object." Cella punctuated her hypothesis with a sort of ta-da gesture, which made her drop her jacket.

Queenie's turn to protest. "None of us ever saw anything valuable in Rocco's room. That's what we told his granddaughter yesterday when she implied that one of us took whatever she was searching for."

"What if Uncle Rocco didn't have it out in plain sight?" Cella speculated. "Something rolled in a sock in his drawer, maybe? I know! Valuable coins. He always liked coins."

That was true enough. I pictured Darren innocently opening the drawer, perhaps helping Uncle Rocco put away clothes, or getting him a pair of socks while he was dressing. The nurse sees a bulky sock, comes back later, while Uncle Rocco's downstairs playing pinochle, to check it out. Why not just steal the sock? Why do murder?

Miss Maggie pursed her lips, a sign that she, too, was skeptical. Yet Queenie jumped on the theory. "You've got the right idea, I bet.

Go question the other nurses. See what they know about Darren." She stood. "I have to get back downstairs. Iggy will wonder what took me so long."

"You were going to show us Wyeth's room," Miss Maggie reminded her.

"Oh, that's right. His room is the one just beyond the nurses' station. On the men's hall. Through these doors and to the left." She pointed to the double fire doors on our right. "You can't miss Wyeth's door. You'll see what I mean."

The nurses' station was deserted. Off giving people their meds? Or, with everyone either watching TV or napping to renew strength for the big Bingo Night, perhaps this was simply a good time for a break.

The rooms had doors wide enough for a wheelchair to pass through easily. On Wyeth's hung a small painting, a nine-by-twelve canvas covered with horizontal streaks of black on slate gray. At the bottom right, "Wyeth Adams" was printed in a scrawl of half-inch orange block letters.

Cella stood back to study it a moment. "Last Saturday when I visited Uncle Rocco, I saw this for the first time. I think it's a portrait of the artist's mother during a blackout."

"And she's in mourning," I added.

"Pshaw," Miss Maggie sniffed. "Just a painting of his signature is all. Elaborate nameplate."

Cella knocked on the door. No answer.

I shrugged. "Maybe he's sleeping?"

"If he paints what he sees in his nightmares," Cella said, raising her hand to knock again, "we're doing him a favor, waking him up."

That's when the door opened. Wyeth Adams stood there, dressed in a white tee and matching sweat pants that were streaked with gray-brown dirt. With a ragged brown washcloth, he was wiping similar dirt from his hands, and little flecks of the stuff stuck to his white beard. Using the smell and his words last night as clues, I deduced clay. We'd caught him at work.

He'd apparently heard our comments, and I got the impression he was amused. With the slack mouth and droopy eyes, you couldn't tell. "Would you like to see the sister work of that painting? Here, on the inside of the door."

He hobbled backward to let us file into his room, then swung the door nearly closed. Sure enough, there hung a sibling—same size canvas, same block letter signature, same black on gray, only this time the streaks were vertical.

"Oh, I like this one better," Cella said, straight-faced. "Much more cheerful."

I bit my lip to keep from laughing, but actually, I *did* like it better. Why, I don't know. Odd, I thought, how he was able to play with emotions with a mere change in streak direction.

I turned to check out the other painting in the room. On the wall opposite the door was the "pencil eraser" work. Not an eraser at all, I realized as I stepped closer, but a gold ingot. The canvas was twice as large as the others and the ingot was in the lower left corner. The background was more black streaks, helter-skelter. The gold bar seemed to float with a hazy glow atop them.

Wyeth had a private room. Over near the window, where in other rooms a second bed would go, he had a sturdy wooden table. On it was his latest project, covered with a wet sheet. From the size, I figured it might be a bust of someone. Then again, given what I'd seen of his style, I wouldn't be surprised to find a 3-D clay interpretation of black streaks.

Another table by the wall held shaping tools, brushes, a spray water bottle, and other necessities of the pastime. Beneath the table were plastic bags of clay. Between the two tables was a padded stool on wheels.

Our end of the room boasted only an Ikea-esque wooden bureau and bed with a plain black bedspread, and black throw rug. Where studio met bedroom, a short white refrigerator stood, with a white phone and small white microwave on top. Very Spartan.

Cella had a like reaction. "Only three paintings? I'd have thought an artist would cover the walls."

"I would if my bedroom weren't also my studio," Wyeth muttered. "Can't have a lot of visual distraction around me. No one expects a composer to listen to the radio while he works, yet everyone thinks an artist should be surrounded by paintings. Besides, I don't paint for myself."

"Did you sell all your works?" Cella asked.

"Sell?" Wyeth's jaw gaped a little more, like he was trying to remember. "Some. Most are on spec in galleries."

"Did you happen to sell my Uncle Rocco a painting by any chance?" So that was Cella's theory, that our great-uncle had invested his life savings in a piece of Wyeth Adams's artwork. Didn't ring true to me. The only pictures I remembered hanging in Uncle Rocco's house had been the free prints given out as promos by the bank where he worked.

Wyeth smiled at the thought, at least, his eyes smiled. His mouth was still slack. "Rocco wasn't a patron of the arts. The opposite, actually. He didn't attach any importance to what I do. Always trying to lure me downstairs to play cards."

"And yet," Miss Maggie pointed out, "you felt close enough to him to attend his viewing last night."

Wyeth didn't quite blush, but he lowered his gaze, embarrassed. "Yeah, well, he was a likeable guy. Even when he was being a pest. Ladies, my clay is drying."

The hint was lost on Cella. "Did Uncle Rocco ever show you a piece of artwork, for an appraisal? Say, something European brought back from World War II?"

Wyeth raised his white brows while he shook his head. "Did he have anything like that?"

"We don't know," Cella admitted. "We think he had *something* of value, though." She looked to me for support, but I still felt that if the source of Uncle Rocco's bucks had been spoils of war, it meant he'd sold whatever it was before we were born. She was more on track thinking our great-uncle had reinvested his money lately.

Wyeth shook his head again, then said straight out that he wanted to get back to work.

Miss Maggie, however, asked one more question. "Did you talk to Rocco last Saturday?"

Wyeth shook his head, but Cella broke in. "Yes, you did. You were talking to him in the hall outside his bedroom when I got there. You were saying something about his night table."

"Rocco had lent me his nail clippers," Wyeth explained, slowly, as if picturing the scene himself. "I'd returned them to him. He was late coming up from dinner, but Iggy was there. I went in and put the clippers on the table. When I came out of the room, Rocco was coming down the hall. I stopped to tell him. That's what you saw. Not a real conversation."

Miss Maggie turned toward the door and, disappointed, Cella and I followed.

15

The nurses' station was still deserted. Cella checked her watch. "You wanna stick around to find a nurse or get to Montgomery Cemetery? We'll be running out of sunlight if we wait much longer."

"Let's go," Miss Maggie said. "We ought to rehash the facts before asking more questions here."

Outside the sun was low in the afternoon sky and the breeze felt cooler. After the unbearable heat of the building, I thought it felt good as we walked toward the car. Miss Maggie bundled herself up once more.

We were no sooner in the parking lot than Cella whacked me on the arm. "When were you planning to tell me Uncle Rocco was murdered?"

"I'm still not sure he was," I told her. "We only have Queenie's word for it."

"What do you think, Cella?" Miss Maggie's voice was again muffled by her scarf. "You know her better than we do."

Cella frowned in thought as she fished her keychain out of her coat pocket. "I think Queenie believes everything she said. I mean, she's not deliberately lying. She just has that kind of pushy personality. You know, gets something in her head and feels she has to convince the rest of us."

"So we shouldn't take her seriously?" I asked.

Cella unlocked the doors on the passenger side of her Neon. We piled into the car and my cousin cranked up the heater for my mentor's sake before answering my question. "Thing is, if we ignore her, I'll always wonder if she was right. Yeah, I can see why you didn't want to tell me last night and I can see why we shouldn't tell Ma or Aunt Sophie or even Beatrice. Not yet. No use getting everyone upset with no proof. But I don't want to read in the paper in another year that somebody else died here under suspicious circumstances."

"You think Uncle Rocco's death was suspicious?" I asked as I leaned forward to help Miss Maggie with her seat belt.

Cella shrugged. "He was a hundred and two and his EKG said he had a heart attack. What could be less suspicious?" She put the car in gear and headed out of the lot. "Maybe I'm just feeling guilty. I was the last of the family to see him alive and he looked fine. No complaints about chest pains or being out of breath. Not even *agita*, even though he pigged out that day, what with both Aunt Sophie and Ma sending food. Nothing I can point to and say 'I saw that heart attack coming.' "

"Tell us everything you saw," Miss Maggie said, "from the moment you arrived."

Cella hung a left onto Germantown Pike and got the Neon up to speed. "Let's see. I stopped at the entrance to sign in as usual. The night shift guard had just come on and he said he'd seen Uncle Rocco in the dining room. When I got there, Queenie said he'd gone up to his room a couple minutes earlier. I took the stairs. Been taking the stairs at work, too, trying to get in shape now that I own a house with three floors."

After another turn, Cella continued. "Uncle Rocco was in front of his door talking to Wyeth. He introduced me. First time I met the guy. I didn't realize until today that he was the one who did the painting on the door down the hall. Anyway, Wyeth went back to his room, and Uncle Rocco and I went into his. Iggy was watching a John Wayne movie. He's got a little portable TV right next to his chair, but he still turns it up pretty loud, so I didn't stay too long. Just helped Uncle Rocco unwrap the pepper-and-egg sandwich and I fetched him some water for his dinnertime pills."

"Pills?" I echoed.

"Do you know what he took?" Miss Maggie asked.

"Not the names," Cella replied, "but I'd seen him take them before—three pills that Darren brought in. Then Uncle Rocco added his usual vitamins and supplements. Saturday he was rather proud of the fact that he'd discovered cod liver oil pills. He told me our great-grandma used to give him and Grandpop the stuff by the tablespoonful when they were little."

"My mother gave us castor oil." Miss Maggie shuddered as she relived the memory. "Oh, that was an awful taste. We used to wash it down with sarsparilla. I still can't stand root beer because of it."

"Apparently cod liver oil isn't great-tasting either. Uncle Rocco said they should have put it inside a pill long ago. He still had trouble swallowing it Saturday, the pill was so big. And I asked Darren about it. He said cod liver oil has tons of Omega-3 and vitamins. It was okay for Uncle Rocco to take it."

"The meds that Darren brought in," I said. "Could you tell if they were the same pills Uncle Rocco always took?"

Cella shook her head. "Wasn't paying attention. Darren *could* have switched meds or even just dosage sizes, I guess. Uncle Rocco didn't notice anything, but he was busy talking to me. But I am sure the multi-vitamin and glucosamine supplement were what they claimed to be, because I opened those bottles for Uncle Rocco myself."

She stopped speaking to turn onto a side road and negotiate an S-curve. When she didn't start talking again, I asked, "Then what happened?"

"Then nothing. That's when I left. Like I said, Iggy had his movie up loud, and with Uncle Rocco being a little hard of hearing, conversation wasn't easy. Plus Queenie came in, too. Just being nosy to see what I brought, I think, but the room's small with only so many places to sit . . ."

Miss Maggie nodded her understanding, yet I wasn't entirely satisfied. I knew Cella well enough—I'd seen her at plenty of loud, crowded, family gatherings—to know that shouting and claustrophobia wouldn't be enough to get rid of her. When she changed the subject the next moment, asking Miss Maggie what in particular she wanted to see at Montgomery Cemetery, I knew my cousin was holding something back. I made a mental note to corner her later.

The last time I'd been inside Montgomery Cemetery, I was about Beth Ann's age. Cella and I never went there when we were in high school. By then the cool thing was to hang out either in her bedroom talking about boys, or down in the basement playing pool with her brothers and their friends.

I recalled the feeling the old graveyard used to give me, like I was leaving reality and entering a kind of dream world, one where nice, living Italian girls weren't entirely welcome. Part of that feeling came from the fact that Montgomery had been derelict for so long. The grass had always been long, many of the stones toppled and broken, with smashed liquor bottles and drug needles in evidence here and there.

Today though, as we drove that last block of Hartranft Street before the gates, I realized the feeling was nearly exactly what I'd felt the first day I entered Bell Run. Like Miss Maggie's estate, a lot of the mood had to do with geography. Both pieces of land were on a hill above a river. The opposite bank here was King of Prussia, Pennsylvania, home to suburbanites and what some locals claim is the largest shopping mall in the known universe, mentally I knew we couldn't simply pass through the burial ground and back out to civilization like we could at St. Patrick's Cemetery this morning.

Not only that, but like all hunks of real estate next to rivers on the Eastern seaboard, Montgomery was often covered in a haze that seemed to clear only on the driest, sunniest days. Today was no exception. The March sun had melted most of yesterday's snow, evaporating it just enough to leave the moisture suspended in a translucent cloud a foot off the ground.

Cella parked in front of the last house on Hartranft. In the middle of the L-intersection with Jackson Street was one of those portable basketball hoops on a pole with wheels, attesting to how little traffic found its way back here.

Behind the hoop were gates of thick cast iron bars, supported by massive stone block pillars. On the black iron arch overhead, "Montgomery Cemetery" was painted white. When I was young, the gates were superfluous, with no equally formidable wall or fence on either side. All you had to do was walk around them to get in. Now the entrance was fixed up, with iron fence several yards on both sides, then hedge, then split rail fencing. Oh, you could still duck between the top and bottom rails of the latter to get in, but at least it kept unwanted cars out.

"They keep the gates locked now, so people can't use this place for dumping," Cella explained as she cut the ignition. "We walk from here. I'll bring my flashlight, just in case."

By the long shadows, I estimated that we had no more than an hour of decent daylight left. With the uneven ground and all, I agreed the flashlight was a good idea. The sun had already sunk behind the two-story gatekeeper's house to our right. That building, I noticed, now sported new siding and windows.

Cella started her lecture at the entrance, turning to face the street we'd just come down. "Imagine these gates transplanted up three blocks on Main, all these row houses in between gone, and instead, a grassy park and a lane lined with sycamore trees. That's what the entrance looked like in its heyday back in the mid-nineteenth century. This street was called Montgomery Drive then. Must have fairly screamed 'Only Rich Folks Planted Here.' It was fashionable to take the trolley out here for a picnic. The train along the Schuylkill stopped here, too. People came from as far away as Philly. First public park in the county, despite being a graveyard."

Cella led us through the smaller pedestrian gate. Inside, where the lane forked left and right, the last four old sycamores stood like sentinels, two on either side. Victorian Norristown had been big on sycamores in public spaces. In my old neighborhood, the boulevard along Elmwood Park still boasts many of its original sycamore trees. They were prettiest, I thought, in the winter, sans their pea green leaves, with their white trunks silhouetted against evergreens or deep blue sky. Here, with the setting coloring my imagination, these giants seemed skeleton-like.

Cella turned to the left along the gravel and dirt drive. "We'll do Hancock's grave first, since it's closest."

Miss Maggie wisely hooked a hand around my elbow. The path was muddy in spots, with puddles along the lower edge from the snow runoff. I didn't see much ice, thank God, but I kept an eye out for it, now that the sun was nearly gone and the temperature was dropping. While I was watching our footing, Miss Maggie was looking all around, not wanting to miss a thing.

Hancock's mausoleum was in the front left corner of the burial ground, set off by itself, away from the other tombstones. In fact, it seemed closer to the backyards of the houses that bordered the cemetery—closer to the living residents of the area than to the dead ones. A dog began barking in one of those backyards, presumably hearing our footfalls or smelling us on the breeze. I couldn't see the animal, but he sounded aggressive, and if the deep throaty woofs were any indication, big.

Cella ignored him, waving one hand at the chain link fence enclosure on our left. "When they restored Hancock's mausoleum, they put this fence up to protect it from vandals. Sort of a shame, but it had to be done, after the money that was put into the restoration. So we can't go inside."

Miss Maggie nodded. "Worth protecting. The man deserves respect, and not simply because circumstances put him in command of the Union center at Gettysburg and he never got the credit he fully deserved for the job he did. He was also in charge of the

Lincoln Conspiracy prisoners after the war. He begged for a stay-of-execution for Mary Surratt, to no avail. Proved to be a thorn in his side in his first run for president. They labeled him 'Lady Killer' and he never got out of the 1868 primary."

This was all news to me. A general turned death row warden turned presidential candidate, from my hometown? Who knew? But apparently Cella did because she jumped into the conversation with enthusiasm. "He won the primary in 1880, but Garfield beat him. I heard there was big time election fraud."

Miss Maggie was thrilled to find an informed student. As they debated the probability of the 1880's equivalent of hanging chads in New York State, Cella led us off the path, downhill and around to the fence's gate. The dog quieted down.

Hancock's mausoleum was built into the side of the small rise. Inside the fence, the grass and small bushes were immaculately kept up. Through the metal bars on the stone facade, we could clearly see two tombs inside: Ada and W. S. Hancock.

"The general's buried with his daughter," Cella said. "His wife's interred out in the Midwest with her family. I heard that on the day of his funeral, tons of politicians from D.C. and Harrisburg arrived by train for it, plus his old army cronies and men who served under him. This place must have been jammed."

Miss Maggie studied the crypt another moment, then with a sigh said, "Okay, who's next?"

"Let's head back to Hartranft's grave," Cella decided. "He's by the river, under trees. Gets dark sooner there. But I'm going to take the high ground instead of the short cut along the edge." My coz led us back up onto the path, heading for the middle of the cemetery, to avoid the lower ground shaded by evergreens on the left. "Bound to be snow and ice back there today," she explained, "not to mention that it's lonely enough to still be a favorite spot for drug deals and prostitution. Today I'm guessing it might be a bit cold for the latter."

We paused to inspect some of the odder Victorian stones on the way—carved angels, roses, lilies, draped urns, ivy, ferns, clasped hands and the ever-popular Book of Life. The farther we walked into the burial ground—the farther away from the houses at the entrance—the more it felt like we were going back in time. The air seemed very quiet and still all of a sudden. A single vulture glided overhead, looking for supper.

The path made three circles in the middle, like traffic circles, strung out parallel to the gates. Cella took us around the middle one, pointing out the family vault among the evergreens in the middle, telling us about the legend of the witch buried in the center of the far right circle. On the other side, she cut over to General Zook's grave.

Miss Maggie was thrilled, and told us all about the Union officer's last moments in Gettysburg's Wheatfield. Cella added how his father had died less than a year after burying his son. Me? I was distracted by the sight of a tall marker a good distance away, back toward the river, that seemed to stick up above the rest of the monuments.

For all the times I'd been in this cemetery as a kid, I must have seen the marker before, but I didn't remember it. The design was plain compared to the surrounding stones. Just a big squarish monolith with no fancy carvings. I couldn't see writing on it because it faced away, toward the river, not that I could have read it anyway, at this distance. Yet, somehow, the marker seemed to be vying for my attention, like a third-grader so sure of an answer, he's practically coming out of his desk chair to stick his hand up higher than his classmates.

The angle of the sun, I told myself.

I kept glancing toward it as Cella led us off the path, winding around the stones and family enclosures. I wanted to see if the illusion changed with our position. It didn't.

My cousin, meanwhile, was saying how Montgomery had only three regular mausoleums, the rest were underground vaults and graves. "In fact," she said, "this place has the largest collection of underground vaults in Southeastern Pennsylvania. They're like buried mausoleums, with a moveable slab above for access. Hey, Pat, how 'bout that time we found one vault broken open and you wouldn't let me climb down inside?"

I pulled my attention back from the monolith to answer her question. "I remember. There was no ladder. I said if you got stuck down there and I had to run back to get your dad to come get you out, we'd never be allowed to leave your house without supervision again."

"Anyway, we got to see inside," Cella recalled. "Shelves with coffins on them."

The memory made me shudder, or maybe I was simply reacting to the cooler zone around the Hartranft family plot as we approached. As Cella had said, the graves were near the river and just under the overhang of the trees. Even without their leaves today, considerably less sunlight filtered down to the earth here. Patches of snow and ice still hugged the north sides of both the low stone wall that surrounded the enclosure, and the tombstones within it. A cold breeze blew up the hill from the water as if to purposefully discourage us from staying long. Beside me, I felt Miss Maggie shiver even as I did myself.

General John Frederick Hartranft had been a governor and attorney general of Pennsylvania. I knew this not from learning it at school, but because those facts were written on the base of an obelisk in the center of the plot, the tallest obelisk in the whole cemetery. Exactly as I recalled from my youth, the bottom of the monument was white and the top plain, unpainted brown stone. A relief portrait was painted too-bright yellow, and a keystone—the symbol of Pennsylvania—was painted copper red. The whole effect was still as gaudy as it seemed thirty years ago.

Cella knew the explanation now. "Some patriotic civic group—was it the Boy Scouts? I can't remember. Anyway, they had the bright idea to paint Hartranft's marker white like the Washington monument. Unfortunately, they were well into the project before they realized they didn't have a ladder high enough to reach the top of the obelisk. Typical Norristonian short-sightedness if you ask me. At some point, I'm hoping the historical society will at least clean the paint off the bronze relief, but right now they need to spend their money stabilizing other stones in worse shape."

Miss Maggie told us juicy tidbits about Hartranft's career. "He led the charge across Burnside Bridge in Antietam, only a colonel at the time. Then he became a Brigadier General and finally at the end of the war, a Brevet Major General. Served under Hancock. For the Lincoln conspirators, he was their jailor and the ranking officer at the scaffold. The day was rainy and dismal as he read the Order of Execution, then clapped his hands to signal the release of the trap doors."

I shivered again and Miss Maggie's eyes sparkled. I knew she was grinning at me under her scarf. She loved getting that reaction to her stories.

As we turned away from the Hartranft plot, Cella said, "Well, we've got three more Civil War generals, the G.A.R. plot, and at least five other interesting graves I wanted to show you, but the cold's starting to get to my bones. Plus we're losing daylight fast. Want to come back Saturday morning?"

Miss Maggie and I were agreeing when I caught sight of the monolith again. "What's that marker?" I asked. "The tall squarish one."

"Oh, that's right," she exclaimed. "We were supposed to check out the Lowell vault. Come on, we can pass by it on the way out."

I recognized it then from the newpaper photo, the large double L on the face seeming to fade into focus. That same moment, I spied a little black cat lounging along the top of the monolith, lazily flicking its tail as if enjoying the last rays of sunlight.

My feet slipped on the uneven wet grass, and I almost went down, pulling Miss Maggie with me. Cella grabbed my coat sleeve in time to steady me.

When I looked up again, the cat was gone, but the message it left behind was clear. I was *supposed* to check out the grave.

As Cella went ahead of us through a narrow spot between stones, I took the opportunity to whisper to Miss Maggie, "Distract my cousin for me a few minutes, will you?"

Her white eyebrows went up, almost touching her wool cap, but she nodded.

The Lowell family plot was surrounded by a matching granite wall, with symmetrical entrances on either side. Granite posts stuck up above the wall at the corners and entrances. Cella pointed to these as she explained, "A heavy iron chain used to run between the posts, but it was commandeered for scrap metal during World War Two."

The monolith was centered inside the back wall, sporting only its double L logo. In front of it was the vault, shaped like a rectangular step-pyramid. The base was maybe eight inches high and five-by-eight feet around. The next step was about five inches high, and on top was a four-by-seven foot slab, carved with the name "LOWELL" in block letters across the middle. A border of intertwined roses garnished the edge, with a nickel-sized hole in the center of each side. I speculated that they might be air holes, either to let out the noxious gases of decomposition, or to calm someone afraid of being buried alive.

As I went inside the enclosure, Miss Maggie kept Cella from following by asking, "This granite looks newer than most of the rest of the cemetery. Is it?"

Cella was happy to tell what she knew. "Lloyd Lowell put up the granite monument and wall in the 1920s, right before the Depression, I think. The vault, though, is one of the oldest in the cemetery. Lloyd's grandfather had it built for his family in the early 1850s."

Names and dates had been carved on the slab below the surname: Letitia and Lucius, who both died in the 1870s; Lawrence, in 1914; and his wife, Mary Constance, in 1918. On the granite monolith, three more names and dates were chiseled into the base. Lloyd: 1885-1933, Loretta: 1893-1952, and Latimer: 1917-1953.

Miss Maggie started plying Cella with questions about the Lowells, beginning with the latest generation. As my cousin was explaining how Latimer had died in a car fire only a year after his mother, I reached out a hand and touched the monolith. The stone felt like ice, but I left my palm there and closed my eyes.

Immediately, I saw a bright flash and flames, startling me so that I almost jumped backward. Then, as if my Other World camera switched to wide-angle, I saw that the flame was nothing but a match and Uncle Rocco was holding it—the young, twenty-something Uncle Rocco of Aunt Sophie's photos. He held the match out, as if to light someone's cigarette or cigar.

The scene replayed itself. Uncle Rocco reaching into his vest pocket, bringing forth a match, doing some sleight-of-hand to make the match burst into flame, leaning forward, and this time, I saw the tip of the cigarette he was about to light for someone.

Then I smelled garlic. Strong.

Then, nothing. I left my eyes closed, hoping for more, but the feeling I got was of a voice saying, "You've got the pieces. Don't be lazy."

"Hey, Pat, you feeling okay?" Another voice. Cella's. Can't distract her for long.

I opened my eyes and, ignoring her query, said, "Seems odd that Lowell put up this monument facing the river, with its back to most of the rest of the cemetery."

My cousin shrugged. "Like I said, there used to be another entrance on this side with a train station. I don't know if it was still here in the 1920s. But maybe if it was, Lowell was thinking, being the richest guy in town, that he had no local peers to impress, so he decided to wow the folks who came to visit from Philly and the Main Line downriver."

Made sense to me. The monolith would be easy to spot as you came out from under the trees after climbing up steps from the railroad tracks.

"Anyway," Cella continued, "this is the vault those orphans were stolen from. On the tour, they said it takes at least three men to move the slab, not to mention having to carry away all the coffins. Probably some kind of gang robbed it."

Reminded of Uncle Rocco by my vision, I thought how he, going down into this vault the next day, had discovered the orphans were missing. I wondered if that had anything to do with the scene I'd just glimpsed. Or with the smell of garlic.

Garlic? No way. That odor was connected with Uncle Rocco's death, not Lloyd Lowell's.

Confused and cold, I let Cella and Miss Maggie lead me back to the car.

"Now everybody has got a scheme to relieve unemployment."

—WILL ROGERS, 1931

March 2, 1933 – Trepani's Cellar

The sleet turned back into snow, dropping another inch or so before it stopped in the early afternoon. Vito and Pip shoveled off the walks around our house and I could hear all our neighbors doing the same.

Del's good clothes were wet when she came home from school, evidence of snowball fights along the way. On a normal snowy day, after she changed, she'd have gone right back outside to practice her fastball using snowballs aimed at Jock Ranelli's head. (She hardly ever hit him, though. He could duck real fast.)

Anyway, that afternoon Del went down the cellar instead. Aunt Gina thought her daughter was going down to fetch the mop and bucket for scrubbing the bathroom floor, but Del had other things on her mind.

Still remembering yesterday's explosion, I wouldn't follow her. I stood at the top of the steps, watching my cousin descend, wondering if another bottle would blow up today. Crisi was already down there, I knew. After lunch, when Nonna brought the boys' shirts down the cellar to wash them, I'd seen Crisi brush by Nonna's legs to get down the steps first. The cat hadn't come back up since.

The light at the bottom went on and Del disappeared out of sight, but I heard her say, "Oh, so you're back in your old spot, Cristiana. Don't you like these shelves anymore, now that Ma's ketchup bottles fight back?"

I wanted to see what Del was doing. I wouldn't go down too far, I told myself. And not wanting Mrs. Roosevelt to get more polka dots, I left her lying on the top landing. Sitting down, I went down one step at a time on my rump, to the fifth tread, until I could just see beneath the ceiling rafters.

With the dreary weather, the cellar was darker today, the shadows deeper. They seemed longer, too, though they couldn't have been. That was only my imagination.

Del had her back to me. She stood in front of the shelves, hands on hips as if conducting an official inspection. Nothing was there to inspect. All the bottles and jars had been moved.

"Doesn't feel hot down here today." She reached through the shelves to touch the wall. "Nope. Not even warm." She looked over her shoulder at me. "So you can come down, Bambola. No glass to break and the wall's cold anyway."

I stayed where I was. Crisi, though, padded across the floor to her.

"Like I said last night, Bambola," Del went on, talking more to herself than me, "this wall shoulda never got hot, even if Rocco had his stove blasting. Between us and him is a three foot wide tunnel upstairs. And I guess solid dirt down here."

Crisi passed the shelves and, in two quick hops, mounted the small barrel and chest. She paused as Del reached out a hand to stroke the fur under her chin, but my cousin was too preoccupied to do more than let the cat rub her face against her fingers. Crisi jumped up again, onto the top shelf, ducked under one rafter and, like yesterday, disappeared.

This time, from my vantage up near the ceiling, I saw where she went. Between the first two beams, a black pipe, maybe four inches around, came down from above before making two ninety-degree turns—sideways and back—to exit through the wall behind the shelves. The hole in the bricks was large enough for Crisi to squeeze through alongside the pipe.

I was surprised enough to let a sound out of my mouth, something between "Hey!" and "Cat!"

Del swung around and stared at me. "Did you *say* something, Bambola?"

I shook my head, but I pointed to where Crisi had vanished.

Del turned to follow the line of my arm. She couldn't see from where she stood, of course. She went over to the coal bin, scooped up the crate she'd been sitting on yesterday, and carried it back to the shelves to stand on. She grabbed onto the shelves to hoist herself up and they rocked, but didn't come down on top of her, thank God.

Del saw the hole then. "Well, I'll be! Crisi? You in there? Come'ere, kitty." She made whispering noises between her lips. Crisi emerged from the hole, back out onto the shelf, stretching her back beneath my cousin's palm.

Del gave her a good rub, all the while studying the hole and the pipe that led into it. "This explains *everything*, Bambola."

16

As Cella drove us back to Main Street, I rehashed what I'd seen and sensed in my vision—Uncle Rocco lighting someone's cigarette, then the smell of garlic. Thing was, Uncle Rocco looked to be twenty-something when he lit that match, but the odor of garlic went with the hundred-and-two-year-old Rocco. What was up with that?

Cella inched her Neon through rush hour traffic on Main until we were past the first bridge, then she cut over a block where travel was moving faster. We were waiting at the Swede Street light when the tune "That's Amore" filled the car.

"Aunt Sophie," Cella said, reaching into her coat pocket to retrieve her cell. Opening it, she handed the phone back to me. "Tell her three minutes."

I did, adding our location.

"I'm gonna warm up leftover meatballs," Aunt Sophie said. "That okay? No more pizza but we still got roast peppers and olives. Maybe I should put on a vegetable?"

Knowing she had leftover desserts, too, I assured her that meatball sandwiches and roast peppers would be plenty. In truth, with the big lunch and all, I didn't feel like eating. And with all the stress, my tummy was feeling like somebody walked on it with cleats.

By the time Aunt Sophie let me hang up we were turning back onto Main. "I'm just gonna drop you off," Cella said. "I told Ma I'd be home for supper tonight. Aunt Sophie knows. Gotta take Joan to her study group at seven, plus I said I'd read over a theme paper Janine has due tomorrow."

Cella pulled alongside Uncle Leo's Olds to let us out. "I'll be back around nine probably. You got my spare key if you want to go over my place earlier."

Aunt Sophie was at the door, waving goodbye to Cella. As she let us in, she said, "I put on some limas. Won't take long. We'll eat in a little bit. Take your things off. Leo's got the news on if you want to watch." She bustled off to the kitchen.

The hallway was as it had been the other night, dimly lit, with the aroma of tomato sauce wafting in along with the sound of the TV. As usual, a table lamp was on in the front parlor and this is where Miss Maggie beckoned me after we hung up our coats.

"I'll need to climb the steps to the bathroom in a minute, but let me rest my legs first," she said. "We did a lot of walking today."

She sounded tired enough that I was instantly concerned. "You okay?"

"Oh, sure." She sagged onto the small sofa on the other side of the treadmill and patted the seat next to her. "Just getting old." Her eyes crinkled into a laugh. "Didn't drink enough liquids today. And I forgot to take my lunch pill. I'll take it with dinner." As I flopped down beside her, realizing I was also extremely tired, she asked, "Now, tell me, what happened at the cemetery?"

I filled her in on everything, from the monument seeming to want my attention, to the cat sighting, to the vision.

That's when I got a reaction. "Oh, I *hated* the matches we had back then! My Jake used to carry them in his pockets, too. I was always afraid he'd set his clothes on fire." She held out her right forefinger. "See that scar below the cuticle? One day when I was doing laundry, emptying Jake's pockets, I accidently nicked a match with my nail. Nasty burn."

"They lit that easily?" I was thinking how that explained Uncle Rocco's sleight of hand.

"*Too* easily. Nearly any surface worked. Jake used his pant leg all the time."

"Uncle Rocco used his fingernail?"

"Apparently. But what's that got to do with what you saw last night next door? Or with your friend the cat, who seems to be following you all over town?"

I knew we didn't have time to sit and analyze the whole mess, but I did have an idea. "Come on, Miss Maggie. Potty break. I'll help you up the stairs."

While she was in the bathroom, I retrieved the photo of the black cat from the shoeboxes in the back bedroom. When we went downstairs, I headed for the kitchen. "Aunt Sophie, I've got a question—"

"Call your Uncle Leo in," Aunt Sophie interrupted as she drained the water from the pot of beans. "Everything's ready."

Stowing the photo in my sweatshirt pocket, I went to fetch

Uncle Leo, then helped my aunt put supper on the table, knowing that until her guests had food under their noses, I'd never get her full attention.

Once we were all seated, with plates boasting sandwiches heaped with meatballs atop leftover rolls toasted a golden brown, I took the photo out and slid it over to Aunt Sophie. "Take a look at this."

Frowning, she wiped her hands on her napkin, picked up the snapshot and held it out, tilting her head back to look through the bottom of her bifocals. Then she pulled the photo right up to her nose and studied it over the top of her rims. "Hey, that's Uncle Rocco. A good picture, too." She held out the photo at arm's length so Uncle Leo could see. He did the same tilting of his head, but never let go of his sandwich. "That's Delphina Trepani next to him," Aunt Sophie told her husband.

"Mrs. Ranelli, right?" I asked as I forked some sweet peppers onto my meatballs.

"Oh, sure, sure," Aunt Sophie replied. "Del married Jock Ranelli. Knew each other since they were kids. Used to play baseball over in his yard. She was a tomboy, that one!"

Uncle Leo scrunched up his nose as if that brought the picture into better focus. "Bet that's the baseball Rocco gave her. Every boy in the neighborhood was jealous. Signed by Lefty Grove of the Ath-e-letics." He pronounced it in four syllables. Always did. He'd say "arthritis" the same way, and so did a lot of other Italians I knew. Something about a "th" followed by a consonant begged for a vowel sound between.

"Me?" Uncle Leo added. "I woulda asked Jimmy Foxx to sign it instead. Jimmy could really swing a bat."

"Signed?" I murmured, reaching up to take the snapshot from my aunt's hand before her arm got tired. "Wouldn't something like that be worth serious bucks these days?" I was thinking about Cella's theory of lost treasure. Perhaps Uncle Rocco got a ball signed for himself, too.

Uncle Leo shrugged. "Wasn't a home run ball. Or even a ball he struck out Babe Ruth with. Maybe not even a game ball. And Lefty wasn't so hot by that time. I remember telling Del too bad she didn't get Rocco to get her a ball a few years earlier, from when the Ath-e-letics were in the Series."

"What year was this photo?"

"Lemme think." Uncle Leo scooped up a piece of roasted red pepper, shoveling the big strip into his mouth whole, figuring while he chewed. "They won the Series in '29 and '30. *Shoulda* won in '31, but the Cards took the last game. '32 they came in second in the League. By '33, they were barely over five hundred."

Aunt Sophie snorted. "How come you remember all that but you forgot to pick up the dry cleaning at Antonelli's last week?"

My uncle ignored the sarcasm. He was too busy reliving his youth. "I remember all those seasons. Mr. D'Abruzzi used to let us listen to games on his radio. And the YMCA took us boys down the city sometimes to Shibe Park. Called us the Knothole Gang." He took another bite of his sandwich, chewed, swallowed, then continued. "But see, during the Depression less people went to the ballpark. Connie Mack started selling off his best players. The Ath-e-letics were never the same after that."

He tapped the photo in my hand with his little finger, the only digit not coated with sauce. "That picture's from '33 or '34."

I caught Miss Maggie's smile out of the corner of my eye. She'd made some connection. I'd ask her about it later. Right now, I voiced my main question about the snapshot. "Tell me about the cat."

"Crisi?" Aunt Sophie asked. "Oh, everybody on the block knew Crisi. Mother of God, could that little one howl!"

"Crisi." I said it aloud to try the name on for size, see if it gave me the willies or anything. No luck. "Was he—"

"She," corrected Aunt Sophie. "Used to sit in Trepani's store window and watch us go by. Or if you went in, she had to inspect you before you could buy whatever it was your mother sent you for. Nosy, that's what she was."

Miss Maggie pursed her lips. "And did curiosity kill the cat?" She wanted to know the reason for the haunting, of course, as did I, but I wouldn't have asked, not wanting to hear the details, especially not over dinner.

Aunt Sophie, though, shook her head. "Not that cat. Lived all of her nine lives and then some. All the way up through the war. Then when she was real old, she simply went off someplace and never came back. I don't think Delphina ever found her."

Maybe that was why Crisi's spirit was hanging around. She was still trying to come back. Yet, I couldn't help feeling she was trying to tell me something. No, I *knew* she was. But what?

"They had real ball players back then," Uncle Leo said, still stuck in baseball-mode. "Pitchers went the whole game. Even extra innings. Not like these guys they got now, get paid millions and can't pitch seven innings. Babies."

"Phillies lose again, Uncle Leo?" I asked sympathetically.

He grunted what I took to be an affirmative. "They're all bums. Sophie, pass some more peppers over here."

After dessert—I ate only three leftover butter cookies, though I craved the devil's food cake in the worst way—I helped Aunt Sophie clean up while Miss Maggie went off to watch the news with Uncle Leo. When the dishes were done, and after I took the garbage and recycling out for my aunt, we all settled in the sitting room to watch *Jeopardy*. I did this only because my mother had taught me that it was impolite to, in her words, "eat and run" when I was a guest for dinner. But I was antsy to go next door before my cousin returned.

Before *Wheel of Fortune* came on, I made the observation that the day had seemed very long. Miss Maggie jumped in, stretching and even producing a gaping yawn that, I swear, couldn't be faked, adding that she was going to turn in early. Aunt Sophie walked us out to the hallway, fussing as we donned our warm outer clothes, reminding us to come for breakfast the next morning.

Next door, as we hung up our coats, Miss Maggie asked, "Well, where shall we begin tonight?"

Without answering, I closed my eyes then and there. Once again I had the sensation of something being very close, right behind me—something that retreated as soon as I, psychically-speaking, glanced over my shoulder.

Discouraged, I said, "I don't know, Miss Maggie. What do you think?"

Shrugging, she set her handbag on the stairs. "The dining room worked last night."

So we headed in that direction, boosting the thermostat as we passed through the sitting room. In the cellar beneath our feet, the furnace rumbled to life.

In the dining room, I took a moment to imagine the space as I'd seen it in my vision, with the big table in the middle. Had there been other furniture? I couldn't remember.

I closed my eyes again and waited. I could see the table, but the picture was from my memory, nothing more. The people around the table were fuzzy still-lifes, kneeling at their places as I'd last seen them, frozen in mid-prayer.

I was about to lift my lids when I got the urge to turn to the right, toward the wall this house shared with Aunt Sophie's next door. I saw a door I hadn't noticed before, hanging open into the room. Some part of my brain that deals with spatial logic deduced that this led beneath the backstairs.

Eyes still closed, I walked over to the doorway and looked inside. To the right, stairs led down into the cellar. A dim light was coming up from below and I could just make out a small, handmade doll, flat on her back on the landing, button eyes gazing straight up. Halfway down, I spied the silhouette of a little girl, a toddler, sitting sideways on a step, gazing down into the basement. She didn't move, didn't take her eyes off whatever held her attention, but I had the impression of an invitation to go sit beside her.

Carefully stepping around the doll, I descended to two steps below the child and sat down to watch.

> "These unhappy times call for the building of plans . . . that put their faith once more in the forgotten man at the bottom of the economic pyramid."
>
> —FRANKLIN DELANO ROOSEVELT, CAMPAIGN SPEECH, 1932

March 2, 1933 – In the cellar

"This explains *everything*, Bambola." Del lifted Crisi from the shelf, turning as she did to follow with her eyes the course of the pipe through the ceiling. "Rocco helped Vito and Pip put that in last year. Remember? Vito said it was a heating vent or something, going up the chimney through the fireplace in the upstairs parlor. I thought it came from *our* furnace, but it comes from Rocco's next door. From his stove. That's how it could get so hot yesterday."

On this last deduction, Crisi decided she wanted to get down. She wiggled her black head under Del's arm and pushed off with her feet, spinning my cousin around in the process. Once on the floor, Crisi came over to the stairs, looked up—I guess weighing her options—then changed her mind and returned to her blanket nest in the crate.

Not distracted, Del continued reasoning aloud. "See, this also explains the voices we heard the other night, Bambola. Rocco, Vito and Pip must have been talking over his place, and the pipe let us hear them up in the parlor. But why would Rocco put his stovepipe up our chimney?"

Up in the kitchen I heard Aunt Gina yell up the back stairs for Tutti to come down and sort coal. Since Del had never finished sorting yesterday, we needed twice as much.

Del heard her mother, too, and realized my brother would soon come down to the cellar. "Bambola, let's not tell anyone about this pipe until I figure it out. We'll keep it a secret between you, me, and Mrs. Roosevelt, okay?"

I nodded.

She started climbing the stairs. "I wonder if Vito and Pip are still in the store. Let's go see."

17

The scene faded to black. I opened my eyes. More black greeted me. I felt warmer than I had in the vision. I seemed to be sitting on what felt like steps, in the dark. The loud rumble of machinery was nearby.

Light was filtering down from above. I turned to look in that direction. At the top of the stairs, a familiar form was silhouetted by the glow coming through a doorway to her right. "Miss Maggie?"

She let out a sigh of relief. "Sakes, Pat, you gave me a scare, opening the door and going down these steps with your eyes closed. I wanted to turn on the light, but I was afraid I'd startle you."

"If there's a switch up there, hit it now so I can see my way back up."

She did, and on the wall above the landing, a sconce with a dingy glass lit up. At the bottom of the steps, another light went on, a bare bulb in a ceiling fixture this time.

Instead of mounting the stairs, I was transfixed by what I could see of the cellar from my vantage point. Where the shelves had been in my vision, Cella's oil furnace now stood, thundering away as it sent steam up into the house above. This modern version of the basement had more junk in it—old furniture, cardboard boxes, decades worth of odds and ends.

Yellow streetlight glare was coming in the window in front, barely illuminating an oil tank with a workbench beside it. Further back in the cellar, in the shadows, a washer and dryer now sat beside the big utility sink.

Instead of going up, I went down for a closer look. As Miss Maggie descended behind me, one step at a time because of her bad knees, I told her about Del, Crisi, and the little girl, Bambola, and even about Mrs. Roosevelt. Somehow I knew she was that doll who'd been flat on her back on the stair landing.

I wandered toward the furnace, raising my voice to be heard over the noise. Spying a pull chain hanging from another ceiling fixture in the front of the cellar, I changed course and yanked the chain, bringing to life another bare bulb. "This was all empty shelves, Miss Maggie. An old chest of drawers was here."

"No furnace?" she asked, coming to stand beside me. "Figured they might have burned coal. Most folks did in the Depression."

The word sparked a memory. "I saw a coal bin over there, where the oil tank is now, and I think the furnace was back that way. But what makes you say the Depression? This house has been here since at least the turn of the twentieth century."

She grinned. "Not only the Depression, but 1933, if I don't miss my guess. First of all, you mentioned Mrs. Roosevelt. FDR took office in '33."

"And he was president a long time," I pointed out.

"Then there's the girl Delphina and her cat. She didn't look older than in the photo of her you had at dinner, did she?"

Remembering that I'd put it back in my sweatshirt pocket, I produced the snapshot now to compare Del to my Other World flashback. "No, she looks pretty much the same, except she was wearing a sweater."

"Your uncle said that photo was taken in '33," Miss Maggie said.

"Or '34, he said. Or he might have been wrong."

"Well, the clincher, Pat, is that Lloyd Lowell died in '33. You had a vision at his grave today. That can't be a coincidence. According to the news article, he died on March first. Today is March second, and since, at your other ghost meetings, you've seen events of the same day, centuries apart, I'll bet the scene you just witnessed here happened on March second, 1933."

I had to admit she was likely right about the day of the month, at least. Last Christmas when I'd seen a ghost's memories, I hadn't necessarily—hold the phone! Was I seeing a ghost's memories now? In other encounters, I usually found myself looking out of the eyes of someone from the past. I hadn't felt that this time. I'd been myself the whole time, allowed to sit in on a memory, but not participate. I recalled that weird mental invitation, just before I descended the stairs.

"Is that pipe still here, Pat?" Miss Maggie asked, shaking me out of my contemplation.

"Well, it's still up on the second floor, running along the back of the parlor fireplace," I replied as I studied the jungle of pipes leading to and from the heater. "That's what Cella found last night."

At last, I pointed to a pipe coming through the ceiling, a black iron conduit that simply hung there, detached, its two elbow joints gone.

"That explains why," my mentor said, "a section of wall behind the furnace has been patched."

I saw what she meant. Part of the wall wasn't lumpy, painted-over bricks like the rest of the cellar. Here was a rough circle, maybe three feet across, of pale green-gray cement.

I shook my head. "This isn't high enough up for the pipes. That second little patch up there . . . see it? That's where the pipes went through."

"What does that suggest to you, Pat?" Miss Maggie asked.

"You mean, can I think of any reason why Uncle Rocco would have sent his stovepipe up through the chimney next door?" I shrugged. "Maybe his own chimney was crumbling and he couldn't afford to get it fixed. This might have been easier."

"After digging through two foundation walls and several feet of dirt between?" Miss Maggie pointed out.

But my attention was on the black pipe, or rather, where it led. "Between here and the second floor parlor is the store, and that's where Del was headed next. What do you say we go upstairs and have a look at it?"

Miss Maggie was game. We retraced our steps back up through the dining room and sitting room, into the front hall. The side hall leading to the back of the store was dim, but once I opened the door, I saw a pull chain practically in front of my nose. Good thing, because the light was necessary for the three steps that led down into a small, walk-through storeroom.

Instead of shop merchandise, though, this room now held a chest of drawers, a highboy and a pair of rocking chairs with wicker seats and backs. On each horizontal surface were cardboard boxes containing things like ornate hinges and fancy glass doorknobs. I knew this because Miss Maggie, nosy-parker that she is, had to look in every box she could reach, pulling out noteworthy specimens for our mutual appreciation.

Opposite was a paneled wood wall, painted white, with a plain wood slat door at the end closest to us. The storeroom had felt a tad cooler than the hall, but when I opened this door, like the parlor upstairs, the cold hit me in the face.

Another pull chain hung directly in front of my nose and when I yanked it, a white globe lamp above my head went on. I could see a dead moth silhouetted inside.

More furniture filled this room, including, if I wasn't mistaken, the dining room table and chairs from my earlier vision. A few other pieces were covered in sheets. On lifting one corner of the nearest item, I found an upholstered sofa. Everything was a bit dusty, but only a bit. Cella probably went on a cleaning jag every time her allergies got bad.

The interest for me in the room were the shelves that lined each wall, eight feet high maybe, with green subway tile above, reaching halfway to the high ceiling. The shelves were nearly empty now, holding only small pieces that my cousin wanted to protect, like picture frames and knickknacks.

I imagined these shelves lined with canned and jarred goods, ready for sale. Closing my lids, I saw just that, and on the floor between the shelves—no more than a ten-foot width—I saw a big pickle barrel, a case of orange soda and open crates of apples and onions. On the back wall hung a big clock, along with a horseshoe for good luck. And on the wide sill beneath the front window, Crisi gazed out on a daylit Main Street, swishing her tail back and forth, as if to let me know I was in the right place. Otherwise, though, the store scene was a still-life, with no people, no action, and no hint that it would liven up in the near future. Disappointed, I reopened my eyes.

"Nothing?" Miss Maggie asked.

I told her what I saw.

"Sounds like the trail is as cold as this room. Time for some hot tea, Pat."

Realizing my nose felt like an icicle, I agreed. She led the way through the house to the kitchen, retrieving her handbag on the way.

As she put water in the kettle, I readied the mugs and sulked, frustrated that I couldn't make sense of whatever this ghost was trying to tell me. Not knowing if I was even *supposed* to make sense of it.

Miss Maggie had her mind on other things. "I really should check my email."

Welcoming the diversion, I hopped up onto the stool beside the counter and booted up the laptop. "Let me see if we have a signal tonight."

A few moments later I was reading this message from Hugh. "Slight change of plans. We're stopping over in Baltimore Friday night. Expect to arrive in Norristown by Saturday noon. Send directions from I-95. Or is there a better way?"

Miss Maggie heard my gasp. "What's up at home, Pat?"

I told her the gist of the message. "Hugh's taking Beth Ann to see Tanya's parents. I mean, I assume he is." I told her about my conversation with him earlier in the week and his cryptic email the other night.

Meanwhile, Miss Maggie retrieved her reading glasses from her handbag on the table and came to look over my shoulder. "That's what he's doing, all right. He wouldn't stop overnight just for a few hours at the Baltimore Aquarium."

Then again, I thought, neither was it like him to dredge up old, painful memories, which seeing Tanya's parents would do.

I looked at the date and time of the message. Last night, 7:21. Hugh had to be wondering why I hadn't answered yet. I moved the cursor to the reply button, then stopped myself. "Here, Miss Maggie. Check your mail first. What with directions and all, my reply's bound to take a while."

Leaving the laptop to her, I went to the stove to pour the hot water.

Miss Maggie pushed the stool aside, unable to mount it with her bad knees. Instead, she stood at the counter. "Been nagging Hugh for ten years to get back in touch with Tanya's folks. Glad to see you could talk sense into him. Beth Ann ought to know her grandparents."

I agreed, but was also aware that Beth Ann had been silent, email-wise, since Hugh said he was going to talk to her. I mentioned that aloud.

"Might have been busy finishing up her science project," Miss Maggie suggested. She didn't look like she believed it. She knew Beth Ann and her moods better than I did.

I latched onto the change of subject. "I wonder how Beth Ann's making out at Science Night."

"Took second place the last two years. First place went to the same boy both times. Her projects were more involved than his, but Stoke County schools still can't quite fathom that a girl can do well in science. Plus the boy's father is on the School Board." Miss Maggie pushed the laptop's mouse around as she spoke, without looking away from the screen. I wondered if I'd be able to multitask like that at her age.

I set her tea beside her, then sipped my own. The hot liquid awoke in me an irresistible case of the munchies. My stomach felt bloated. Nerves. I retrieved the bag of pretzels from the cabinet. Chunky sourdough, the kind that would give my molars a workout.

I took a seat at the table to chomp and mull over recent developments. I couldn't help worrying about Beth Ann. The thought of meeting her mother's folks was likely causing serious gastronomic butterflies. Not that she'd admit it. Oh, Hugh was doing the right thing, finally, but he wouldn't be real sensitive to her fears. Or if he was, I couldn't picture him handling it well. They'd be yelling at each other all the way up the Baltimore-Washington Parkway.

What could I do to help? (And how often, I wondered, for the rest of Beth Ann's teenaged years, would I ask myself that question? Or maybe I'd be asking it the rest of my life. Aunt Lydia was no doubt thinking the same about Cella these days, and my mom surely thought the same about me, every time I had trouble at work or a bad date or a fender-bender with my car.)

Mom. I wished she was still around, now that I'd be a mom, too. I had a zillion questions for her.

"Consarnit!" Miss Maggie grumbled, pushing herself away from the counter, bumping me out of my reveries.

"What's wrong?" I asked.

"The usual. Living forever is a great thing, except all the medicines keep you in the bathroom half the day. And I hate being interrupted when I'm doing something interesting." She tottered over to the steps. "Be right back."

"Take your nighttime pills while you're up there so you don't forget later."

"Good idea."

I watched Miss Maggie climb up the stairs, thinking how fond I was of her, thinking I ought to take advantage of the years she had left to ask her all my Beth Ann questions.

I was turning my head back to the pretzel bag when my eye caught movement at the window over the sink. In that split second, I could have sworn I saw, peeking over the half curtain, two feline eyes on a face of black fur. A faint, throaty meow came to my ears, more of an echo of sound than the real thing.

I dashed to the window, yanking the curtain aside, hoping to spot a flesh and blood cat rubbing up against the glass.

Outside, the streetlamp on Penn combined with a single parking light in the lot next door to show two big freight trailers parked in the center of the gravel, behind the silhouette of the chain link fence. Nothing stirred. No cat.

I almost called for Miss Maggie. Silly, I told myself. She can't come down right away, and by the time she does. . . . If something had happened on March second, 1933, at precisely this time—something that Crisi, or whoever, wanted me to witness—maybe it couldn't wait for Miss Maggie.

Yes, the ridiculousness of that time paradox occurred to me, but I didn't take the time to laugh at it. I closed my eyes.

Another meow, and a gentle though insistent scratching at the door.

"Okay," I said aloud, "whatever you want." Opening my eyes, I moved around to the door, and as I pushed *that* half curtain aside, I shut my lids again, wondering why I was bothering to touch the curtain at all.

But this time I saw Uncle Rocco's house, and two small, shadowy figures beside his back stoop.

> "The working classes didn't bring this on, it was the big boys that . . . overbought, overmerged, and overcapitalized."
>
> —WILL ROGERS, NOVEMBER 1931

March 2, 1933 – In back of 347 East Main

"Come on, Bambola," Del said as we came through the yard of the house next door. "Get out of the wagon. I don't want anyone to hear us."

Del had wanted to start investigating the mysterious pipe in the cellar right away that afternoon, but Aunt Gina made my cousin scrub the bathroom floor first. Del tried to get out of the chore, saying her backside still hurt, but Aunt Gina wasn't buying it. She said you scrubbed floors on your hands and knees, not your rear.

So after supper, after we'd all knelt at our chairs and recited our rosary again, Del asked if she could go out on Main Street and get an early start taking orders for Easter eggs. See, Mr. Bean down on Beech Street made chocolate eggs in his cellar every year, and some of us kids would take orders for him during Lent, then he'd pay us. Usually we began later, maybe a month before Easter, and Aunt Gina at first said it was too icy out. But Del pointed out how all the walks had been shoveled already and promised she'd stay on this block. Uncle Ennio backed up his daughter, saying it was good that Del wanted to get a head start. Aunt Gina finally agreed. Anything that would bring a little more money in for the family was always encouraged.

What they didn't know was that Del only wanted an excuse to be outside once it got dark.

"Take Bambola with you," my aunt said. "The neighbors all like to see her." She meant, with me along, Del always got more orders. The neighbors would stop to say how cute I was and ask about my father, holding still long enough for Del to go into her sales pitch. Once she got going, nobody could say no to her.

Nonna wrapped me in a blanket so I wouldn't get cold, and Del put me in the little wagon that Pip used if anybody bought heavy stuff at our store and wanted their order delivered. The wagon wasn't much more than three two-by-sixes on the bottom and slat sides, all a little warped with age and missing most of the original red paint, but the wheels were sturdy metal covered with rubber. They didn't make too much noise. I liked being pulled around in it.

I gazed up at the puffy white clouds that filled the darkening sky as Del pulled the wagon west on Main Street, knocking at the doors of the houses on our side. Small mounds of shoveled snow ran parallel to the walk, either up against the houses or along the curb. In between, patches of ice clung to the pavement here and there. Del watched her steps. The breeze felt cool on my face, I recall, but the rest of me was warm beneath the blanket.

Del got four orders right away. I remember one of them was for fifty penny eggs. Del wrote the orders down carefully on a piece of paper that she brought along, using the nub of one of last year's school pencils.

What with Del explaining to each neighbor who asked how my father was still out looking for work and hadn't come back yet, and no, we hadn't heard from him in months, and yes, wasn't it a shame for him to leave his two little ones behind like that, well, by that time all the streetlights winked on.

As if that was a cue, Del stopped knocking at doors and pulled me down around the corner, up Arch Street to Penn, strolling so as not to attract attention. She couldn't go too fast anyway 'cause of the ice. She went back up Penn toward our yard, stopping only once, when she spied Jock Ranelli out behind his house. He was dumping a bucket of coal slag on their ash pile at the end of the yard.

Jock asked her if she'd heard that the Phillies wanted to move out of the Baker Bowl to Shibe Park.

"Sez you!" Del was so scandalized, she almost forgot her mission. "The Phillies can't move into Shibe! Where would the Athletics go?"

"The two teams would share the place," Jock replied. "Can't blame the Phillies. The 'Toilet' Bowl's all run down."

"Yeah, but those losers are bound to put a curse on Shibe," Del argued. "The A's shouldn't allow the Phillies inside."

Jock let her have the last word on the subject. He always did. He asked Del if she wanted to come in and listen to their radio. Uncle Wip was on, I think, or maybe Kate Smith. Del said she had to get home. Another few years, though, and she'd be over at their place practically every night listening to the radio, just as an excuse to be over there. But she was too young to be sweet on him yet.

By now it was dark. The streetlight on Penn was enough for Del to see her way up to the house next door to ours, the one Rocco lived in.

She pulled the wagon onto the snowy slush covering the grass and lifted me out. The snow started seeping through my shoes right away. I couldn't walk and hold the blanket around me. Del threw it over her shoulder, then took my hand.

The yard didn't have steps like our yard. Instead, the grass made a long slope down to a cement slab, maybe fifteen feet out from the door stoop. This patio was a step lower than the side porch off our kitchen, which meant that, unlike our house, there was room for a cellar window beside the stoop. On the other side of the window, Rocco's iron stovepipe chimney came out of the wall and went up along the corner of the house past the second floor windows.

Del felt the metal pipe with her bare hand. "It's cold, Bambola. If it's blocked or something, you'd think he'd just clean it out, instead of using our chimney."

She turned her attention to the window, which was only about a foot high. You couldn't see in because Rocco had a couple towels tacked up over the inside, like curtains. A few months back, though, when Rocco thought he'd lost his key, he'd lowered my brother Tutti through that window, so he could run up the stairs and open the door. Rocco found his key later, in the lining of his coat. The pocket had a hole in it and the key had fallen through. But the incident with Tutti was how Del knew that the window would be unlocked.

In the light of the streetlamp behind us, the cement in front of the window looked wet. Del stooped down to touch it. "Ice," she mumbled. She spread out the blanket over the patch and knelt down on it. I followed suit, with an odd notion that maybe she meant to pray here. I could feel the cold right through the wool.

She pushed gently at the bottom of the window. It was the kind with a hinge at the top. With a little scraping noise, it gave way. When it was free of the frame, Del paused, listening.

". . . this'll work fine," Rocco was saying, his voice faint, like he was way over at the other end of the cellar, but we could still make out his words. "Nobody'll try the stuff for at least three months. Not if they want to get their money's worth. All we gotta do is find a way to get it out to the cemetery tomorrow night. Orazio picked a dandy time to land in jail."

"Doesn't matter if they don't try it," Vito argued, sounding close enough to the window that I felt Del stiffen beside me, scared of him hearing her. "The smell's all wrong."

"That's why we need to mix everything together," Rocco replied. "Get me that funnel, will you, Vito? Over there to your left. We mix it and they won't notice. No way am I going to more trouble than this for a lousy three bucks. We'll let Junior do the explaining. Serve him right. I'm betting he was the one who broke into the crypt the other night."

"Bratimer?" Vito said.

"Who else? Figure, he must have seen his pop serving this stuff after dinner to important guests. Maybe wonders where it came from. Even Junior could put two and two together."

Pip spoke up. "He couldn't move the slab himself."

"I got ideas about that, too. Remember those tracks we saw out next to the tomb on Wednesday, Vito?"

"The article in today's *Herald* didn't say anything about tracks," Pip said.

"That's because I didn't tell Joyce about them."

"You calling that doll by her first name already?" The way Pip said it, I could picture his eyebrows rising like helium balloons. He always did that when he was surprised.

"She told me to last night." Rocco's voice was smug. "When I walked her home."

Pip let out a whistle. "You move fast. Gimme lessons?"

Rocco laughed. "Your brother needs 'em more— Vito, whaddya doing? The funnel. To your left, I said."

"Yeah . . . sure . . . I got it . . . Here you go, Rocco." Vito's voice kept getting softer, like he was walking away from the window.

"Thanks. What? . . . right . . . So, Pip, anything else interesting in today's *Herald*?"

"Huh?" Then Pip spoke up loudly. "Oh, yeah. Senator Walsh died on the train on his way to Washington for the Inauguration. Isn't that something? He just got married last week, it said."

The whole time they were speaking, Del had slowly inched the window open far enough that she could lower one hand down around the bottom of the frame. She gently pushed the towel-curtain back from the wall until we could see something. I couldn't view much from my angle, plus it was kind of dark inside, because Rocco only had one lamp. But that lamp was on a table right below the window, and next to it was—

"A coffin!" Del whispered. Sure enough, the shape was right, though the box was no more than three feet long.

All of a sudden the back door opened. "Delphina!" Vito hissed. "Aw, geez!"

He sounded sore.

18

When I came back from the past this time, I knew right away I was outside. I was freezing, for one thing, and my hands were clutching what felt like a cold, rusty, metal chain link fence. Opening my eyes confirmed it. I was looking into the lot where Uncle Rocco's home had stood, staring down the grills of the trucks parked there.

Behind me, the back porch light of Cella's house clicked on. I turned toward it, absently, like a moth, still caught up in what I'd seen in 1933.

That's when the screaming started. No, more like shrieking, out in front of the house. I knew Cella's vocal cords were producing those high-pitched screeches. I recognized the attitude.

Dashing down the tunnel toward the street, I skidded over icy patches, nearly going down flat on my face twice.

"Let go!" I could hear her screaming. "No! You can't!"

I pictured her being assaulted by a whole gang of big, burly thugs, so I wasn't prepared, when I came out of the tunnel, to find her getting the better of what amounted to a simple tug-of-war with one not-so-burly, unthug-like guy wearing shorts. Ron.

Between them was a small, thin, rectangular box. Cella was unfairly using her pocketbook in a flank attack to get Ron to let go of his end. He had his free arm up, protecting his head.

"Hey!" I yelled, and they both turned to look at me. Neither one let go of the box. "What are you two doing?"

"He was stealing my box of chocolates," Cella said.

"Was not," Ron countered, also speaking to me. "I saw the box sticking up out of her mailbox and wanted a look at who sent them. Man's got a right to know who's sending his wife gifts."

"You got another box of candy?" I asked Cella, troubled, wondering if she really was having an affair. Clean out an attic and sure, you might get one box as a thank you. You don't get two. But this box was too small for a serious Don Juan. No more than a dozen chocolates inside, I reckoned. Cella wouldn't put up with an illicit lover unless he sprung for at least one-pound boxes. Size matters when you're talking seduction via chocolate.

Cella ignored my question in favor of making her case against Ron. "He was stealing. I caught him carrying them back to his truck."

"Was not," Ron repeated. "I was taking 'em out under the streetlight to read the writing."

"Like fun. He wasn't anywhere near the light."

"I didn't have time. That's when she pulled up behind me." Ron gestured with his free hand out to the street where his delivery truck and her Neon were both double parked. His truck was off with its hazard blinkers on. Her car was running and the dome lamp was lit, meaning she hadn't even stopped long enough to shut the driver's door all the way.

Cella took advantage of his guard being down to whack him good with her purse. When his grip loosened, she yanked the box away from him. "None of his business who's sending me candy."

"Remind her that she's still married, Pat."

"Tell him I don't *feel* like I'm married."

I wasn't sure if I was supposed to be a referee or a switchboard operator. All I knew was that I was feeling the cold more and more through my sweater. Wrapping my arms across my chest, I tried to sound sane. "Listen, how 'bout if you two just come inside and—"

"No!" Cella butted in, her voice breaking. The show of emotion only made her angry with herself, and more stubborn. "Tell him to go back to what's-her-face and leave me alone. Once and for all."

Ron looked directly at her, stunned. "You gotta be saying that for Pat's sake. I *know* you can't believe it." Spinning on his heel, he headed for his truck. As he swung himself up into the driver's side, he paused, standing, to yell over the windshield. "For the record, the only person I'm seeing is a guy named Sanjay."

Ron slammed the door shut behind him, gunned the truck to life, put it in gear and rumbled off up Main.

Cella let out a sigh, then seeing dazed confusion on my face, she said, in a voice that came out sounding too rational and calm, "No, he isn't gay. Sanjay's his new doctor."

I had no time to ask even one of the zillion questions that the scene had generated because Aunt Sophie pushed open her storm door and poked her head out. "Oh good, you're both here." Apparently she hadn't heard the argument or seen Ronny's van, and she was too distraught to wonder why Cella and I were standing out in the cold. "Beatrice called. Her husband—what's his name?"

"Ozzie," Cella and I said in unison.

"Right. They took him to the hospital. He got real sick, throwing up something awful. The ambulance guys said it might be a heart attack, but Beatrice is sure it's food poisoning. She asked me if garlic could go bad enough to make a person sick—"

"Garlic?" I cut in. "Why garlic?"

Aunt Sophie shrugged. "I guess that's what he ate last."

"Madonne!" Cella whispered, thinking the same thing I was. Ozzie was violently sick to his stomach and garlic somehow played a role, just like Uncle Rocco. And Queenie claimed Uncle Rocco had been poisoned. Beatrice's husband, too?

Aunt Sophie, of course, didn't know any of the sinister implications. Still, she wasn't simply broadcasting the news. No, she wanted a ride. Neither she nor Uncle Leo were allowed to drive after dark anymore, but she was determined to go out to County Hospital to be with Beatrice. "So she won't have to wait all alone," my aunt asserted. "Now that her grandfather's gone, she's got no family at all."

Cella and I weren't fooled. Aunt Sophie intended to scoop her sisters, plain and simple.

"Get your coat," my cousin told her. "My car's ready."

As Aunt Sophie vanished back into her hall, Cella turned to me. "You realize, if Ozzie *was* poisoned like Uncle Rocco, then Beatrice is suspect number one? Motive and opportunity. She had the chance to poison both. And since she can't find Uncle Rocco's money, now she's after her husband's."

Cella could make a case, I had to admit. "Let me grab my coat. I'll come with you."

She shook her head. "You know how emergency rooms are. Uncomfortable chairs and you wait forever. And you don't want to leave Miss Maggie here by hersel—"

As if the name conjured the person, Miss Maggie appeared in the doorway above us at that moment, making so little noise, I realized she must have had the door open a crack already. Probably she'd heard the whole scene.

"Leave us your phone, Cella," my mentor said, with an uncharacteristic gloom in her voice. In the shadows, her expression seemed apprehensive. "That way you can call us from the hospital. And I want you to leave the chocolates here, too. We won't eat them, you don't have to worry. But I have a good reason for asking."

Cella looked at me for an explanation, but all I could do was shrug.

"I guess if I take them, I'd have to share with Beatrice. Okay, here. Put 'em in the kitchen." My cousin handed me her candies, then fished her cellphone out of her purse. "Plug it in to recharge. I'll let you know what I find out."

Aunt Sophie came out. Cella took her arm to help her over the ice in the gutter. I stayed outside just long enough to watch them pull away, then, frozen to the bone, went in.

"You need more hot tea," Miss Maggie said, leading the way back to the kitchen, where she added, "Set that box here on the table so we can have a look at it."

I did as she asked. Now, under the light, I could see that the box was one of those Easter selections you could get in any drug store this time of year. The box was red, with the manufacturer's logo on the front along with a photo of the yummy stuff inside—chocolate covered cherries, liquid center. Someone had wound a thin red ribbon diagonally around the corners and tied the ends with a simple bow. On another corner of the box, in black ink and small, fancy calligraphy, was written, "For Marcella, Happy Easter."

The "Marcella" proved it wasn't from somebody close, which relieved my mind considerably. To Miss Maggie, I said, "Um, what exactly are we looking for?"

"Go read what's on the laptop screen, Pat."

Curious, I went over to the counter, scooping up my nearly full tea mug en route so I could reheat it in the microwave. I also plugged Cella's phone into its charger, then turned my attention to the laptop, which was in sleep mode. The screen was black. I hit one of the arrow keys and a page titled "Phosphorus Poisoning" faded in.

I read the title aloud, not liking the ominous way it sounded in that depressing little kitchen, hoping somehow Miss Maggie would say I was supposed to be reading a web page on chocolates and this was the result of a computer virus.

Miss Maggie retrieved two spoons from the drawer. "I got to thinking about that vision you had, about the lighted match. Back when I was a kid, the newspapers were full of warnings not to let babies suck on match heads because they were made of poisonous white phosphorus. Look at the symptoms, Pat."

I read them aloud. " 'Nausea, diarrhea, vomiting, heart irregularities'—*Madonne!* This says the breath and excretions have a garlic odor!"

"Bingo. *That*'s what your ghost was trying to tell you."

I couldn't get my brain around it. "The cat wanted me to know that the match Uncle Rocco lit was poisonous?"

She shook her head. "By that time, white phosphorus matches weren't being made anymore. They used red phosphorus instead. But that web site says that the friction from striking a match heats up the red phosphorus, which turns it into white phosphorus."

I turned away from the laptop to see if she was serious. Her wrinkled face showed obvious worry. "You think a cat who lived next door to Uncle Rocco during the Depression came back from the dead to let me know my uncle was poisoned with phosphorus last week? Not only that, it chose vague symbolism for a chemical concept that I couldn't possibly know about? Even if I thought cats become chemists when they die, Miss Maggie—"

"I know, I know, it's not a great theory. But maybe the cat is warning you that your family's still in danger." She punctuated the thought by jabbing an arthritic finger toward the chocolate box.

"You think those chocolates have phosphorus in them?"

"Cella's received two anonymous boxes of candy since your Uncle died, correct? If this were an Agatha Christie novel, you'd be yelling at the characters not to eat any." Miss Maggie tried to push the ribbon off the box with her spoons and failed. "Oh, pshaw. Here, Pat, push off the ribbon and open the lid. Your fingerprints are already on the box anyway."

"Along with Cella's, Ron's, and everyone who touched it at the factory, distributor's and store."

"That's where you're wrong. At the store and distributor's, at least, this would have been shrink-wrapped."

Miss Maggie was right, of course. I'd never seen this manufacturer's boxes in the stores without shrink wrap. The fact sent a chill down my spine. After I removed the lid, she lifted one of the chocolate cherries out using both spoons, then flipped it over onto the table.

My imagination had already conjured a neat hypodermic needle hole in the bottom, dramatically oozing with deadly venom. But no, the bottom of the candy was unbroken and perfectly smooth.

"Oh." Miss Maggie squeezed all of her disappointment into one syllable. Using her spoons, she flipped over the rest of the chocolates. Same result.

"Oh, sugar," she said. "I was so positive."

I took a closer look, my nose a mere two inches away from one of the little goodies. "I could swear the chocolate on the bottom is slightly lighter than the chocolate on the sides." I told Miss Maggie about the time Cella and I had helped our cousin Isabella throw a baby shower for her sister Nicola. We got a container of microwave chocolate for dipping strawberries, the kind of chocolate that hardens after, so it isn't as messy. "Wouldn't be hard to patch evidence of tampering with something like that, Miss Maggie."

"Hand me a knife, Pat. Or better yet, I saw a screwdriver on the paint cans in the next room. Nobody'll be using that on food later."

I retrieved the tool from the dining room, placing it into her palm handle first, feeling like an OR nurse as I watched her dissect one of the candies. The screwdriver wasn't the neatest instrument for the purpose, but it worked. Inside with the liquid and cherry was a chocolate blob, small as a baby pea.

Miss Maggie carefully scooped the nugget out with the screwdriver. "Pat, put a napkin here on the table." When I obeyed, she smashed the morsel onto it. "Turn out the top light. Leave the range hood on."

I did as she asked. In the darkened kitchen, bits of the streak glowed.

"Ingenious," Miss Maggie said. "According to that website, phosphorus can be stabilized by storing it in oil. Looks like our killer used chocolate instead, the same stuff he patched the bottoms of the candies with afterward."

"Could that drop kill a person?"

"Only took two match heads to kill a baby. If this is a purer form, well, probably a tiny amount is lethal. Your cousin might have eaten several without noticing an unusual taste. She might have even swallowed these bits whole."

I sat down at the table, stunned. "Someone's trying to kill Cella."

Miss Maggie crossed to the switch to turn the lights back on. "Time to call the police, Pat."

I agreed, even though Norristown's Finest were bound to have questions I couldn't answer. Telling them about the cat was out. I went back to the counter and reached for Cella's phone, then punched in Aunt Florence's number. She was also bound to have questions I couldn't answer, but I didn't intend to tell her about the chocolate box.

I was lucky, though. My cousin Paulina answered. "Pat! Good seeing you last night."

I got past the preliminaries—yes, it was nice to be back in town, yes, I was excited to be engaged, and no, I didn't need to talk to her mother. "Actually, I wanted your brother Ant'ny's phone number." His name was Anthony, but our family always dropped the "ho" from the middle.

"Ant'ny?" Her tone implied that nobody ought to want to intentionally get in touch with Ant'ny, that maybe bumping into him in the supermarket might be nice, but call? You weren't serious, right? Unlike the rest of our nosy family, her brother tended to stay to himself. Why would anyone seek him out?

"I've got a question for him," I said, "about when to pick *cadunas*." That's how we Montellas pronounce the weed called cardoon that our family considers a delicacy. "I found a patch of them growing at Bell Run." In truth, Beth Ann said she knew where they were and hadn't actually shown me yet (fear of me making her eat vegetables), but Paulina didn't need the details. "Didn't Uncle Dom used to bring them around in March or April?"

"End of March he brought us *dente di leones*. You know, dandelions. You pick the greens before they flower. I think *cadunas* were after. Ant'ny always forgets and picks them too late. Last year he brought them in June and they were tough."

"Well, let me have his number anyway. Maybe if I remind him tonight, you'll get nice tender ones this year." I was right. That was all the incentive Paulina needed.

"He's probably still at work," she cautioned after giving me his home number. "That's why he didn't come to the viewing or the funeral. I tell him he likes his dog better than us."

I asked if he was still with Plymouth Township and she said yes. Ant'ny was a police K-9 officer. If he was at work, so much the better. When I got off the phone with Paulina, I looked up the number for Plymouth Police on the laptop and called there first. Yes, Officer Grandinaria was in, I was told, and when he picked up, I could hear dogs barking in the background.

"Ant'ny?" I raised my voice to be heard over the yapping. "This is your cousin Pat . . . Pat Montella . . . Yeah, Tricia. Listen, I need some advice from a policeman. Just don't tell me I'm nuts 'til you hear me out, okay?"

"He said he's coming over to see for himself," I told Miss Maggie as I rehooked Cella's phone to the charger.

In the version of the story I told Ant'ny, I was snitching one of Cella's chocolates and thought it didn't look right. Miss Maggie and I cut it open, spied the glowing innards and did a cyber-search for phosphorus (that being the only substance either of us knew of that glowed in the dark). On reading the symptoms of poisoning, we remembered one of Uncle Rocco's cronies saying she'd smelled garlic after he started barfing.

"Nothing we can do but sit and wait," Miss Maggie said.

I noted the bag of pretzels still open on the table and recalled that my tea was still in the microwave. Knowing poison was in the room, I'd lost all appetite and thirst. "Let's go sit on the steps in the front hall, Miss Maggie. We'll be able to hear the door better."

"First I want you to tell me your latest vision. When I came back down the stairs, this door was open and you were outside. You saw something else from 1933, didn't you?"

I explained about Delphina and Bambola sneaking a peek through the window into Uncle Rocco's basement apartment. "He had a child's coffin, Miss Maggie. Does that mean Uncle Rocco had something to do with the grave robbery?" The thought of poison aimed at my favorite cousin had made my appetite disappear, but the image of my great-uncle carrying the coffins of children out of a grave in the middle of the night thoroughly sickened me.

Miss Maggie looked pensive. "In a way, I suppose. But what I think is—"

The laptop chimed, directing my attention to the screen where an instant message had popped up. The sender was "AngelTrumpet" and the note read simply, "I WON!!!!"

"She won," I said aloud. "Beth Ann won!"

Miss Maggie beamed. "Well, don't just sit there, Pat. Answer her."

I clicked on the IM box, typed "CONGRATULATIONS!!! from both me and Miss Maggie" and hit enter.

AngelTrumpet: "got a TROPHY with a spaceship on it. soooo cool."

Me (resisting the urge to scream about using capitals): "What was your project?"

AngelTrumpet: "had to do with the side of a plant facing the sun versus the side that doesn't. can't explain here. i'll tell you saturday, okay?"

Me (hesitating a sec, but needing to know): "Are you okay with going to visit your mom's parents tomorrow?"

Her pause was long enough that I knew the answer was complicated. She finally replied with "should be fun. gotta go. homework to finish then bedtime." The connection vanished.

Clicking open the email screen, I dashed off a quick note to Beth Ann. "Since you'll be off email tomorrow night, you and your dad can reach me on my cousin's cell." I reached for Cella's phone again, flipping it open and hitting the menu to get the number, which I typed in. I congratulated Beth Ann once more, signed off and hit send, feeling unsatisfied and helpless.

Not wanting to worry Miss Maggie with problems neither of us could do anything about for the moment, all I said was, "Beth Ann had to go do her homework."

The way Miss Maggie nodded gave me the impression that not only could she read perfectly well between the lines of my sentence, but that maybe she'd telepathically read my instant messaging and email, too. I bet that nod came in handy back when she had to listen to the excuses of eighth-graders.

I changed the subject quickly. "You were about to tell me what you thought of Uncle Rocco and the coffin."

She smiled to let me know she recognized the diversion, but said only, "Come on, out to the front hall. But I'll tell you this—I'm certain that coffin was never used to bury an orphan."

19

No sooner had we crossed the threshold into the front hall than someone knocked at the door. Unlike Aunt Sophie's house that had front windows, here you couldn't spy on who was on the stoop. If Cella was going to live in this neighborhood, she needed to install a peephole or intercom or something.

I took the chance, hoping I'd find Ant'ny on the other side. My cousin was there, decked out in an unbuttoned police parka and winter hat, and he'd brought a furry, four-legged friend on a short leash. The dog was a German shepherd with a puppy-like expression in his eyes and a badge on his collar.

"Tricia, how you doin'?" Ant'ny said, sounding, as usual, very Rocky Balboa-ish. This cousin was younger than I was, in his early thirties. I hadn't seen him in ages. I swear he'd grown, though he was always a big guy to begin with. He had one of those distinctive pear-shaped heads, all jowls, along with a single Neanderthal eyebrow.

"Hope you don't mind me bringing Nero in. Too cold to leave him in the car." He gave the impression, though, that he and the canine were inseparable. Addressing the dog, my cousin said, "Nero" followed by a word I didn't recognize, that sounded like *k'NOza.* Nero stepped up into the vestibule with Ant'ny right behind him. They squeezed past me and I closed the door.

"Nero, *SEDnyi*," my cousin said, and the dog sat. Ant'ny scratched him behind the ears. "*HodeNAY*."

Miss Maggie raised an eyebrow. "If I'm not mistaken, you're speaking Czech."

Ant'ny was impressed. I was, too, despite having observed in the last year Miss Maggie's ability to understand words in a variety of languages.

"We get a lot of our dogs from Germany and the Czech Republic," Ant'ny explained. "They have the best breeds for police work. Nero here also got his early training in his homeland. Easier for me to learn a few words of Czech than for him to learn a whole new set of commands."

I introduced Miss Maggie, adding her place in the scheme of my life. As I suspected, Ant'ny was out of the loop enough that he didn't know I'd been living in Virginia the last year.

Ant'ny took off his hat, more because he was getting warm, I think, than from manners. "You're in Virginia, and Cella's living here now? Since when?"

"She's not living here full time yet," I replied. "Still fixing the place up. She's mostly living at her mom's. So are her kids. You know she and Ronny are separated, don't you?"

"No way! Not Ronny and Cella." Lowering his voice as if maybe he'd committed a *faux pas*, he said, "Is Cella upstairs?"

"No, she's not here."

Ant'ny looked at Nero quizzically. I realized the dog had been gazing intently up the stairs, his ears forward and alert, nose dilating to catch any subtle scents. As I watched, Nero's eyes seemed to follow an invisible something down the stairs and over toward me.

Feeling the sudden urge to get out of that room, I headed for the kitchen, motioning everyone to follow, explaining on my way about Cella taking Aunt Sophie to County Hospital because Beatrice's husband took sick tonight. "That's the other thing, Ant'ny. We think Ozzie might have been poisoned, too. Aunt Sophie said that Beatrice mentioned garlic, same as Uncle Rocco."

"You don't know for sure that Uncle Rocco was poisoned," Ant'ny pointed out.

"Well, no, not for sure, but look at what we found." We reached the kitchen and I did a Vanna White at the chocolate smeared on the napkin. Miss Maggie flipped off the top light and the glow was evident.

Ant'ny frowned. "Turn the light on again." He commanded the dog to lie down by the doorway (or at least, I assume that was the command since that's what Nero did), and unhooked his leash. Normally, I'd have been a bit nervous, having a large police dog loose within lunging distance, but then my cousin pulled a dingy yellow chew-toy shaped like a pretzel from his pocket. Nero took the toy like it was a long lost treasure, happily thumping his tail on the linoleum as he worked his big teeth over the rubber. He looked like a happy, well-trained puppy. The intimidation factor was lost. Ant'ny repeated the word "Hodenay," which seemed to be some sort of praise, because more ear scratching went with it.

Then my cousin strode over to the table to examine our evidence, moving his nose to within an inch of the chocolate, sniffing, making me wonder if he'd been hanging around canines too long. Next, he turned his attention to the writing on the box lid, careful not to touch anything.

"Show him the web page, Pat," Miss Maggie suggested.

I did. Ant'ny skimmed over the words, then turned back to the candy, rubbing his chin in seeming indecision. "You said on the phone that Cella got another of these boxes."

I nodded. "Tuesday. Aunt Lydia said she was going to put it in her freezer." My stomach turned, hoping neither of Cella's girls, not to mention my aunt and uncle, got the urge to sample those goodies tonight.

"That one was also anonymous?"

"That's what Aunt Sophie said."

He pondered a moment longer, then said, "Here's the deal. *That*," he gestured toward the smear, "definitely looks suspicious, especially with no card or anything to say who sent it. I'm going to call Norristown Police to come get it so they can have it tested. I'll also suggest that they contact County Hospital and tell Ozzie's doctors to check for phosphorus, and that they should retrieve the other box from Aunt Lydia's."

"She'll freak if a policeman shows up at her door, let alone this time of night," I pointed out.

Ant'ny agreed, not so out of the family loop that he'd forgotten Aunt Lydia's idiosyncrasies. "I'll see if they'll let me tag along." Ant'ny made the call through the radio on his shoulder, sending a formal request through his own dispatch. While he talked, he turned his back to achieve pseudo-privacy the way folks do when they use cellphones in elevators.

While he straightened out the logistics, Miss Maggie silently beckoned me over to where she stood by the sink, whispering, "Watch the dog."

Nero still held his pretzel between his forepaws, but instead of chewing on it, he was staring at the open door to the back stairs. After a moment, he cocked his head to one side, as if not sure what he saw. Me? I didn't see anything, but I had to wonder if a certain cat held his attention.

"Look at the direction of his eyes," Miss Maggie murmured.

I saw what she meant. If you drew a straight line from the back of the dog's head out through his corneas and over to that door, the line would hit the door around knob high, not down close to the floor where Crisi would be. I imagined, say, a small table occupying the space in 1933, the feline on top of it, hissing down at the intruder.

Nero cocked his head the other way, letting go a befuddled whimper, which made Ant'ny turn around. The dog, seeing that he now had his master's eye, whimpered again, as if asking for permission to go inspect whatever was by the stairway door. Nero punctuated the question with a bark.

My cousin frowned again. "Nobody's upstairs?"

I assured him that we were the only ones in the house, which was true if, like Ant'ny, you were talking about live people. Miss Maggie backed me up, saying, "I just went up to the bathroom a little while ago."

"Did you go all the way up to the top floor?" he asked. Of course, neither of us had. He insisted on checking it out.

"Knock yourself out," I replied.

He told his dispatch the new development and asked us where the light switches were in each room.

I gave him the switch schematic for the second floor. "If it's light you want, better go up the front stairs."

Using the *k'noza* command again, which I was thinking might be "heel," Ant'ny pocketed Nero's slobbered-on toy and we all headed out to the hall. Ant'ny sent his dog up ahead of him. The canine immediately veered right, into the bedroom Miss Maggie and I were sharing, and began barking. To my ear, the sound wasn't growling or threatening. Curious, I'd call it, or maybe even, "Hey, guys, look what I found!" However one says that in dog-Czech.

By the time Ant'ny reached the top of the stairs, he had his handgun at the ready, pointed up toward the ceiling. With his free fingers, he reached around the corner, flicked on the overhead lamp, then followed Nero in. The theatrics made me wonder if we really did have an intruder, but a moment or two later, after Nero had stopped yapping, we heard Ant'ny say, "What the hell were you barking at?"

Since he was speaking English, I figured the question was rhetorical.

We saw Ant'ny and Nero cross the top of the landing, toward the front of the house, and heard them take the steps up to the third floor. In less than ten seconds, we heard them come down again. From there, they apparently checked the bathroom, closet and front parlor. Nero appeared again, recrossing the landing into our bedroom, nose to the floorboards.

Ant'ny was right behind him, firearm still up but now with less expectation. "We'll meet you back in the kitchen."

Miss Maggie and I retraced our steps, in time to find Nero and Ant'ny coming down the back stairs. The dog again had his pretzel in his mouth and, in place of his police special, my cousin's fingers now held a doll gingerly by the foot of one leg. To be precise, a handmade ragdoll, faded with age. She now wore a different shift-like dress knitted from blue yarn, dotted with moth holes, but I recognized her right off.

"Mrs. Roosevelt!" I exclaimed.

Ant'ny raised his face-wide eyebrow at my reaction. "This is yours?"

"Um . . . no . . . I—"

Miss Maggie broke in before I stammered out more than either of us could explain. "Where did you find her, Ant'ny?"

"On one of the beds in the middle room." My cousin's eyes narrowed. "Where the suitcases are." Deducing, correctly, that it must be the room where we were staying.

"Cella probably found Mrs. Roosevelt and left her on the bed for us to see." Miss Maggie said. "You see, Pat saw an old picture of the doll earlier and she was curious."

Ant'ny latched onto one word. "How old was the photo?"

"1930s. Hence the name 'Mrs. Roosevelt.' " Miss Maggie's tone implied that if she'd had my cousin in her classroom, he'd have made the connection at once.

Ant'ny scratched the back of his head. "Regardless, Nero took an interest in this doll. I'll need to open her up, to look for controlled substances."

"You can't!" The thought of tearing the doll open turned my stomach, as if my cousin had suggested an autopsy on a live baby. And I suspected that Nero's reaction wasn't to the doll itself, but to the ghost who'd left it. "She's an antique," I argued. "You'd destroy the value."

"Mind if I have a look at her?" Miss Maggie held out her hand with the manner of a teacher wanting to see a note being passed behind her back. Ant'ny was too well trained to give in. Not until

Miss Maggie added, "Fingerprints aren't an issue. All fabric. No smooth surfaces," did my cousin shrug and allow her to take the doll.

Miss Maggie gingerly rolled the dress up until we could see Mrs. Roosevelt's torso. "Pat, turn on the range hood light."

I did, and she shuffled over to inspect the seams under the brighter bulb. Ant'ny and I looked over each of her shoulders, while Nero settled down to chomp on his pretzel.

The doll had been fashioned from sturdy white cotton. "They used to make grain sacks from this type of cloth," Miss Maggie told us as she slowly turned the doll. "Either of you see any obvious repairs?"

The hand-stitching on the seams was tiny and even, and the thread was yellowed and soiled in the same places as the cloth. The face had black button eyes and nose, a hand-embroidered mouth, and brown yarn for hair, but I noticed that light orange stains overlapped the thread on both neck seams. I said as much.

Miss Maggie nodded. "Nothing in this doll that wasn't put there the day she was made. Here," she gave Mrs. Roosevelt back to Ant'ny, "let the dog sniff it again and see what happens."

My cousin crossed the room and hunkered down next to Nero, slipping the doll under the dog's nose. I held my breath, hoping the canine's canines wouldn't transfer from pretzel to cloth, but after two whiffs, Nero gazed up at his master as if wondering what was being asked of him.

Ant'ny stood up, bewildered. A banging on the front door, loud enough to be heard in the kitchen, brought him out of his thoughts. "That's Norristown. Nero, *COMinyeh*." He set the doll on the counter and strode off to answer, dog on his heels.

Miss Maggie grabbed Mrs. Roosevelt and shoved her at me. "Here. We'll need her later, I'm guessing."

I set her on the counter behind me, leaning against the wall, like she'd always been part of the decor, but back near the corner where she wasn't obvious.

For the better part of the next hour, we told two Norristown cops the same answers to the questions that Ant'ny had asked about the chocolates. In the end, they packaged up the candy and box, and even wrote down the phosphorus website URL. Before they left, they took Miss Maggie's and my fingerprints so they'd be able to eliminate them from those on the box.

The only glitch was when they wanted to know Ozzie's last

name and I couldn't for the life of me remember it. I had to call Aunt Lydia for the information.

"You're calling this time of night to ask that?" was her first response. "You're making me miss *FOX News*."

I apologized, but knew she'd appreciate a more germane broadcast. "Beatrice's husband is in the hospital."

"I know. My sister Sophie called an hour ago. Is she there? She hear anything yet?"

"Cella drove her out to the hospital. They haven't called yet." I hated to be the one to tell my aunt that her sister was getting an exclusive without her, but I fed her a tidbit to hold her over. "There's a chance Ozzie might have been poisoned, Aunt Lydia. That's why I need his last name. I can call the hospital and tell them."

She ignored all the words after "poisoned" and that one she repeated twice, loud enough for Ant'ny to hear four feet away. Rolling his eyes, he held his hand out for the phone, which I relinquished.

"Aunt Lydia, this is Ant'ny. . . . yes, your sister Florence's Ant'ny. . . . Right. . . . I'm coming out to your place tonight. I'll be there in about a half hour. . . . Yes, tonight. . . . I'll tell you all about it then, I promise, but I need Ozzie's name *now*." Something about the way he said "now" must have worked because a moment later he said goodbye, hit the "end" button on the phone and handed it back to me.

"The name's Zimmer," he told his cohorts. "Let's roll." He didn't give Mrs. Roosevelt a second look, either having forgotten her or maybe deciding she wasn't worth the trouble, since he was out of his jurisdiction and hadn't had a search warrant or permission from Cella.

I walked them to the door. Outside the Norristown patrol car was double-parked, still running, with all its lights going. Across the street I could see blinds up and curtains yanked back as neighbors watched and wondered. Next door, though, no sign of curiosity. Uncle Leo was likely in the sitting room, asleep in front of the TV.

No sooner did the combined police forces drive off than Cella pulled up. As she was parking in the empty spot in front of Uncle Leo's Olds that Ant'ny had vacated, I walked up to the passenger side so I could help Aunt Sophie out.

"What are you doing outside, Tricia?" my aunt asked. "And without a coat. Gonna catch your death."

"Long story," I replied. "Come inside and I'll fill you in." I had to at least tell Aunt Sophie everything Aunt Lydia knew or be scolded about it later.

"You come over my place. You and Cella. Miss Maggie, too. I'll make coffee."

"None for me," Cella said. "If I drink coffee now, I'll be in the bathroom all night. And I have to work tomorrow."

My cousin, I noted, looked exhausted. The day had been long and tiring enough, even without that scene with Ronny.

"This will only take a few minutes," I assured both of them, then, having a brainstorm, I added, "Besides, Aunt Sophie, I have something I want to show you."

Inside Cella's place, after my cousin shed her outer garments, I led everyone back to the kitchen. Miss Maggie was seated at the table, looking pensive. Aunt Sophie, though she refused to take off her coat, sat down and made herself comfy. Waving my cousin into the remaining chair, I asked how Ozzie was.

My aunt answered. "No good. They put him in Intensive Care. Beatrice went in with him, but they'd only let two people in and his brother was there, too, so we came home."

I didn't know Ozzie *had* a brother, but I let that go and got down to business, telling almost the same story I'd told Ant'ny. I didn't say I was snitching one of the candies this time because Cella knew I'd given up chocolate for Lent. Miss Maggie covered for me.

"I thought it was odd," my mentor said, "that Cella had received two anonymous boxes of chocolates this week. I had Pat open this one so we could inspect the goods. That's when we saw they'd been tampered with."

Things went downhill from there, with Aunt Sophie exclaiming, "Mother of God!" every few seconds as I went on with my tale. As for Cella, despite the distress evident on her face, she said disturbingly little, that is, until I mentioned summoning Ant'ny.

"What?! You let him bring his dog into my house? Are you nuts? I'll be up all night vacuuming dog hair."

I'd forgotten all about her allergies and hastened to apologize, then gave her the worse news, that Nero had been all over the house, especially up in the bedroom where her sleeping bag was still on the floor.

"Aw, Pat! Where'm I gonna sleep tonight?"

"You come sleep over my place, Marcella," Aunt Sophie said. "I got that room up on the third floor I keep nice for when the grandkids sleep over."

Miss Maggie eagerly supported the plan, which made me suspicious of her motives. "Pat and I will clean the whole house first thing tomorrow morning."

Cella, of course, only saw that a ninety-one-year-old woman was volunteering to do her work for her, which made her Italian guilt glands overflow. "No, that's okay. I can do it. I mean, I know you guys just got spooked—"

Ironic choice of words, I thought.

"—you know, what with somebody sending poisoned chocolates and all. I don't blame you for wanting Ant'ny to check out the house before he left." She stood. "I'll go get my toothbrush and stuff, Aunt Sophie."

I watched Cella retreat up the backstairs. My cousin was putting up a brave front, but the chocolate incident terrified her. Not that I could blame her. Yet something else was bugging her, too.

"Mother of God," Aunt Sophie murmured again. "I can't believe it. Who'd want to poison our family? You told all this to Lydia, right? Ant'ny is gonna get that other box?"

I assured my aunt that everything was under control (and hoped I was right). Then, to get her mind off the subject, I reached back onto the counter and brought out the doll. "Aunt Sophie, did you ever see this before?"

"Mrs. Roosevelt! Where'd you find her?"

"Actually, Ant'ny's dog found her." I placed the ragdoll into my aunt's outstretched hand.

Just like a little girl would, Aunt Sophie smoothed Mrs. Roosevelt's hair and dress as she smiled down on the button face. "What a coincidence, you of all people finding her."

I didn't try to correct my aunt again. If she said I found the doll, that's the way history would be written.

"And look how good she looks," Aunt Sophie continued. "Must have been put away someplace, nice and careful. Looks just like she does in that picture I have. You remember, Tricia."

"What picture?" I did a mental scan of the multitude of photo frames on Aunt Sophie's end tables and dining room buffet. No dice. They were all of her kids and grandkids. No dolls.

"In my album upstairs. Didn't I ever show you? Got a picture in there of my two brothers and the three youngest Trepanis, and your mother and her brother, all of 'em sitting on the steps out front."

Cella came back down the stairs toting a plastic grocery bag stuffed with clothes. "I'll come back over tomorrow morning to change and get my phone and—"

"Look at this, Marcella." My aunt held up Mrs. Roosevelt. "Look what Tricia found upstairs. Her mother's doll."

"My *mother's*?!" I exclaimed.

"Sure," Aunt Sophie said, nodding. "Didn't you know? I thought that's why you asked me. T'resa, when she was little, she took Mrs. Roosevelt everywhere with her."

"Why was her doll in my house?" Cella wanted to know.

Aunt Sophie shrugged. "I guess she left it here. Come to think of it, I don't remember T'resa carrying Mrs. Roosevelt around after her father came home. That's when she and Tutti went to live with him up the street over Ronca's bar. Tutti was what we called Sal when he was a kid. Otherwise he'd get mixed up with all the other Sals on the block."

"Wait." I sat down, dazed, trying to make sense of this new development. "She left it here? Are you saying my mother *lived* in this house?"

Aunt Sophie looked surprised. "I thought you knew. Didn't she tell you? During the Depression, your grandfather couldn't find a job around here and couldn't feed his kids. He left your mother and Tutti with his sister—"

"His sister?"

"Yeah, yeah. His sister Gina. She married the Trepani man and they lived next door."

"That's what you said the other day, Pat," Cella reminded me. "You said one of the Giamos married a Trepani."

"I never knew which one. Or maybe Mom told me when I was too young to understand."

"Mrs. Ranelli was your first cousin-once-removed," Cella deduced.

I asked Aunt Sophie one more question, because I had to know for sure. "Did my mother have a nickname back then?"

Aunt Sophie nodded. "Sure, sure. She looked so much like a little baby doll herself that we all called her Bambola."

After my aunt and Cella left, Miss Maggie and I closed up the house behind them, lowered the thermostat, then climbed the front stairs to go to bed. I carried Mrs. Roosevelt up with me. I couldn't seem to keep my eyes off her.

Miss Maggie had been quiet through the whole earth-shattering conversation, remaining mum as we each used the bathroom and got ready to sleep.

Once the light was out, to break the silence, I said, "Is it my mother who's doing the haunting, Miss Maggie?" I think I was actually trying on the theory to see if I believed it.

"What do you think, Pat?"

I did some mental fact-sorting. "It would explain why, every time I've tried to make contact, the ghost—" No, I didn't like thinking of my mom as a ghost. "—the *spirit* seems to be so close to me. Physically close, I mean. But it—*she*—seems reluctant to tell me anything. My mom was like that. She never talked about herself, about her childhood or anything. Her whole life was always about me and my dad. I thought maybe my brother's death made her that way. You know, made her more guarded about herself."

"Bound to, if you ask me."

"Okay, if it *is* her," I mused, "what's up with the cat?"

Miss Maggie chuckled in the darkness. "I guess if I were going to come back and haunt someone I loved, I'd try not to be too scary about it. Sending a non-threatening messenger on ahead seems like a good idea."

Made sense. Ma would know I'd freak out if she simply popped out of nowhere. In our family, even a hint of the eerie stuff like that and you start lighting votive candles and spritzing holy water around. But send a cute, furry kitty to smooth the way . . .

I rolled on my side, staring out toward the hall, toward the light coming in through the doorway, as if trying to illuminate the dark corners of my brain. "I thought she was at rest, Miss Maggie. She died a little over two years ago. I've been out to visit the grave dozens of times since. I came to Aunt Sophie's house nearly every week until I moved to Virginia. Yet I never saw that cat before. Why would she come back now?"

"Your family's in danger, Pat."

"You think that's it?"

"I do. I'd do the same for my son. And you'd do the same for Hugh and Beth Ann, wouldn't you?"

The radiator across the room, cooling down for the night,

clanked twice, startling me. I let Miss Maggie's words sink in. If true, why hadn't Ma shown up last spring or summer when I was in danger in Virginia? Here, the danger was more to Cella, wasn't it? Then again, if not for my Lenten fast, maybe I *would* have been tempted by those chocolates tonight. Ma would have understood that weakness of mine better than anyone.

"But why would she come back as a tot?" I mused aloud. "Why show me her earliest memories, like the cat? Because this is the house where she was living at the time?"

Miss Maggie's even breathing could be heard from the other bed. She'd already dozed off.

Closing my eyes, I pulled Mrs. Roosevelt closer under the covers, expecting her to smell of dust, or worse. She didn't. Instead, I caught phantom whiffs of tomato sauce, Thanksgiving turkeys, anise pizzelles baking. All the comforting aromas of my childhood. Memory scents.

Then I dozed off, too.

"I think this would be a good time for beer."
—FRANKLIN DELANO ROOSEVELT, MARCH 1933

March 2, 1933 – Rocco's apartment

"You gonna let me come in, Vito?" Del pushed herself to her feet. "Or do I tell the whole neighborhood what I just saw on Rocco's table?"

"Aw geez!" he repeated, seeming frozen to the spot. Del took my hand and marched us up the steps, leaving the blanket where it was. She squeezed past her brother to get inside, pulling me after her.

We were in a dim hallway. That's what that house was like before Rocco bought it later and opened it up. Running the length of the house was this hall, lit only by a single Edison bulb high up on the wall in the middle, next to a square stairway leading up and down to the apartments.

Del led me down the steps to Rocco's apartment door at the bottom, which Vito had left open a crack. She pushed it open and walked right in.

Like our cellar, you entered this one in the middle. Rocco had put old rugs down over the dirt floor. The front of the cellar was blocked by a curtain. That, I later found out, was where Rocco had his bed. Toward the back of the cellar was a kitchen, if you could call it that. The table we saw from outside was under the window. In one corner, on a bureau with drawers, was a basin with a big metal water ewer, the only sink. Beside the basin was an open tin can, the dregs of pea soup obvious around the lip. The smell of that soup still hung in the air along with the aroma of slightly burnt coffee, and the burning oil in Rocco's lamp. He didn't have electricity in his cellar.

When we went in—with Vito following close behind us—Pip was standing to our right, his shadow huge on the front curtain behind him. Rocco was sitting at the table, looking like he'd been there all along, dressed as usual in his work clothes with his hair slicked back. The coffin was gone, but Del didn't mention that because something else got her attention. Next to the door was a small, black stove, cold and empty.

"That's not your stove," Del said to Rocco.

"I wish you were right," he replied. "Man who sold it to me yesterday didn't mention that I wouldn't be able to get it to work right."

"Did you get rid of your other stove?" She pointed to the stovepipe, hanging disconnected from the back wall, the inside end stuffed with rags to keep out the draft.

"You don't see it, do you?" Rocco smiled, the same smile he used when he was playing cards and wanted you to think he had a handful of trump.

"Was this little one the one you were using yesterday when it got so hot in our cellar? I felt the heat clear through that wall. I don't see how, since there oughta be maybe four or five feet of bricks and dirt between. But it was hot enough to break a ketchup bottle on our side."

"I told them I brought you pine knots," Pip said. "That's why it got so hot."

Rocco nodded. "Pretty warm in here, wasn't it, Vito?"

"Sure. Like July," Vito said. "Come on, Delphina. Time for you to go home."

Before he could lay a hand on her, though, from somewhere behind the front curtain came a bloodcurdling yowl.

"Crisi!" Del cried. Pip turned toward the sound and Del, seeing her chance, ran right at him, going down into a headfirst slide at the last moment, right past his feet. That's how she always stole bases, headfirst. When she played ball in Jock's yard, she had to do it careful, though, 'cause second base was the streetlamp pole on Penn Street. She'd wrap one arm around the pole to stop herself.

Here she just kept going, her feet disappearing under the curtain before Pip could blink. All three men ran after her, yanking the curtain aside, shouting her name. I toddled after them, laughing when I saw that Del had slid all the way under Rocco's bed. Beds were higher up off the floor in those days and Del, being skinny and agile, could easily maneuver in the space beneath the double frame.

Pip and Rocco got down on their knees on either side and tried to reach her. Del stayed in the very middle so they couldn't get a good hold.

When I got down on my knees, too, Vito picked me up and sat me on his hip. "Don't go under there, Bambola. You don't want to get Mrs. Roosevelt all messy, do you?"

I shook my head. True, I would have gotten filthy, since no

rugs covered the floor under the bed or in front of it.

"Look what I found!" Del exclaimed. I'd seen enough in those few seconds I was on my knees to know what she meant. The coffin was underneath the bed.

"Delphina Mariana, you come out of there," Pip said. "I'm gonna tell Mama you were crawling around on the floor."

"No, you won't. Not unless you want me to tell her what I found, you won't. Hey, this isn't a real coffin at all. It's made of slats from Pop's fruit crates." All of a sudden we all heard glass rattling, then Del added, "And it's got bottles inside 'stead of bones."

Another one of Crisi's howls arose, this time seeming to come from the wall behind the bed. Instead of painted stone like the rest of the cellar, this wall had wooden panels. Strangely enough, one edge of the panel right behind the bed was sticking out an inch. I watched as it swung another inch, until the panel hit the wooden bedstead and couldn't open further.

"Crisi's stuck," Del said. "I can't get her out. Pull the bed away from the wall, will ya? Wait. Never mind, I can push it with my feet." The bed inched along the floor and the panel swung open another half foot.

"Aw geez," Vito mumbled as Crisi came out from under our side of the bed. Pip had to use both arms to push the cat away from his face.

"*Now* I can see Rocco's stove," we heard Del say. "Holy cow. Is *that* what a still looks like?"

All three guys said, "Shh!" at the same time and Vito, still carrying me, hurried across the room to make sure he'd closed the door. By the time we got back to the bed, Rocco and Pip had pulled it out farther and Del, covered with dirt from head to foot, stood up beside the open panel, gazing into a small secret room dug between the foundations of our two houses. The light of the oil lamp shone through the opening, glistening off two metal macaroni pots and lots of copper pipes.

"Here's how I got it figured," Del reasoned. "Yesterday, you three had both stoves going in this little secret room. That's why it got so warm on our side. But the second stove didn't work, or maybe it just got too hot or something. I don't know. Anyway, now you're just using the one to make your bootleg whiskey."

"It's not whiskey," Pip said.

Del swiped a hand across her dirty face, making it worse. "Gin, then."

Rocco shook his head. "Not gin, either. We're not making nothing. Look." He squeezed past Del into the room, ducking his head because the opening was low. He brought out one of the macaroni pots. "Just your Pop's wine. That's all."

"Yeah," Vito agreed. "Pop's wine. No law against that."

Del was skeptical. "If it's only wine, why are you hiding it in that room? And what are you doing with all those pipes? And if you've been stealing Pop's wine all along, he would have noticed and had a fit. No, you gotta be making some kinda liquor."

Her face lit up as she continued thinking. "Yeah, you took the rotten fruit from the store and made liquor from *that*, then you put bottles of it in these children's coffins you made, and you put them in Mr. Lowell's crypt, saying you're burying orphans. Only you're not. You've been burying liquor. Then I guess some rumrunner came and got it each time. Which explains why there were no orphan coffins in the vault yesterday except that last one you put in on Monday." Del nodded. "Yep, that's how you've been doing it. Am I right?"

"Now, Delphina," Rocco said, "you go around telling a story like that and you'll be getting your brothers in serious trouble. You don't want the cops coming around, do you?"

"Who said anything about the cops?" Del replied. "Do you guys make a lot of dough doing this?"

"Whaddya want? Money?" Rocco asked. "If I give you two bits, will you promise not to tell anybody?"

"A quarter? Holy cow!" But then Del seemed to reconsider. "How much more would you give me if I tell you a sure-fire way to get that coffin out to the cemetery tomorrow night?"

20

"Pat, wake up!"

Realizing that someone was shaking me, I opened my eyes. "GAH!" Understandable reaction. Back lit by the hall light, Cella's face was less than a foot from mine and covered from her nose down with a dust mask.

She sat back on her knees, looking up at me. "What? Did I scare you?"

Half-asleep, I glanced over at Miss Maggie's bed, which was empty, the covers thrown back.

Cella read my mind. "She's already next door having breakfast with Aunt Sophie."

I stretched my legs under the covers. "What time is it?"

"Eight-thirty."

The radiator was hissing softly, reinforcing the fact that it was morning. My brain woke up enough to realize my cousin was wearing her overalls and sweatshirt. "You aren't going to work?"

"You kidding? Somebody's trying to kill me. I'm staying here where it's safe. Except for dog hair, that is."

Conceding what seemed like a prudent idea, I hoped she had enough sick days and notes from Alphonse to cover this week.

"Speaking of that . . ." Cella swung her legs around in front of her, then bunched up her knees and wrapped her arms around them, a definite gesture of insecurity. Unusual for her. "You know how I told you the other night that I assumed Ronny left that first box of chocolates?"

I pushed myself up on my elbow so I could nod without the pillow getting in my way.

"Last night when I drove up, Ronny was up on the stoop with the box in his hands," Cella said. "Despite what he said, he could have been leaving them there himself."

"You think Ronny's trying to murder you?" That sounded ridiculous to me, but the estranged husband is always the prime suspect, right?

Cella was frowning, uncertain, under her mask. I couldn't see her mouth, but I could tell. Her eyes showed pure misery. "I told him I absolutely won't divorce him."

"You did?" Some part of my sleepy brain wasn't getting this. In the months since her separation, my cousin had given everyone the impression that she'd thrown her hubby out, not the other way around. And from what I heard the other night, Ronny was the one stalking her, not vice versa.

She nodded. "I told him even if he moved far away and I never saw him again, I was gonna stay married to him. That gives him a motive, doesn't it?"

I rubbed my eyes with the palm of one hand. "Back up a sec. Why would Ronny have killed Uncle Rocco? I mean, same poison, right? So we're talking the same poisoner. Or why would he want to kill Ozzie? And remember, nobody saw Ronny at Evergreen Manor last Saturday."

"That's not entirely true." She paused, either for dramatic effect or to let me react. I waited her out, until she added, "*I* saw him there. When I pulled into the parking lot, my cell rang. It was Joan, wanting to know if she could go to the movies with her friends. That was a no-brainer. She didn't have her English paper done and it was due Monday, and she'd handed in her *last* paper late. But she haggled with me, maybe five minutes, I don't know. When I finally got out of my car, I saw Ronny's truck. I figured he must have followed me into the lot. Thing is though, he could have been there already. Uncle Rocco didn't mention seeing him, but—"

"You sure it was Ronny? Not some other delivery van?"

Cella rolled her eyes. "He pulled into the space behind me, Pat. I stopped to talk to him. He asked if I wanted to get some coffee. He wanted an update on the girls. Could I say no? He's their father."

"Ah. Which explains why you didn't hang around visiting Uncle Rocco longer. You had a date."

The skin I could see around Cella's mask turned crimson, but she didn't deny my deductions.

"Why didn't Ronny go inside with you?" I asked.

My cousin shrugged. "Said he was expecting a call."

"He was still there when you came out?"

Cella nodded.

"So you went out for coffee with him?"

"Um . . . no."

"You had a fight instead?"

"Not . . . not exactly." Cella shifted positions to stretch her knees out. She looked down at her legs, not at me. "We started talking about where we should go, but . . . well . . . in the middle of it, I just . . . kissed him. I mean, there he was, you know? And it had been so long . . . so . . ."

"You kissed him," I prompted. "Did he kiss you back?"

"Ohyeah." One word. All she needed, really, but Cella, trying to rationalize, kept connecting the dots for me. "See, there we were. End of the day. I knew his van would be nearly empty, and . . . and it had been so long . . ."

"You had sex in his van?" I was beyond simple prompting. I was imagining what cold metal felt like on a late February evening.

"We tried. Or at least, *I* tried. For the gazillionth time in the last two years."

Prompts deserted me this time. I just let my mouth gape open. Cella, unable to judge my reaction from listening to me, stole a peek in my direction, so my gesture wasn't lost.

"Ronny can't," she said simply.

"And hasn't been able to for two years?" Back to prompting.

"Not with me, anyway." Cella bunched her knees up again, as much as she could, given her Montella thighs. "He keeps swearing there's been nobody else, but I'm starting to wonder."

"What about that girl from the Acme?"

Cella wagged her head back and forth. "We made her up. I mean, we had to tell our families something about why we were splitting. Another woman they could understand. And that way, Ronny kept his pride. You know how Italian stallions are."

"He'd rather be called a *porcellóne* behind his back? What about *your* pride?"

The way she shrugged, I had an epiphany. My cousin was an Italian mare. Some part of her believed that her own sexual skills should have been able to fix the situation. Easier for her to let the rest of us think that another woman was to blame instead of herself.

I switched to a different track. "Okay. Ronny has ED. What about all the drugs they have these days?"

"He tried them all," Cella said glumly. "Minimal success. At first we were thinking, hey, he spends every day lifting heavy boxes. A few years ago, he even had a hernia operation. Oh, he was fine afterward," she blushed again, "you know what I mean. We thought maybe this was from another injury. But every doctor he went to ran the same tests. No apparent injury, no disease. One doctor even told him flat out it was psychological. Not that it matters. Ronny's health plan won't pay for treatment of sexual dysfunction without proof of disease or injury. We're talking thousands and thousands of dollars, Pat. *Tens* of thousands if they have to do surgery. And we've still got eighteen years on our mortgage, one car to pay off, and our home improvement loan from three years ago. We put money in the kids' college funds, but that's off-limits."

My cousin, the budgeting wizard, had met her match in the health care system.

"That's why Ronny wanted to sell this house right off when I got it," Cella continued. "I said, 'Don't be a *stupido.* We'll sell the house with the mortgage.' More marketable anyway, and we could let out the store downstairs here as an investment. But no, Ronny gotta have his big house in the 'burbs."

So, I thought, the crux of their breakup wasn't sex, or lack of it, but the old story, money. Then again, sexual dysfunction was also doing a job on both their self-esteems. I steered Cella back to her original concern. "Do you think Ronny had anything to do with those chocolates? Or with Uncle Rocco's death?"

Cella shrugged. "I can't picture it. That's *so* not like him. Poison, I mean. He'd have to plan it out. I'm the planner in the family, not him. But I could see him maybe asking Uncle Rocco for a loan. Which might explain why Beatrice can't find her grandpop's money."

"You're saying Uncle Rocco gave all his bucks to Ronny?"

Her head wagged back and forth again, like she was trying to clear the confusion out. "I still think Uncle Rocco invested in something, a piece of art, whatever. Ronny asks for a loan. Uncle Rocco gives him the artwork, trusting Ronny to go pawn it, then bring back the excess cash."

"And Ronny kills Uncle Rocco so he can keep all the funds?"

Cella visibly winced at the suggestion. "Okay, maybe somebody else actually killed Uncle Rocco—they *must* have—but Ronny kept the money."

"Then tried twice to poison you with your favorite food?"

"Oh, I don't know!" Cella moaned in frustration as she put her hands on either side of her head and squeezed. When this had no medicinal effect, she pushed herself to her feet. "Come on, let's eat. I can't think on an empty stomach. I swiped some of the bagels and cream cheese left at Aunt Sophie's yesterday. They're downstairs."

That signaled the end of our tête-à-tête. I sat up in bed to stretch. My left arm was still hugging Mrs. Roosevelt.

"You slept with that doll?" Cella asked. "Wasn't she dusty?"

I shook my head. "She's in surprisingly good shape for an old doll. Like she'd been carefully packed away all these years." And that's what Ma would have done, I thought.

"Where'd the dog find her? I could have sworn I searched every nook and cranny of this house, and I never saw her before."

"Let me get washed and dressed, then I'll not only tell you where Nero found her, but some other surprising revelations about your house." I'd decided to let my cousin in on what Ma had shown me so far. Gently. She'd freak if I just flat out told her the house was haunted. But I thought I might need Cella's help later on if I wanted to tune in on the next installment.

The kitchen smelled of Lysol. Cella was at the table, already noshing a poppy seed bagel with strawberry cream cheese, her dust mask hanging down around her neck, proclaiming this a dog-hair-free zone.

I sat Mrs. Roosevelt at the back of the table, next to the little TV, to keep her clean.

"You gonna carry that doll around with you?" Cella asked. "If you are, that's weird."

"You have no idea *how* weird," was all I said as I picked up the plastic bag of bagels. Three were left—raisin, whole wheat, and one with everything. I chose the raisin, which reeked of garlic and onions from the everything one, and had flecks of poppy seeds that had strayed off of Cella's. All three bagels were cold. Aunt Sophie always puts leftover bread in her fridge right away, even in winter.

"Wrap it in a damp paper towel and nuke it for ten seconds. Be good as new." Cella can't cook, but she knows as many household hints as Heloise.

I was folding a moist towel around the bagel when we heard the front door. Miss Maggie called, "Only me!" She'd apparently taken Cella's spare key from my coat pocket. A minute later, she shuffled into the kitchen bearing a photograph in one hand and a large mid-twentieth century vintage Thermos in the other. "Your aunt sent over some fresh, hot coffee."

"Bless her," I murmured with feeling and retrieved mugs from the cabinet.

When I set my load of cups on the table, Miss Maggie handed me the photo. "Sophie said to show you this."

Here was the snapshot my aunt had mentioned the night before. Seven kids on the two steps out front: my dad and Uncle Sal (about the same age they were in their Confirmation photo), Uncle Mario, Delphina Trepani and, in the back, two teenaged boys who I assumed were two of her brothers (also my cousins, I reminded myself). On the bottom step was a little girl dressed in a too-big, hand-me-down sweater that nearly covered her knee-length skirt, and wool socks that seemed to reach all the way up her legs. She was the only one in the photo not smiling, instead wearing an expression of intense and blatant curiosity. Mrs. Roosevelt was on her lap and with one hand, the girl clutched the doll's stubby right arm, as if making her wave to the camera.

I knew what Miss Maggie was waiting for, so I said, "Yeah, that's her," confirming that this was Bambola from my visions.

Cella, of course, didn't realize that. She stood to look over my shoulder, saying, "That your mom? Man, she was a cutie."

She was indeed. I could see where she got her nickname. This was the earliest snapshot I'd ever seen of Ma. Now that I studied it, I could see my mom's eyes looking out of that small child. Oh, the wisdom wasn't there yet, and these orbs candidly admitted not knowing much. But they'd already felt hurt, I could see that. They'd already lost one parent and were afraid the other might never come back. Wow.

Miss Maggie, I noticed, was studying my face as closely as I was studying Ma's. She wanted to know if I'd found out any more.

Cella had turned back to the table, where she was pouring coffee for herself.

I addressed my comments to my cousin. "What if I told you that the pipe holding your chimney flue open in the parlor upstairs was never connected to your furnace? What if I told you that pipe used to go down to your cellar, through your foundation wall, and into a secret room dug underneath the tunnel between this house and Uncle Rocco's? Not only that, but during the Depression, it was the chimney pipe for a still."

"I knew it!" Miss Maggie exclaimed, her eyes dancing. "Back

then, a pipe going through a wall and hidden in the back of a fireplace was bound to have a bootlegging still at the root! Why, my brother ran his stillpipe up to the roof through two closets." When I raised my brows, she added, "He's the brother who took after great-granddaddy Fletcher. Supposedly made the best corn whiskey in three counties, not that any of the rest of the family knew for sure. None of us drank."

"What are you two talking about?" Cella asked, sitting down again, sipping her coffee, as she looked from me to Miss Maggie and back again.

I explained. "In 1933, Uncle Rocco and the two older Trepani sons were apparently making some kind of liquor. One of Uncle Rocco's get-rich-quick schemes that he never told us about. I'm guessing the Trepanis's father knew, too. His name was Ennio." I remembered hearing that during my first vision. I now realized he was my great-Uncle Ennio. "Anyway, they used overripe fruit leftover from the store and Uncle Ennio's wine."

"Making brandy," Miss Maggie deduced. "Brandy was hard to get during Prohibition, 'less you knew somebody who'd sneak it across the border from Canada. But to be any good, brandy has to be aged. Otherwise it's just hooch."

I nodded. "That's what Uncle Rocco said. He said something like, 'If they want their money's worth, they won't touch it for at least three months.' I think, after Mr. Lowell died, they were going to make one more batch, but didn't have time to do it properly. The plan was to substitute watered-down wine, maybe mixed with some of the fruit juice, or even water, hoping no one would notice right away."

"Lowell?" Cella asked. "Lloyd Lowell?"

I then told everything I knew, for Miss Maggie's benefit as well as Cella's, all about how, once a month or so, Rocco and the Trepani brothers filled enough bottles with liquor to put into small coffins, which they'd bury in the Lowell's family vault. Presumably they were picked up by, as Del called them, rumrunners, who then paid Mr. Lowell and he paid Uncle Rocco, Vito and Pip. I surprised myself, actually, because I seemed to know even more than I'd witnessed in the visions. I figured that was my mom filling in the blanks for me, because as wild as my imagination was, I didn't think I knew enough about Depression history to elaborate on my own.

What I didn't mention was my sources. And naturally, that's

what my cousin wanted to know.

Cella had her bagel back in her hand, redistributing the cream cheese with her knife. "If you're right, Pat, you've solved a mystery that's three quarters of a century old, about the disappearance of those orphan coffins. Where'd *you* find all this out when nobody else could?"

I hesitated, but only a second. "What if I told you that Ant'ny's dog, Nero, found Mrs. Roosevelt up on one of the beds we've been using? Probably mine."

Cella frowned. "*I* didn't put it there."

"Neither did we," Miss Maggie said, grinning.

I nodded my agreement. "Bizarre as it sounds, I think my mom put it there. Her spirit, I mean."

Cella had been on the verge of taking a bite. Her jaw stayed open, the bagel unchomped. "Your mother's spirit? Haunting *my* house?" See, she had no trouble believing my mom was back from the grave. Only the location she questioned. That was her Italian upbringing at work.

Miss Maggie replied before I had a chance. "I don't think so. She's haunting *Pat*, specifically. The house only comes into it because this is where Pat's mother was living during the first week of March in 1933. Somehow the events of that week are related to the events of this week. When Pat learns what that connection is, her mother will rest in peace."

Cella seemed to view my learning ability with doubt, maybe remembering all the times she had to help me with algebra homework. "You still haven't mentioned how you found out about the still in the basement."

I knew all along she'd come back to that point, but was I ready with a convincing answer? "Um . . . I kind of . . . I saw it in a dream last night."

Cella's expression went from simple doubt to full-blown disbelief. No, beyond that. She grinned, figuring she was seeing through an elaborate joke.

Miss Maggie defended me. "She's not kidding, Cella. That's how Pat sees ghosts, or what I like to think of as segments of actual history. She sees events unfold either in sleeping or waking dreams. This past year at Bell Run, she's shown a real talent for it. Why, last May she described a battle of the Civil War in details she couldn't possibly have known on her own."

My cousin's mouth gaped again and her eyes widened. "*Madonne!* You used to do that when we were kids!"

"Do what?"

"When we'd play in Montgomery Cemetery," Cella said, "you'd tell me gruesome things about how some of the people died or—"

I laughed. "I made those things up to scare you. Only they never did. You loved morbid stuff. The grosser, the better."

"You *didn't* make everything up," my cousin argued. "I found out when I started going on cemetery tours. Remember how you told me that graverobbers took Donald Fetter's skull in 1902? You were right. And what you said about Elsie Bingleman dressing herself in her husband's best suit before she hung herself, because she didn't want to ruin her own clothes? Turns out she'd sent her entire wardrobe to her church that morning, with a note to distribute the garments to poor women from broken homes."

I laughed again, a self-conscious giggle this time. "I probably read about those incidents before I told you. Or somebody else told me first."

"That's what Pat always says as an excuse," Miss Maggie told Cella, like a teacher discussing a naughty child with a parent. "But it makes sense that she had episodes in the past. Only reason she realized her talent at Bell Run was because I could tell her the history was true on the spot."

Cella eyed me with new interest. "Ought to be a way you could make money doing this."

"Well, until I figure out how," I said, "don't tell the family, okay?"

"No way," she agreed. "Aunt Sophie would cart you off to the priest for an exorcism."

Miss Maggie reached for the Thermos. "So what shall we do now, Pat? What's the next step?"

"I need to go back to Montgomery Cemetery."

"We were gonna do that anyway tomorrow," Cella pointed out. "I guess we could go today instead. The kids'll be safe with Aunt Sophie."

"What kids? Yours?" Placing my bagel in the microwave, I hit the reheat button.

Cella nodded. "I told Ma to keep 'em home from school, so we can make sure they don't eat anything suspicious. My mom still wants to do her grocery shopping today. The world would stop turning if she couldn't pick up her order on Friday afternoon. So they're dropping the girls here after lunch."

This reminded me of the poisoner. "Any word about Ozzie?"

"Aunt Sophie called the hospital first thing," Cella replied, "but since she's not immediate family, they wouldn't answer questions. I called Ant'ny, too. He didn't know anything, either. Just said to be careful."

Meantime, we Montellas were hunkering down behind our walls here on Main Street, eating only meals prepared by our own hands, which was no big hardship because Aunt Sophie had a basement filled with canned and frozen foods, and she was a primo cook. No doubt we could survive a siege. Still, I was glad Hugh and Beth Ann would be stopping over in Baltimore 'til tomorrow.

The microwave beeped and I removed my breakfast. "Actually, I want to go to Montgomery Cemetery tonight. After dark."

Cella nearly spit out a mouthful of coffee. "What are you, nuts? Druggies and prostitutes hang out there at night. And cops looking for druggies and prostitutes. We'd probably get arrested. And even if we managed to avoid that, one of us is bound to break a leg tripping over a tombstone in the dark."

I shrugged. "The next phase of my mom's story happened at that cemetery on the night of March third. Or at least, I think it did." Funny, I thought, how so much of this ghost stuff ended up linked to my intuition. Still, my gut feelings, ghost-wise, had usually been right in the last year. "I'll go alone. Just let me borrow your car."

"What if I don't?"

"I'll borrow Uncle Leo's. Or I'll walk if I have to. I'll be all right. Ma came back this week because the family's in danger. She's not going to let anything happen to me. She's not a ghost, she's a . . . a guardian angel."

Cella and Miss Maggie both frowned at that theory. Truth to tell, all the logic-lobes of my gray matter were frowning, too. But I had to believe it. Why else would Ma be here?

Cella picked up her coffee mug again. "Let's worry about tonight when tonight comes." Translation: she intended to talk me out of it. "Meanwhile, I want a look at the basement wall downstairs. Maybe that secret room's still there."

She smiled then. Back in Indiana Jones mode.

21

I wanted to follow Cella downstairs, to keep her from demolishing, in her enthusiasm, any wall that might actually be holding up the house. I would have, except she dropped hints to remind me that I'd promised to clean up Nero's sheddings. Remembering our earlier conversation about Ronny, I wondered if she was just looking for time alone, to mull things over.

After breakfast, I returned to the bedroom to strip the beds of their quilts, bringing them and the sleeping bag over to Aunt Sophie's backyard to hang on her clotheslines for airing. All the snow was gone, the ground now squishy under my boots. The day was sunny and breezy, however, and that was all that was needed to dissipate dog hair.

Miss Maggie had volunteered to follow me through the rooms, vacuuming after I dusted and dry mopped. I carried Cella's Hoover upstairs, and crawled under the corner table to plug it in. We started in our bedroom, then did the back room before crossing the landing to do the hall and front parlor.

Meanwhile, I could hear the sound of hammering rising from below, gentle tapping at first, then more aggressive whacking. I revised my theory. She wasn't mulling things over, she was taking out her frustrations.

The front parlor was still cold, all the more so since Cella had lowered the thermostat to keep the furnace from going on as she worked beside it. Miss Maggie had added her sweater underneath her sweatshirt.

I walked over to the hearth, noting that the tarp my cousin had placed over this fireplace was, at least, keeping out the draft. I could hear her talking to herself two floors below as she worked, not the words, but the rise and fall of her tones. Feeling mischievous, I pushed the tarp aside and stuck the dry mop to the back of the fireplace, using the handle to bang on the pipe three times.

The hammering and talking stopped below. I pictured my

cousin thoroughly spooked, looking over her shoulder for the source of the ghostly rapping. Unable to resist, I steeled myself against the draft and crawled back to the pipe, cupping my hands against the icy cold iron.

"Marcella Napoli Emilio," I crooned as eerily as I could. "This is the Ghost of Giamos Past."

She replied with a rap on the pipe loud enough to make me jump, banging my head on the bricks. Then she yelled, "Hey, Pat! Can you hear me?"

Her voice was muffled but clear. Better than a lot of cellphone connections, in fact. Rubbing my noggin, I replied, "Yeah, I hear you."

"Come down and see what I found."

She sounded excited enough that I didn't need further goading. Miss Maggie had heard, too, and the two of us rushed downstairs as fast as my mentor's arthritic knees could manage, me holding back to stay even with her, afraid she'd try to hurry faster and stumble if I went ahead. At her age, her bones would shatter like light bulbs on impact.

As we descended the basement steps, I noticed that the cellar was brighter today, the morning sun streaming obliquely through the front window. Now I could see details around the workbench, like the old tools that hung from a peg board on the wall above. Leaning against the wall beside the oil tank was a sled like the Flexible Flyer I used to ride, reminding me of winter afternoons spent getting soaked to the skin on Elmwood Park's slopes, before they fenced in the ballfield and ruined the best sledding terrain.

"Oh," Miss Maggie sighed, half out of breath from our fairly quick descent, half disappointed. The source of the latter was the new hole in the wall behind the furnace. The breach was breast-high, Z-shaped, and only the size of two overlapping bricks.

"That's it?" I asked, having pictured something more on the lines of a secret stone door leading to a chamber of treasures.

Cella stood beside the hole, flashlight in hand, safety glasses over eyes, dust mask over mouth, and fine grey dust over her overalls.

"The cement was easy to chip off," she said, indicating the pile of shards on the floor below the hole. A hammer and old nicked chisel leaned against the wall to one side. "Nothing more than the standard pre-mixed stuff, with hairline fractures all over it, probably from being near the furnace. But before cementing over the top, somebody filled the hole with bricks and mortar, and made a darned good job of it. Took a lot of elbow grease just to push two bricks through. I didn't go further because, well . . . come here, I'll show you."

She stepped aside as we approached. "Stick your arm through the hole."

"No way." First of all, I didn't think the gap was big enough to accommodate my limb past the elbow. Second, I had no clue what was on the other side of the hole. My imagination conjured spiders and rats.

"*I* did it," Cella said.

"So?"

My cousin rolled her eyes like she used to when I'd refuse to go along with one of her weekly bad ideas in high school. "Okay, I'll *tell* you what I found. This brick patch is only two courses thick. The foundation wall is about double that. Behind the replacement bricks, I could feel something metallic. I'm afraid if it's loose and I hammer at these bricks again, I might knock whatever it is into the space behind. Then I'd have to make a hole big enough to get through and, this being a load-bearing foundation wall, and me having invested mucho-bucks into this house already—"

"Not an option," Miss Maggie said. "Shine that flashlight here again."

Cella flicked on her torch and panned it over the wall.

"The patch looks to be . . ." Miss Maggie held her hands apart, estimating width and height. " 'Bout two foot tall. Not quite as wide. Pat, how big was the pipe that went through the wall in your vision?"

"Same size as this one." I pointed to the other end, still dangling from the ceiling. I saw what she meant. "And the cat had just enough space to climb through beside it. And it was up near the ceiling. This hole wasn't here at all."

"So someone made it," Miss Maggie mused. "To put something inside? I wonder. What we need is a periscope."

Cella agreed. "Better yet, something like one of those surgical scope thingies, you know, that we could snake inside, then watch on my laptop. Alphonse should have been a gastroenterologist instead of a podiatrist."

"Too bad your cellphone doesn't take pictures," I said.

"Wouldn't be enough light anywa—" Cella froze. "I'm such a

dope." She ran for the stairs, climbing them two at a time.

Miss Maggie and I followed at our own pace. When we reached the dining room, we could hear Cella talking in the kitchen. She was on her cell, trying to convince her mom to put Joan on.

A moment later, Cella was saying, "Joan, bring your digital camera when you come today. . . . Because my camera's too big, that's why. . . . Too big for what I need it for. For Pete's sake, I'll show you when you get here, okay? And bring the cord so I can download the pictures onto my laptop. Oh, and maybe fresh batteries. Go check and see if you need them. . . . Yes, now, while I'm on the phone with you. . . . It's a portable phone, dearie, requiring only that you stand and walk with it."

Cella rolled her eyes again and, as an aside to me, added, "*Sure* you want to be a mother?"

While waiting for Joan and Janine to arrive, Cella and I finished the cleaning, leaving Miss Maggie in the kitchen with the laptop so she could answer the emails she'd received last night. Three of the missives were from her editor about her manuscript and could wait no longer.

Around eleven-thirty, when Cella and I were trying to decide if Ant'ny would have taken Nero all the way into the store, the pocket of her overalls started playing "That's Amore." Aunt Sophie was calling to say lunch was all planned. Aunt Lydia and Uncle Gaet were already on the way over with Cella's girls, and Cousin Angelo was bringing goodies from his pizzeria.

We washed up, fetched Miss Maggie, and headed next door, arriving a minute after Aunt Lydia's crew and three minutes before Angelo walked in. He carried two Sicilian pies, which are big, square pizzas with inch-thick crust. In most local incarnations, the crust around the edge was somewhere between toasted and downright jawbreaking, but Angelo had figured a way to keep it the consistency of good, chewy Italian bread. People regularly traveled from all over the Delaware Valley for my cousin's version. Our family never got extra toppings. Angelo's pizzas didn't need them.

Angelo set the boxes up on the counter beside a stack of paper plates, and we all paraded past, helping ourselves while the pies were hot and the mozzarella gooey. Then we squeezed in around the kitchen table, already set with glasses of ice, a pitcher of water, and a bowl of salad that my aunt had tossed for those minding their LDL cholesterol (everyone in the older generation and Angelo who, at forty-eight, already had high blood pressure). Cella, her kids and I perched at the table's corners on chairs carried in from the dining room.

While Aunt Sophie was still fussing—making sure everyone had what they wanted, asking who wanted soda instead of water—Cella leaned across Uncle Leo to ask Joan if she'd brought the camera.

Joan reached inside her V-necked pullover and brought forth a school lanyard with a tiny camera fastened to it. "I don't see why you couldn't use yours."

Aunt Lydia sided with her grandchild. "Joan needs hers for her school project."

While we were cleaning, Cella had told me about the photography course Joan was taking this semester. Her daughter had shown an avid interest in photography the past year. Cella had given her a good camera last Christmas. I'd wondered why we hadn't had courses like photography when I was in high school. I gladly would have traded, say, gym class for it.

"My own camera's too big," Cella explained. "Got a little hole in one of my walls, and I need to see what's on the other side before I do anything else."

"Smart," Uncle Leo said. "Gaet, remember the time you, me and Pat's father put in the bathtub upstairs? When we knocked down the side wall, we didn't realize the chimney was so close."

Cella's father smiled at the memory. "Carmen put his sledgehammer right through the bricks. What a mess that was."

"We couldn't use the furnace," Aunt Sophie added. "It was October and a cold spell hit the next day. Carmen got his brother-in-law to come and patch it up quick."

"My Uncle Sal?" I asked. Mom's brother died before I was born. I never knew much about him.

"Sure." Aunt Sophie sat down in her usual seat. "He was a bricklayer. Got us the bricks cheap and always did good work."

We all fell silent a moment as we satisfied hunger. Then Aunt Sophie gave us the family version of the News at Noon. "Finally got hold of Beatrice. When I called the hospital the third time, they put her on. She told me, once they heard about the phosphorus, they pumped out Ozzie's system, but he's still not good, they said. Still in Intensive Care."

"A real shame," Uncle Gaet murmured. "Young fella like that. Still got his life ahead of him." We all agreed, even though Ozzie was on the far side of fifty years.

"But," Aunt Sophie went on, "the doctors think the phosphorus was in a cod liver oil capsule Ozzie took. Beatrice said Uncle Rocco had a bottle of them, which was in with the things she and Ozzie took home from Evergreen Manor. Ozzie said he heard they were good for you. He thought he'd try them."

"*Madonne!*" Cella exclaimed. "Uncle Rocco took one of those pills Saturday night. I got him a glass of water for it."

Aunt Sophie nodded. "Beatrice said the hospital's testing the one capsule left in the bottle today."

So, I mused, Ozzie's poisoning might not have been intentional, unless, of course, Beatrice knew about those capsules and persuaded Hubby to take one. Nonetheless, Cella *had* been deliberately targeted. I reconsidered Ronny as a possible suspect. He might have motive, but like Cella, I couldn't picture him going to all the trouble this sort of murder involved. Heck, I couldn't even picture Ronny as a heat-of-passion killer. Then again, a guy who wore shorts all year long must be hot-blooded, right?

". . . so I invited Beatrice to supper tonight," Aunt Sophie was saying.

Uncle Leo grimaced. "Aw, whaddya go and do that for?!"

"Hush you," Aunt Sophie replied. "Like it or not, Beatrice is a Montella. What with Rocco dead and her husband so sick, she's got nobody else now. She's family. We gotta take her in. Besides, it's Friday and it's Lent. I can't let her eat at the hospital. They'll have meat."

"Doesn't matter," Aunt Lydia said. "Beatrice won't come. She never does. We're not good enough for her."

Used to be, I could down three pieces of Angelo's Sicilian pie. Now one and a half made me feel uncomfortably stuffed. I was getting old.

After lunch, Angelo went back to work, Aunt Lydia and Uncle Gaet went off to do their grocery shopping, and Janine plopped herself down in Aunt Sophie's sitting room to watch TV. Miss Maggie also decided to stay at Aunt Sophie's, since it was warmer there. After lunch settled, she planned to take a stroll on the treadmill, she said. But she made me promise to come get her if anything exciting turned up.

Joan came next door with us to see what her mom had planned for the precious camera. Once she viewed the wall in the basement and comprehended the situation, she said, "No way are you putting it through that hole, Mom. You'll drop it."

"I will not," Cella retorted. "Here, I'll wrap the lanyard around my wrist. Geez. Not like I wouldn't buy you another one if I let anything happen to this one."

I knew darn well that my cousin's budget couldn't handle another digital camera. Not a decent one, anyway.

But Cella's forearm wouldn't fit far enough through the hole to allow her to get a photo of much of anything. Joan had a smaller limb, so she tried. Her pictures were better, yet all we could tell for sure was that a small room had been dug out on the other side of the wall. More of a niche, really, slightly larger in floor area than a bathtub. Looked a lot smaller than what I'd seen in my vision from the other side, but that was because, as we could see in Joan's photos, Uncle Rocco's foundation wall had been neatly re-bricked. I wondered if my Uncle Sal had done it.

None of the photos, however, identified the metallic object that Cella had felt. Whatever it was reflected light. All we saw was a white glob in the foreground.

We were pondering our next step when Aunt Sophie's ringtone once more interrupted. She was, as usual, already thinking ahead to dinner. Fish, she'd decided, but then claimed that Uncle Leo had no clue how to pick out good seafood, so would Cella mind going? Suspecting my cousin's fish shopping experience was limited to fast food sandwiches and frozen fish sticks, I said I'd tag along. Besides, if need be, I could prevent Cella from taking candy from strangers. Not that I thought she'd be stupid enough to do so, knowing now that phosphorus might be lurking beneath the surface.

We brought back two nice, fresh hunks of salmon and, because Cella claimed her kids wouldn't eat it (translation: *she* wouldn't eat it), also a pile of already-breaded flounder filets.

Since the afternoon was nearly gone, I stuck around to help my aunt get dinner ready. The day had been frustrating so far, and I was getting antsy in anticipation of my evening trek. I needed the therapy that working in the kitchen brought. Today I mostly peeled and chopped carrots. Cella turned her nose up at K.P. duty. She went off to find Miss Maggie, who our aunt said had been upstairs for the last hour, still sorting through photos and news articles.

Aunt Sophie was the one who'd taught me how to cook fish. She sprinkles the flesh lightly with olive oil, parsley and oregano, then stuffs each piece into a roasting bag with onion slices, sealing the bag with a twist tie, but leaving space for steam to surround the fish. (When I do it, depending on my mood and the species of fish, I vary the type of oil or herbs.)

To cook, you can just float the bag in boiling water, maybe flopping it over once as a way of basting. Tonight, though, Aunt Sophie set her bags on a roasting pan in the oven, along with a Pyrex dish holding the flounder filets.

The top of the stove was reserved for large pots of brown rice, green beans, and my carrots, seasoned with dried tarragon. Enough food to feed a whole high school football team, bench players, cheerleaders and all. Aunt Sophie wanted to be ready if any of her kids or grandkids dropped by for dinner (not that they would without calling first). We all assumed, correctly, that Cella's parents would stay. Aunt Lydia would need to satisfy her curiosity, to see if Beatrice really did come.

As it turned out, Beatrice *didn't* come. Oddly enough, though, she did call her regrets, just as we were all sitting down to eat. She told Aunt Sophie that Ozzie had gotten worse and she was afraid to leave him.

Aunt Lydia was skeptical. "Making excuses, that's all. She just called to stay on your good side, Sophie, in case you find Rocco's money first."

"Maybe," Aunt Sophie conceded. "Not that I'd know where to look. I told Beatrice that. Still . . ." My aunt let her eyes drift to the phone. Even though she'd hung up the receiver five minutes ago, it symbolized a link to our black sheep cousin. "She didn't sound like herself."

At the mention of Uncle Rocco's missing fortune, Cella spoke up. "That reminds me, Miss Maggie and I sorted through that last bag of his clothes up in the back room, Aunt Sophie."

"Find anything?" I asked as I passed the bowl of beans to Aunt Lydia.

"One raincoat, a windbreaker, and a pile of old, ratty sport coats," Cella replied. "If you know of a high school doing *Guys And Dolls* in the near future, the coats would be perfect. Vintage Damon Runyon. All the more so because the pockets were stuffed with a trillion lottery tickets."

Janine rolled her eyes. "She's always telling me *I* exaggerate."

Cella stuck her tongue out at her youngest. "All right, maybe not a trillion, but lots of them, and all kinds—Daily Number, Instant Game, Pick-Six. . . . You could tell when Uncle Rocco wore each sport coat last by how old the tickets were. And in one especially ugly lime green polyester jacket, I found a voucher for the buffet at The Sands."

Uncle Leo let out a grunt that was half laugh. He finished chewing his current mouthful, swallowed and said, "Rocco always forgot to go to the buffet when he took the casino bus. Too busy playing blackjack."

I swallowed a mouthful of salmon. "Uncle Rocco went down the casinos?"

"Oh, sure," Aunt Sophie said. "We all did when they first opened, back in . . . what was it? 1980? Remember, Lydia? Few times a summer we'd go down."

Uncle Gaet answered for his wife. "The bus cost ten bucks, but they gave you a roll of quarters and a voucher for the buffet. Free ride down the shore *and* a meal. Can't beat that."

"They don't do that anymore, do they?" Uncle Leo asked of nobody in particular. "Casinos don't need the business now."

Aunt Lydia nodded. "Sophie and me, we used to go see the shows, then, while these two" —she gestured to my uncles— "played the slots, we'd go stroll on the boardwalk."

"I always liked the Ocean City boardwalk more," Aunt Sophie lamented. "Better fudge."

Aunt Lydia agreed. "You remember Watson's? Best seafood down'a shore."

"Margate was nice, too," Aunt Sophie sighed. "We used to bring the kids down to see the elephant when they were little. Too bad the bus only went to Atlantic City."

Before they digressed too far down the Jersey coast, I asked my uncles, "How'd you two do at the slots?"

"Aw, I always lost," Uncle Leo said. "Gaet, here, he brought home thirty bucks once."

So it was rarely a free ride, I thought. I wondered how much my uncles fed the one-armed bandits beyond the gratis roll of quarters. "How 'bout Uncle Rocco? Did he win at all?"

Aunt Sophie nodded. "Oh, sure. He was good at blackjack."

"Money loved him," Uncle Leo said again, repeating his eulogy from Tuesday night. He scooped up a forkful of rice, losing half of it on the flight to his lips.

"Oh, you know Uncle Rocco," Aunt Lydia put in. "Always claimed he won. Never admitted it when he lost."

"He *must* have lost sometimes," Cella said. "Did he only take the casino bus when you did? Or more often?"

"Every two weeks," Uncle Leo replied. "Like clockwork."

"Naw, he didn't," Aunt Sophie argued.

Uncle Leo, of course, dug in his heels and insisted he was right. So did Aunt Sophie. All we heard for the next two minutes was "Yeah, he did" and "Naw, he didn't."

Aunt Sophie broke the deadlock first. "Only in nice weather. His doctor told him not to go out in the cold. Stirred up his angina."

"Couple'a years later," Aunt Lydia said, "he had to stop driving at night. He couldn't get home from the casino bus unless someone gave him a ride."

"Beatrice never would," Aunt Sophie added. "She didn't want him gambling. She was scared he wouldn't be able to pay off her college loan."

"Did he?" Cella asked. "Pay off her loan, I mean."

"Oh sure," Aunt Sophie replied, then Uncle Leo cut in, explaining, "Rocco put her through college. Her own father wouldn't. Didn't think girls ought to go past high school."

"You were the same way with Lu," Aunt Sophie reminded him. "Made her go to secretarial school instead."

"She *wanted* to," Uncle Leo countered.

Aunt Lydia saved us from another argument. "I thought Beatrice's father couldn't afford to pay her schooling. I heard he spent all his money on Zoe's medical bills."

Aunt Sophie nodded. "That, too."

Miss Maggie, who'd been quietly listening while devouring her supper with obvious delight, spoke up. "Which college did she attend?"

"Brock School of the Performing Arts," Aunt Sophie replied.

I didn't ever remember hearing that. Brock was a prestigious, not to mention exclusive, college in Philadelphia. You had to have serious talent to get in. "Performing? You mean, like acting? Beatrice?"

Aunt Lydia shook her head. "She wanted to be a . . . whatchamacallit . . ."

"A director," her husband finished for her.

"Naw," Uncle Leo said, "a stage manager. Or maybe a theater manager? Something like that. She likes bossing people around."

Cella cut to the bottom line. "Brock's not cheap."

Aunt Sophie went on. "She got a scholarship, at least her first year, and she had a summer job. Same place she's working now. Took her full time when she graduated. Making good money."

Beatrice had never used her degree, I mused. Not that I was being judgmental. I didn't use my liberal arts degree either my first decade and a half out of college. The seduction of a steady paycheck right after graduation had made me forget high school dreams. Was the same true for Beatrice? If so, maybe she was as ready for a mid-life crisis now as I'd been a year ago.

"... the real effect of the bank closings seemed to be a test of who's got a dime ..."

—*Boston Post*, March 4, 1933

March 3, 1933 – Trepani's kitchen

The next day, Pip and I were eating lunch in the kitchen when Vito came in. We had Pip's favorite that day—eggs cooked in tomato sauce. Aunt Gina liked it 'cause she could feed us a good hot lunch that was both fast and fairly cheap. I thought it looked like lumpy orange mud myself, so I never ate much. My favorite lunch was fried bologna and egg sandwiches, but it was Friday. We couldn't have meat.

Anyway, when Vito came in, he told his brother, "Pop wants you to go get change soon as you're done."

Pip smeared a piece of bread through the last of his sauce. "Already? You just went a couple hours ago."

Vito sat at the table. "He decided we'd better change those two fivers in the cash drawer, too, since the bank's closing."

"Closing?"

Vito nodded. "Rocco got sent home early today, and they told him to take tomorrow off. Peoples is gonna be closed in honor of Roosevelt's inauguration, they said."

Pip looked grim. "Sounds like an excuse."

Aunt Gina set a steaming bowl in front of Vito, along with a spoon. He sprinkled on some grated cheese and scooped up a spoonful. "Rocco says the other banks are doing the same thing. He's worried Peoples won't open again."

"Is he out of a job?"

"He'll be okay. You know Rocco. He's a talker."

Pip didn't look so sure, but all he said was, "What are we gonna do for change?"

Vito swallowed his mouthful. "I told Pop, worse comes to worst, if we get a big bill, I'll go over Atmore D'Allen's store and buy a stick of gum to get change."

Other than the concern over a neighbor being put out of work, the bank closings were only a minor inconvenience for our family. Talk at dinner was more about how Bondi's Barber Shop got robbed the night before. The thief broke the window and got two dollars and thirty-five cents. Uncle Ennio never left money in the store after hours, but that very night he started putting a sign in the window saying so.

Pip told us all about other news in the *Times Herald* that evening. The County Emergency Relief Board was planning to supply gardens to the unemployed. Aunt Gina and Nonna already kept a vegetable garden out back in the summer, but my aunt wanted Pip and Vito to try for one of the Relief gardens. They wanted to plant extra tomatoes and beans. The boys agreed reluctantly. They hated gardening, but they liked to eat. Uncle Ennio volunteered his younger sons to help with the weeding.

Del was quiet through the meal. She'd come home on time that day, and had not only done all her homework for the weekend without being told, but also folded laundry and helped Nonna with the ironing. Now, as we were finishing supper, she asked, "May I go out tonight to take Easter egg orders again?"

"I don't know," Aunt Gina said, looking at her husband for guidance. "It's Friday." My aunt considered Fridays during Lent to be sort of like holy days. First Fridays of every month were special, too. Today was both, which was why she and Nonna had taken me to Mass that morning, not that I wanted to go.

Del had thought her case through. She repeated how she wanted to get a head start so she could sell more, and pointed out that it was a nice night. Actually, the whole day had been cloudy, but what she meant was, the air had warmed up enough that the walks were clear.

"Plus," she said, "Vito and Pip said they'd walk me up Main to where the rich people live. I can ask at their houses before any of the other kids get there."

Uncle Ennio liked that his daughter wanted to take the initiative and expand her sales territory, especially the part about selling to rich people. Not that he voiced any of that. His only comment to his wife was, "Let her go." The words "We need the extra money" didn't need to be said.

After our rosary, I was bundled up in a blanket again, like last night. Pip carried me and Mrs. Roosevelt outside and put us in the wagon. I sat up higher tonight 'cause, while we ate supper, Rocco had layered his bottles of liquor on the bottom of the wagon, stuffing rags around and between them so they wouldn't rattle. He put cardboard on top for me to sit on. That way nobody would see the bottles if they happened to look inside.

The wagon was heavier, of course, which would have been obvious if Del had tried pulling it herself, especially up the hill on the other side of Stony Creek. Vito and Pip took turns pulling me and the liquor, both of 'em trying to look like they weren't working up a sweat. We didn't have to go too fast, though, since the distance was only a mile and a half. Del actually did stop and knock on a few doors, figuring she better bring back some orders or her parents might be suspicious.

Del had been to the far west end of town before. We all had, last summer, when the Wild West Show was at the Car Barn, which wasn't a barn at all, but an empty field alongside the end of the trolley line. We got free tickets to the show 'cause Uncle Ennio let them put their posters in his store window. All of us walked up Main Street that night, except me. The adults took turns carrying me.

Taking the same route tonight, I recalled how I'd been half scared and half fascinated by the galloping horses and the yelling Indians. I recalled, too, how Del had straggled behind us on the last few blocks of our walk, to study the large, single houses at this end of Main Street, with all their gables, turrets and porches, and wide lawns surrounding them.

She did the same tonight. This time she didn't have the benefit of late summer sunlight. By the time we got within a half mile of Montgomery Cemetery, night had settled in completely. Oh, sure, the streetlamps were on, and the headlights of cars and trucks going up and down Main. The left over snow from yesterday, in mounds on the north side of the street and on the grass in shady areas, helped reflect what light there was. But back from the road, the big houses sat in darkness, lamplight occasionally peeking out from between heavy, expensive drapes, as if to emphasize the economic barriers between their occupants and us.

That, of course, didn't stop Del from running up onto their porches and knocking. Only one door opened to her, and that was to tell her no, they didn't want Easter eggs. She didn't care. She'd gotten a peek into the foyer beyond, with its chandelier and fancy carpet and wide stairs.

As Del joined us again, she asked her brothers, "How many rooms do these houses have?"

"Dozens," Vito replied. "Everybody who lives in them gets four bedrooms apiece. Nobody has to share."

"And they got two dining rooms, too," Pip said. "One for the servants."

"And two bathrooms."

"Per person."

"Yeah. Marry a rich guy, Del," Vito said. "Then you can have a house like that and we'll all come live with you."

Del didn't say anything, but I think she was picturing something similar, except for the part about her brothers living with her.

Only the big square house on the corner of Hartranft and Main showed any signs of life. The circular drive was lined with cars, and between wide, pyramid-like stone pillars, the porch light was on, as well as all the interior lights, which could be seen through the fancy stained-glass windows flanking the doors and chimneys. On the porch, black mourning cloth hung on either side of the steps.

"That's the Lowells'," Vito said needlessly. Everybody in town knew the Lowells lived there. They also owned a big mansion in upper Montgomery County where they spent their summers, and a hunting lodge in the Poconos.

"I didn't know he had that many relatives," Pip commented.

Vito laughed. "They ain't relatives. They're vultures. All of 'em jockeying to be on Mrs. Lowell's good side, now that she's inherited a bundle. Betcha half those cars belong to politicians."

We continued around the corner and down three blocks, past a row of modest new houses built last decade, before the Depression hit. Some seemed empty, unoccupied. One had a sheriff's sale sign in the window. Hardly any cars were parked here, and no one was outside. Like I said, my wagon wheels didn't make much noise, but the warped frame rattled a bit, especially on uneven ground. Tonight, on this quiet street, that rattle sounded like a Tommy gun going off.

No streetlamps lit this neighborhood yet. The farther we got away from Main Street, the more we were enveloped by darkness. The skies were still cloudy, with no stars, and a half moon only peeking through now and again, looking spooky up in the sky with fat, gray streaks across it. Here and there, dim lamps could be seen under plain, white shades or through sheer curtains.

Between these spots of scant illumination, at the end of the street, the cemetery waited, looking like a black cave. As we approached, though, we saw a pinpoint white flash near the ground, then a glow that looked like a small, fuzzy, yellow ball.

"There's Rocco," Vito said, grabbing the wagon's handle to help his brother pull faster.

As Rocco stood, I saw that, instead of his Fedora and nice coat, he had on a heavy dark sweater, and a cap like my brother Tutti always wore, and around one shoulder was a coil of rope. He lifted his little oil lantern by the handle, then draped a square, black cloth over the light. I'd been staring at the glow, so the resulting darkness seemed inky to me. I hugged Mrs. Roosevelt tighter with one hand and reached the other out of my blanket, grabbing at Pip's pant leg. He put a hand on my shoulder to calm me.

Vito, meantime, was fingering the cloth over the lantern and laughing. "Isn't this part of your fake nun's get-up? Sure does come in handy on these little jaunts, doesn't it?"

"I needed something to cover the lamp," Rocco explained, "plus I figured, it's brought us luck in this cemetery before."

"And this time," Pip said, "you don't have to wear it."

"Amen to that," Rocco agreed. "Any trouble walking here?"

"Naw," Vito answered. "With Del along, and Bambola in the wagon, we looked as innocent as babies."

"And most people," Pip added, "once they realized Del was selling something, they crossed the street to avoid us."

"Good. Here." I heard the jingle of coins, then Rocco said, "Here's fifteen cents, Pip. Treat the girls to a trolley ride home."

"Holy cow," Del breathed out in a half whisper.

But Pip wasn't anxious to leave. "Won't you need help with the slab on Mr. Lowell's vault?"

"The Bratimer can help us," Vito said. "Where is he, anyway? You seen him, Rocco?"

"Not yet. Unless he's already in there. Go on, Pip. We'll be all right. I'll pay you soon as I can. You too, Del."

"A whole dollar," she reminded him. "Don't forget. And make sure you bring the wagon home, Vito, or Pop'll have fits."

Pip hesitated a moment more, long enough to say, "One article in the *Herald* today I neglected to mention at dinner. Two brothers got arrested yesterday for transporting whiskey up in Eagleville."

"You had to mention that *now*?" Vito asked.

I felt Pip shrug. "Just be careful, okay?"

22

"Lemme borrow your car?" I asked Cella as soon as I got her alone after dinner.

I had volunteered the two of us to take out the garbage and recycling. Then I noticed that I'd forgotten to take in the quilts. That's what we were doing when I asked her. We hadn't bothered donning our coats. We were hurrying, shivering as we unclipped the clothespins.

In the streetlight's glare, I saw Cella roll her eyes at me. "You're still bent on going out to Montgomery Cemetery?"

I nodded stubbornly, jamming my hands into the fold of one quilt for warmth, only to find the cloth ice cold. "I need to find out what happened there. It has something to do with Uncle Rocco's death and your chocolates. I know it does." When she didn't argue back, I added, "I'll be nice to your car. Promise."

"Right. Like I'd let you go by yourself." She waved me toward the door with her free arm. "Okay, let's go get bundled up and grab my extra flashlight."

Janine and Joan had already left with their grandparents. We only had Aunt Sophie to contend with. Cella told her our evening plans were to visit former playmates and—she actually said this—"check out an old haunt." We let our aunt innocently interpret that to mean we'd be hanging out with high school chums at a pizza or ice cream place.

As for Miss Maggie, she'd listened to us in silence, then followed us out to the front hall. When I knew Aunt Sophie couldn't overhear, I began, "Miss Maggie, I—"

"You don't want me coming out to the cemetery with you. You're scared I'll fall on the uneven ground and break one of these old bones. Am I right?"

I pursed my lips, wondering how to answer that without getting swatted. One did not remind Miss Maggie of her age when one could avoid it.

Before I could get a word in, though, she said, "Sensible of you. I'd distract you. Worrying about me when you need to concentrate." She turned to Cella. "You're going with her?"

"Yes, ma'am," my cousin replied, rather solemnly, as if swearing an oath.

"Keep alert. Be her eyes and ears. And keep your cellphone handy. Understand?"

Cella's brows rose a half inch, but she merely nodded.

We carried the quilts next door and brought them up to the bedroom first, then went down to the hall to don hats, scarves and gloves. Cella had left her flashlight in the cellar that afternoon. When she ran down the steps to fetch it, I walked into the kitchen with the idea of taking the doll with me. If Ma had been to Montgomery Cemetery the night of March third, 1933, then in all likelihood, so had Mrs. Roosevelt. The link might help me see more.

But Mrs. Roosevelt wasn't on the table where I'd left her. Or anywhere else in the kitchen, for that matter.

The doll hadn't been on either bed upstairs.

I met Cella as she came back up the steps. "I was going to take Mrs. Roosevelt, but I can't find her."

"Gone as mysteriously as she appeared?"

"Apparently."

My cousin gave a little shiver. "Let's go before I change my mind about this trip."

I was lost in my own thoughts as we drove up Main, wondering what I'd "see" at the cemetery, hoping we weren't off on a wild goose chase, and a little scared at the prospect of running across drug or sex deals in the making. Oddly enough, I wasn't scared otherwise, even though a murderer was stalking my near and dear. I really did believe if my mother wanted me in Montgomery Cemetery that night, she'd watch out for me.

Cella didn't let me ponder very long. "So what'dya think, Pat? Did Uncle Rocco lose all his money gambling?"

I shrugged. "Even if he just played a couple dollars on the lottery each day . . ."

"Seven hundred and thirty bucks a year," Cella concluded. She was always good at math. "Over the last twenty years, that's more than fourteen grand. Not counting extra tickets for instant games or

Powerball or whatever. And not counting money lost at the casinos."

"Assuming he didn't win like Uncle Leo claimed. He *was* good at cards, Cella."

"Nobody's that good. He had to lose sometimes."

I shrugged again. "Maybe he set limits for himself. If so, his going down the casinos to play blackjack was no worse than . . ." At that moment a Hummer pulled out of McDonald's lot and in front of Cella. I took advantage of the visual. ". . . than a person who buys a big gas-guzzler and has to spend a fortune on fuel each week."

"Speaking of which," Cella said as an aside, "this Neon gets nearly fifteen miles more to the gallon than my old minivan. I'd love it if it weren't a total sieve on wheels."

"Is it leaking oil yet?" I asked, thinking of my own car.

"Oh, swell. Do I have *that* to look forward to?"

"This is America, cousin. You're *supposed* to throw your money away on cars. It's unpatriotic not to."

She drove across Route 202, then uphill, past the firehouse. "Back to Uncle Rocco. What you're saying is, his gambling was just a hobby? That, if he had the extra bucks, why not spend it on what he enjoyed? Part of the whole Pursuit of Happiness thing. Like people who buy houses that cost five mil and have to get all the latest gadgets for their kiddies. Like that?"

"Happiness *is* expensive these days," was my editorial.

"Don't I know it." Cella mulled that over until she stopped for the light at Hamilton. On the corner was Alfredo's Restaurant, a pizzeria inside one of the nice old Victorian houses left in this neighborhood. At last, she said, "I wonder how much Uncle Rocco shelled out for Beatrice's education."

"And he probably gave her other money since. I mean, if he lent money to the Garcias across the street—"

"He'd make darn sure his own granddaughter wasn't hurtin' for anything."

"You'd think."

A minute later we turned down Hartranft. As a kid, I'd seen this street in the dark lots of times, when our family had come to visit Aunt Lydia's. Tonight was the first time I focused on the cemetery. At the very end of the last block, a streetlamp cast a circle of light on the small intersection, the basketball hoop and the side of the gatekeeper's house. Spotlights on the opposite side of the gatehouse sent beams out into the old burial ground, but they didn't penetrate far. Beyond their reach seemed to be a deep black hole.

I knew I'd never noticed the effect before, but oddly enough, I had a feeling of *déjà vu.* On instinct, I closed my eyes. Sure enough, the streetlights faded and the newer houses on the right side vanished completely. I was seeing this neighborhood as it had appeared in 1933, when that black hole was even more forbidding. The darkness had frightened even Bambola, who didn't scare easily because her worst nightmares in those years involved more horrifying things, like missing parents.

The scene evaporated and I reopened my lids. Cella, meantime, had driven around the last block in order to park on the cemetery side of Jackson Street, right beside the rail fence.

"We aren't going in the front gates tonight," she explained. "I don't want any neighbors seeing us and calling the police. We can duck between the fence rails here."

Had I been a nosy neighbor, I thought, I'd be more suspicious of strangers ducking between fence rails than marching up to the front entrance like they belonged. As I got out of the car, I could see that the side windows of the two row houses closest to us were either dark or shaded.

The spots on the gatehouse gave us plenty of illumination to begin with. Under their glow, I felt like a trapped prisoner in a bad remake of one of those World War II stalag escape films. No, come to think of it, I identified more with "Chicken Run."

Even after we got out of range of the spots, we only needed Cella's flashlight to keep out of puddles. I tucked the smaller torch into my jacket pocket.

The sky itself wasn't all that dark, even with the sun set completely more than an hour earlier. Above us were the kind of white clouds you see on winter nights, atmospheric ice crystals reflecting ground light, in this case from the parking lot at King of Prussia Plaza across the river. Against it, the taller monuments and obelisks were silhouetted jet black. The flashlight seemed to pick up only shades of gray. All that black-and-white cemented my earlier old-movie fantasy, only this time, in this Victorian setting, the genre was gaslight.

I heard a dog bark, probably the one over near Hancock's grave, but he was obviously a good distance away, reinforcing in my mind that we'd entered the land of the dead. The only other sound was our footfalls. My other senses were heightened. I was all too aware of how chilled my face felt, not to mention the clammy touch of the breeze, both sensations bringing mental images of cold, dank tombs. The smell on the air was of wet earth and decaying leaves. I pictured fresh-dug graves.

"What was that?!" Cella stopped and spun around, waving her flashlight beam over the path behind us.

"What?"

"I heard a twig snap. Somebody's following us."

We both stood frozen, listening. The dog was still barking, and a car door slammed over in the same general direction. Other than that, nothing. From where we stood, I couldn't even see the closest streetlight anymore.

"Maybe it was an animal," I suggested.

"Could be. And you know what kind of animals hang out in places like this, so close to the river, at night?"

I hadn't even thought about the possibility of rats. "You *had* to say that, didn't you?"

"Well, we could turn back. Get in the car and go get coffee somewhere? What'dya say? I can hear a pair of nice, steamy lattes calling our names."

She sounded so hopeful. To tell the truth, I was tempted, but instead I said, "Used to be, *I* was the wuss. You were the one who wanted to climb down into crypts."

"I'm not scared," she lied. "Just cold."

"I have to go through with this, Cella. You can go wait for me in the car if you want."

She sighed and started walking forward again. "As if. Miss Maggie knighted me. I'm bound by sacred duty. I'm sticking to you like dog poo."

"Lots of that in this graveyard, too, I'm guessing."

Cella laughed. It came out a tense giggle. She flashed her light ahead. "Look, the witch's grave. We're more than halfway there."

We stepped up our pace and covered the rest of the distance in silence, both of us listening for unnatural sounds behind us. Thing is, surrounded by acres of graves, and both of us having huge imaginations and loads of inbred superstition, all sounds seemed unnatural, even the drone of an airplane hidden in the clouds above, or that dog, still barking over near Hartranft. The more I listened, the more the night became filled with noise—traffic from Main Street, the muffled honk of a fire horn up in Jeffersonville. I wanted to tell them all to shut up so I could hear if a murderer was stalking us.

As we neared the Lowell monolith, another racket came from in front of us, a squealing trill followed by an eerie, trembling wail.

"What the hell was *that*?" Cella gasped, her voice cracking.

"Calm down. Only a screech owl."

"Lemme guess. Your step-kid-to-be told you."

"We've heard one in the woods at Bell Run. Beth Ann calls him Screechums. This one must have a nest in those trees and doesn't like us being so close."

"Geez. You've become a walking-talking PBS documentary. Not that I mind. Better to know it's a screech owl than think it's a banshee and somebody's gonna die soon. This wouldn't be a great time to think something like that."

She was babbling out of nervousness, and I had to handle that before I could get down to the task at hand.

Cella read my mind. "I need to shut up so you can concentrate, right?"

"It would help."

"Okay. I'll just stand here, next to the stone, okay? And I'll turn off the flashlight to save the batteries."

My turn to read her mind. She was turning off the light so we wouldn't be sitting ducks, and beside the tall stone, we wouldn't be silhouetted against the sky. "Perfect. I won't be long. Promise."

"Go on. Do what you have to." Just before she flicked off the light, I saw her turn her back, as if to give me privacy, like she equated my seance with things best done behind a bathroom door.

The night seemed to close in around me, the monument blocking residual light from the gatehouse. I reached out to touch the Lowell monument like I had yesterday, only this time my instinct was to ground myself, to give my mind a spatial reference, since I couldn't see. When I closed my eyes, it was more to shut out the darkness. Thing was, darkness was also what Bambola was seeing on the Other Side.

> "It's bootleg while it's on the trucks, but when your host . . . hands it to you on a silver platter, it's hospitality."
>
> —Al Capone, 1930

March 3, 1933 – Montgomery Cemetery

Del and Pip, who was carrying me, blanket and all, started retracing their steps back up the street, going slowly and practically walking backward so they could watch Vito and Rocco disappear into the cemetery. Actually, with Rocco's lantern shaded, we couldn't see them after only ten seconds, but we could hear the rattle of the wagon frame as they pulled it over the bumpy path.

Del stopped walking first. "If me and Bambola weren't here, you'da gone with them, right?"

"Yeah. So?"

"We could follow them a little. Make sure they're okay."

Pip wanted to. You could tell just by the way he stopped walking and didn't answer right away. But another duty called. "I have to bring you two home. It's late."

"If we're taking the trolley, we'll get back in no time," Del pointed out. "We can spare fifteen, twenty minutes."

"Vito sees us, he'll kill me."

"How's he gonna see us in the dark?" Pip didn't answer that. Del knew she was winning the debate. "Fifteen minutes," she repeated, "then we leave." What she didn't say was how they'd time the interval, since neither one owned a watch.

"Okay, listen," Pip said at last. "I only want to see if Junior pulls a double-cross." Pip knew about stuff like that from reading his penny novels. "I don't trust him. We'll watch from a distance. Nobody has to know we're here. Got it?"

Del agreed and we headed into the cemetery, hurrying to keep up with the sound of the wagon. At least, hurrying as much as we could considering how muddy the ground was. The moonlight obliged us a tiny bit, highlighting patches of snow wherever tombstones or trees shaded the ground. The light was enough so we could stay on the path 'til our eyes got used to the dark.

I don't remember the walk through the cemetery. Likely, warm in the blanket, with Mrs. Roosevelt in a comforting snuggle against my stomach and with the rocking motion from riding on Pip's hip, I dozed against his shoulder. But when the motion stopped, I opened my eyes again.

Del was hunkered down behind a tombstone that had an open book carved in the top. I figured that's why we stopped, because Pip always read everything he could get his hands on, and he wanted to read this book, too.

He was standing beside a taller monument, leaning against it, peering around the corner. I looked up and saw the statue of an angel above us, one arm up, pointing upward. I thought she was trying to point at the moon, though she wasn't even close.

Hearing voices, I craned my neck to look in the same direction as Pip.

" 'Bout time you two wops arrived." The speaker was Boris/Kenny, dressed like Rocco in a heavy sweater and cap. He wore leather gloves, too, and on top of the cap rested a pair of goggles. Latimer was beside him, wearing the same coat and hat as yesterday, trying to look every bit the grownup tycoon. Failing miserably.

I could see everything 'cause Rocco now had the shade off his lantern. On either side of the tallest monument in the cemetery, not more than thirty feet away from us, the two pairs of men faced each other, like a showdown in a Gary Cooper movie. We were downhill from them, off to one side, behind Vito and Rocco, who responded with, "These things can't be rushed."

"Funny looking coffin." Latimer nodded at the wagon.

"That, gentlemen, is merely our mode of transportation," Rocco explained. "We're gonna use the empty coffin that we left inside the crypt the other day."

"I wasn't planning on opening it up," Latimer said. "My father was interred only this morning, remember? Wouldn't be respectful."

Vito laughed, then realized that he sounded callous. "Just seems funny, you turning sentimental all of a sudden. More like you're afraid of ghosts, I'd say."

Boris took a menacing step forward, clenching his fists, but, since that one step was the extent of the threat, the other three ignored him.

"We're fulfilling your father's final wish," was Rocco's take on the situation. "And we can't just leave the bottles sitting here on top of the grave, can we?"

Latimer shook his head. "No need. I sent word to our business associates from downriver. Told them to come early tonight and to bring their money with them now instead of sending it later. That way we can do a simple exchange—money for goods—with no need for complications. Much easier than all the rigamarole my father insisted on."

"You mean the rumrunners are gonna be showing up now?" Vito asked. "While we're still here? Are you nuts?"

I could tell Pip wasn't pleased either by the way he shifted me on his hip, like he was restless just standing here, listening from a distance. Or maybe his feet were getting cold from standing in snow.

Latimer puffed out his chest. "Like I said, I don't have my father's love for the dramatic. I prefer to keep things simple."

"Simply stupid, you mean," Vito countered. "Your pop was smart enough to know nobody was gonna arrest us for burying a coffin. Nobody was ever gonna look inside it."

Rocco nodded. "An exchange like that, even here in the dark, anybody sees us, they'll be calling the cops."

The notion must have upset Boris. He looked all around, like he expected to see glowing eyes behind every tombstone. He missed us 'cause Rocco and Vito were in the way of the lantern's glow.

"Nobody'll see us." Latimer spoke with an authority born of arrogance. "As for the police, if it comes to that, the Chief will believe whatever the Lowell family tells him. The mayor and borough council will tell him to believe it. At this very minute, half of them can be found at my house, pledging their loyal support to my mother in her time of grief, because they know the Lowells hold the purse strings of the entire county. But if you two are scared, why don't you just leave that wagon and go home now?"

" 'Cause you won't pay us," Vito said, stating the obvious. "And when we *do* leave, the wagon goes with us. Too many people saw me walk up Main Street pulling it. I want 'em to see me walk home with it, too."

Rocco agreed. "Meaning we still need the coffin. If you gentlemen would give us a hand moving the slab . . ."

"I told you, I don't want the crypt opened," Latimer insisted, stamping his foot like a little kid.

"Doesn't matter what you want, Junior," Vito said. "Necessity says we gotta."

"If you're feeling squeamish, Latimer—" Rocco made his tone gentle, understanding. "—you just stand back. We'll do it. Kenny can help. Better yet, we can use your motorcycle to pull the slab off, like you did Monday night."

Latimer shuffled his feet. "What are you talking about?"

"Monday night," Rocco repeated. "You opened the vault and took the bottles out of the coffin."

"Somebody saw you," Vito added without batting an eye. Not that we could see his eyes from where we were, but we'd known him long enough to know when he was putting somebody on. Aunt Gina would've made him go to confession for it.

"Who saw us?" Boris roared, not realizing he was practically admitting their guilt.

"Nobody you need worry about," Rocco assured them, in a way intended to make them worry more.

Suddenly, apparently alerted by some noise, all four of their heads turned toward the river. Me? I didn't hear anything, but I felt Pip get all tense.

"Time's wasting, fellas," Vito said.

Rocco agreed. "Come on, Kenny. Lend a hand."

Boris looked to his boss for guidance. Latimer grudgingly nodded.

Rocco set his lantern atop the granite wall surrounding the Lowell plot, then shrugged the rope off his shoulder. He and Vito unwound the coil, which had an angular hook in one end. Rocco carried that end inside the enclosure and fitted the hook into a hole in the end of the vault's slab. I couldn't see the holes from where we were that night, but I saw them later and figured it out.

Anyway, Rocco got the rope hooked up, then climbed over the wall and chain to join Vito and Boris. "Tug-of-war time, boys. Don't yank it all the way off, Kenny. We only need an opening big enough for me to climb in."

The three of them lined up along the rope on the other side of the wall and put their backs into tugging. The thin slab moved slowly, but fairly easily, until a three foot hole gaped open.

Rocco grabbed the lantern again, and he and Vito walked over to the open vault. Boris stayed outside the wall, still holding the rope, waiting for further instruction from Latimer.

"Hey," Vito said, looking inside the hole as Rocco held his lantern close. "Where's the ladder?"

"I had it removed this morning," Latimer stated.

"Removed," Vito echoed, unbelieving. "Oh, well that's just swell, Junior. How're we supposed to get in?"

"You're *not* supposed to." Latimer's smile was haughty. "I told you, I didn't want the tomb opened."

"Well, what'dya know?" Rocco mused. "Maybe he *is* afraid of ghosts, Vito. Good thing I'm not a suspicious person or I'd have to wonder why."

"I am *not* afraid!" Latimer stamped his foot again.

Vito was all set to tease him some more, but didn't get the chance because a tall man appeared on the other side of the wall, at the edge of the lantern's circle of dim light. He was dressed all in black, and the turtleneck sweater he wore stretched over hulking muscles. The neck of his sweater was long, pulled up to his mouth, and his black cap was tilted down over his eyes. All anyone could see was his upper lip and bulbous nose. In fact, now that I think of it, he blended into the shadows so well that we heard him speak before we saw him.

"Youse guys orta whisper." His voice was croaky but higher than you'd expect, like he was trying to disguise it, or like somebody had tried to strangle him once and he didn't fully recover. "You never know who can hear you these days."

One of his forearms was up, at a right angle to his body, which made no sense until Del tugged at Pip's pant leg and hissed, "He's got a gun!" Because of the Wild West Show, I knew what a gun was, but this wasn't like the pretty, white-handled pistols the cowboys had. This one was so tiny, the man's hand hid most of it.

"Are you . . . ?" Latimer left the question open. He wasn't being lordly anymore. He sounded unsure now, scared. Even from where we were, even with all the stark shadows, you could still see his Adam's apple bob in his throat.

"Who I am ain't the point," the stranger replied. "You're s'posed to have something for me."

Vito, who'd always believed bravado was the best cure for fear, said, "According to Junior here, you're supposed to have something for us, too."

"I might at that." The big man turned to Latimer. "You're the one who arranged this little meeting?"

Latimer's only response was another bob of his Adam's apple.

"I gotta tell you," the stranger continued, "my boss was real upset at you changing our regular plans. He don't like change.

Not when the old way worked so well."

"We can—" That came out almost a squeak. Latimer paused to swallow. "We can go back to the old way. Whatever way you want."

The man grunted as he nodded. "Goes without sayin'. Show me what you got."

Latimer pointed. "Over there, in that wagon."

"Wagon?" We couldn't see the stranger's face, but I knew he was frowning.

"That was Junior's doing, too," Vito assured him. "The coffin we wanted to use is in there," He gestured to the open tomb. "But Junior here took the ladder so we can't get it."

"I become unhappier by the moment." The man turned back to Latimer. "Wagons do me no good where I'm headed. I need the coffin."

Latimer swallowed again. "We'll get it for you. Kenny, jump down inside and hand the coffin out to us."

"Me?" Boris groused.

"Yeah, you. I'm paying you, remember?"

"But how do I get out?"

"We've got a rope," Latimer told him. "We can pull you out."

"Yeah, Kenny," Vito said. "You don't think we'd leave you in there, do you?" Somehow, though, he made it sound like leaving Boris in the tomb was a brilliant idea.

The chauffeur inched closer to the opening, darting glances between the dark depths, his boss, and the stranger's firearm.

"Come on," the man ordered, impatiently waving his gun hand. "The longer this takes, the twitchier my finger gets." To Vito, who'd been eyeing the rumrunner's tiny pistol, he added, "Don't anybody be thinking this Brownie wouldn't plug a good-sized hole in any of you guys. Though, even if I missed, I got two buddies as backup. One's packing a Luger his old man brought home from the War and the other's got a Thompson."

Vito, Kenny and Latimer surveyed the black woods behind the man and the taller tombstones nearer at hand, looking for signs of accomplices. Del and Pip looked around, too, hoping not to find us surrounded.

Only Rocco kept his gaze on the stranger, saying, "Makes sense he wouldn't be alone. He'd need help moving the slab if this was business as usual." Rocco handed Vito his lantern. "I'll get the coffin. Lemme use the rope."

Still eyeing the rumrunner, the way he always kept eye

contact when he was playing cards, Rocco fetched the rope and pushed the hook into a hole in the inside end of the slab. "Vito, make sure this doesn't slip, will ya? Kenny, I need to borrow your gloves."

Boris balked. "What? They cost me two bucks."

"Do it!" the stranger ordered, with another wave of his pistol. Then Boris couldn't get his gloves off fast enough.

With Vito holding the hook in place, Rocco climbed over the stone lip and slowly lowered himself into the hole. A moment later Vito lifted out the small coffin.

"Excellent," said the big man. "Put it right there on the ground. Now, the rest of youse climb into that grave, too."

"What?!" This time the shriek came from Latimer. "What for?"

" 'Cause I said so." The rumrunner lifted his weapon until his arm formed a straight line between his nose and Latimer's head. "You either get in yourself, or I shoot you and toss your dead body in. Which is it?"

Latimer stood frozen, but Boris needed no more incentive. He didn't even ask Rocco to toss his gloves back up so he could use them on the rope. He just swung his legs into the crypt opening and jumped. We heard his exclamation of pain when he landed, even over where we were hiding.

Vito complied too, smart enough to reach for the gloves from Rocco. He lowered himself carefully down the rope, scowling at the rumrunner all the while.

Latimer was staring at the tomb in horror as the stranger once more waved his gun. "Your turn, Daddy Warbucks."

That brought Latimer out of his shock. "I've got money. Actually, I don't, but my mother does. Tons of it, now that Father's dead. I can get you whatever you want."

The man lowered his pistol. "Yeah? You're saying if I kidnapped you like the Lindburgh baby, she'd pay ransom?"

Latimer gulped again, not wanting to end up like the Lindburgh baby. "I was thinking we could skip the kidnap part and I could just bring the money to you. Or . . . or leave it someplace for you to pick up."

"And trust you not to change plans again? No, I like you coming with us better. Pull that rope up outta there. Come on. Unless you want to join your pals below."

Given the option, Latimer decided he preferred the company of the rumrunners and retrieved the rope. If Rocco, Vito or Boris protested, we couldn't hear them from where we were.

The stranger waved his free hand and two boys came forward, as if materializing from the shadows. They might have been around Charlie's age—younger than Pip anyway—and were alike enough in appearance to be brothers, both with blond crew cuts and close-set eyes. In build, though, they were like the older man. Latimer took a chickenhearted step backward.

They were wearing sweaters, too. No coats. No place to hide a Tommy gun, for certain, and probably not a Luger either. Latimer was too lily-livered to make the observation, but I bet Vito would have, had he seen them.

"Gonna shoot 'em?" the taller boy asked, with a hopeful grin on his mug.

"Yeah," said the other, "you ought to. Serves 'em right, crossing us up that way."

"If Daddy Warbucks here behaves, nobody gets hurt." The rumrunner gestured his two accomplices forward. "Now, howzabout the three of you push that slab back in place?"

The boys eyed Latimer with doubt and one said, "He ain't strong enough."

The big man leveled his gun at Latimer's head. "You strong enough, Daddy?"

Latimer nodded and sidled over to the slab.

The two younger men joined him, one on either side, and all three bent their backs to the stone.

"Aw geez," Pip whispered. "They close that up, we'll never get 'em out." He meant him and Del alone. He'd have to go home and fetch Uncle Ennio and Charlie. And maybe, since Charlie was on the scrawny side, he'd have to find somebody else to help, too. All that would mean explaining to Aunt Gina. Which wasn't an option.

What we didn't know was, since the guy with the gun showed up, Del's hands had been busy making snowballs. Now, just as that slab inched forward, she stood and let one of her projectiles fly. She didn't aim for the men, but lobbed the snowball over their heads, like she was firing one in from center field to home. Then she ducked back behind the book-tombstone.

The rumrunners and Latimer didn't see the snowball flying. All they noticed was the "thunk" it made when it hit a grave marker off to their right.

"What was that?!" one of the boys hissed. All of them stood stock-still, listening.

"Nothin'," the man replied at last. "Some animal."

They were bending back to the slab when Del lobbed another snowball, off to our left this time. It clipped the point of an obelisk and plummeted to the wet leaves below.

The men at the Lowell crypt all swung around at this new noise. "If it's an animal," the tall boy said, "it moves fast."

"Quiet, too," the other agreed. "Unless there's more than one."

"It's the witch's ghost," we heard Vito call. "You don't want to get her mad."

The rumrunner stepped forward, alongside the vault. The glare of the lantern was behind him. "Who's there?!" he bellowed. "Show yourselves or I'll shoot this kid here."

He meant Latimer, but his mistake was that he didn't point his pistol at his threat. He was too intent on trying to peer into the shadows. The muzzle of his gun was toward the last sound, then he swept the firearm slowly left and right. I'm guessing, from what happened next, that he reminded Del of a batter taking warm-up swings.

No lob this time. She let go a screamer straight at the man—straight, that is, until the last blink of an eye, when the icy missile curved down and inside, whacking the stranger square in his crotch. As his knees buckled, he dropped his pistol neatly into the open crypt beside him.

For a full second, everyone else up on that rise stood in a frozen tableau, jaws gaping, until we heard Vito yell, "Let go, Kenny! I got it!" A shot sounded, not loud, but like the "pop" made when my brother Tutti hammers a cap on July Fourth.

The rumrunner had been flailing around with his right hand, trying to grab the edge of the vault to steady himself. Now that hand flew upward, as if he was hailing a taxi, except we could see blood splattering out of his palm. Off balance, he fell to the ground sideways.

As the two young thugs ran to help the older man, Latimer, either wisely seeing his chance to escape or, more likely, simply letting hysteria take over, bolted. He disappeared into the shadows on the far side of his family plot, and a few seconds later, we all heard his motorcycle roar to life.

"Shit!" The shorter boy's voice cracked in panic. "Think he'll bring back the cops?"

"Never mind the cops," his brother hissed. "Something else is out there and we don't have a gun anymore."

"Let's go."

The other agreed. "Help me get Dad on his feet. Then I'll

take him and you get that wagon."

Del said later that they cleared out faster than school does on the last day before summer. We heard the three of them lumbering through the woods to the river, stumbling as they ran, cursing, dragging our creaky wagon after them.

Even before they were out of hearing, Pip set me on the ground beside Del, saying, "Stay here 'til I make sure it's safe," before he ran over to the Lowell vault.

Del obeyed the command for the time it took her to lift me onto the book-stone, turn around and pull my arms around her neck, so she could carry me piggy back. Then she hobbled after Pip uphill to the open vault.

He was smart enough not to stick his head over the edge. "Hey, Vito! It's me, Pip. Don't shoot, okay? Anyone hurt?"

"Kenny's out cold," Vito called back. "See, I had to let him run his face into my fist. And we couldn't shoot you if we wanted to. This Brownie only had one bullet in it."

Pip picked up the rope, secured the hook, then tossed the length back into the crypt. Vito climbed out and, after a few moments, so did Rocco. He'd tied the end of the rope around Boris's armpits, so the three of them could haul the unconscious chauffeur out. Even in the lantern light, we could see Boris was already sporting a big shiner. Del said his nose looked like Jack Dempsey's after a fight, but Vito said it wasn't broken.

After Rocco put the coffin back inside and they'd pushed the slab back in place, Vito got the bright idea that they should place Boris face-up atop the closed vault, arms across his chest, like some slain Viking.

That's how we left him as we headed home, Rocco carrying me this time, Vito toting the lantern. When they heard Del and Pip's side of the story, Vito told his sister, "I agree with Jock Ranelli. You're as good as Lefty Grove. No. Better."

Del shook her head. "I blew that pitch." A fastball was what she'd intended, she claimed. "Shoulda been straight and true, to whack the man's hand and send his gun flying." She blamed the snowball, saying it was less spherical than Jock's leather hardball and too slippery to control properly.

Rocco disagreed. "That pitch was perfect and don't let anyone tell you different. You saved our skins, Del. Tell you what, I can't pay you the dollar I owe you right now, but soon as I get some money, I'll give you double. No, triple."

That's when it hit the bunch of them that the whole night's fiasco had made them all poorer instead of vice versa. And with

Peoples Bank closing that day, they knew Rocco would need every penny he could scrape together just to survive.

"You can have the Brownie, Rocco," Vito said, patting his coat pocket where the pistol now resided. "You can pawn it."

Del agreed. "And keep the money. I don't want it."

In the lantern's glow, I saw Rocco's smile, not the roguish grin he always used to sweet talk the ladies, or even the neighborly, "glad to help out" beam that everyone on East Main knew him for. This smile said he was touched that he had good friends. "I'll get you something better'n money, Del. You wait and see."

I don't remember any more 'cause I fell sound asleep, but Del said the trolley ride home was swell.

23

I knew, even before I opened my eyes, that my mother could tell me nothing more about that night. Still, I had the sensation of being interrupted because the first thing I heard was a phone's ringtone. Cella's, I presumed. This time the tune was "Strangers In The Night."

By the time I wrestled my thoughts completely away from the past, I could hear my cousin saying, "*Who*? . . . Oh, jeez. Pat can't talk now. She's um . . . *you* know about her ghost thing, right? . . ."

That really brought me back. "Who is it?" I asked, opening my lids and turning toward Cella's voice. She still had her flashlight off, but my eyes had adjusted to the dimmer world of 1933. My night vision seemed better than usual. The cemetery now looked like a night scene from an old movie, the kind where it's obvious they filmed it in broad daylight with a dark filter. Except those old movies never had the eerie glow of a cellular screen in them.

Cella held out her phone to me. "Stepkid-to-be."

"Beth Ann?" I put the receiver to my ear. "What's wrong?"

The connection was filled with static and missed words, but I did hear, ". . . you pl . . . ing with ghosts ag . . . n? Dad'll freak!"

"Where are you? I can barely hear you." I plugged my free ear with the other hand, in an attempt to catch her words.

"Wait." More static, then, when it faded, "That better?"

"Slightly." Less interference, but her voice was still distorted. "Where are you calling from? Are you in Baltimore?"

"I'm in my grandparents' upstairs bathroom. Well, actually, I've got my head out the window. Better reception that way. I'm calling from my cell."

"You don't have a cell."

"YeahIdo." One word. "Dad got it for me this week for winning first place at Science Night. Cool, huh?"

Knowing Hugh, I wondered whether the phone was a reward for Science Night or a bribe to get his daughter to go to Baltimore without whining. All I knew was, distortion or no, I detected insecurity in her tone. I mean, she was calling from a bathroom. I pictured her barricading herself inside with a towel rack.

Resisting the urge to yell "What's wrong?" again, knowing that would make Beth Ann go into denial, I said, "So, what do you think of Nonna and Pop-Pop?" I purposefully used my own family nicknames for maternal grandparents, to make her laugh.

She didn't, but I thought I heard a reluctant smile color her garbled tones. "They're, um . . . they're *intense*."

Beth Ann was logical enough that she'd realize that needed more explanation. I waited her out.

"I think I've been hugged a zillion times in the last two hours," she went on. "And not only by my grandparents. Three aunts, two uncles, and seven cousins, too."

She wasn't used to smothering family affection like I was. This was probably only the tip of the iceberg. A starting point, at least. "They're Italian," I quipped. "Comes with the territory. When you come here tomorrow, all my relatives will hug you. Hundreds of them. Wear thick clothes."

"Mom's folks are only half Italian," she said, as if genetic accuracy would earn extra credit on the final test. "My grandmother's Polish. She made *pierogis* for dinner. She said they used to be Dad's favorite."

Hugh liked Polish food? Who knew? But Beth Ann apparently didn't like Polish food, or more likely, *thought* she didn't. Her inflection made the dumplings sound like a synonym for curare. "Did you try them?" I asked, guessing the answer.

"They had *sauerkraut* in them! And *onions* on top!" Worse than curare. Nuclear waste.

I vowed to work on her food phobias. I'd grown up with Pennsylvania Dutch friends and was willing to bet I could get my hands on a homemade sauerkraut recipe even Beth Ann would like.

Suddenly Cella grabbed the sleeve of my coat, unplugging my non-phone ear. "What was that?!" she hissed, head alert, gaze sweeping the darkness toward the cemetery entrance.

"What?" I asked, and of course, Beth Ann, assuming I was talking to her, repeated her lament about the sauerkraut.

"There's someone out there!" Cella whispered, each syllable high and taut.

I didn't hear a thing, except for Beth Ann whining in my ear and that dog who was still barking in the distance. With my improved night vision, though, I glimpsed someone darting between tombstones, light facial skin reflecting what little light there was. The figure was running toward us, fifty, sixty feet away. Too close to give me time to confirm the sighting.

Cella still had my sleeve in a death grip. I headed downhill to my left, pulling her along. "Follow me."

"What?" a confused Beth Ann said in my ear.

"Not you. Hold on a sec." I led my cousin toward the spot where I thought I'd find the book-stone and angel that had hid my mother, Pip and Del more than two-thirds of a century earlier.

"Is this a bad time?" Beth Ann asked. "I could try to call back later." She sounded pretty sure she wouldn't, likely thinking, with all those relatives in the house, that the bathroom might not be free the rest of the night. Her voice also held a hint of disappointment that I wasn't dropping everything to deal with her problems.

"No, no," I assured her. "Stay on the line. Tell me more about your grandparents." Meantime I kept moving, scanning the silhouettes of the taller stones, searching for the angel my mother saw. I heard the dog bark again, sounding closer this time. He must have jumped his backyard fence, and now was bounding toward us, maybe having gotten a whiff of fresh meat.

"Are you running?" Beth Ann asked. "You're breathing hard."

I didn't reply because Cella stumbled behind me. Letting out a shriek of pain, she let go of my sleeve. When I turned, she was bent over, rubbing her right ankle with both hands.

I wrapped my free hand around her waist to give her support, saying, "Here. Get down behind this tombstone."

"Tombstone!" Beth Ann exclaimed. "Wait. You're talking to ghosts in a *cemetery*? In the dark? *And* running? Away from the ghosts or toward them?" She was absolutely intrigued. On the bright side, I'd made her forget her estranged kin woes. Even the sauerkraut.

Once more, I didn't have a chance to answer. From up on the hill came the sound of thuds and grunts. I assumed at first that our pursuer had fallen, too, the ground being uneven, muddy, and dotted with grave markers. But then we heard a voice yell, "What are you doing stalking my wife?!"

"Ronny?" Cella called, turning so she could head back up the hill toward him, even though she was hopping on one foot. "Pat, gimme a hand. We have to help Ronny."

From the sounds of the scuffle up on that hill, *someone* needed help. I couldn't tell if it was Ronny or the other guy. I also couldn't tell if the other guy was armed, but it occurred to me that, if he'd been deliberately following us, he might be our poisoner, and therefore intent on killing us. Wasn't too far-fetched to assume he'd brought along a weapon for the purpose. From Cella's point of view, of course, that was all the more reason to limp to Ronny's aid. Me? I pictured our three bodies riddled with bullets and no one left to rescue.

Moreover, I could hear the big barking dog getting closer. He'd head for the sweaty, scuffling men, wouldn't he? So I wanted to stay put.

In the seconds these thoughts took to squirt through my brain, one of those sweaty men managed to get to his feet. I could see the lighter skin of his face reflect the dim light. He wasn't Ronny, I knew, because first of all, he took the opportunity to plant two nasty kicks on his opponent. Ronny wasn't the type to kick somebody who was down. Second, as our stalker turned to run away, his legs didn't reflect light like his face, meaning he wasn't wearing shorts.

"Can you get to Ronny by yourself?" I asked, already knowing the answer. Even if Cella were paralyzed from the neck down, she'd drag herself to her beloved using her teeth alone.

"You're not going after that guy?!" Cella yelled as I trotted up the path.

I called back over my shoulder. "I have to see who it is." A forlorn hope, I knew. I'm not a fast runner and he had a head start. I also had no intention of confronting him. Still, I could try to get a look at his car.

I'd barely reached the path and begun to pick up speed when one of my knees gave way. I let out a curse at the pain, slowing to a limp. From a point behind me and to the right of the Lowell tomb, though, a voice bellowed "Police! Freeze!" followed by "*STOO-ee!*"

Stoo-ee? Was that a name? Even so, I froze.

Another bellow: "Nero, *drzsh!*"

Ant'ny! Had to be, of course. I mean, how many dogs named Nero who understood non-English commands could there be?

Apparently *stoo-ee* or *drzsh* or the combination meant *sic 'im*, because, parallel to me on my right, I heard Nero making a beeline for the guy.

I saw our quarry reach the path maybe forty yards ahead. He

would have done better to stay on it, but as the lane began to curve back in, the guy veered off to the left, away from the dog.

Ant'ny yelled another command to Nero. With my knee throbbing as I scuffled along the muddy lane and my heart thumping in my chest, I didn't catch his words, but Nero paused to wait for his master, whimpering, then barking as if to say, "Aw, I almost had him!"

The man ahead of me, whether he still thought the dog was after him or just saw his chance to get away, doubled his speed, hurdling a knee-high stone in front of him. Unfortunately, he caught his back foot on it. The momentum took him headfirst into a four-foot pedestal. The rest of him flopped to the ground.

By the time I shambled up, he'd rolled to his back with a moan, then lay still. Nero and his master trotted up behind me.

Ant'ny had a flashlight, reminding me of the unused one in my pocket, but I had no inclination to add more illumination to the scene. His beam showed more than enough.

The pedestal that had stopped the man's head was a Greek column purposely left unfinished at the top. From the point where he'd made contact, a smear of blood ran down the column to the words "Rest In Peace" around the bottom. The guy's head had more than a smear—his forehead was bleeding profusely.

Ant'ny's light also showed the man's green jacket, embroidered with "Evergreen Manor" over the breast.

I scanned what I could see of his face. "Darren King."

"You know him?" Ant'ny stooped to check his pulse.

"He was Uncle Rocco's weekend nurse. Is he . . . dead?"

"No, but he needs to get to a hospital before his brain swells." My cousin put his gloved hands over Darren's wound to stem the bleeding. "Anyone else hurt?"

That made me glance back toward the Lowell monument, calling, "Cella! Ronny!"

"We're coming!" Cella replied. "Where are you?"

"You guys all right?" I took my torch out of my pocket at that point, flashing the beam down the path.

They hobbled into view, each supporting the other. Cella was now putting weight onto her hurt ankle, with only a slight gimp. Ronny was limping more, and trying too noticeably to keep his hands off his crotch.

"Call 9-1-1, will you, Pat?" Ant'ny said. "Just tell them the minimum for now. Man with head injury in Montgomery Cemetery. Bad concussion."

My right hand still clutched Cella's cell. I put it to my ear. "Beth Ann, you there?" Static. "Listen, I can't hear you, and I have to get off the phone. Call me back later, okay?"

"We've got 'em on the line, Pat," Cella said. Ronny held his own cell, which had apparently survived combat, and had already punched in 911. Cella took it from him and started relaying instructions.

Too late. The static in my ear was now a dial tone.

We heard the sirens coming across town long before the paramedics arrived. Ant'ny jogged out to the gate to meet them, leaving Nero with us, as protection, I suppose. Then again, none of us knew a word of Czech. I remembered "k'noza" and that it might mean "heel." Fat lot of good that would do me in a crisis.

I spied red, white and blue lights—flashing dots in the distance, over near the entrance—and remembered that the vehicles would be stymied by the locked gates. Sure enough, my cousin returned with two paramedics and three township cops, all on foot. One of the cops had been a police academy classmate of Ant'ny's. Because of that, the rest had pretty much taken my cousin's explanation as gospel and didn't ask many questions, thank goodness. In fact, the sticking point of their curiosity was what Cella, Ronny, Ant'ny and I (for they assumed we'd all come together and we didn't tell them different) were doing in the graveyard after dark.

"Looking for ghosts," Cella quipped, with a "duh" implicit.

Ant'ny's buddy laughed. "Find any?"

"What do *you* think?"

They took her answer for no, but seemed satisfied with the explanation. Apparently they'd come across other folks ghosthunting here in the past. One of the other cops suggested that they ought to write us all up for trespassing after hours.

"You can't go ghosthunting in broad daylight," Cella pointed out, adding another silent "duh."

Ant'ny made them forget the trespassing charge by telling about the poisoning and attempted poisoning cases, and how he figured Darren here might be the perp, since he'd been following us tonight and had ties to Uncle Rocco.

By this time Darren was strapped to a stretcher and the cops were needed to help carry him out to the ambulance. Ant'ny also helped, while Cella and Ronny limped behind and Nero and I brought up the rear.

Once out at the gates, Cella insisted Ronny go in the ambulance, too.

"I'm okay," her hubby protested. His voice still sounded like he was in a choke collar and at the end of a short leash. None of us were convinced. The paramedics sided with Cella. They wanted to take her, and me, too, but we both insisted we were fine.

Ronny gave her his car keys. Instead of his delivery van tonight, he'd brought his black Monte Carlo. Less noticeable, though it always reminded me of a Mafia car.

So that's where we all parted, Cella chasing off after the ambulance in Ronny's car, Ant'ny and Nero likewise, at a more sedate pace. I drove Cella's Neon back to Aunt Sophie's.

I knew I'd have to explain why I was walking in the door without my cousin. I'd have to tell the whole saga, because Aunt Sophie never settled for summarizations. And given my aunt's penchant for interrupting to question minute details, my story was bound to take a good while. As I drove back, I was looking ahead in my mind to when I could get Miss Maggie alone and tell her all about my vision.

That's how I'd stacked up my priorities. With Darren in police and hospital custody, the danger to my family was over. Granted, where the poisonings were concerned, I couldn't account for every loose end. Darren certainly had opportunity in Uncle Rocco's case. He was on hand that day and could handle Uncle Rocco's meds without suspicion. The police could ferret out means and motive, both for Uncle Rocco's death and Cella's attempted murder. They'd find something, I was sure. After all, counting Ant'ny, we now had three police forces on the case.

So instead, I was focusing on the loose ends of 1933. What, for instance, was Ma trying to tell me? I mean, sure, finding out that Uncle Rocco had made bootleg brandy was fascinating. The fact that Ma had been involved, especially during that last adventure at Montgomery Cemetery, was amazing. But what was the point of me knowing all this?

I took the last parking spot, behind Uncle Leo's Olds. I hadn't parallel-parked in ages. It took a while, backing in, pulling out, 'til I got the angle right.

The outside light was on. I was mounting Aunt Sophie's stairs—slowly because my knee had stiffened up—when Miss Maggie opened the door.

Her brows went up. "Cella?"

"Long story." I wanted to explain just once, in front of everyone, but I added, "She's okay."

"Your cousin Beatrice is here."

"Beatrice?" My inflection was more disbelief than question. I'd come through the vestibule and into the hall. The sound of loud moaning hit my ears.

Miss Maggie nodded. "In the kitchen. Her husband passed away. She didn't want to go home to an empty house, I suppose."

I couldn't blame my cousin. Hadn't I done the same when Ma died? I'd stayed with Aunt Sophie until after the funeral, only going home for fresh clothes and to take in the mail and newspaper. After the funeral, I'd sold the house as soon as possible and moved into an apartment.

I hung up my outerwear and followed my mentor back to the kitchen. In the sitting room, the TV was tuned to the Christian network Uncle Leo always got when he wanted ABC and punched in the numbers backward. The sound was on mute. He was in his chair pretending to sleep. I knew he was faking it because his mouth was closed. Translation: he didn't want anything to do with Beatrice but couldn't fade into the woodwork.

As if my thoughts had stoked the emotional energy in the house, the moaning grew louder.

"Oh why did this *happen*?" Beatrice was keening, a good octave and fifty decibels above her normal tones. As we entered the room, I saw that, as at the viewing, she wore a professional suit with a frilly blouse. They now looked like she'd worn them more than twenty-four hours. Her hair was mussed, flatter in the back, as if she'd been dozing in a hospital chair all day. And her face was tear-streaked and puffy. Not a good overall look on her.

"Two in one week!" she shrieked. "I can't handle it!"

"There, there. Here, drink this." Aunt Sophie was setting a fresh cup of coffee in front of Beatrice. I hoped it was decaf. "Tricia, get the red pizza out of the fridge. That's what she needs, poor thing. Bet she hasn't eaten all day."

Like I said, my family uses food medicinally. My only surprise was that we had leftover tomato pie. I could have sworn we'd finished it.

"On the bottom shelf," Aunt Sophie directed over Beatrice's lamenting. "Under the crisper, on top of the egg cartons. I saved a few pieces, just in case."

Just in case. Great Depression training, I presumed. Ma used to do the same kind of squirreling away. Me, I was all for eating food fresh, then if needed, buying more. But I was a member, albeit one of the last, of the Baby Boomer generation.

I found three slices under plastic wrap on a plate. I transferred the whole assembly to the microwave to take the chill off and soften up the crust.

Beatrice meantime was clutching the coffee mug, still wailing like a banshee. I understood that grief was at the root, but the unrestrained display made me antsy. I'd always expressed grief by clamming up.

While the tomato pie was warming, I fetched the bowl of leftover M&Ms from the dining room buffet. My thought was that if Beatrice had any real Montella blood in her, plugging her mouth with chocolate would be sheer genetic instinct. I was right. Her technique was even less subtle than Cella's rapid-fire system. She reminded me of a hamster stuffing its cheeks.

The sudden silence gave Aunt Sophie the chance she'd been waiting for to utter her usual platitudes about all this being God's will.

"God's will?" Beatrice mumbled, full-mouthed yet suddenly angry. "Well, then *God* can just pay for the second funeral." She gulped down the candy so she could continue her rant unobstructed. "How'm I supposed to bury Ozzie? What I still owe on Grandpop's funeral is gonna empty my bank account." This sent her back into wail-mode. "Oh, what am I gonna *do*?"

Beatrice looked straight at me this time. I felt obliged to answer, though I let myself off the hook by asking an obvious question. "You're saying you can't afford to bury your husband?"

"Do you know what funerals *cost* these days?!"

Oh sure, I was disconcerted that money seemed to be her main focus, but I presumed she was using it as a distraction to keep her emotional brain off the fact that her husband had just died. On the other hand, money worries do tend to march to the front of one's thoughts and demand attention. Hadn't I found that out whenever I tried to envision my wedding?

The microwave dinged. I went over to fetch the tomato pie, saying, "I know what they cost a few years ago when Mom died. They sure aren't cheap."

Beatrice snorted. "It's a goddam racket!"

Aunt Sophie frowned at the language but said nothing. Had it been me, I'd have been told to keep a civil tongue.

Beatrice ignored the plate of pizza I put on the table in favor of another handful of M&Ms. "Not like you can shop around. Even if you could, they all got the same prices. They know you can't bargain. Not like going out to buy a car where you can hem and haw and say 'Lemme sleep on it for a week.' Plus everybody else has to get their piece of the action—the church, the cemetery, even the newspapers. Do you know that they charge a mint for obituaries now? Like you're taking out a goddam ad!"

"Newspapers are no good nowadays," Aunt Sophie editorialized. "Nobody reads the write-ups anymore. You gotta make sure you call everybody to tell them about the funeral."

Beatrice looked dazed. "You mean I shouldn't put an obituary in the paper?"

"No, no," Aunt Sophie said in total contradiction. "You gotta. Everybody's gotta have a write-up when they die."

Beatrice looked to me for clarification, but it was Miss Maggie, sitting at the table, reaching for a piece of tomato pie, who explained. "As a historical record. For most people, the obituary is the only written clue of what their life was about."

Aunt Sophie nodded, repeating, "You gotta have a write-up."

"That's the problem," Beatrice moaned. "I have to have *everything.* Churches, cemeteries—*everybody*—has rules about what has to be included. Besides the obituary, there's the flowers, the sealed casket, the overbox, the hearse, the embalming, the viewing, the funeral mass *with* organist *and* singer, the grave opening—Good God! Ozzie and I don't even have a burial plot!"

Aunt Sophie wagged her head back and forth, sympathetic "tsks" coming from her lips. "That and a tombstone's gonna set you back at least an extra five grand. That's what Pinky Messalina shelled out when he buried his wife last December."

Beatrice put her face in her hands and let go another wail, this one with more sincerity than I thought her capable of.

For the first time that I can remember, I felt sorry for this cousin. The cheapest funerals cost about the same as the cheapest new car, only here no dealership was falling over backward trying to offer you financing you could live with. I recalled for my mother's how the funeral parlor needed money down so they could pay everyone else. Luckily, after Dad died, Ma had the foresight to put my name on her bank account.

"Insurance?" I suggested. "I know you need up-front money, but if you have insurance bucks coming, you can get a loan—"

"Ozzie's policy is only five thousand." Beatrice yanked a napkin out of the holder to blow her nose. "Just yesterday, after we saw what Grandpop's funeral cost, we were saying we needed to buy more insurance. I can't get a loan. We've already refinanced the mortgage twice and we're paying two car leases. And with my job now . . ."

Miss Maggie, Aunt Sophie and I exchanged glances, but I did the prompting. "Your job?"

"They're moving our office in April, consolidating with our New Jersey operations. Half my department's going to get laid off. We don't know who. That's why I've had to be at work practically every minute the last two months."

That brand of office blackmail was all too familiar to me. I'd been put through similar shenanigans by my last employer. Beatrice and I were compatriots in the great Corporate Wars.

No wonder she'd been searching for her grandfather's money.

It was on the tip of my tongue to suggest cheaper alternatives, specifically a mausoleum drawer and cremation. My family didn't approve of either. With the former, you wouldn't be able to plant flowers at the gravesite. With the latter, going the cheapest route, you wouldn't have a viewing so my aunts could gawk at a corpse.

Before I could say anything, though, Aunt Sophie chimed in. "It's late. We'll sleep on it. Everything'll look better in the morning." She went on to insist that Beatrice stay overnight (another moan, this one from the direction of the TV room), and assured her that we'd all help out, naming a litany of cousins, which is when it finally occurred to my aunt to ask, "Hey, where's Marcella?"

My turn to tell tales, but at that very moment, I heard my cousin's cellphone in my coat pocket out in the front hall start playing "Strangers in the Night."

24

Excusing myself, I ran to answer the phone, assuming Beth Ann was calling back.

"Pat, it's me," Cella said when I picked up.

"Where are you calling from?" If "Strangers in the Night" was her default tone for numbers she didn't have programmed in, she couldn't be using Ronny's phone. I'd seen enough this week to know she'd have his number in her cell 'til death do us part, programmed to ring something like "All The Way."

"Got a phone here in Ronny's room in the ER," she replied. "Not allowed to use a cell. Listen, they said Ronny's gonna have surgery tonight. He's got internal bleeding. The nurse said he'll be okay, though," she added hurriedly, desperately wanting to believe it. "They just gotta open him up."

"Ronny'll be okay, Cella." I hoped I was right.

"So I'm staying at the hospital tonight. I mean, you don't need me for anything, right? You got my key."

I assured her that Miss Maggie and I could tuck ourselves in, and I didn't tell her about Ozzie. Cella had enough on her plate. "Want me to bring you anything? A change of clothes? Something to read?"

She thought it over for a full two seconds. "You wouldn't mind running some stuff out here?"

"Just tell me what you want."

"In the hall closet across from the bathroom," Cella directed. "There's a backpack with some clothes. Got a sudoku book in it, too. Maybe that'll keep me sane while I wait."

"Okay. I'll be out in a bit. I just have to tell Aunt Sophie about Ronny going to the hospital and everything first."

"What? You didn't tell her yet?"

"We got distracted. I'll explain when I see you."

"No rush. I'm not going anywhere."

I hung up and walked back toward the kitchen, but met Miss

Maggie at the stairwell.

"Your aunt took Beatrice upstairs to find her a nightgown and get her settled in," my mentor explained.

"Oh, great," I murmured. "If I wait for her, I'll never get out of here." Miss Maggie's eyebrows rose, meaning she wanted enlightenment. I gave her the salient points: Ronny was in the hospital, Cella was with him, I promised I'd bring Cella some things. I'd made my way to the sitting room as I explained, and when I got there, Uncle Leo was sitting up, alert.

"Ronny's in the hospital?" he asked. "He okay?" Then he added, "Stupid question. If he was okay, he wouldn't be in the hospital, right?"

"He got kicked in the groin," I said, shying away from mentioning surgery. No use getting everyone worried.

"Ooh." Uncle Leo involuntarily moved his own legs together. "Listen, you go do what you gotta. I'll tell Sophie."

"You sure?" My aunt would ream him out for not getting all the details, but I also didn't want to be waiting all night.

"Yeah, yeah, get going. She'll be upstairs a good half hour, putting clean sheets on that back bed and finding Beatrice a toothbrush." Proving he *had* been eavesdropping.

Miss Maggie followed me out to the hall and began donning her own outer garments. "Mind if I tag along?"

Translation: debriefing time. Exactly what I needed, but being dutiful, I asked, "Sure you're not too tired?"

"I've spent a third of my life sleeping, Pat. It can wait." Meaning, yes, she was tired, but curiosity won out.

We went next door where we both hit the bathroom and I picked up Cella's backpack. My cousin's hall closet was as freshly painted as our bedroom and she'd installed one of those wire organizing systems. The clothes she'd worn this week were neatly hung, even her overalls. Cella and I may act like twins sometimes, but here's how we differ—the organization thing.

Two minutes later Miss Maggie and I were in Cella's Neon, pulling away from the curb. I cranked up the heat to stave off both the cold of the night and the odor of mildew in the car.

"Start with Ronny," Miss Maggie directed from behind her muffler. "Cella didn't kick him, did she?"

I shook my head. "Darren King did."

"Darren? The nurse from Evergreen Manor?"

I told about Cella hearing someone following us, and how it turned out to be two people, Darren and Ronny, the ensuing fight, the Mounties showing up in the form of Ant'ny and Nero, the chase through the cemetery, and Darren's headfirst trajectory into the broken Greek column.

The story sounded completely implausible to me, but Miss Maggie only questioned one point. "Darren King? You think he's the poisoner?"

"Looks like it." I stopped for the light at Dekalb, which was 202 North through town. You wouldn't think there'd be much traffic after ten o'clock at night, but the line of cars going by seemed endless. No right-turn-on-red tonight. "Darren had the opportunity to kill Uncle Rocco," I said, "and he could have easily put the chocolates in Cella's mailbox both times."

"Opportunity, certainly," Miss Maggie agreed. "Those chocolates were dropped off by someone with mobility."

"Mobility," I echoed as I made the turn at last. "You mean somebody with a car?"

"More than that," she said. "Even with transportation, once you get to the house, there are still steps up to the mailbox. Picture somebody with a walker climbing them."

"Or someone with arthritis like you?"

I caught her nod out of the corner of my eye. "They aren't easy. Coming down is twice as difficult. Cella doesn't have a railing on her side, either."

The light at Airy turned yellow four cars before me. They all went through, but I braked. "Well, anyway, Darren wouldn't have trouble with the steps."

"No, and for all we know, he might have dandy motives for both crimes."

Or he might simply be flat-out psycho, I wanted to say. Miss Maggie's tone stopped me. A "however" was implicit. "So what's the problem with the case against him?"

"Means, Pat. If I were a nurse in a geriatric facility, with access to all kinds of medicines, and therefore capable of making a murder look like an accidental overdose with relative ease, why would I go to the trouble of using phosphorus? Apart from the fact that it's dangerous to handle and store, where would he get it in the first place? They stopped making glow-in-the-dark things from phosphorus decades ago."

Good question. "Maybe online? I mean, you can buy pretty much anything on the Internet, can't you?"

"I checked yesterday morning. Finally found a handful of manufacturers in China."

The light turned green, I hit the gas. "So you *can* buy it?"

"Yep, if you don't mind taking it in two-hundred-kilogram steel drums. Fifty-five gallons," she added, as if she thought my metric conversion skills not up to the task. And granted, she was right.

"In other words," I said, "if UPS dropped one off on Darren's porch, his neighbors would definitely notice."

Miss Maggie chuckled through her scarf. "Especially since you have to buy a whole shipping container, at least eighty drums apiece. I don't think you can buy just one drum. Even if you could, our Homeland Security folks would likely frown on individuals ordering phosphorus if they aren't connected to a business with a legitimate need for it, like fertilizer or flare manufacturing. At least, I *hope* they'd frown on it. You hear way too many horror stories these days about our ports being unprotected. Ooh, gaslights!"

She was squinting into the darkness outside her window. Big turn-of-the-century townhouses, once occupied by well-off business and factory owners, sat just beyond wide sidewalks. The borough had redone those sidewalks a couple years back and added tall, black, simulated gaslights. Their glow was too bright, and superfluous with the regular streetlights still above them, but the visual effect was nice. Very period. Hid the fact that the neighborhood had grown a lot poorer in a hundred years.

But I was still stuck on the Darren-versus-means problem. "What if Darren knows someone who works, say, at a fertilizer factory? I think there's one in the area somewhere."

"And he got his friend to swipe some phosphorus for him?" Miss Maggie asked, her head still turned to gaze out at the night, even though the gaslights had only lasted a few blocks.

I saw her point. Like asking a friend in the explosives industry to swipe some TNT. Unless the friend was in on the scheme. . . . "Okay, what if Darren himself worked at the fertilizer plant? We don't know what he did before becoming a nurse. People bring home all sorts of things from work."

Miss Maggie wasn't responding. I wondered if she'd heard me, or even if she'd fallen asleep. But at last, she swivelled her head back in my direction, as far as her scarf would allow. "I was thinking back to when I was a teacher. Mr. Colbert taught ninth grade science. His room was three down from mine. Awful smells came from there at least once a week." She paused, and I pictured her wrinkling her nose behind her scarf. "A short, plump man he was, everything about him round. Had a flair for the dramatic. Used to perform science tricks for his students, just like a magician. *He* kept a small supply of phosphorus. Didn't need all that much to demonstrate how it reacted when exposed to air. Science teachers aren't like that anymore, though, not with the cost of insurance and everyone so safety-conscious these days. And like I said, with the difficulty of getting hold of phosphorus in the first place."

The vision I'd had on the first Montgomery Cemetery visit replayed itself in my brain. Uncle Rocco reaching into his vest pocket, his dextrous sleight-of-hand, the bright white flash of the match. "At the beginning of the twentieth century," I mused, "people carried phosphorus around in their pockets. *Everyone* had access to the stuff then. But Uncle Rocco was murdered in the twenty-first century."

"What did you see at the cemetery tonight?"

I didn't have enough time to tell her the whole story. We arrived at the hospital as I got to the exciting part, where the rumrunners showed up. Miss Maggie didn't seem to mind waiting a bit to hear the end. I suppose she thought perhaps we shouldn't walk into the ER talking about bootlegging.

The waiting room was more than half full, mostly people in their twenties and thirties. I pictured them having brought in kids or parents, not that overly-adventuresome spouses were out of the question. All those people made the usual warm hospital air seem even more stifling. I unzipped my jacket.

We waited our turn at the desk, then I told the receptionist we were there to see Ronny, explaining that I'd brought some things for his wife, all the while trying to give the strong impression that I was immediate family without actually lying. I mean, as far as I'm concerned, Cella and I *are* immediate family. Miss Maggie and I, too, for that matter. Most folks seem to have funny ideas about the definition of immediate.

"Room 10-A," the receptionist said. "I'll buzz you through the door." She was eyeing Miss Maggie more than me. My mentor had unwound her scarf, yanked off her cap, and put on her sweet-little-old-lady face, which worked better than a "World's Best Grandma"

T-shirt.

I'd been in this ER way too often with one or the other of my parents in the last two decades. The rooms formed a square around a central nurses' station, with entrances at each corner—two coming from the hospital, one from the outside for the ambulances, and the one we were using, from the ER waiting area. I knew I'd find room ten not quite halfway around the square to the right. Bed A would be on the left as we walked in. Dad had been put in 10-B the night he passed out at the dinner table. Turned out he needed a pacemaker.

Behind the desk were three nurses and one doctor, one on the phone, the rest doing paperwork. As we passed room three, another nurse was coming out, but considering all the folks out in the waiting area, things looked pretty calm back here.

We were maybe two steps from room ten when I saw one of the cops from the cemetery come in through the hospital entrance at the end of the hall. What stopped me in my tracks was who was following him—small, furry, black, with a little white spot on the chest.

I *knew* they didn't allow cats in the hospital. Yet Crisi looked like she owned the place. When the cop stopped at the nurses' station, the feline sat down in the middle of the corridor, lifted her back leg and proceeded to lick her privates.

"What's wrong, Pat?" Miss Maggie asked.

Lowering my voice, I replied, "You don't see a cat over there, do you?" I didn't take my eyes off the creature this time, expecting her to vanish as she had so many times before.

"You see Crisi?" She wanted to shout, I could tell, but she made her voice a half-whisper. "What's *she* doing here?"

"I guess I'm supposed to go find out the rest."

"Give me the backpack. I'll stay with Cella. Come back here when you're done."

"You don't want to tag along?"

"Last night, Crisi waited until I'd left the room. Then you found out a lot. She's more comfortable with you alone." Miss Maggie, I knew, meant my mother, not the cat.

I agreed, handing her Cella's stuff. "I won't be long."

Crisi, seeing me walk toward her, abruptly stopped her ablutions and trotted back through the doorway. I followed her into the hall beyond, which led only to a couple of elevators and a corridor to Radiology.

The moment the doorway got between me and the cat, I lost sight of her. Both elevator doors were closed, one sporting an "Out of Order" sign. The hallway was deserted. Thing was, this part of the hospital had been added after World War Two. In 1933, I would have been outside.

Looking for guidance, and since no one was around to see me, I closed my eyes.

"Now don't you worry, Mr. Montella. We'll take good care of her."

The voice was calm and so close, I jumped. In my mind's eye, figures materialized in front of the elevator. A nurse was pushing the metal elevator button. She wore a Cherry-Ames-ish uniform dress, white and starched. The nurse's other hand rested on the handle of an old-fashioned wheelchair which was occupied by my mom, in her twenties, very pregnant, squirming from the discomfort, crying out when a contraction hit. She was wearing a wool coat over a large flannel nightgown, with slippers on her swollen feet. My dad stood by looking scared and helpless. He'd taken the time to put on pants and shoes, but a pajama top lurked behind his unbuttoned overcoat. He hadn't combed his hair.

"First child?" the nurse asked.

Dad just nodded. The nurse's smile was meant to be comforting, I'm sure. It reeked of superiority.

Now I knew why the corridor was here. I wasn't witnessing 1933. This was the night my brother was born.

The elevator doors slid open and the nurse backed the wheelchair inside. As Dad followed, a voice from Emergency yelled, "Hold that elevator!" Dad, finally glad of being given a useful task, gallantly slapped an arm across the door to keep it in place.

Two male attendants in white shirts and pants rushed a gurney out of the ER and into the elevator. Another man, slightly older than Dad but just as disheveled-looking, hurried along with them, anxiously gazing down at the patient whose face seemed to be hazy, out of focus. Of course, if this was Mom's memory, she hadn't been able to see the patient from her wheelchair.

The worried man kept asking the attendants if the patient was going to die. They kept saying things like "We'll do everything possible," but never actually answered him.

I heard my mom gasp, the imminent birth of my brother Lou momentarily forgotten.

25

The vision ended as the elevator doors closed. I waited a moment before opening my eyes, thinking there must be more. I'd have tried longer but I heard someone coming through the door from the ER. Rather than be mistaken for an epileptic in petit mal, I opened my lids and tried to look like I belonged where I was, like the wallpaper behind me. No, come to think of it, the wallpaper had been chosen because some designer thought it looked homey and comforting, and in this environment, that was completely out of place.

Two men in blue scrubs pushed an elderly woman on a gurney past me. "Just taking you back for a CT scan," one was assuring the patient loudly. The patient squinted as if trying to read lips. He repeated it even louder.

No sooner were they around the corner than the doors on the working elevator opened.

No one was inside.

Sure, this happens to everyone, and I know there's a logical explanation. Someone upstairs, either to be helpful or mischievous, must have hit the first floor button as he/she got out of the elevator. Always seems a little creepy to me, though.

Tonight, my overactive imagination got the distinct impression that this was an invitation. Did I hear a quiet meow from inside? I didn't question further, but walked right in.

My only choice was the second floor, which I knew was The Floor Where They Did Things To You. Outpatient Procedures, Maternity, the Cardiac Center, and the OR were all up there. I thought I knew what to expect. Hadn't I fidgeted in the second floor waiting room through two major operations and five same-day procedures for my parents, and through two babies for Cella?

Thing was, I'd never taken the Emergency Express elevator before. I didn't realize it would open right in front of the nurses' station.

"Can I help you?" The three nurses within querying distance all had the samc question on their faces. The closest one, an athletic-looking brunette holding an ear thermometer, voiced it.

Before I could come up with an answer, someone to my left spoke up. "Looking for Darren?" I turned to see Ant'ny's academy classmate strolling toward us. He gestured over his shoulder as he got into the empty elevator. "They're prepping him for surgery."

"Oh, you're family?" The nurse gave me the once-over, trying, from the way the cop addressed me, to peg me as Darren's mother, aunt, or way-too-old-for-him girlfriend. "You can sit with the patient a few minutes before he goes in, if you want."

I nodded, letting that answer all her questions. What I wanted was to get out of the open hall so I could close my eyes again and see what year Crisi/Ma would take me to next. Besides, nods were safe. If asked later, I could say I simply had a stiff neck, or that I was practicing to be a bobble-head impersonator.

She led me down to the fourth door. These rooms were cubicle-like, fully enclosed, but tiny, only as wide as the door and a two-by-two foot window next to it. The windows were double-paned with a Venetian blind in between. I supposed the blinds could somehow go up and down, and their slats open, but in my lifetime, I'd only ever seen them closed. I never quite understood why the windows were there at all.

Inside, the room was smaller than Cella's bathroom, only as deep as the length of a gurney, one chair and a few inches of maneuvering room. Chair and gurney were on the left.

Darren was stretched out on the latter, unconscious, head half covered with a dressing that still couldn't hide the hideous swelling and dried blood. He now wore the standard hospital gown, white with an uninteresting blue print, designed, I swear, to make a patient look as frail and vulnerable as possible.

Darren was tethered to an I.V., oxygen tube and a vital-signs monitor. I was relieved to see that the latter showed his heart beating at a steady 82 beats per minute, a blood oxygen level of 99, and a 112 over 63 blood pressure.

"He's young and strong," the nurse said to assure me, gaving the impression that she was leaving a lot unspoken, like how many head injuries she'd seen, and the ratio of full recoveries to brain damage, or to fatal complications. "I'll be back in a little bit."

I nodded again, watched the door close behind her, then immediately ducked into the restroom, the door of which was on the right wall. The lavatory was no more than a toilet and sink and was shared with the next room over, but I figured I'd have more privacy in here. The doorknobs had push-in locks.

Once closed in, I shut my eyes once more.

Nothing.

I took a deep breath, letting it out slowly, trying to clear my brain by counting backward from a hundred. Before I got to ninety-five, the image of Darren lying helpless in the next room floated in front of my mind's eye, in vivid 3-D, like I was gazing into a virtual reality visor.

Okay, this wasn't going to work. Was I merely in the wrong place? Would I somehow need to sneak down the hall to Maternity? Could I do that this time of night without someone stopping me?

I doubted it.

I was asking myself these questions as I reopened the bathroom door. I didn't initially notice that another person was, at that moment, slipping quietly into Darren's room. I looked up, he turned at the same moment and both of us, startled to see the other, let out "oh"s of surprise.

"What are *you* doing here?" That came out of my mouth involuntarily, because he didn't fit into my twenty-first century world. I recognized him as the man I'd seen in my vision downstairs, the one getting into the elevator with the gurney in 1952, despite the fact that he was now fifty-plus years older and completely bald. Now the only hairs on his head were white tufts sticking out of his ears.

The answer might have been obvious since he was dressed in black pants and a white shirt, like all the hospital's senior citizen volunteers, but that was the wrong answer. He fumbled with something in his hand, which I realized was a small hypodermic needle. Removing the protective plastic tip, he raised his hand menacingly toward me. That's when I made my second mental match on his face. I'd seen him earlier tonight, in my vision at the cemetery, and on Wednesday, too, in a news clipping in Aunt Sophie's back room.

"Latimer Lowell!" Another case of involuntary speech escaping from my lips, this time in a horrified whisper.

He scowled. "Back away from that door."

I was already backing away, from the needle, whose clear chamber was loaded with a half inch of something yellowish. Phosphorus, I imagined, probably in some kind of oil suspension to keep it stable. Problem was, the room was so small, I couldn't back away as much as I wanted. And my comfort zone with that needle would have to be measured in miles.

My right brain was opting for panic mode, fully grasping the corner I'd backed myself into (literally). My left brain, though, still busy making logical deductions, had made a third mental match, after recognizing the voice and the hazel eyes.

"Wyeth Adams!" Another whisper, hoarser than the first.

His eyes narrowed. "You didn't know I was Wyeth Adams?"

"You shaved." An understatement. I tried to remember how he'd looked with his Santa Claus-like white hair and beard. His face had seemed wider then, and his eyes droopy. That effect must have been all eyebrows, which had also been shaved off. Now all his wrinkles showed, deep furrows between his eyes, and double rows of laugh lines around his mouth. He looked like he hadn't laughed in two decades. Without the beard, the slackness of his jaw was now more pronounced, giving him a perpetually out-of-the-loop expression.

As if to emphasize that effect, his next words were "But you *knew* I was Latimer Lowell?" He lowered the needle a fraction.

If I kept him asking questions, I wondered, would he lower it some more? I mean, he *was* elderly. Less oxygen getting to his brain, slower reasoning and reaction time. Ought to be to my advantage. Unless he was more like Miss Maggie than Uncle Rocco.

"I saw your picture," I said, moving only my eyeballs as I assessed my options for getting help (the nurses' call-button was way out of reach) or for weapons (could I fend him off with an I.V. pole? Could I even lift an I.V. pole? How much did one of those suckers weigh, fully loaded like that?).

Meantime, I kept babbling. "Saw it in the newspaper, like Uncle Rocco did. That's why you murdered him, right? He said he saw your photo in the papers. Maybe as Wyeth Adams you never got into the paper. Uncle Rocco recognized you as Latimer Lowell, only he didn't realize it. He got confused like that—"

"Where'd you see my picture?"

Good, I thought. Another question. "Same place Uncle Rocco did. He kept clippings and—"

"Clippings?"

This was easier than I thought. "Yeah, clippings. I was looking through them and—"

"Where *are* they?" The needle jerked upward again, to within a foot of my chest.

Resisting the urge to zip up my jacket, as if that could protect me, I retreated another step, until I could feel Darren's monitor behind me. Monitor? I snaked an arm behind me as if trying to get my balance, yanking at the first cable I grabbed. It came out of the monitor and hung limp in my hand. Okay, the nurses would see a change in Darren's vital signs and someone would rush in to investigate. I just had to keep my hand behind my back and keep Latimer/Wyeth distracted so he wouldn't notice. Keep him talking, that was all. But one thing was certain, if I told him where Uncle Rocco's clippings were, he'd have no reason to ask more questions.

He read my mind. "If you don't tell me, I'll stick *him* with this needle." Wyeth/Latimer swung the hypo toward the prone form on the gurney, stopping mere inches from Darren's bare leg. Those insane hazel eyes, though, were glued to mine. He could so easily have poked Darren by accident. Of course, he'd come in here wanting to kill the younger man anyway, but he probably intended to inject the phosphorus at the I.V. needle site. No suspicious second puncture hole that way.

To change the subject away from threats, and because I was now thinking about Darren, I said, "He delivered the chocolates to Cella for you, didn't he? Was he aware he'd be an accessory to murder if she ate them?"

"You know about that, too?" His frown deepened his face wrinkles hideously, then he let out a grunt that might have been a laugh. "The only thing Darren was aware of was how much credit card debt he'd gotten himself into."

"So you promised him money. That's how you get other people to do your dirty work. Like Kenny."

His eyes opened wide. "Who told you about Kenny?"

I didn't have a ready answer for that question, mainly because I was busy thinking that the nurses should have shown up by now. Should I tell him about my visions, I wondered? Would freaking him out be a good option?

He didn't give me a chance. "That's why you went out to the cemetery tonight, isn't it? You know about Kenny."

Say *what*?

Then my brain made a final match, not with his face this time, but with all the events revolving around the Lowell family since the 19th century. It was like finding, all at once, every sock lost in the dryer over a quarter-century stretch. *Now* I knew what Ma had been trying to tell me.

"I know Kenny was a school chum of yours," I said. "One night during the Depression, he helped you steal bottles of bootleg brandy out of your family vault, right? That same week you hired him to be your chauffeur."

"That same week?" He scrunched up his eyes, like he was trying to remember. His age was an advantage, I realized. A younger person would already have seen where I was going with this. Though, if he was anything like Uncle Tonio, he'd be able to bring a memory from seventy years ago into sharper focus than something that had occurred last month.

"Same week," I repeated. "The week your father died. You remember *that*, don't you? You poisoned him with phosphorus." Another vision stole into my mind's eye—little Bambola peeking out the door to view Lloyd Lowell as he sat on the stoop, ill. When he spoke to her, I could smell the garlic. "White phosphorus, left over from when your grandfather owned a match company. That's what lucifers were. Matches."

Latimer/Wyeth scowled again, but not at me this time, at the memory of his ancestors. "My grandfather was an idiot. That's what Mother always said. She got Father to invest in other ventures, long before L.L. Lucifer went belly-up, after the Match Tax was signed into law. But after Grandfather died, Father insisted on keeping the leftover match inventory. He built a special stone vault for them in the basement, where they wouldn't burn the house down. We had *hundreds* of boxes of matches down there when I was a kid. Cook was scared to use them. Mother had to light the stove for her each day."

Still no nurses coming to my rescue. What was keeping them? I steered the subject back to Lloyd Lowell. "Why did you poison your father?"

Wyeth/Latimer didn't deny it. "I didn't know the matches would kill anyone. I'd read that phosphorus could make things glow in the dark. I'd been experimenting, that's all. Not much success with my paints. I never wanted to be an artist, you know. Mother had insisted I take lessons from an early age. Said I had talent. But I wanted to do something more . . . more . . ." He made a fist with his free hand, as if trying to grasp at a lost dream.

Keeping him on track was like herding goldfish. I prompted him. "After you tried your paints, then what?"

"I tried rubbing alcohol, then Father's liquors. Even though it was Prohibition, he kept all sorts in his cabinet." The needle lowered again as his mind rambled through his memories. "You have to scrape the match heads off while they're submerged or they'll ignite. I used a shot glass. Ours were dark green cut glass. You couldn't see through them. I filled it with Father's smuggled Canadian whiskey, scraped a bunch of match heads into it and stirred. Then I heard someone coming. I left the glass next to the cabinet and hid behind the sofa. The someone was Father, home early. He'd just found out about our cemetery vault being opened and he was more than a little upset. He spied the glass and figured Mother had poured it for him, since he always drank a shot as a cocktail every night. Never mind that dinner was still a good hour away, he tossed it down. I can still see the face he made. He *knew* it didn't taste right, yet in those days, bootleg was often passed off in bottles of something like Canadian Club. That's what Father assumed. Never knew he'd been poisoned."

"But *you* knew." That was the gist of the whole situation. Little Latimer Lowell had grown up feeling entitled to the power he thought his family's money would give him. He hadn't wanted to be an artist, he'd wanted to be a boss, a tycoon, a mogul. An emperor. What he'd found that week in 1933 was that his greatest power over people lay in the knowledge of how to kill them. So (since no one seemed to be watching the monitors down at the nurses' station) I asked the obvious question. "How many others did you kill with those matches after your father?"

That got a laugh. "None. Mother got the fire marshal to take them all away the day after the funeral."

"But I know you killed my Uncle Rocco, and my cousin Ozzie. They both took the cod liver oil capsules that you doctored. That's what you left for Uncle Rocco last Sunday. Not nail clippers."

Wyeth/Latimer kept laughing. "Rocco was willing to try any of those natural cures. I found that out the day I moved into Evergreen Manor. That's when I knew how easy it would be. That shocks you, doesn't it? Sure, I had to kill Rocco before he figured out who I was, but that wasn't *why* I did it. I'd always dreamed of getting even with him and Vito Trepani, for humiliating me. The war robbed me of the pleasure of killing Vito, and I never got my chance with Rocco, not until last January. I gave an art talk out at the Manor and there he was. Soon as I could, I arranged to move in."

The image of him stalking Uncle Rocco these last months

sickened me. "And you wanted to kill Cella because you thought she overheard you telling our uncle that the capsules were on his night table. You were afraid that sooner or later she'd make the association."

"I couldn't take the risk," he spat out defensively.

What could I do? My monitor brainstorm hadn't worked. Maybe the cable hadn't been connected to a vital sign. Clutching it behind my back was starting to make my fingers go numb. Either Ma or my own brain tried to steer my thoughts away from the discomfort, because another vision swam around inside my noggin: Kenny/Boris the last time Bambola had seen him, in his Viking warrior repose atop the Lowell vault.

"What about Kenny?" I asked. "He's buried in your family's tomb, isn't he? Buried under your name?"

That got me a shrug. "Latimer Lowell needed to die. The police were starting to ask questions. I'd inherited Mother's estate by then, but most of it was property and investments. I took my time turning it into cash. Kenny had become an alcoholic. Couldn't keep a job or a wife. I told him I'd pay him. All he had to do was grow a full beard, put on the quintessential artist's clothes I sent him—full cape, black scarf, dark glasses, and big-brimmed flamboyant hat—and show up at my door. I passed word around that an art friend named Wyeth Adams was coming to visit. I named him after two of my favorite artists, N.C. Wyeth and Herbert Adams." He was amused by that, the same way he'd been when he showed us his paintings at Evergreen Manor. Now I could see that the only part of his face that was smiling were his eyes.

"So you killed Kenny in a car fire and became Wyeth Adams," I concluded.

He shook his head. "I killed him before the fire, so I could shave him and dress him in my clothes. They didn't fit him well, but it didn't matter. The fire did a thorough job. Phosphorus burns hot."

"Where did you get *that* phosphorus?"

He wrinkled up his already-wrinkled brow and, I swear, his jaw dropped another half inch. I couldn't tell if he was trying to remember, or thought the answer was obvious, or if this was his I-ain't-talking look. I was losing patience. You can only interrogate someone with clogged brain capillaries for so long.

Miss Maggie's story about Mr. Colbert came back to me. "You said you were an art teacher. What about the science labs where you taught? Is that where you got the phosphorus?"

More wrinkles, this time on his nose. "They kept all their chemicals under lock and key, but I found out from them the scientific company that sold phosphorus. Mother wrote the check. She would buy me anything if I claimed I needed it for my art. Remember the gold ingot painting in my room? The way the metal seems to glow against the black background? Complete illusion, done with a mix of yellows and a bit of crushed glass in the top layer of paint. But I told Mother the phosphorus made it glow like that and she believed me." For the first time, his gaze dropped, and something like grief, or at least regret, crossed his features.

Put together with my vision in the elevator, I came to another conclusion. "You poisoned your own mother, too?"

"She began to suspect after two of my old girlfriends died—" He gave a sudden start, taking a wobbly step, looking down at his feet. "What was that?"

"What?" My eyes were focused on the needle, now waving wildly again, and closer to my chest.

"Something brushed my leg. There it is again! My God, what *is* it?! It feels like . . . like . . ."

Like a cat? I wondered. I didn't look down to check. Instead, I took advantage of his distraction to whip the cable I held around in front of my body, slashing it as hard as I could at the hand that held the needle. The cable's metal tip met with the inside of his thumb, breaking his grip. The deadly little syringe dropped, clattering on the floor.

Latimer grabbed at my jacket, both to capture me and stay on his feet. I didn't care, as long as he didn't go after the hypo. Seizing his wrist, I lunged for the nurses' button, slapping it, yelling, "Where the hell *are* you people?! Get in here!"

The next instant, all the doors burst open. The two policemen, guns drawn, came out of the restroom. Miss Maggie, Ant'ny, and the three nurses came through the door from the hall. I'll never know how they all fit into that tiny room. I didn't care. All that mattered was that Ant'ny and his buddies took Wyeth/Latimer-the-serial-killer and his nasty little needle away.

Two of the nurses wheeled Darren off to surgery. The other fussed over me. I assured her I was okay, although I took advantage of the chair, sinking down into it to relieve my shaking knees. Then the nurse turned her fussing on Miss Maggie. Apparently she'd never met a nonagenarian who didn't swoon or have a heart attack when exposed to stress. Of course, before I met Miss Maggie, I hadn't either.

My mentor was wearing a stethoscope, still plugged into her ears. She raised the other end to her heart and listened. "Still ticking. Here, take this and go find another victim." She handed the instrument to the nurse before shooing her away. "Those gizmos are great for listening at doors, Pat. Remind me to order one when we get home."

"Is that where everyone was? Outside listening? How did you know Latimer was in here?"

"I didn't, but I spied Wyeth. Saw him follow you up in the elevator. Recognized his limp. Your cousin Anthony was in with Cella and Ron, and his police friends were still at the desk. I rounded them up and we came upstairs. Just as we got to the nurses' station, Darren's oxygen monitor blacked out. One of the nurses turned on the intercom and we listened."

"So why didn't anyone come in sooner?"

Her brow creased with remembered worry. "Latimer said he had a needle. We didn't know how close he was to you or Darren. The police decided to enter through the lavatory, hoping to get between the two of you, but the lavatory door to the next room was locked—"

I groaned. "My fault. I did that."

"Not much of a snag. The nurses all know how to poke the lock open from the outside, of course. They have to. The problem was trying to get everyone into position silently. Meanwhile, your cousin, the nurses and I heard Latimer's every word here at this door, as did the rest of the second floor staff down at the nurses' station. His money won't do him a bit of good where he's going."

I stood. "Let's go, Miss Maggie. I'm bushed." I didn't say it, but as we rode the elevator downstairs, I was mulling over Latimer's long list of victims. The ones I knew about, that is. Likely he'd killed others. Now he was old, at the end of his days. Somehow a life sentence, or even the death penalty, wouldn't mean all that much.

"... the only thing we have to fear is fear itself..."
—FRANKLIN DELANO ROOSEVELT, MARCH 4, 1933

June 12, 1944 – 349 East Main Street

The twelfth was one of those beautiful days, the kind you get early in June, reminding you that summer was coming. School was almost over for the year and nobody wanted to work, students and teachers alike, not with balmy breezes wafting in through the high school's open windows, smelling like honeysuckle and mown grass. Especially since the week before nearly every day had been cloudy. Benny Gordon, who sat behind me in homeroom, kept staring out the window, musing how the nice days always missed the weekends and hit Mondays.

I think we were all grateful that the perfect weather gave us something to talk about besides the war. Everyone I knew had at least a half dozen close relatives and friends in uniform. We were all in a constant state of worry, all the more so after hearing of a big battle. When somebody we knew got bad news, like when Benny's older brother was killed in the Gilbert Islands last year, you couldn't help feeling as if that faraway nightmare would knock at your front door next.

For the last week, the papers had been brimming with stories about the Allied D-Day invasion, all about troop movements and strategies, and how we had Hitler on the run. Nothing about casualties yet, in fact, no negative reports at all. You'd think the Germans were all lying down without a fight. Everyone knew better. Bad news would show up eventually. We were all cringing inside, waiting for the blow.

I walked home that day with my usual gang of friends, chattering with them the whole way. My family used to tease me, saying I was making up for those early years when I wouldn't talk, before my papa came home.

My friends all lived on Marshall or Penn or one of the cross streets, so for that last block down Walnut, I was always alone. Tomorrow would be my last test of the year, in history. I carried the text and my notebook. As I was about to cross Main, somebody yelled "T'resa!" The only person who called me

Bambola these days was Papa. I told him not to, because I felt all grown up and it was a baby name. But not too many years from now, Carmen Montella would start calling me Bambola for different reasons, and I would encourage him.

Down the block, I saw my brother Sal (nobody called him "Tutti" anymore). He was wearing one of his short-sleeved shirts with the stripes in front. With his dark hair and mustache, he looked like a short Clark Gable. Everybody said so. He had scads of girlfriends.

He was standing in front of Aunt Gina's, beckoning with his arm. Del was sitting on the steps. She had a factory job and should have been at work. In fact, she still wore her overalls. Her normally lithe figure was hunched forward, and her arms were gathered on her lap like somebody had just punched her in the gut. From a half block away, I could tell something was wrong. I ran toward them, awkwardly clutching my books to my bosom, my pocketbook banging against my side. We had little purses then that hooked over our elbows, just big enough for a hanky, pencils and lunch money, and maybe a compact and lipstick if you used makeup. I wasn't allowed. Papa said I was still too young.

As I got close, I saw Crisi curled between Del's arms. She was an old cat and acted more like a kitten now than when she'd been one. She stretched one black forepaw toward me, as if to wave hello, but didn't move otherwise.

Being out of breath from running and in expectation of terrible news, I only got one word out. "Who?" I was pretty sure that was the right word. All four of Del's brothers were overseas someplace, as was her husband, Jock. The two of them got engaged right after Pearl Harbor and were married while he was on leave between basic training and being shipped out. Uncle Ennio was a possibility, too. He'd been getting chest pains sometimes when he climbed stairs, ever since the day Gussie's draft notice came.

"They got a telegram from Charlie in England," Sal explained. "Said Vito was in the invasion and his troop carrier was reported missing."

I set my books on the Montellas' steps and sat down, stunned. Sure, we'd all heard stories about missing-in-action servicemen who'd turned up later, healthy and breathing. That's what you *wanted* to believe would happen. But we all knew that most times "missing" was just a precursor for "killed in action."

Del held her hand up in front of Crisi's nose, letting the cat rub her face against the palm. "Ma went over Moore Street to tell Vito's wife. She's gonna be broken up something awful."

Yes, I thought, but wives can get married again. Brothers and cousins can't be replaced.

None of us could think of anything else to say. Sal, hands deep in his pockets, was gazing down the block, squinting into the sun like something fascinating was going on at the L.A.M. lodge. I knew he was doing his darndest not to show emotion. Like when he was seven, he still had a need to look tough.

Del must have noticed, too, because she asked, "You still all gung-ho to ship out?"

Eyes still pointed west, jaw set, he nodded. "Shoulda gone already." Sal had wanted to join up a year ago, the day he reached enlistment age. Papa wouldn't let him. Our father never talked about his part in World War I, but he'd tell us things like "You don't want to go to war until they *make* you go."

Sal didn't understand that it was Papa's experience talking. My brother only saw the argument. The two of them could never agree. In fact, Sal looked for things to argue about. He'd never forgiven Papa for leaving us when we were little. Ever since the day our father came home, the summer after F.D.R. first took office and local jobs could be found again, Sal had been, at best, a difficult child. At worst, a holy terror.

Papa was to blame, too. Most of it was his Sicilian hard head. But he never seemed to be well, either, his stomach always upset, his muscles always sore, his joints puffy. He'd get such pain in his legs and hands at night, he couldn't sleep. Doctor Fabbri called it rheumatism. Aunt Gina said it was from her brother being in the first war. Whatever it was, Papa was often tired and miserable, and sometimes downright crotchety.

Anyway, when Carmen Montella, my brother's best friend, got drafted, Sal walked down to the Naval Recruiting Office and signed up. He told our father that night. Papa must have seen it coming, since he gave in pretty easily. He also seemed relieved that Sal had chosen the Navy, thinking it was safer than the Army or Marines. Sal didn't tell him he picked the Navy because he wanted to fly planes off the big carriers.

Long and short of it was, Carmen had left on the Army train for basic training this morning. Wednesday, Sal would head for the Navy's Allentown facility.

"You know that space between the basement walls?" Del asked out of nowhere.

Sal seemed happy for the change of subject. "You mean

between your house and Rocco's? The one I bricked in on Rocco's side when he was home on leave in April?"

Del nodded. "We got a hole on our side of the wall now. When the Boy Scouts came around last week collecting scrap metal for the war effort, Pop told 'em about the pipe and stove inside the wall. Told 'em they could have it if they could get it out. They came this morning. Took everything but the chimney pipe. Couldn't budge that. But now we got a three-and-a-half-foot hole in the wall. Can you fix it before you leave?"

"Sure. Tell Uncle Ennio it won't cost a thing. I got mortar mix left over from Rocco's job and I know where I can lay my hands on some old bricks." Sal's hands came out of his pockets, in anticipation of action. That's all he needed, something to keep his fingers busy. "I'll go get them now."

"Wait." Del ran both her palms along Crisi's back, one at a time. The cat stretched out as long as she could to take full advantage of the rubdown. "I want to make a time capsule. I'm gonna take something of Jock's, and each of my brother's, and mine. Maybe Ma and Pop, too. And you both, if you want. I'm gonna put everything in that hole before you seal it up."

We didn't question her motives. She wanted a memorial for Vito, and while she had the chance, for her other brothers and her husband and Sal, in case none of them came back. And for us, in case the war came home and this block ended up looking like the newsreels of England and France.

Sal scratched his head. "I don't know what I could give you. Gotta think about it. How 'bout you, T'resa?"

I didn't have to think at all. I knew exactly what to put into that time capsule.

26

Miss Maggie had brought my beloved and stepkid-to-be straight to my side the moment they arrived. They still had their coats on, which was smart since it was cold down in Cella's basement with the thermostat turned down. Miss Maggie had on her mittens, scarf, hat, and extra sweater. Her reading glasses were perched atop her cap, their thick lenses distorting the pattern in the wool.

Beth Ann held out a humongous, bulging freezer baggie as an offering. "These are *really* good." She was smiling. Always a good sign.

I took off my safety glasses and pulled down my dust mask to get a better view of the bag's contents. "Ooh, Polish *chrusciki*! Yummy." I recognized the ribbons of fried dough, crisp and coated with powdered sugar, because every Polish friend I'd had in school had a grandmother who made them. "How was Baltimore?"

She shrugged. "Okay." In her adolescent afraid-to-show-emotion way, she was saying she'd had a good time after her initial trepidation. The *chrusciki* had apparently made up for the *pierogis*. And maybe she'd even liked her mom's kin. I vowed to weed more out of her later.

"I thought we were going to meet your relatives," Hugh said.

"You will. No one's home right now. Cella's still at the hospital with Ronny, Aunt Sophie went with my cousin Beatrice to the funeral home to make arrangements, and Uncle Leo went over his son's to watch the Phillies on Angelo's hi-def—"

"Funeral arrangements?" Hugh unzipped his jacket. He gets warm when he's confused. "I thought the funeral was Thursday."

"Uncle Rocco's was, but this one's for Ozzie. Beatrice's husband. I don't have to stay for it. I wasn't that close to Ozzie." I felt a twinge of regret as I said it. Beatrice was a Montella. I *should* have felt close. Had this been the spouse of any of Uncle Tonio's grandkids, I'd want to go to the funeral. Or at the very least, send a nice mass card.

"Not to change the subject," Beth Ann began, "but why are you knocking down that wall?" She used her non-*chrusciki* hand to indicate the wall behind the furnace, where an L-shaped hole the size of thirteen bricks now gaped.

First thing I'd done this morning, after waking from a dream about my mother and Del in 1944, was call Cella to tell her I needed to see what was behind her basement wall before I left. Seeing I was determined, Cella, in turn, called her brother Pasquale, who was not thrilled to be awakened before nine-thirty on a Saturday morning.

Pasq was even more of a do-it-yourselfer than his sister, and he liked me enough not to want me to bring Cella's house down on my head. After breakfast he showed up with some two-by-fours to shore up the basement ceiling. He also brought a stack of hard hats, three pairs of safety glasses, and a power drill with a bit for mortar, then worked with me until eleven-thirty, when he had to leave to pick up his son at wrestling practice. After lunch at Aunt Sophie's (nice, hot, pasta fagiol' soup), Miss Maggie and I had come back to the basement, me to work, her to shout encouragement, until she climbed the stairs to watch for Hugh and Beth Ann's arrival.

"I'm digging for treasure," was my reply to Beth Ann. "Wanna help?"

"What kind of treasure?" Hugh was skeptical, as always.

"The kind my mom would have buried in a big old spaghetti pot. Come on, grab a hard hat, glasses, and a dust mask. I'll explain all while we work."

Now, Hugh is the kind of guy who tends toward the notion that pulling down walls is man's work, and that if any task needs to be done where brute force is a possible solution, then it's the *only* solution. He is educable, God bless him. I instructed him in the need to work slowly, to make sure the bricks all fell toward us into the basement, not backward into the hole. Pasq said he'd repatch the wall for his sister with cinder block, Cella thought she could reuse the bricks elsewhere. I was trying not to break them.

While we were perforating mortar with the drill, then carefully chiseling and prying each brick free, I began to tell them the whole story of Uncle Rocco, Latimer Lowell, the Trepanis, and Bambola. Miss Maggie supervised both our work and my storytelling while she munched *chrusciki*, which she'd never tasted before. (Knowing the ribbons contained whole eggs, sour cream and other cholesterol carriers, I kept her from downing too many by telling her to save some for Cella and Aunt Sophie.)

What with all the noise we were making, we didn't hear the front door. Cella announced her presence by trotting down the stairs, yelling, "What did you find?" Her eyes looked like she could use some sleep, so I was surprised at her energy. Seeing Hugh and Beth Ann, she gave a war whoop and enveloped the younger in a smothering hug. Beth Ann turned beet red and winced at the blatant affection.

Cella pushed her away, but only far enough to study Beth Ann at arms' length, lifting off the hard hat for a better view. "*Madonne!* What *gorgeous* red hair. I'm so jealous. I'm Pat's cousin, Cella. The one you talked to last night on the phone. In the cemetery. Remember?"

"Cemetery?" Hugh put on one of his scowls.

I hadn't gotten to that part of the story yet. Pushing my glasses up and mask down again, I said, "I'll tell you in a second. First, Cella, how's Ronny?"

If her good mood hadn't been evident, the grin she put on next would have clinched it. "Flirting with the nurses when I left him. He had his surgery and they found *scar tissue*!" To my blank look, she added, "Left over from his hernia operation, Pat. *Scar tissue.* You know, interfering with . . . things. Don't make me spell it out. There's a kid here."

I got it then. "So he's not only okay from last night . . ."

Cella nodded, beaming. "He's perfect. Or supposed to be. Good as new. Or good as middle-aged is supposed to be. And insurance oughta pay since this was emergency surgery."

Hugh and Beth Ann both had at-sea looks during the exchange, but Hugh was too much of a Southern gentleman to say anything. Beth Ann, though, asked, "What are you talking about?"

"Ask me in three years," Cella replied, then changed the subject. "Come on, show me what you found."

I handed her the flashlight. She directed the beam into the hole, which was now about a little over a foot in diameter.

"A stew pot?" My cousin sounded disappointed.

"Why not?" I said. "If I were burying a time capsule, I'd want something waterproof. And with the pot's porcelain coating, it wouldn't rust."

Cella stuck her flashlight arm, then her face through the hole. "Looks like the pot's on top of an old milk crate." Her face reappeared. "Let's get more of these bricks off."

So we went back to work, and I told the rest of the story. I put a glossy spin on the episode in the hospital with Latimer, though, making it sound like I wasn't alone with him that long. No use getting Hugh upset after the fact. Miss Maggie agreed. I caught her nod of approval when I glanced at her.

I should also mention that I kind of skimmed through the ghost parts of the story, not intentionally, but because I always find my other-worldly encounters hard to put into words. I mean, I'd been seeing and sometimes feeling the ghost of a cat, but communication-wise, my mom was definitely on the other end. The physics of the whole thing was beyond me. What I was afraid of was Beth Ann asking me questions I couldn't answer.

But being a teenager, Beth Ann already had the answers. "This is just like that time last summer, when a ghost showed you where to dig in Miss Maggie's yard and you found a skeleton."

"Skeleton? *Madonne!*" Cella whacked my arm. "Tell me we aren't gonna find bones."

"No bones. Swear to God," I replied. "At least, not people bones. I can't make promises about dead sewer rats."

Hugh involuntarily pulled his hand away, and Beth Ann let out an "Eew!" She stepped back from the hole, but craned her neck to look in, curiosity winning out over repulsion.

My cousin? Sewer rats didn't phase her. You didn't have to get the priest in to exorcize rat spooks.

"What do you think?" she asked. "Is the hole big enough to lift that pot through?"

Hugh stuck one arm in, turned the pot so the handle was facing us and tested its weight. "Not all that heavy." He tipped it until he could get his other hand underneath, then lifted it over the bricks. Despite his claim, I could tell the pot wasn't light either. *Something* was inside.

Cella reached through the hole behind him, yanking the crate through as well. It was made of wood slats, with a gap between each. We could see nothing was inside but spider webs. I'd used a crate just like it, painted bright blue, as a nightstand in college. The bottom of this one was rotted, apparently having stood in water several times in the last six decades.

So we all focused our attention on the pot.

"Bring it over here, under the light," Miss Maggie ordered. Hugh obeyed with us in his wake.

As soon as Hugh set the pot on the floor, Cella whipped off the lid. Underneath it, a piece of red and white checked oilcloth was tucked in around the edges. I carefully pulled that up, only to find more underneath. Apparently the cloth had been used to line the pot, to protect the contents from dampness.

Beneath the inside flap was the front page of a *Times Herald* with the giant headline: "Allied Invasion!" The date was Tuesday, June 6, 1944, validating what I'd heard Ma talking about in my dream. Granted, I'd been sure enough of that vision to knock down a wall today, but this blatant affirmation was a reward in itself, like a tangible hug from my mom. I stared down at the page, blinking back tears.

"Read it later." Cella pulled down her dust mask, pretending impatience, but not fooling me for an instant. She knew I was all choked up and was trying to save me embarrassment. "Let's see what else is inside."

I lifted the paper to reveal packages all wrapped in the kind of long white paper my parents had used for lining kitchen cabinet shelves. On each bundle, in smeary fountain pen, someone had written "This belonged to" and the owner's name.

On top were two packages, one marked "Teresa Giamo." I snatched it up, already knowing it would be soft under my fingers. I knew what I'd find even as I stripped away the paper.

Mrs. Roosevelt.

"I don't believe it!" Cella exclaimed, gaping in amazement.

The doll wasn't an exact twin of the doppelganger that Nero had found the other night. The other one had been in better shape, the way Ma had remembered her. The doll I now held was slightly yellowed, and two seams needed repair. Likely all the cotton thread would want reinforcing eventually. I didn't care. Even the fact that I hated sewing didn't faze me. I would take her home and mend her and sit her on my bed. Maybe I'd pass her on to a granddaughter someday, with the story of how she'd witnessed bootleggers, rumrunners, and a poor but loving Italian family's battle with the Great Depression.

"You can have anything else in that pot," I told Cella, "but Mrs. Roosevelt's mine." And because I'd skipped over the doll's part in the synopsis I'd given Hugh and Beth Ann, I simply said, "She was my mom's."

Miss Maggie slipped her arm around my back and gave me a

squeeze. Now *she* was all choked up.

Cella undid the second bundle, which boasted the name "Ennio Trepani." It was about six or seven inches across, bulky and awkward, and slipped from her fingers, hanging down below the wrapping.

"An accordion!" Beth Ann exclaimed, kneeling on the floor for a better look.

"To be precise," Miss Maggie corrected, "a concertina."

"Uncle Ennio's squeezebox." Handing Mrs. Roosevelt to Miss Maggie, I knelt down on the dirt floor beside Beth Ann. The little instrument had seen better days. Now its red leather was tattered, with splits here and there along the folds. Half of its white bone buttons were missing.

Cella was already fiddling with the package underneath. " 'This belonged to Luigina Trepani,' " she read aloud. " 'Wedding present from Ennio's sister, Ernesta.' "

My cousin held up a pretty little crucifix, dark wood with a bronze Jesus. Looked like new. I took that to mean that either Aunt Gina had cherished the gift, keeping it carefully stored away all those years, or that she hadn't liked her sister-in-law enough to display the crucifix on the wall. Considering that Aunt Gina had let her daughter bury the cross in the basement, I thought I could guess the correct scenario.

"That will go on the wall in one of the girls' bedrooms," Cella declared. I imagined Aunt Gina turning in her grave.

"This one's heavy," Beth Ann said as she lifted out the next small package. "It says 'Vito Trepani.' " Flipping it over, she neatly folded the paper back until we could all see the tiny pistol on her palm, shiny gray steel, with polished wood grips.

Hugh reacted first, heroically seizing the firearm before it could harm his daughter. "How the hell do I tell if this is loaded?"

Miss Maggie, handing Mrs. Roosevelt back to me, took the gun from Hugh before he hurt himself. "A Mossberg Brownie," she said with admiration. "My Uncle Willie carried one of these. Back when my brothers were bootlegging."

"Brownie?" I repeated. "That's the pistol Vito got from the rumrunner. Rocco must not have pawned it. Or he did, then got it out of hock and gave it back."

"Looks like Vito took real good care of it." With complete competence, Miss Maggie opened up the back and checked inside.

"No bullets, but let's make sure." She closed it up, aimed it at the back wall and pulled the trigger. Four clicks later, she swore it was safe. "I remember Uncle Willie saying his pistol cost him five bucks in 1924. This is likely worth a few hundred now, Cella."

"Yeah?" My cousin took the weapon and set it beside the crucifix. Talk about odd couples.

The hard-packed floor was doing a job on my knees. I brought my feet around to sit cross-legged. Beth Ann did likewise and, undaunted by her last discovery, she reached for another bundle. "Hey, look, a baseball."

Balancing Mrs. Roosevelt in my lap, I scooped up the wrapping to confirm what I already suspected. "That's Del's. The ball in the photo. And she added here, 'A present from Rocco Montella, for saving his skin.' "

"Got a signature on it," Hugh said, looking over his daughter's shoulder.

I craned my neck for a gander, too. Lefty Grove's John Hancock was centered on the sweet spot between the seams, the "Lefty" big and bold, the "Grove" all scrunched up, looking more like "Grork."

Beth Ann handed it to Cella who appraised it with a critical eye. "Good shape. Think Uncle Leo's right about it not being worth much?"

"You kidding?" Hugh replied. "That's a vintage Official American League ball. If the signature's genuine, collectors like my brother would line up for a chance at it. In fact, I'm pretty sure he doesn't have a Lefty Grove autograph."

"Well, since you're almost family," Cella said, "I'll give him first dibs. Fair?"

Beth Ann had already lifted out the next item, which had no wrapping, but was only a small, tin cigar box that said "Bayuk Philadelphia Phillies Perfectos" on the label. Balancing it on her lap, she raised the lid. A yellowed piece of notebook paper covered the contents and, in a bold scrawl, read, "If you aren't Charlie or Gus Trepani, HANDS OFF!! (This means you, Delphina.)"

Laughing, Beth Ann moved the paper, then, getting a glimpse of the contents, let out another "Eew!"

The rest of us leaned in to see. Under the paper in the box were a bunch of small animal skulls.

"See? We got bones after all," Cella said, lifting one out. "That's a turkey head."

"How do you know?" I asked, remembering that my cousin hadn't been a stellar student in biology.

"Don't you remember? That one Thanksgiving that Grandpop brought Dad a fresh-killed turkey, head, feet and all?"

I shook my head. "If we're talking Grandpop, Cella, we weren't older than five."

"Right. Anyway, Grandpop took the skull, bleached it in the sun, then gave it to me for show-and-tell that year."

Beth Ann was surveying the other skulls with a scientific eye. "These four are mice and that's a rat—"

"Rat?" Cella repeated, making a face and giving me a look like it was my fault for mentioning them earlier.

"—and I think these are turtles," Beth Ann continued. "The big kind you see in streams. And that one's a squirrel."

Cella's jaw dropped at Beth Ann's knowledge. I smiled proudly, saying simply, "She *did* win the Science Fair."

"Yeah?" My cousin feigned a look of celebrity awe. "So can you do a CSI thing and tell me how they died? Or maybe I don't want to know I've had murder victims in my basement."

Miss Maggie held out a hand toward Beth Ann. "Let me have a look see." My mentor lowered her reading glasses and brought the tin closer to the light. A moment later she said, "Half of these seem pretty porous. See? These three have worse osteoporosis than I do."

"So they died of old age?" Cella asked hopefully.

Miss Maggie nodded. "Likely. The turkey was in his prime. I'm guessing, like your specimen, the rest of him was dinner. The squirrel was young, too, but he has head trauma."

Cella made a face. "*That* doesn't sound good."

"Roadkill?" Hugh suggested.

"Probably." Miss Maggie tapped another skull with her mittened fingers. "This is a skunk, and nobody's fool enough to mess with a live one just to supplement a bone collection. As for these mice noggins, well, there *was* a cat in the house."

"Good enough," Cella declared. "No inquest needed. I can dispose of the remains—"

"Don't throw them out!" Beth Ann exclaimed, horrified. "I'll take them." Her father rolled his eyes, making me wonder what else I might find if, after we were married, I decided to dust Beth Ann's room. No, I'd make her clean her own stuff.

"Keep 'em," Cella said, lifting out the next package. " 'This belonged to Giuseppe (Pip) Trepani,' " she read aloud, and revealed what proved to be a first edition of Raymond Chandler's *The Big Sleep*. Horrible condition, though. From what I knew of Pip, he'd probably gotten it second or thirdhand, then read it through four times himself.

Cella had the same opinion. "I'll give it to Ronny to read while he's recovering. What's next?"

Beth Ann handed her a small white envelope. On the outside, Del had written, "This belonged to my husband, Joacquim Ranelli."

The envelope flap had been secured with cellophane tape that was now so dried out, it fell off as my cousin touched it. Raising the flap, she said, "Stamps."

"Postage stamps?" That was my beloved, his antennas twitching with interest. "Can I see?"

"That's right. You're a mailman." Cella handed him the envelope. "Tell me if these are worth anything."

"Mostly three-centers," Hugh murmured under his breath. "A 1939 New York World's Fair. Vermont Statehood. Baseball centennial. Boulder Dam, 1935. A thirty-three Kosciuszko—"

"That's pronounced *Kostchewstsko*," Miss Maggie corrected, sounding as Polish as the *chrusciki* she'd been eating. "Thaddeus. Colonel in the American Revolution. Chief engineer. Wouldn't have won Saratoga without him. Congress made him a general afterward and he became a naturalized citizen."

Hugh was too engrossed in the little squares in his hands to care. "Ooh, here are all three 1940 'For Defense' one-centers—"

"Yes," said Cella, "but are they worth anything?"

"None of these are very rare," he replied with a shrug. "And they're all canceled."

"So they're not even worth the postage?" Cella sighed. "Keep 'em if you want 'em."

"Here's the last thing." From the pot, Beth Ann took a file folder, its original olive-brown color darkened with age. On it, in a faded bold scrawl, was written "Property of Salvatore B. Giamo." She flipped it open to reveal a comic book.

"Action Comics," Beth Ann read.

"That's Superman on the cover," Cella exclaimed.

"Let me see." Hugh bent over his daughter's shoulder. "Look, in the corner. 'Number one.' The first Superman."

"You sure?" I asked.

"He's sure," said Miss Maggie. "I recognize it, too. My son Frank read them. Started coming out in the late '30s."

"Really?" Cella held out her hands to receive the folder from Beth Ann, then gingerly turned the pages. "Awesome condition. Betcha it's worth a lot."

She meant money, of course. I was thinking about an uncle I'd never met, who'd somehow felt enough of a bond with Superman to leave pristine evidence in a time capsule. I glanced at our other relics, representing the Trepanis: Vito the tough guy, Pip the voracious reader, Gussie and Charlie the typical big brothers, and Del, tomboy with an arm like Lefty Grove, Rosie the Riveter, and eventually Mrs. Ranelli, the skinny neighbor in bowling shirts who'd chat with my mom over the back fence. All my cousins. Even the mouse heads, representing Crisi. Plus Aunt Gina and Uncle Ennio. This family had welcomed my mom and her brother into their home when simply making ends meet had been a weekly challenge. How trivial my own money worries seemed compared to theirs.

"Hey," Cella said, "we all got a souvenir except Miss Maggie."

"Not true," my mentor said, her eyes twinkling. "I'm claiming the newspaper. To historians, they're like diamonds."

"So we're all good," my cousin said.

I gazed down at the doll on my lap, somehow knowing her presence meant I wouldn't be visited by a certain small black feline anymore. The family was safe. Ma was at rest.

I gave Mrs. Roosevelt a big hug. "Yeah, we're good."

EPILOGUE

Bell Run, Virginia – Present Day

Miss Maggie's house seems afloat in a sea of crocuses, a patchwork of purple, white and yellow. In the side yard, the tulip bulbs I planted last fall are poking through the dirt, along with enough dandelion greens for a week's worth of salads.

That last night in Norristown, I had one more dream. Nothing vivid, just a glimpse of Ma and her papa, and my brother Lou, who was maybe five years old. My grandfather looked ill—way too thin and pale, and he walked with a cane. He was telling Ma he wouldn't eat bread anymore, that it made him sick to his stomach. Made his legs hurt worse. She was humoring him.

That was it. Whole dream probably took less than a minute. But I got the message. Ma wasn't quite at rest. Grandpop had achy knees, so did I. He got major *agita*, I did sometimes. I promised Ma I'd make an appointment to see Hugh's doctor sister soon and I'd tell her the family connection.

By the time I left town, Aunt Sophie had stopped speaking to Beatrice again. My cousin not only sensibly opted to have Ozzie cremated, but decided to forego all burial fees by putting his ashes into a decorative vase which Aunt Lydia swore Beatrice bought at Dollar City. Beatrice's idea is, when she dies, someone else can pay to inter both of them at once. Shrewd.

Uncle Rocco's fortune is still missing, though in with the last of his clothes, Aunt Sophie found a copy of his contract with Evergreen Manor. Technically, it says they have a legal right to anything else he owns. If extra bucks do surface, Beatrice may have a court case on her hands. Personally, Cella and I both think they won't find a thing. He played with whatever money he had—gambled with it, gave it away, *enjoyed* it. Flashed it around so it looked like more, sure, but really, he was as middle class as the rest of us and we know it.

Whatever value the time capsule has, Cella says she's going to put it toward fixing up her house. Ronny is now all for selling their other place to get rid of the mortgage. As my cousin says, men are so much more reasonable when they can have sex. Women, too, I'm tempted to remind her. Together, they'll save 349 East Main from the wrecking ball, raise their girls there, and be close for Aunt Sophie and Uncle Leo as they get older, which gives the rest of us some peace of mind.

Cella also promised me a finder's fee. Oh, I don't want much. The wedding's going to be simple, I decided. I don't know where or when yet, but I absolutely refuse to spend a mint on it. On my wedding day, I don't want to feel like a consumer. I want to feel like a bride.

Then again, if that finder's fee covers my income taxes, I won't say no.

THE END

ELENA SANTANGELO is the author of the Agatha Award winning *DAME AGATHA'S SHORTS: An Agatha Christie Short Story Companion*, which was also nominated for Anthony and Macavity awards. In her Pat Montella mystery series, *BY BLOOD POSSESSED* was also an Agatha Award finalist. Elena's short stories have been published in the United States and Japan. She was co-editor of the short story anthology, *DEATH KNELL IV*. Many of her short stories are now available for Kindle. You can read her weekly blog at www.elenasantangelo.blogspot.com.

CPSIA information can be obtained at www.ICGtesting.com
Printed in the USA
LVOW041501100412
276999LV00002B/14/P